The Voyage
of the
Chianti

Also by B. J. Morison
from North Country Press

CHAMPAGNE AND A GARDENER
PORT AND A STAR BOARDER
BEER AND SKITTLES
REALITY & DREAM

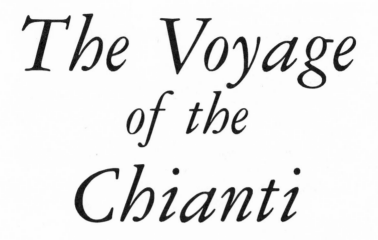

The Voyage
of the
Chianti

• A LITTLE MAINE MURDER •

B.J. MORISON

NORTH COUNTRY PRESS • THORNDIKE, MAINE

Library of Congress Cataloging-in-Publication Data

Morison, B. J. (Betty Jane), 1924–
    The voyage of the Chianti.

    I. Title.
PS3563.087167V69   1987   813'.54   87-24888
ISBN 0-89621-110-X (alk. paper)
ISBN 0-89621-112-6 (pbk. : alk. paper)

COVER DESIGN BY ARMEN KOJOYIAN

SET IN GARAMOND TYPEFACES BY SHORELINE GRAPHICS / ROCKLAND, MAINE

This story is dedicated to Jane Austen at the request of Elizabeth Lamb, who has herself been called "shrewd and observant." E. L. feels it may help take the sting for Miss Austen, wherever she is, out of her remembrance of a letter once written by Charlotte Brontë: "Why do you like Miss Austen so very much? I am puzzled on that point. . . . I should hardly like to live with her ladies and gentlemen. . . . Miss Austen is only shrewd and observant."

Acknowledgments

The author expresses grateful appreciation for help to Mark Kandutsch, M.D.; to Chief Dan Herrick, B.H.P.D.; to Jay Emlen, who provided the plan of a yacht on which the mythical *Chianti* was based; to Cordelia Drexel Biddle Robertson, who years ago spoke of the "Black Death"; to Malcolm Forbes, who permitted inspection of his *Highlander*; but most of all to Chris Vincenty, who provided invaluable information on technical matters.

Foreword to a Well-Favored Reader

Dorothy L. Sayers, so I have been told, received some criticism of her masterpiece *Gaudy Night* when it was published. Allegedly there were those who said that in a book presented as a mystery there was too much about Oxford University, as well as too much of the ineffable Lord Peter Wimsey's pursuit of Harriet Vane and of her evasion of His Lordship. But those very fascinating details of academic life and of how people lived and spoke, ate, dressed and courted in the '30's are relished by present-day readers, as, indeed, they were by most of Miss Sayers' contemporary fans. (It may be noted that she subtitled her next, *Busman's Honeymoon,* "A Love Story with Detective Interruptions." Perhaps she was stung by the criticism, if it existed; writers are sensitive people.)

Sometimes you, dear reader, overlook the warning in *my* subtitles ("A Little Maine Murder") when you react as if you had expected a straightforward thriller with most of the narrative centering on the crime. I warn you that the (little bit of) murder is subordinate to the comedy of manners. Without expecting that I could ever receive a fraction of the deserved acclaim awarded the immortal D. L. S., I hope that years from now someone may unearth a battered copy of one of my little murders and enjoy the picture of the manners, customs, dress, and speech of certain classes — if I dare use that offensive term — in the late '60's and '70's. (As there are readers today who also do, they write me, relish the entertainment I try to provide as much as the touch of murder.)

In this book, well-favored reader, there appears a gentleman who may — or may not — be a member of a (currently) much-publicized organization. You may say that no one who might have belonged to it could conceivably be as he is depicted. Possibly that's correct; possibly not. Regarding that organization, I must say, in Will Roger's phrase: "All I know is what I read in the papers."

Except for one instance of trivia a child of mine related at the

7

dinner table, during a conversation about flowers, as having been told her class by a teacher whose daughter had been often in the company of a young man described as a member. Although I was six years away from beginning *The Voyage of the Chianti,* I was already plotting it — (you may laugh sardonically here) — and dashed to the school the next day to see if the lady, wearily departing homeward after her struggles with the fifth grade, could give me any more interesting facts, for authenticity. She excitedly denied any knowledge, even denying the conversation with the class had ever taken place. There went my one supposedly true fact. (Of course, I used it, just the same.) But one can't deny some persons or facts just might be as I have described them; only a few might know for sure, and I bet they'd invoke the Fifth — and I don't mean the grade.

P.S. I wish I could include for you a letter I got the other day from a British fan who had just discovered my first book, *Champagne and a Gardener.* She asks plaintively, "where is it written that a mystery book absolutely must have its murder early on?" Why not "more books like yours, with fascinating characters we'd like to meet in real life and literate talk" — (I do love this person!) — "where the delicate clues as to who's going to be done in and whodunnit are laid on for us and we wait in delicious anticipation for the murder?" She says *Champagne* "was like getting two books for the price of one."

Well, I have usually, as a critic once wrote of me, "refused to walk a tightrope," so here is another unorthodox murder mystery, along the line of *Champagne and a Gardener.* May you, the English lady, and my other two or three fans enjoy it, while realizing that, as usual, all the persons, places, and events are figments of my imagination except for the verse on page 146, which was contributed by my sister-in-law.

B.J. Morison
BAR HARBOR, 1987

The Characters in the
Order in Which They Appear

ELIZABETH LAMB WORTHINGTON — *an observant twelve-year-old girl.*

ELIZABETH WORTHINGTON — *her grandmother.*

VITTORIO (VITO, V.V.) VINCENTIA — *a man now retired from most of his interests. Perhaps.*

VIOLA VINCENTIA — *his granddaughter.*

CIOCCOLATO — *her kitten.*

ALICE — *Mrs. Worthington's cook.*

EBERLY TIBBETS — *a friend of Mrs. Worthington's. A fiduciary trustee.*

PAYSON PROUTY — *a young acquaintance of Mrs. Worthington's. From Maine.*

PERSIS HALSTEAD — *Elizabeth Lamb's cousin, also twelve.*

ANNIE DONELLI — *Mr. Vincentia's secretary.*

CAPT. SENNO KNUDSEN — *the master of the* Chianti.

JULIA VINCENTIA — *Mr. Vincentia's daughter-in-law, widow of Viola's father.*

PAUL COOPER — *her great-and-good friend.*

AMY DANNIVER — *a writer of mystery books.*

JAKE AARONSON — *an old friend of Mr. Vincentia's.*

THE HONOURABLE MONICA THORNHILL — *an uninhibited guest on the* Chianti.

CHRISTOPHER GRENVILLE — *her escort. One of Mr. Vincentia's many godsons.*

ROBERT TEMPLETON — *another of her escorts.*

JIM DARROW — *an employee of Mr. Vincentia's* Placido Press, *and Mrs. Danniver's editor.*

LIEUT. ALFRED (BUZZIE) HIGGINS — *a detective with the Maine State Police.*

Also servants, crewmen, sinister on-and-off-stage characters, and incidental innocents.

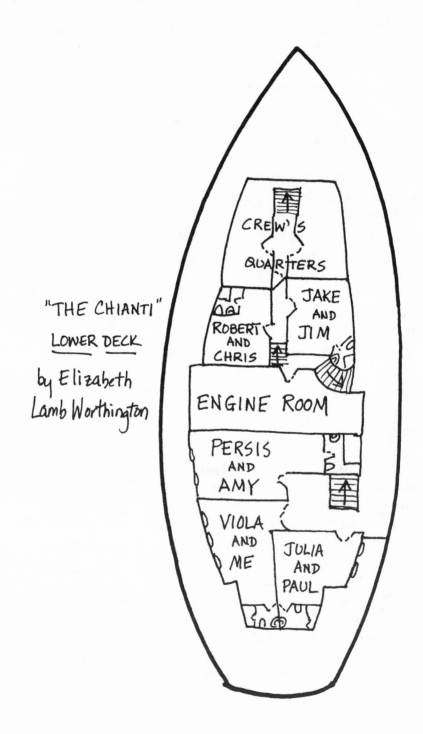

"THE CHIANTI"

LOWER DECK

by Elizabeth
Lamb Worthington

CREW'S
QUARTERS

JAKE
AND
JIM

ROBERT
AND
CHRIS

ENGINE ROOM

PERSIS
AND
AMY

VIOLA
AND
ME

JULIA
AND
PAUL

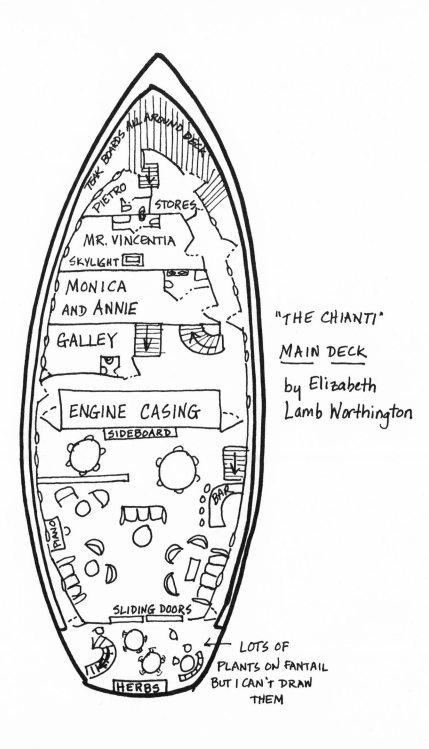

TEAK BOARDS ALL AROUND DECK

PIETRO

STORES

MR. VINCENTIA

SKYLIGHT

MONICA AND ANNIE

GALLEY

ENGINE CASING

SIDEBOARD

PIANO

BAR

"THE CHIANTI"

MAIN DECK

by Elizabeth Lamb Worthington

SLIDING DOORS

LOTS OF PLANTS ON FANTAIL BUT I CAN'T DRAW THEM

HERBS

• CONTENTS •

1 SOME TIME BEFORE   15

2 OVER THE GARDEN WALL   18

3 DINNER ON BRIMMER, 1   34

4 DINNER ON BRIMMER, 2   58

5 MOTLEY CREW   81

6 ALL AT SEA   103

7 A WHOLE NEW CAN OF PEAS   131

8 BETTER TO TRAVEL   150

9 UNDER SIEGE   177

10 J. AARONSON QUOTES A. HITLER   199

11 A TROUT IN THE MILK   245

12 JUDGMENT   267

13 SOME TIME AFTER   299

• CHAPTER 1 •

Some Time Before

THE TALL, red-haired flight attendant had partied too late and too well the previous night. Ashen-faced despite her skillful *maquillage,* she went mechanically about her duties, stumbling occasionally and biting her lower lip to keep control. As the captain made the customary landing announcements in the customary cheerful, confident voice, she sank thankfully into one of the staff's seats at the very back of the plane, and closed her eyes. The other stewardess in the section had joined even more enthusiastically in the night's revelry and now, against regulations, locked herself into a lavatory. The attendant listened sympathetically to the moans and gasps heard faintly through its door.

The captain was saying that there was a delay in getting clearance for landing; the plane began a slow circle, hundreds of miles wide, of the airport. The *No Smoking* light went out, but the one ordering *Fasten Seat Belts* remained on. The passengers groaned, or laughed ironically as they good-naturedly accepted their plight.

"'If time to spare, travel by air,'" quoted one of the occupants of the last row of passenger seats. Another person chuckled. "Or," idly speculated the attendant, who wrote short stories, sometimes

15

published, when she was not flying or celebrating, "would one describe it as more of a giggle?" She dozed.

A jolt in the smooth circling woke her just as the voice spoke again: "Well, now we're for it, *caro*. You've got to face up: our — friend's got to go." The voice was rather high, for a man, but low for a woman. She could not remember who was sitting where. "The way I feel, it's a bloody wonder I remember who *I* am," she mumbled, to herself. "Never again!"

"For God's sake, be quiet!" This voice, too, could have come from someone of either sex. "But agitated, and, almost, fearful," the girl thought. "Why?" She opened her eyes a slit and got a glimpse of a head half-turned around the edge of the back of the last aisle seat, several feet in front of her. Longish hair — male — female?

Obviously only the empty seat beside her, to her left, had been in the person's view, for now the second voice spoke again, more calmly: "It's all right; she's in the w.c. Sounds more than a bit off-color, too." Another chuckle — or giggle — rather unpleasant.

"So," the first voice said, lower, but the attendant was now fully awake and listening as closely as she could, "it's agreed you'll do your part? God knows this flight has given you plenty of time to consider the necessity. It's given me time to invent your alibi, too. The police could be a bit difficult, but we'll be able to act it out successfully for —" the voice dropped to an unintelligible murmur.

"Alibi?" the attendant thought. "Police? My God, what are they up to?" Frightened, she shrank further to her right, pressing against the door of the unoccupied lavatory in case the head turned again. Her fellow, still gagging and pressing a tissue against her mouth, noisily emerged from seclusion and fell into her seat. Quickly, mouthing "Quiet," and shaking an admonishing head, the first girl unfastened her belt and slipped into the lavatory. If the head turned again, and more completely, only the girl who had obviously just sat down would be seen.

The attendant hid for a good five minutes after the aircraft had finished taxiing to the terminal building. When she emerged, briskly, wearing a detached, professional expression, the last of the passengers on her side had reached the very front of the plane and the other girl was busy straightening up the galley.

16

The passengers were intermingling far down the aisle; was that pair of men looking into their hand luggage the two people who had been in the back row? Or had it been the man and woman standing almost beside them? She considered the origin of the flight and shook her head, puzzled: there hadn't been much, if any, of an accent.

"Who were the two in the last row, right in front of our seats, as we were landing?" she casually asked the girl in the galley. "There was a lot of changing-around during the flight, long as it was, with so many empty places."

"Dunno," she was answered. "I was right out of it almost the whole damned time. Gawd, what a party! Why d'you want to know? They didn't complain, I hope?"

"Doesn't matter. You know how I always like to look at people. Helps me write. That's all."

"Well, if you'd been looking at them," the other began slowly, "then wouldn't you know —"

"Oh, never mind. I've got such a head I can't think straight, much less talk straight. Say, how about stopping at Nino's for a touch of the hair of the dog? It'll help me forget — help us forget our troubles."

• CHAPTER 2 •

Over the Garden Wall

IT WAS the 20th day of June and a sultry afternoon in Boston. Elizabeth Lamb Worthington languidly waved a pleated parchment fan in front of her flushed face as she leaned back into a latticed verdigris iron chair placed in a far corner, against Lime Street, of her grandmother's little walled garden. She lifted her eyes to a burning blue sky, glimpsed through the low-hanging leaves of the dusty tree above her, and tried thought-control to battle the indigestion she had been feeling for several hours, after an unwise indulgence in quantities of cold cream-of-cucumber soup and green-grape tart.

Thought-control was not working. She turned up the volume of a small radio set on the brick paving at her feet, to distract herself from her discomfort with the news announcer's happy recital of the difficulties the city was having securing fuel distributors who could supply its municipal vehicles. He switched cheerily to an announcement that the heat wave would continue for an indefinite period. His voice rose in ecstasy: "And no — that's no, no, *no* relief in sight, listeners!"

Elizabeth Lamb sighed and tossed the ineffective fan toward a large clay pot of geranium and lobelia. After a singer chanted a few bars of *Lucky Man,* the announcer came on again, with national news. He informed his audience that Jimmy the Greek was giving odds of "a thousand to one against impeachment; two hundred to one against resignation." He then, with a merry laugh, prophesied gasoline rationing by the end of the summer.

Elizabeth Lamb sighed again. She turned the radio up even higher and picked up a pristine notebook and a gold pen from the wicker table beside her. Unlike the majority of her generation, she was more stimulated in concentration by the spoken word, however unpleasant the thoughts it was expressing, than by loud sounds that passed for music.

She headed the first page: *My Novel for the Summer.* Under that, she wrote: *Title: A Case.* She tapped the top of the pen against her teeth while she reflected. She had been involved in several incidents which a professional investigator would have described as "cases" and since the very advanced school she attended had assigned "a short novel" as a summer vacation task she thought she might as well get the tiresome chore begun. The strain of literary composition — for who but a bad writer ever claims to "love to write"? — might conquer not only the cucumber-and-grape pangs and the heat but also the regret she still felt when she thought of the second of her three cases.

She chewed the top of the pen, an expensive birthday gift from her parents, presented with some guilt when they had been obliged to fly to Spain a week before, although her twelfth birthday was not until the 22nd. She swung her long legs, scuffing her proper little-girl-brown-leather-buckled-sandals back and forth against the paving. Five minutes of this made some inroads on their soles but not on her regret. "I'm just not ready to write about it yet," she thought. "'When in doubt, don't,' as Grandmother says. I'll just," she decided, "make up a whole new mystery, starting today. And what's wrong with that?"

She smoothed back her damp hair, took in a deep breath of the heavy air, grimaced, and wrote: "It was the 20th day of June and a sultry afternoon in Boston."

"Then what?" she thought. She considered with annoyance the axiom that a work of fiction should never begin with a description of the weather. "Oh?" she said aloud. "But what about: 'It was a bright cold day in April and the clock was striking thirteen'? Mr. Blair knew a thing or two. He must have, since we still have to read the book, depressing as it is. And it's eleven years before 1984, too."

There was a light rapping from the open bay window at the other end of the garden, a half-story above the brick paving. A slim figure inside the house beckoned to her. Elizabeth Lamb rose dutifully and advanced to peer up at her grandmother.

Elizabeth Worthington spoke quietly but clearly. "Why are you talking about a 'Mr. Blair'? Do we know him? And do turn that radio down a bit. We have new neighbors, you know, and they may be disturbed by it. Really, Elizabeth Lamb!" She gestured toward the yard at her left, from which could be heard the low murmur of voices.

"I'm sorry, Grandmother. I was thinking of *1984.*"

"What in the world — oh, of course. I met the young man once, years ago. I never did ask him why he wrote under 'George Orwell' when his own name, Eric Blair, had quite a distinguished ring to it. So many people demand to know all sorts of things about writers, often very impertinently. Have you ever read his *Down and Out in Paris and London?* I liked it very much."

"No, Grandmother. But Mummy and I were once down and out in Paris, you remember. Maybe I don't have to read about it."

Her grandmother's laugh was youthful and lilting. "I remember, Elizabeth Lamb, although you and your mother were too brave and enterprising to be very far down. Now, I want *you* to remember that Mr. Tibbets is coming to dinner, at seven. Change your frock before then, please. I think we'll do without tea today. It is so hot, and Alice gave us a very substantial lunch — why are you making such a peculiar face?

"I will be up in the studio until dinner. There's much to finish before my Paris showing and only two days left till I leave. Now, dear, do lower that radio."

Elizabeth Lamb went back to her chair and cut off the announcer in the midst of his gleeful international report that gold was up to an unheard-of $127 an ounce in London. He could almost be heard to rub his hands together in satisfaction as he went on to say that the American dollar was so weak that a famous candy shop in Paris was refusing to accept dollars for its overpriced confections.

"I guess Grandmother won't bring me back any sugared almonds," she thought wistfully. She considered with gloom her ten days alone in her grandmother's Brimmer Street house, with only the hostile cook for company and with little hope of her favorite sweets at the end of them. She regarded the sentence she had written, chewing her pen again and sighing. A chuckle and a clink of glassware sounded from the adjoining garden.

Elizabeth Lamb put down her notebook and appraised the heavy, ancient grape vine espaliered against the garden wall. She had not, in the week spent with Elizabeth Worthington, achieved a sight of the wealthy old gentleman another neighbor had reported to have recently bought the house next door, nor until today heard a sound of him. She was possessed of not only a talent for observation but also a great curiosity; both attributes had nearly proved fatal to her in the first of her cases.

She took off her sandals before she stealthily climbed the vine. As her head rose above the nine-foot-wall, she was tempted to duck down again, but she had never yet retreated from an action, however ill-considered, unless she believed it might prove dangerous — and not always then.

The elderly man staring, with a smile, straight into her eyes did not appear dangerous. He rose from a white iron chair beside the wall fountain across the yard from her, placed one hand over his heart, and bowed with elegance. "Ah!" he said merrily, "The Little Girl Next Door! I knew there was one, but I had no idea that she would be so *bellino*. The cook of your house has told my cook about you, though."

"What did Alice say?" Elizabeth Lamb asked with interest. The cook was not one of her most ardent admirers, since she considered that a pre-teenager should be more receptive to boiled beef with "my good floury potatoes" than to "furrin stuff" like *pâté* served with thin, buttered toast, accompanied by avocadoes dressed with olive oil and vinegar. And she certainly should, so Alice had opined, be more fond of Coca-Cola, "now that they took the dope out of it, some years back," than the contents of her grandmother's wine-cellar.

21

"It was not entirely clear to me," the old gentleman said regretfully, "since Rosa has almost no English, and your cook no Italian at all. Allow me to introduce myself, please, *signorina*. I am Vittorio Vincentia, your grandmother's new neighbor." He bowed again. "And you?"

"Elizabeth Lamb Worthington. Everybody calls me Elizabeth Lamb." She hoisted herself atop the wall and thoroughly scrutinized Mr. Vincentia. She glanced only cursorily at the dark, stocky young man who leaned again on Mr. Vincentia's little blue wooden door into Lime Street. He had stiffened when her head first appeared over the wall and she had also noticed, in her initial view of the garden, that his right hand had moved quickly into the left side of his loose dark cotton jacket. He now clasped both hands behind his back and looked stolidly up at a second-floor window, just inside which another man in a navy-blue jacket had appeared.

Mr. Vincentia stood with graceful poise, smiling at his visitor. He was tall and slim and dapperly dressed in white gabardine trousers and a short-sleeved cream silk shirt, which revealed sinewy, very brown forearms. A wine-colored Ascot scarf was tucked into his open collar, and he had pulled a matching necktie through the loops of his trousers to serve as a belt. His lined, dark-skinned face was agreeable; his eyes were narrow, the pupils very black, as was his thin mustache and his heavy, rather long, glossy hair, which displayed as few strands of white as did Elizabeth Lamb's seventy-three-year-old grandmother's similar hair.

Mr. Vincentia's black eyes regarded a slim, graceful child whose intelligent green eyes were so large as to be startling in her pale, oval face. Her brows were in dark contrast to her long silver-gilt hair, and she wore a rumpled sleeveless linen dress that matched her eyes.

"Will you not join me for tea?" he asked. "It will be served soon, whenever my granddaughter gets back from her lesson. Benno will help you down." He motioned to the man against the door, who moved quickly to the wall and held up his arms. Elizabeth Lamb lowered herself into them and was gently deposited beside her host.

"Thank you; I will," she said. "I'm getting sort of hungry again, and Grandmother isn't having tea today. Stomachs are very unreliable things, you know," she confided to Mr. Vincentia, who laughed pleasantly. "One minute they're hurting and the next, they're wanting to be filled up again.

"But what is that you were drinking, Mr. Vincentia?" She peered at the bottle beside a small crystal glass on an umbrella-shaded table. "I never heard of *Grappa.*" She sat down beside the table and produced what her grandmother called her "society smile," used when the social situation was difficult or, as now, when she wanted something.

Mr. Vincentia appeared to understand her motive. "It is not for young girls," he informed her. "*Grappa* is made from wine lees, and is very strong. I have a little each afternoon because my doctor wishes it; my heart is not as predictable as when I was young.

"But my stomach is as good as it ever was. Mine has never been unreliable, as you say; it consistently wanted food when I was a boy, when there was little to be had, and it demands it now, when there is much."

He lit a small brown cigarette. "*Grappa* is loved by Sicilian peasants, as I was born. We have many of its characteristics. I wanted to name my boat the *Grappa,* but my son had slightly more — ah, more refined tastes. He preferred wine of any type, but he loved chianti."

"You don't have much of an accent at all. What kind of boat do you have?"

Mr. Vincentia smiled, a little ruefully. "A very large one. My daughter-in-law — my former daughter-in-law, that is — had luxurious tastes to match my son's refined ones. Perhaps I pay too much attention to my family; that too is a Sicilian characteristic."

"A Bostonian one, too," his guest informed him, frowning. "My grandmother has to go to Paris for almost two weeks, and my parents are in Spain, so I have to stay here with that awful Alice because my aunt tells my grandmother that I shouldn't go alone to Maine and be by myself there, or maybe with Persis, till Grandmother comes back and goes up. And she told Grandmother I'd be too much bother to take along to Paris.

"Goodness, I lived there for years and know it very well. I'd be fine going around by myself. Grandmother wouldn't have to tend me. Aunt Sarah is just too bossy."

"Why do you not stay with this aunt? Does she live far away?"

"No, just out in Dedham. But she broke her leg, a bad break, and she's very nervous and fussy. She doesn't like me much, either, so I'd make her worse." She frowned thoughtfully. "Even Persis makes her nervous now, though, and she simply and utterly dotes on Persis," she added quaintly. Mr. Vincentia concealed a smile.

"And who is Persis?"

"My cousin. Her daughter. She's just exactly a week younger than I am. We'd like to go up to The Bungalow and be on our own for a while, but Aunt Sarah says we'd get into trouble, with only Dora — she's the housekeeper — to watch us."

"And would you? You seem to be an adventurous young lady. That wall is rather high."

"Oh, of course we wouldn't. Persis and I are *quite* mature. It is really ridiculous, you know, because Mount Desert Island is so lovely in June, and all the local people around Grandmother's camp are our friends; well, as much our friends as they let themselves be to summer complaints, as some of them call summer visitors.

"But we get along with them, because Persis and I are not show-offs or bossy. Like some people I could mention," she concluded, with a glance toward the general direction of Dedham.

"This Bungalow is on Mount Desert Island? But that is indeed a coincidence! My granddaughter and I and some guests leave for there day after tomorrow. We shall stop only to leave off several of the party, and then the *Chianti* goes on to Canada, where I have business, although not as much as I used to."

"Oh, I wish you'd take Persis and me up! You said your boat was very large." The society smile was produced again. "That would cut into the time we'd be alone at The Bungalow. And Grandmother's cove is so beautiful that you might want to stay there a few days. I just bet you would! We're awfully good at sailing and could work our passage, too."

Mr. Vincentia smiled. "That would not be necessary. I have a crew of four, and a captain. And I usually have a boy to help the cook, but recently — no matter."

He considered. "This might be very agreeable for my grand-

24

daughter — to have two young ladies on board. The rest of the company is old, though not as old as I. I am very, very old." He grimaced comically and then smiled again.

"Is Miss Persis as charming as you?"

"Oh, much, much more so." Elizabeth Lamb was earnest. "And you don't seem so old, only as old as my grandmother, and she acts quite young. But your granddaughter might not like me. Not everyone does. She might like Persis more, though."

"I cannot believe that," Mr. Vincentia answered gallantly. "But here comes Maria with our tea. That means Viola is home, and we shall see about this voyage for you. Remember, though, your grandmother might not permit her family to set sail with a stranger. I say 'set sail' in the poetic sense; the *Chianti* is diesel-powered."

"Oh," Elizabeth Lamb began, "she'd first thoroughly check up on —" She stopped, reddening, as Mr. Vincentia chuckled knowledgeably and nodded.

"Ah, here is Viola," he said quickly. "And it is always good to see you, Anne. Can you stay for tea?"

Two young girls had entered in the wake of the fat, middle-aged woman who wheeled the tea wagon out from a door set flush with the yard. Elizabeth Lamb wished that her grandmother's basement floor was not set below ground so that the temperamental Alice sometimes might, just might, be persuaded to bring out tea to their garden.

The older girl was tall and darkly handsome, her brown eyes somber and her smooth brown hair braided into a bow-tied plait that hung down her back. The other, who dutifully kissed Mr. Vincentia's cheek, had a childishly-plump pink face and limpid, rather vacant, round violet eyes, beautifully set off by long, dark lashes. Her red-blond curls stood out in a damp aureole. She had a petulant expression which changed, as she looked Elizabeth Lamb up and down, to a hostile one. She picked up a macaroon and chewed it, staring sullenly. Both girls wore short-sleeved mesh riding shirts and khaki breeches. Elizabeth Lamb thought their high, brilliantly-polished boots unsuitable for riding on such a hot day.

Before Mr. Vincentia could present her, she addressed the tall girl with pleasure and no mention of boots: "Hullo, Anne, do you

25

remember me? Elizabeth Lamb Worthington. I met you once when you and your mother were at my Aunt Sarah Halstead's."

"You are already friends?" Mr. Vincentia asked, as Anne smiled a greeting. "That is good. Viola, *caro,* this is the young lady who at present lives in the house over the garden wall. You have heard her name. Elizabeth Lamb, my granddaughter, Viola Vincentia."

He looked at his granddaughter with a slight frown. "Will you not pour for our guests before you eat any more cakes, my dear?" Viola crammed a third macaroon into her pretty, pouting mouth, with no regard for the crumbs that fell on to her shirt, before she reluctantly seated herself at the table on which the maid had placed the tea accoutrements. Maria's small black eyes thoroughly examined the visitor from over the wall before she left for the kitchen. She evidently liked what she saw, for she ducked a sort of curtsey at Elizabeth Lamb.

"None for me, please, Viola," Anne said. "I must get home to Mother, Mr. Vincentia. She wasn't feeling very well when I left for Viola's lesson."

She sighed as she regarded her pupil. "Viola, you must be sure to tree your boots today. I suppose you won't want any more lessons for her for a while, Mr. Vincentia?"

"I will telephone when we return," he answered. "And I will send my doctor again to your mother. She seemed better when I called on her just after his last visit. I suppose it will take a good deal more time for her grief over your father's death to pass.

"My dear, I'm really very sorry you cannot sit and rest a moment. You look thinner than when you last brought Viola home, only two days ago. Teaching my granddaughter to ride must be very exhausting. I love her" — he turned with a smile to Viola, who made a face at him — "but I know she can be as wilful as her father. Tell me, is she improving?"

"She still bounces awfully," Anne began tiredly, as Mr. Vincentia walked with her to the garden door, held open by Benno. "Here is Antonio with the car," Mr. Vincentia said, shaking his head in a cautioning manner but gently patting her arm. "I heard him bring it around; he will take you home as usual.

"Perhaps it would be better to tell me about her progress when you are riding with me, Anne," he continued softly, although heard by both Elizabeth Lamb and Viola, who stuck out her tongue at Anne's retreating back. "But I want you to continue with her, of course; she could have no better teacher. And would you exercise Omerta for me while I am gone, at the same rates as when I was in Europe last month? I would take it as a kindness, my dear."

Benno peered nervously into the street until Anne had passed through the little door and entered the waiting car. Mr. Vincentia returned and stood while he thirstily drank the cup of tea his grand-daughter handed him. Elizabeth Lamb sipped hers and thought him much more kind as well as much more charming than the sulky Viola. "Your horse is called Omerta?" she asked. "Why — because it doesn't talk?"

Mr. Vincentia laughed gaily. "You have read the book of the *paisano,* I see. Yes, perhaps that is why. But it might be because I always enjoy what they call a play on words; Omerta is a mare."

Now Elizabeth Lamb laughed as she held her cup to be refilled. "There isn't any more," Viola said ungracefully.

"My dear, that is the hot water jug. Of course there is more tea, in the teapot." Mr. Vincentia beamed happily at Elizabeth Lamb. "I have a great love for tea, so Rosa always gives us much. I became addicted to it when I lived in England."

More soberly, he addressed his granddaughter. "How would you like to have this young lady as company on our cruise, as far as Maine? And perhaps her cousin, too? If we can persuade her grand-mother and her aunt to let them come with us, that is."

He and Elizabeth Lamb looked expectantly at Viola, who peered into the heavy silver teapot, ignoring them. "Oh," she said finally, after a thorough examination of the inside of the pot, "it would be all right, I guess." She appeared to think. "As much as she can think," Elizabeth Lamb, who had as yet achieved no very high regard of Viola Vincentia, muttered under her breath.

Quite suddenly, Viola lifted her head and smiled charmingly. "Yes, Grandfather, I'd like very much to have her — and the cousin. Maybe they could help the cook, or know someone who would, since you were so mean and sent Alberto home." Then she frowned and angrily banged the teapot down on the table. "And for no reason! I really didn't like him at all! He was stupid, and you are stupid, too!"

Mr. Vincentia was appalled. "Viola, we do not discuss our troubles in front of guests — nor require them to act as cabin-boy. We will find a helper for Pietro before we leave. I have made inquiries.

"And it would not be a disaster for anyone if you, yourself, helped Pietro set the table, and so on, you know. A little work is good for young people; too much, which at your age was my lot, is not."

Viola attacked a piece of grape tart moodily, again spattering crumbs. Elizabeth Lamb, with a shudder, refused a portion Mr. Vincentia offered her, and ate bread-and-butter sandwiches.

"You have simple tastes," her host approved. "And I, myself, think there is no tea so good as that from a plain brown earthenware pot. I learned about tea from my English friends. But it pleases Rosa to set a lavish table, always; sometimes so lavish that Maria gets quite confused waiting on it.

"Now, how shall we go about persuading your grandmother to let you come with us?"

"You could start by sending her flowers," Elizabeth Lamb suggested. "She loves white roses."

Behind them, Benno sniggered softly. He attempted to turn his amusement into a choked cough as Mr. Vincentia turned angrily to him and forcefully exclaimed what sounded to Elizabeth Lamb like, "*Stattizitta!*"

"That means 'shut up,'" said Viola, grinning. "He won't let me say it, though. He says it's common."

"Why's the man laughing?" asked Elizabeth Lamb, whose stomach had been soothed by bread-and-butter and was now sending signals demanding a large cream-filled pastry decorated with candied violets.

"In my — family," Mr. Vincentia answered, frowning, "white roses are sent only — white roses are regarded as unlucky.

"We are very superstitious, I suppose, we Italians. For instance, my grandmother instilled in me a fear of cats as evil creatures, a fear Viola does not share. She keeps one, and my blood runs cold when it comes near me."

As if on cue, a piercing "Meeeoww!" came from the screened door

Maria had shut behind her. Viola ran to it and secured a fat brown-and-white kitten. She pried open its little jaws with one hand while with the other she attempted to cram into them a strawberry from the bowl on the tea table.

"I swear that girl is mentally deficient," Elizabeth Lamb thought as Mr. Vincentia spoke loudly: "Viola, you have been told what he should eat! You will make him sick — again. The last time, he ruined my Bokhara!"

Viola pressed her face into the struggling kitten's fur and kissed it, with a loud smacking noise, before she thrust him at her grand-father. He pushed the animal away, with an angry exclamation, and walked to the marble wall fountain, staring at the stream of water that poured gently from the lion's mouth at its center. His arms were rigid at his sides, his hands tightly clenched.

"I cannot understand why you are so attached to that animal," he said over his shoulder. Viola put it down and took another macaroon. The kitten ran to hide under Elizabeth Lamb's chair.

"Because I got him at my school," Viola answered sweetly. She began to chant: "I – love – my – school – and – I – love – my – teachers – and" — her voice rose loudly with emotion and she ran all her words together — "Ilovemostofallthedearonewhogavehim-tome." She smiled triumphantly at Elizabeth Lamb. "So there!" she ended.

"I did not know you were that fond of any of your teachers," her grandfather said. "And it is cruel of you to insist on keeping that cat when you know how I fear him. I feel you must really dislike me."

Elizabeth Lamb thought that only a much too overly-indulgent grandfather would endure the presence of something he so dreaded. She wondered where Viola's parents were and why Mr. Vincentia would have accepted the responsibility of raising such a difficult child. "Why doesn't he put her in a girls' boarding school?" she thought. But aloud she asked politely, "Where do you go to school, Viola?" following her grandmother's example of always introducing the pleasant side of a difficult subject, if there were even a hint of one.

Viola, who was scrambling about in front of the boxwood bushes along the Lime Street wall, making loud coaxing noises at her invisible kitten, ignored the question. "At the Exceptional School, near Canton," her grandfather answered.

"Oh," said Elizabeth Lamb, "that's nice." Remembering vaguely that a married couple who were among her Aunt Sarah's friends ran the school — people named Bath, was it, or maybe Bisk? — and that she had once heard her aunt rather acidly telling them that she thought it most unfair to bright children that retarded ones were termed "exceptional," she said no more.

"But I'm slipping," she thought. "I should have seen at once that that poor girl is not normal. She's so pretty, though, that one doesn't immediately catch on. Or maybe it's the heat; I think it's melting my mind, or something."

Another fat, dark woman appeared at the doorway and spoke rapidly in Italian to Mr. Vincentia. His answer was as rapid and his expression a mixture of amusement, annoyance, and gratification. He waved the woman inside and gave directions to Benno, who followed her after a signal to the upper window.

Mr. Vincentia poured himself more tea and turned, laughing, to his guest. "I have a quantity of Spanish onions flown over each month from land I own in Sicily; they are the best in the world, and Rosa uses many onions in her cooking. But today, my friend whose plane brings them just left six times the usual amount. My entrance hall is overflowing with bags of onions, and Rosa is distressed. Benno will have to put them down in her room, which is the coolest, since we have not enough space in the basement bins."

"You could put some in my grandmother's wine cellar," Elizabeth Lamb suggested. "It's cool, and it's sort of empty now because my father was staying with her for a time — wait, I know! If you gave her a bag or two of onions, it would be a better present than flowers. She loves onions, and do you know how much Spanish onions cost now? Alice won't even order them, they're so expensive."

"They are thirty dollars for fifty pounds, wholesale," her host answered promptly. "Last year it was six dollars. The onion-growing land had severe flooding last winter. I have some little interest in the vegetable markets," he added.

"Are you retired now, mainly?" Elizabeth Lamb asked with the usual frank curiosity her family deplored. "You must have made a lot of money, because this house was up for sale a long time, the price was so high."

Mr. Vincentia raised his eyebrows, although he smiled gently. "I see you do not observe the Bostonian *tabu* against discussing money, private money, that is. Friends of mine who are what we outsiders call the Baked Beans will talk of city or national or international monies, and sometimes of their business finances, but never, never of their personal means.

"But, yes, I am somewhat retired and, yes, I was prosperous in many business interests when I was younger. Now I concentrate on my publishing house and on my candy factories. You have perhaps heard of *Cioccolato da Vincentia?*"

"My goodness, yes! They are *so* good. They beat Belgian chocolates by a mile, but they do cost an awful lot. My father bought my mother a big box a couple of weeks ago, after he'd done something terrible and because he was trying to get her to go look at the new mine in Spain with him, and my Aunt Sarah said it was a shameful extravagance. She said he should just have gone to Bailey's, where they have very nice candy."

She grinned. "My mother didn't offer her any, after that. She and my grandmother ate the whole box — three apiece after dinner every night. My mother did give me two of hers, once."

"Well, then, I am somewhat known to your grandmother. That is good. I have more hope of your joining us."

"Grandfather," said Viola, who had given up her pursuit of the kitten and was rapidly finishing all the pastries on the tea table, "I wish we could stay awhile in Maine, not just leave her and the cousin off. You would like anchoring in a pretty cove and I could spend more time with this nice girl and see her grandmother's place." She produced what Elizabeth Lamb recognized as another "society smile."

Mr. Vincentia was pleased. "But, come, Viola, you must eat up these strawberries. Rosa tells me again that each time I am not with you for lunch or dinner, you send away the vegetables and fruits. You will be sick if you go on like this, eating only meat and sweets."

"She could take vitamin pills," Elizabeth Lamb said helpfully, as

31

Viola shook her head and made a face at the bowl held for her by her grandfather.

Viola stamped her boot so loudly that the emerging kitten hid himself again. "I will *not*. They give my mother pills in that place where she is kept and they make her crazy. And you put her there, Grandfather!"

Mr. Vincentia sighed. "Viola, it was necessary. Now, come, I will feed these to you." He held a berry to her lips, and then another and another until the bowl was empty. Viola immediately seized it, filled it with milk from the pitcher on the table and set it on the paving with dangerous force. Elizabeth Lamb was shocked, for the bowl was of very old paste-ware, decorated with painted berries, and obviously valuable.

"She will take things she dislikes only from the hand of someone she loves," said Viola's grandfather, beaming fondly at his grandchild. "And who loves her, as I do." Viola rewarded him with a charming smile. "Brat," thought Elizabeth Lamb.

"Well," she said, spurred somewhat by Maria's standing just inside the door, patiently waiting to clear away the remains of tea, "I have to go. Thank you for a very nice time, Mr. Vincentia. I hope to see you soon, Viola.

"I'm going home to start figuring how to make Grandmother let me go to Maine with you. Don't forget the onions, Mr. Vincentia. Maybe Viola will bring them over." Viola stuck out her tongue.

Mr. Vincentia courteously accompanied his guest to the garden door. Benno rushed from the house and put himself between the door and his employer, as he held it open. Elizabeth Lamb walked slowly around the corner to her grandmother's front door on Brimmer Street. The late afternoon sun had made the brick sidewalk uncomfortable to her bare feet. She took in a deep breath and wondered what was vaguely puzzling her. Something — something somebody had said that didn't seem right?

"It's so awfully scalding hot in Boston that it makes me feel all disoriented," she thought. "I've just got to get up to The Bungalow. I could think there, and get that dumb novel started. If I weren't so hot, I'd understand why that nice old man has that tough-looking Benno hanging around. He acts just like a bodyguard, but maybe he's only a poor relative who needs a job.

"I wonder why their garden is so much cooler than ours? It can't be the 'luck of the Irish,' either, as Alice is always saying. It must be because he's so rich. Daddy says money can't buy you everything but that it certainly can alleviate all of life's miseries. Maybe it could even tone down a heat wave."

She rang the bell, putting the Vincentias from her mind and concentrating on thoughts of a cool bath, to help her brush off the awful wrath of Alice, roused from her afternoon rest.

• CHAPTER 3 •

Dinner on Brimmer, 1

ELIZABETH WORTHINGTON descended the stairs from her fourth floor studio almost as nimbly as she had over fifty years before when she was a young bride and the place a refuge from her mother-in-law's authority over all the regions below it. Her seclusion in the large, bare room, the high windows of which revealed only sky, and the chimney-pots of other Back Bay houses, had given her the sense of security she needed to begin the creation of the little enameled paintings on precious metals and the hand-wrought jewelry for which she was now uniquely famous.

She paused on the third floor to smile at her granddaughter's coaxing voice, accompanied by loud splashes, coming clearly through two closed doors, and wondered why Elizabeth Lamb, in her bath, was making what sounded like a most persuasive speech.

On the floor below, she quickly washed her hands and face in her own bathroom and applied face powder, green eyeshadow and a pale lipstick. She brushed her shining black hair and re-knotted it low on her neck before she changed her cotton trousers and smock for a short, tiered beige chiffon dress and matching moiré slippers.

"Sleeves," she thought, smoothing down hers, "were invented for women over forty."

She regarded herself in the mirror, wryly pushing up the skin on her cheeks so that she looked almost as she had long years ago. "Oh," she said aloud to her image, "how terrible it is to have almost the same feelings and reactions one had at sixteen — even the same fears, except also new ones! — and yet, to the world, to be an old woman. But since it is only Eb Tibbets tonight" — the reflection wrinkled up its thin, aristocratic nose — "who cares?"

She went more slowly down to the first floor, feeling some disquiet: the lamp on the table in the entrance hall below her was throwing a fat, ominous shadow, its arms akimbo, up against the wall at her right. "Now what?" she thought, casting her mind among the possibilities that might have upset her volatile cook.

Once, after reading that Winston Churchill had said, in reference to General deGaulle, that "the heaviest cross I have to bear is the Cross of Lorraine," she had murmured to her husband that *her* heaviest cross was a sturdy Celtic one. "And," she had gone on, "unusual in that the horizontal pieces are triangular, because her hands are always on her hips!"

Otis Worthington had not agreed with his wife. Alice had been a scrawny, big-eyed, humble fourteen-year-old come over from Ireland to help her aunt in his mother's kitchen when he was a young man. He had been sorry for the child and insisted she attend school and then learn cooking, when schooling was abandoned by her. He had always found her agreeable, as she had been, to him. But women, even her idol's mother and, later, his wife, were to her another kettle of Irish cod.

Almost nothing the widowed Elizabeth Worthington did or even suggested to Alice was ever acceptable as what "the mister" would have wished. Had his wife not promised the ailing Otis to keep Alice until retirement — "one year nearer now," she whispered to herself every New Year's Day — and had she not always been able to find some humor even in Alice's most outrageous acts and pronouncements, the cook would have long since been sent packing.

"Begorrah!" came loudly up the stairwell. Elizabeth frowned in apprehension. She had once told Alice that never, in her several

35

visits to Ireland, had she heard an Irishman, even a stage Irishman, proclaim, "Begorrah!" Alice had replied that "the air of the Old Country, 'tis fair calmin'" — (to the nerves of the sensitive Irish) — "and Boston's ain't," so there was no need to say it Over There. After that, though, it had been reserved for occasions when Alice was most violently enraged, which occurred at least five or six times a month.

"Good-evening, Alice," she said equably, upon reaching the foot of the stairs. She produced her lovely smile. "I know you have an especially good dinner for Mr. Tibbets tonight. He does so love the sauce you make for fried soft-shell crabs and you were very clever to get the last crabs the fish store had."

Alice did not trouble to explain that the crabs were slated to rest in the refrigerator in their packaging because she had felt in the mood for chicken salad. She swept one plump arm around in a violent semi-circle, keeping the other antagonistically on her hip.

"Look!" she said loudly, adding a defiant, "Begorrah!"

Elizabeth looked. A dozen or more large canvas sacks were strewn about the hall floor. "What ever did you buy?" she asked quickly, knowing that, with Alice, a good offense was better than even a superlative defense.

"Buy?" shrilled Alice. "Me? Not nuthin' did I buy. As ye well know, I do me level best to keep yer expenses down. Gettin' on, y'are, and would do well to put somethin' aside fer yer old age." She considered, and added, "Ma'am."

"But what are all these? Where did they come from?"

"The Black Hand," Alice replied sinisterly. "That's where they come from. And wot it means, I do not know." As her employer began to smile again, she raised a grim hand.

"Smile, if ye like — ma'am. But 'tis no smilin' matter. The bell rings, I git up from me bed, me pore bones still achin' from all that good cookin' I done fer lunch — I already bin woke up once by that Elizabeth Lamb, in 'er bare feet, do ye mind — "

"What in the world do Elizabeth Lamb's bare feet have to do with all these bags? What's in them?"

"It's onions what's in 'em. The bell rings, as I was tryin' me best to say. This dark Eyetalian says these onions is fer you. He drags 'em in, tips his shofer's cap — civil, he was; I'll say that for 'im — and drives away in a big limmerzeen, round to Lime Street. I run to the winder and watched. And leaves me with thousands of onions. No doubt stolen," she added with relish.

"The man who bought the house next door has a large car he keeps in a garage on Lime Street. And didn't you tell me he was Italian? He must just have sent his chauffeur over with a neighborly present. And a very nice one," she said, taking the offense again. "Haven't you been complaining about how much onions cost? But I wonder where he got so many?"

"No doubt they're hot," Alice replied knowledgeably. "He's gettin' us to hide them fer 'im. Prob'ly made all his money shakin' down pushcart vendors. I seen movies."

She glared as Elizabeth Worthington began to laugh uncontrollably. "When ye git done, tell me — ma'am — wot I'm to do with these. Me back won't stand fer me to hist them down to the basement, and we got comp'ny comin' —"

The doorbell rang. Alice blanched. "MarymitheraGod, not more!" She collapsed on the bottom stair, which creaked loudly.

Elizabeth sighed and opened the door. A tall, thin, gap-toothed, sandy-haired boy removed his baseball cap and grinned at her. "Evenin', Miz Worthington," he said. "I jest came by for a little visit, like, 'fore I try to git back to the island."

She was at first disconcerted. Then she recognized the boy as the oldest child of a large clan of Mount Desert Island natives who lived near her summer home. He was at least a head taller than when she had seen him the previous fall, but the grin was unmistakable. In Maine, it had often accompanied the gift of an illegal portion of venison.

"Why, it's Payson," she said pleasantly. "Payson Prouty, you're all grown up! I'm awfully glad to see you, and we'll certainly have a nice little visit. Before my dinner guest comes," she added firmly, aware that Payson might have inherited his father Varner's tendency to come for "a little visit" and to stay until the liquor ran out or weariness closed his hostess' eyes.

Payson came in, grinning wider than ever, and then fell back a step at the sight of Alice, now sprawled over several stairs. "She

37

fainted, ma'am?" he asked uneasily. "But her eyes is open."

"Why, no, Payson. Alice just got upset at having to carry all these bags down to the base — cellar," she ended, remembering that to many who had gone to school on Mount Desert Island, "basement," for some reason lost in the mists of antiquity, meant "lavatory."

"Wouldn't you do it for us? And then I know Alice will fix you a snack" — she looked firmly at her cook — "which you can have in the drawing room with me, since she has to set the table in the dining room."

Alice heaved up her pore bones, with all their lavish covering, brightening at the sight of a male, especially a useful one. "Foller me, bhoy," she directed, "and wot is it you might be fancyin' t'eat, now?"

"I don't suppose you got any clams to fry up, ma'am?" Payson was easily carrying three of the sacks down the basement stairs. "My mouth's ben set fer some good ones ever since I got here. Somehow, them at the Hojos' ain't as tasty as Mumma's."

"Like crabs? Got some of 'em handy. Could fry you up a few, fer a sandwich, in some nice butter. My, ain't you the strong one! Jest throw them sacks in this closet. Be the time they're all down here, I'll have you a nice little supper."

Elizabeth was in the kitchen getting beer and a glass for her guest. She shook her head as Alice lumbered up the stairs. "There aren't enough crabs for dinner and for Payson, too. Can't you make him a sandwich out of these capons? Eileen and her husband and I hardly touched them last night."

"They're fer me special chicken salad. *Which* Mr. Tibbets thinks a sight more of than crabs. Said so onct, he did." Alice put her hand to her forehead and groaned resoundingly. "Oh, me nerves is ever'-which-way! If I git enny more upset, I'll have to take to me bed."

Her employer accepted the hint and went to await Payson in the drawing room. He came in, grinning as always, and sat beside her on the sofa, his grin broadening at the two frosted bottles on the low table in front of him. "Them'll go down right good, Miz Worthington. It was that hot, hitchin' to the subway stop, and then them trains was like ovens." He poured beer and sipped with pleasure, looking around him appreciatively. "This room is some old elegant. I wrote Mumma about how the ceilin' is all gold-like; from old tea-papers, you told me. I know she'd admire to see it."

"She's welcome any time Varner brings her along when he comes down to see a baseball game. You said you're going back to Maine, Payson? Didn't you get along with Dr. Oliver? When I heard last fall he needed someone to help his kitchen staff, I thought sending you to him was a wonderful idea. I knew you'd done cooking in Bar Harbor and I thought you might get to be his head cook someday, though I suppose cooking for restaurants differs from institutional cooking."

"Oh, it ain't so different, and at Doc Oliver's nobody was as fussy as them tourists and summer complaints — summer visitors is, over to Bar Harbor. I got along with him and everybody else jest finest kind, even them pore little blind buggers what couldn't hear good neither in that wing what had to hev a special nurse who knowed that writin' that's all dots. I made a couple of tasty dishes for 'em special, onct or twice.

"Funny, too, because I never afore could stand bein' around sick people. Wouldn't ever go see Mumma or the kids, times they had to be in the hospital back to home." He looked sadly down into his glass. "I jest hev a turrible hankerin' to git back to the island right now, fer a time, is all. Thought you might know somebody goin' up I could git a lift off'n"

He glanced sideways at her. "It's about time you was leavin' fer the island, ain't it, ma'am?"

"I'm not going for two weeks, at least. Couldn't you fly, Payson, or take the bus? You've saved some money, haven't you?"

Payson blushed. "I hev, but I'm tryin' to keep aholt of ever' cent, almost. I — I got a girl." He ducked his head.

Elizabeth Lamb had entered just behind Alice, who put before Payson a large tray laden, Elizabeth Worthington saw with annoyance, with not only three enormous sandwiches that must have held a dozen of the hard-won crabs but also a huge chunk of the imported whiskey cake she had recently been given and directed be left sealed in its tin till the autumn. It was wedged on a plate beside a bowl containing at least a pint of the rich, hand-cranked ice cream she loved and now enjoyed only after the rare occasions when Alice's busy niece Eileen came to dinner.

Twenty years ago Eileen had been hired to make the ice cream every Saturday after her catechism class; later, as a college student, she had made it as often as she could, in gratitude for help with her tuition. Now a successful criminal lawyer, each time she was a dinner guest she insisted, to her aunt's rage and her old friend's delight, on coming an hour early and leaving the dining room frequently to return to her familiar haunt in the basement where the ancient freezer awaited.

Elizabeth Worthington wondered, in well-controlled anger, how much of the gallon Eileen had made the night before remained for dinner tonight. She had just determined to speak up when her granddaughter, perhaps luckily, forestalled her.

"Hi, Payson!" she cried. "Did I hear you say you've got a girl? And you promised to wait till I grew up! Oh, Payson, you *are* bad."

Payson blushed again. "Now, I never, Elizabeth Lamb. Not never!" He grinned. "Too wild fer me, you are. Jest like a rambunctious, thorny wild rose, up to home. I like ladies that is more tame-like — quiet, same as your grandmumma here. She allus reminds me of one of them sweet-smellin' white flowers ladies pin on them sometimes when they go out to eat." He blushed again. "My Pansy is real quiet, and sweet, too."

Mrs. Worthington thought that Payson must have inherited his poetic streak from his father, who composed verse when he was not engaged in poaching deer, robbing lobster traps, fighting those who offended him, drinking beer, or other pleasurable pursuits. Very pleased at being compared to a sweet-smelling flower, she said gracefully, "Why, you're awfully kind, Payson. Now eat up those sandwiches before they get cold."

"Cold!" Alice snorted. "In this heat they ain't goin' to chill down much. That there ice cream fair melted away onct I set it out of the fridge —"

Elizabeth rose quickly, motioning her cook toward the door. "Elizabeth Lamb, you entertain Payson while I speak to Alice a minute. I'll be right back."

When she returned, with only a faint touch of angry red on her high cheek-bones, having firmly put the ice cream in the refrigerator's freezer and Alice, more or less firmly, in her place, Elizabeth Lamb was so excited as to be incoherent.

"Grandmother! Payson wants to get back home and — what do you think! — that nice Mr. Vincentia next door is cruising up to Mount Desert day after tomorrow! And he needs someone to help the cook on his yacht and Payson's worked in kitchens and he invited Persis and me to go up with him, too!

"Oh, Grandmother, I'd like so much to get away from — the heat — and Payson could watch out for Persis and me on the boat — if Mr. Vincentia hires him, and I just know he will! — and he'd be around to check on us at The Bungalow — he says he will and I bet Mr. Vincentia would let him get off in Maine — and I just want so much to go! Oh, please." She excitedly took several swallows from Payson's glass and began to hiccup loudly.

Elizabeth Worthington looked impassively at her before she walked to a side table where a slightly subdued Alice was placing drink preparations and an insulated silver ice bucket. She poured what was, for her, a large amount of whiskey into a glass before she added an orange slice and ice cubes, on which she dropped Angestura bitters. She returned and sat, sipping her drink and regarding her granddaughter. "Between this child and Alice," she thought humorously, "me nerves is ever'-which-way. But I can't blame her for wanting to get away from Alice."

She spoke severely: "Elizabeth Lamb, do I understand that you have taken it upon yourself to intrude on our new neighbor and that you are probably responsible for the hundred or more dollars worth of onions now in our cellar? Did you ask for them? And did you invite yourself and Persis to travel with him? Haven't I told you never, never go up to people and introduce yourself? There is such a thing as privacy. And hold your breath so those distracting hiccups stop!"

She paused to smile reassuringly at Payson, who was looking both embarrassed and anxious, as well as a little pleased. "She certainly *is* rambunctious, Payson, but you mustn't let our discussion spoil your supper.

"Now," she turned to her granddaughter, "let's hear what you have to say. And before you begin, Elizabeth Lamb, certainly you may not go off on a total stranger's boat, with or without Persis and Payson. You surely know that."

Elizabeth Lamb let out her held breath forcefully. "Oh, Grandmother! I want so much to go!" She assumed a pitiful expression that almost made Elizabeth smile, and shifted her attack. "But won't you just call Mr. Vincentia and tell him about Payson? It would be so kind to Payson and Mr. Vincentia, too — and you always do say to be neighborly. He's awfully nice. He just suggested sending you some onions because *he's* being neighborly."

She thought. "And he isn't really a stranger. He's *Cioccolato da Vincentia!*"

"He's *what?*" Elizabeth's glass halted half-way to her mouth.

Payson choked on his cake. "But that's the kitten's name!" He blushed in anguish as the two astonished Elizabeths stared at him. He drank some beer and went on nervously, "I heard somebody callin', 'Here, kitty, kitty' and then she said, 'Here, Cheeoc—' she said that name. Next door, it was, when I was ringin' your bell."

"His granddaughter Viola has a kitten," Elizabeth Lamb informed them, "and I guess it's named that, after the candy. But, Grandmother, he makes those chocolates you love and he's *so* charming. Won't you call him about Payson? So Payson can sleep tonight," she added, her voice dropping in effective pathos.

"Please, ma'am?" Payson asked anxiously. Elizabeth Worthington relented.

"You call him then, Elizabeth Lamb, and tell him you've found someone, and be sure to tell him I much appreciate the gift of the onions. But, wait — he's just moved in. His phone won't be listed."

"Oh, Grandmother. There's such a thing as Information. Or Directory Assistance, or whatever they call it." She busily left for the telephone in the hall cloakroom.

Elizabeth poured Payson more beer. The doorbell rang. "Oh, no," she thought, "not more onions!"

Alice came into the drawing room, staggering under the weight of a large gardenia tree in full bloom, its pot set into a handsome pink-and-white flowered *faience* bowl. "That's it — that sweet-smellin' flower I said you was like!" Payson cried.

"What — where did that come from?" Elizabeth asked Alice's retreating back. Her front immediately appeared, clutching a sheaf of long-stemmed red roses to it. "At least two dozen, I bet," she announced. "I'll put 'em in the biggest vase. And wot the mister would've said, I do *not* know. Fine goin's-on."

"My God," said Elizabeth, who seldom took her Maker's name in vain. Her granddaughter came in, smiling.

"Mr Vincentia says he hopes you like the flowers. He didn't know if they'd got here yet. He's very pleased about Payson, because he hasn't been able to find anybody, and he would like to talk to you. He said if it's not inconvenient. Please, Grandmother?"

Elizabeth Worthington, still staring at the gardenia tree, slowly left the room. As she passed Alice, now precariously holding a huge crystal vase with one arm while the other was extended its full length the better to squint at a slip of pasteboard held in its hand, she absently took the card, murmuring, "Do be careful of those roses, Alice." An indignant "Huh!" followed her. While she was gone Elizabeth Lamb assured Payson that his new job was practically certain, that she'd love to meet his Pansy, and that she'd help him finish his beer.

"He'll probably ask to see you, Payson, and you shouldn't have too much to drink. And you'd better rinse out your mouth in the cloakroom lavatory, too, just to be sure he doesn't smell it on your breath. Now, let's decide what you should say to him. You have to make sure he knows you want to get off when we — I mean he — gets to M.D.I., but don't worry because he knows people in Canada and can probably get a cook's helper there for his trip back."

They were still rehearsing Payson's approach when Elizabeth returned, looking somewhat dazed. She still held Mr. Vincentia's card, which she laid on the table as she picked up her drink.

Elizabeth Lamb seized it and ran her thumb over it. "It's engraved, Grandmother. See what a gentleman he is!"

"Really, Elizabeth Lamb! It's vulgar to do that. And vulgar to think engraving means someone is a gentleman; it may only mean he has the money to afford it, and you ought to know that money has nothing to do with being a gentleman!"

"Aunt Sarah does it," her granddaughter replied, unabashed. "But I'll remember. What did Mr. Vincentia say?"

"He's certainly charming. Somehow I — I invited him to dinner tomorrow night. I can't think what came over me." She frowned in puzzlement and sounded a little angry, although she was half-smiling somewhat wryly.

"But what did he say about Payson? Does he want to see him?"

"Yes, he does. You're to go over now, Payson. It's the next house around the corner; just turn right when you leave here. Finish up, dear, because he's leaving for an engagement at eight. Goodness, it's well past seven now; where is Eb Tibbets, I wonder?"

Payson seized his napkin, which had stayed folded on the tray throughout his meal, and nervously ran it over his face. He inquired worriedly of Elizabeth Worthington if he should mention all the places he had worked, "'specially Doc Oliver's, him bein' the last?" and on being told, rather grandly, that her recommendation should suffice, grinned with relief. He slicked down his hair with his fingers and grinned again as he expressed fervent thanks. He almost ran out the door.

"Make me another old-fashioned, please, Elizabeth Lamb," her grandmother requested. She was obeyed with alacrity. One of the first fatherly duties Peter Worthington had undertaken toward his then eight-year-old daughter, on his return after an absence of three years in a South African mining venture, had been to train her as an expert and willing bartender. She wondered, as she carefully measured whiskey, when would be the propitious time to produce the persuasive speech she had carefully composed in her bath. "Maybe it won't work now," she thought sadly. "Maybe I've blown it, with this Payson thing. Darn it, why did he have to show up tonight—" The doorbell rang.

"More flowers, I'll bet," she thought, running to the hall. "Oh, I hope he's not overdoing it." Then glumly, "Oh, hello, Mr. Tibbets."

Eberly Tibbets came in jauntily, followed closely by Alice, who sent an adoring simper in his direction before she reluctantly returned to the kitchen. He was very tall, with narrow shoulders and a lean, brown face topped by a shock of well-brushed white hair. He had been told he resembled Senator Leverett Saltonstall and always did his best to arrange his expression so as to further the impression. He wore the bow tie favored by proper Boston lawyers and trustees above a soft blue shirt and a rumpled grey-and-white seersucker suit.

Elizabeth Lamb, who disliked him because she found him "smarmy," to use her father's term, and because he had paid assiduous court to her grandmother ever since his wife's death (more assiduous after each quarter the Worthington investments took an upswing), noticed with pleasure that he was developing a pot-belly. Her grandmother found bulging stomachs in men unpleasant, saying often that only women who had borne a number of children had earned the distinction — though not completely.

With a flourish, he presented Elizabeth Worthington with a small cone of waxed paper and sat down in the most comfortable chair. "Good evening, my dear. You're looking lovely, as always. These are from my little back garden; know they're your favorite. Beautiful ladies deserve beautiful flowers. Ha!"

Elizabeth, smiling pleasantly, unwrapped three small white roses and directed Elizabeth Lamb to put them into a little vase that already held a few shiny green leaves. Elizabeth Lamb then moved to the fireplace, to bend over the enormous bouquet of large red roses Alice had placed before the folded paper screen that covered it in summer, before she walked gracefully to the gardenia tree. She put her nose to a bloom, inhaling loudly, and then prettily asked the guest if she could make him an old-fashioned.

Mr. Tibbets looked from the roses to the gardenias, his lantern jaw dropping. "Somebody died, Elizabeth? Looks like a Polish funeral in here. And, no, Elizabeth Lamb, I'd much prefer a Negroni. Too hot for whiskey.

"You know, my dear," he turned petulantly to his hostess, "that I always drink gin. Low of me, of course. Ha!"

"Oh, Eb, I'm afraid Peter drank it all when he was here, and I forgot to order more. And *your* roses are simply beautiful."

Alice bounced in, flipping up her starched white apron to exhibit a bottle. "I hid this from Mr. Peter, I did. Remembered Mr. Tibbets likes it and I knew he'd be comin' over soon." She fawned upon him as he told her she was a sweet Irish rose and if she'd find Campari

45

and Cinzano, why then he'd be in like Flynn.

Alice, with more simpering, produced them and Elizabeth Lamb made the cocktail. "Who's Flynn, Mr. Tibbets?" she asked, with her usual curiosity.

"Don't know. Somebody apocryphal." Mr. Tibbets, appeased by the taste of the Negroni, was more his, so Elizabeth Lamb thought, fake-jovial self. "Maybe he sent all these flowers?" He raised bushy white eyebrows at Elizabeth Worthington. "They look real enough, though. Cost a bundle, too, hothouse roses in June, not to mention that tree. Somewhat gaudy, don't you think, Elizabeth?" He buried his long nose in his glass and sulked, waiting for his indirect question to be answered.

Elizabeth sipped her drink, still smiling pleasantly. She remembered a story told her by her husband about Eb Tibbets' economical habits: that he had, years ago, become enamored of a secretary in their firm of fiduciary trustees and bought tickets for a musical — for the cheapest seats in the Colonial Theatre, Otis had assured her — and invited the young woman to spend the night with him at a Boston hotel. He had felt secure doing so since she was leaving for a better job in a few days. For the same reason, she had accepted, thinking (so Otis' secretary, his source of the tale had said) that the encounter would make a good story at the farewell luncheon her fellow workers were planning.

But when she found that the drink with which she was to be lasciviously plied consisted of, not champagne from room service, but a bottle of domestic sherry Mr. Tibbets produced from his briefcase, she had pleaded a sudden headache and left, laughing all the way down in the elevator.

"Oh, no, I think the flowers are lovely," Elizabeth answered cheerfully. "And it was so very charming of my neighbor," — she glanced at the card — "Vittorio Vincentia, to send them."

"V.V., hey? Well, he can afford it. Awfully brash of him though, I'd say. He's only just moved in."

"Oh, you know him?"

"Client of mine. Set up a couple of trust funds for him. I see him at lunch now and then, always as his guest. Nice, that: we're used to treating the clients to lunch, though they pay in the end, of course. Ha! V.V.'s got pots of money and's a good feller — 'spite of his background, which was pretty much lower class."

"Daddy says," Elizabeth Lamb observed, "that the only difference between the lower class and the middle class is that the middle class keep their appointments."

Her grandmother smiled at her. "But what is his background, exactly? Alice said something about the Black Hand, but you know Alice. And there isn't such a thing anymore, is there?"

Eb Tibbets frowned thoughtfully. Elizabeth reflected that although in many ways he was extremely foolish, in his knowledge of financial matters no one was sounder; he had, moreover, an amazingly wide range of knowledge coupled with a good memory, as well as being a fairly good judge of character.

"Doubt it," he answered. "Bit old-fashioned, that. It was an extortion scheme set up by Italian criminals in this country — oh, seventy or eighty years ago — to get money out of decent, hardworking Italians by threatening them or their children. Now we have the Cosa Nostra, as that informer — what was his name, oh, Valachi — let out a few years back.

"Elizabeth Lamb, you can make me another of these. Delicious, my dear."

"What's the Cosa Nostra? What does that mean?" Elizabeth Lamb asked, taking his glass.

"Means 'our thing' or 'our affair,' I believe. It's what outsiders refer to as the Mafia."

"The Mafia? Is Mr. Vincentia connected with it?" Elizabeth Worthington did not seem perturbed, merely inquiring, but Elizabeth Lamb would willingly have emptied Mr. Tibbets' new Negroni over his neat hair instead of courteously handing it to him. Always fair, she recalled that she, herself, had asked him to define the term.

"We-e-ll, there have been rumors. Of course, there always are about any Italian who started from nothing and is now a millionaire several times over. I have no personal knowledge that he is; but then, how could I? And everything I've handled for him was perfectly sound.

"If you want my guess, only a guess, I'd say he could have been, at one time. Usually though, once you're in, you're in. Or so they say."

"But doesn't the Mafia always live together, sort of; in a community, like? With gate-keepers and all? They do in the movies." Elizabeth Lamb hopefully regarded Mr. Tibbets as she questioned him. "Mr. Vincentia lives right next door, and anybody could knock on the door." Then she thought of Benno, her heart sinking, and hoped that Alice had not observed him and described him to her grandmother.

"He lived in the North End, up to when he became your neighbor," Mr. Tibbets replied. "When he wasn't at his house in London, or travelling. Spends some time on his yacht, too; big as a minesweeper, I'm told. Don't know if it has armor-plate and guns, though. Ha!"

He drank deeply and signalled for another. "And you certainly might call the North End an Italian community. I happen to love it; love the restaurants and the vegetable stores and coffee bars and the whole air of the place. Often thought of moving there from Mount Vernon Street, now that Priscilla's gone. No violent crime; they won't stand for it."

He became pensive. "There certainly are car thefts, though." He brightened. "But, then, I don't have a car. 'Specially in *this* city; Boston's getting famous for car thefts."

"*Who* won't stand for crime?" Elizabeth Worthington asked.

"Italians are very peaceable people," her granddaughter answered quickly. "You say that. You like to walk to the North End when we go to Faneuil Hall Market, and you say how nice and friendly everybody is. When we ask where to get *cannoli* or the best expresso, they even take time to go with us and show us."

"Better things there to eat than light bulbs, Elizabeth," Mr. Tibbets observed. "Ha! D'you know there's been another rash of eating them at Harvard? God, the more things change, the more they stay the same. When my son Jack was there—"

"Dinner, ma'am," Alice announced; her pale red hair, usually screwed into a top-knot, was now frizzily around her face, in honor of a gentleman caller.

The chicken salad was proclaimed by Mr. Tibbets to be even better than that served at his sacrosanct club. "And the *Sancerre* —

Elizabeth, it's a '59! As some lucky feller's wife, you'd make him a superb hostess." He bugged out his small grey eyes, smirking as he faced her across the round old mahogany table.

Elizabeth Lamb, between them, kept her eyes on her plate and her mind on what she would say to her grandmother after her suitor left, both about him and going to Maine. "Phone call for you in the kitchen," Alice told her, entering to hold a basket of soda bread beside Mr. Tibbets. "Better take it; I couldn't make 'er understand you was at table. Sounded like a little kid. I didn't know you could be bothered with ennybody yer own age."

By the time she returned, the soda bread had all but disappeared. "And it looked light for once, too," she thought. At her grandmother's inquiring glance she explained, "That was Viola Vincentia. She must be at least sixteen but she's — she's young for her age. She wants me to come over early tomorrow morning and do something." She added, in a surprised tone, "She really sounded happy — as if she meant it."

"Whether she meant it or not, go," Mr. Tibbets advised. "Don't think it's revealing any secret to say she's going to be a very rich young lady, as soon as she's twenty-one, or married. You needn't tell her I said that, you know — or her grandfather."

He happily accepted the remainder of the bread and got up gallantly to pour more wine for his hostess. To Elizabeth Lamb, he gave about a quarter-inch and more advice. "Not that I'm conscious of money, my dear — no one could call me mercenary — but sometimes it's as well to keep in with those who have it."

Elizabeth Worthington shook her head, both faintly annoyed and faintly amused. "Speaking of financial matters, Eb, have you brought those powers of attorney for me to sign? I thought it best, even though I'll be gone only two weeks, at the most."

"Of course, of course, Elizabeth." Mr. Tibbets was offended. "Would have suggested it, if you hadn't. Not that anything is likely to come up, of a business nature, but the way the world is going, anything could happen to anybody." He hastily removed his finger bowl and the doily under it from his dessert plate and avidly helped himself to ice cream. "A woman's safest in her own home — her husband's home, that is.

49

"Ah, this is delicious! But no chocolate sauce, Alice? No Bostonian worthy of the name can eat vanilla ice cream without chocolate sauce, Elizabeth! *My* dinner guests would demand it, my dear. Y'know, I've heard that coffee ice cream, with or without sauce, sells better in Boston than anywhere else. As the feller said, 'You can do just about anything with statistics;' I've never known anyone who's ever even tasted coffee ice cream, including myself. Ha!"

"I don't think Eileen's superb product needs any embellishment," Elizabeth replied, serving herself a large amount. By the time Alice reached Elizabeth Lamb with the bowl, it was almost empty. She regarded her portion with gloom and as she very slowly ate it wondered with deeper gloom if, by the documents about to be signed, should her grandmother be put in a hospital by a rampaging Paris taxi, would she end up under Mr. Tibbets' parsimonious care? And, with less vital foreboding, "Oh, I do hope Mr. Vincentia knows what to do with a finger bowl tomorrow night!"

Alice appeared again, the bowl re-filled. "It's the last of it," she announced with some satisfaction, offering it first to the guest. "And, Mr. Tibbets, here's something to go with it, 'stid of choc'late." To him, and him alone, a large slab of whiskey cake was presented.

In the drawing room he was still glowing with the satisfaction of being a favorite while Elizabeth signed the papers he had brought. With great charm, and a tender pat on her arm, he flattered Alice by asking her to witness the signatures, which resulted in his favorite brandy being unearthed from its anti-Peter-Worthington hiding place.

"We goin' to get a East Wind tonight, sor?" she asked, her voice dropping with the awe in which Boston residents regard that useful zephyr. "It would, of course, take away this muggy air," Mr. Tibbets answered heavily, as if the thought were original with him, "but" — ponderously placing his finger tips together and pursing his thin lips — "they say not."

"You can get me a brandy glass too, please," Elizabeth Worthington informed Alice, to head off her disposition to enter into long weather discussions with single gentlemen guests. "Eb, tell me more about my neighbor. Was he born in Italy, and how did he become so successful?"

Mr. Tibbets loved dispensing information. Elizabeth Lamb, giving up the slim hope of brandy, made herself small in a corner and prepared to listen intently, hoping to hear something that would advance her case.

"He and his widowed mother left Sicily when he was about ten, and went to London with some English people she'd done occasional cooking for. They'd taken a house for a while near Catania, where she lived. V.V. remembers she was expected to marry his uncle, whom she disliked, and so she secured her youngest boy and got out. The English family moved to Canada after a year or so but she stayed in London, since she had brothers there. She went out to work as a charwoman and V.V., at twelve, started work in a factory in north London that made boiled sweets, as the English call them. You know, Elizabeth Lamb," — the listener in the corner had not escaped his all-seeing eye — "they're sort of what we term barley sugar.

"Ten years later, he owned the place. It did well, he went on to acquire other candy factories, opened a gambling club, started a publishing firm, of which he set up an American branch when he moved here to live, about twenty years ago — oh, he's had a finger in a good many pies, all of them successful. Has some connection with Canadian oil interests, too. Can't think what else.

"Of course," he smiled and raised quizzical brows, "these are only his — concerns that I know about."

"But what do you know to his discredit?" Elizabeth asked. "How, for instance, did a poor little boy who worked in a candy factory manage to become the owner in ten years? And, really, Eb, do you think he is, or was, in the Mafia?"

Eb Tibbets narrowed his already too-narrow eyes. "Why so interested, my dear?" He laughed uneasily. "Not thinking of him as a subject for romance, are you? Don't think you'd get far. Although his wife died seven years or more ago, he told me himself, one day over lunch, that he could never have an interest in another woman. Very frank and out-going, these Italians, when they want to be, that is.

"Of course, he does take his secretary, a youngish widow, with him when he travels. And he had me arrange to transfer his house in the North End to her when he bought the one next door. A gift for a decade of faithful service, he said." He frowned disapprovingly and shook his head. Elizabeth Lamb wondered if his displeasure was caused by Mr. Vincentia's trips with "a youngish widow" or by his affronting all Mr. Tibbets' standards by giving anything away.

"Nonsense, Eb," her grandmother answered. "I'm hardly romantically interested in someone I've never met. I'm inquiring because evidently he's invited Elizabeth Lamb, and possibly Persis, to be guests on his yacht as far as Mount Desert Island. I'm almost," she glanced at Elizabeth Lamb and sighed, "tempted to let her go. I'm merely inquiring what you know about the man that might influence me against her accepting the invitation.

"Of course, I wouldn't rely entirely on your appraisal, exact as I know it would be, so you mustn't feel too responsible. He's coming to dinner tomorrow night and I flatter myself I'm a pretty acute judge of people."

Mr. Tibbets got up quickly and lavishly poured himself more brandy, as if determined that the next night's guest should not get much of it.

"Well, Elizabeth, I wouldn't say that this dear young lady would be in any danger, if that's what you mean. Even if V.V. had been associated with the mob, he's about the age the younger members, so I gather, refer to as 'mustache Petes' or 'greaseballs' and don't regard as too much of a threat, to them or the organization. He's certainly concerned with many other interests now, whatever his past may have been. And—"

"Greaseballs!" Elizabeth Lamb burst out indignantly. "No one could call him that. Mr. Vincentia is one of the most civilized men I've ever met!"

"Be quiet, Elizabeth Lamb," her grandmother said calmly. "Mr. Tibbets is speaking. Any more rudeness and I will not bother myself any further with your wishes. I probably should not even be considering them. Go on, Eb."

"And," he continued, "they have a tradition of not — ah — harming women, certainly not children. If V.V.'s yacht should be swarmed over by Cosa Nostra pirates" — a chuckle here, at his own wit — "I'm sure Elizabeth Lamb would be spared."

He regarded Elizabeth Lamb, so she thought, as if he almost hoped she would become a break in an otherwise fine tradition. "And I doubt there's any cause for piracy; I gather V.V. is going on a pleasure cruise?" He looked questioningly at her. Elizabeth Lamb nodded emphatically. Remembering Mr. Vincentia's saying he had "business in Canada," she hoped her grandmother had overlooked Mr. Tibbets' reference to Canadian oil interests.

"I can say he's really a charming feller, and would take good care of your granddaughter, or granddaughters. You might mention me, if you go with him, Elizabeth Lamb — that I spoke well of him. Whatever he was, he's now a most responsible citizen. He's most upset at this confounded fuel shortage, which I personally, by the way, think is rigged, and I'm not alone in that feeling. He was saying just the other day that it is disgraceful that Boston, with which he has been made to feel *compatibile,* as he said, is having trouble getting gas and oil for its fire trucks and police cars, and so on."

Elizabeth Lamb groaned inwardly. It was entirely possible that Mr. Vincentia's trip was to arrange something to relieve the problems of his chosen city and if the "riggers" Mr. Tibbets believed in existed, or her grandmother suspected they did, she might well regard an association with him as, indeed, dangerous. Before Mr. Tibbets could say more, or let his very agile mind connect with thoughts of Canadian oil, she jumped up and went quickly to him with the brandy.

"Why thank you, my dear child." Mr. Tibbets was slurring just a trifle: "child" emerged as "shyld." He took a hearty swig from his glass. "Now, what was I saying, Elizabeth?"

"You were going to tell me, once you finished wandering 'all around Robin Hood's barn' — I wonder, by the way, where that originated? Oh, now I'm doing it! You were about to tell me anything you know discreditable to Mr. Vincentia. How," patiently, "did he manage to acquire that first factory? Any rumors?"

"Oh, yes, yes; of course. Well, as you know, I don't accept just anyone as a client, even with an introduction, as V.V. had, no matter what his monetary position is, or appears to be. And I don't go by rumors, Elizabeth." He leaned back in his chair and closed his eyes, smiling happily. "I checked on his origins with my London contacts, of course."

Elizabeth Worthington was aware that the net of Worthington, Peabody, Tibbets & Tibbets was widely flung, and not only in financial centers. A client of her husband's had once proposed settling a large sum on a lady he described as a worthy but indigent young relative of his wife's; unfortunately, he and the lady had been observed by one of Otis' friends behaving most amorously in the elevator of a Manhattan hotel. Otis had discreetly persuaded his client to wait a few years before making the settlement.

And one of Eb's friends and clients, burning to take funds out of sound investments to put them into a venture in Maine that proposed to distribute frozen scallops at high prices, had been informed that a good friend of Eb's, cruising the Maine coast a week before, had just happened to look up several of his cronies in the scallop factory town. They had gleefully and proudly informed him that the factory's new owner was bound to "clean up, 'fore he gets caught" because the "scallops" were circular chunks cut out of halibut.

"Now I'm wandering," Elizabeth thought, firmly putting aside her glass. "Yes, Eb," she said loudly. "And, so?"

Mr. Tibbets opened his eyes. "Well, the factory V.V. first bought had been having a great deal of labor trouble. Especially among its truck drivers; distribution had been almost at a standstill for several months. And a number of the trucks had been wrecked. Customers were having to pick up their own shipments, those who could, and they weren't about to do it forever. So V.V., with some help from his mother's brothers, got it cheap."

"His uncles had funds?"

"As it happened, by this time they were running a very successful fleet of — trucks."

"I see. And the labor relations improved?"

"V.V. raised wages in the plant. *And* fired the remaining truck drivers. Then his uncles took over the distribution and hired them back."

"Indeed. Complex. What would you say about all this?"

"Could be merely a series of coincidences. Shortly after this, he opened a chain of small loan offices, to make loans to Italians who couldn't get credit from banks."

"And that wasn't against British banking regulations?"

"Way it was done, it was perfectly legal. If there were any suspicions of 'shylocking,' as the loan shark racket is called, none of the customers complained."

"And the gambling club?"

"There are widespread private casinos in London. Again, no complaints from anyone.

"Well, Elizabeth," he rose a trifle unsteadily, "I've got an early morning appointment tomorrow. My thanks for a most delightful dinner." He picked up his briefcase. "I'll see you as soon as you return, I hope. I'll send a car to Logan to meet your flight; I'll get one that won't cost you much. There's no one whose company I enjoy more than yours, my dear. Would like," his voice dropped meaningfully, "to have it always."

"Always is a long time, Eb," Elizabeth smilingly replied, as she gracefully turned her head so that his somewhat noisy goodbye kiss fell upon her cheek. "Goodnight."

"Grandmother," Elizabeth Lamb asked as soon as the street door closed, "you wouldn't ever marry him, would you? Because he's—"

"Elizabeth Lamb," her grandmother interrupted, "you don't need to describe Mr. Tibbets to me. Remember the admonition: 'Don't teach your grandmother to suck eggs.' You have a tendency, dearest, to take too much on yourself."

"I know." Elizabeth Lamb was unabashed. "But what about my cruising to Maine with Mr. Vincentia? And Persis, too, if Aunt Sarah lets her? She would if you said so. Because he's really, really very—"

"Elizabeth Lamb, what did I just say? I'll decide tomorrow, after dinner. It won't take you long to pack — if you go, that is." She frowned. "But don't put all your hopes on it.

"Alice, do I remember you're going out tonight? Rather late, isn't it?"

Alice was loading a tray with coffee cups and glasses. "It's the Hibernian Sisters Charity Lodge again, ma'am. They meet late, all of the Sisters bein' hard-workin' women. Now, you," — to Elizabeth Lamb — "if ye're goin' gallivantin' termorrer mornin', jest remember yer breakfast is on the table at eight-thirty, jest after I take yer grandma's tray up. I an't servin' it before *or* after that."

She looked appraisingly at her mistress. "Oh, but Mr. Tibbets is a lovely man. It'd be a pure pleasure—"

"Thank you, Alice." Elizabeth had transferred her frown as she wondered if Elizabeth Lamb would get any breakfasts at any time, once she was safely enroute to Paris. "Elizabeth Lamb, I'm going to my room to list what I'll be packing. Although my plane won't leave till late, the day after tomorrow, I think I'll pack tomorrow morning. I must take something gala; there will be many prominent people, M. Cavalle assures me, at the opening. Better go to bed soon."

"Yes, Grandmother. I'm just going to read awhile." When they were on the second floor landing, safely out of Alice's acute hearing, she informed Elizabeth Worthington: "You know, Eileen told me last night in the basement that there is no Hibernian Sisters Charity Lodge. She thought you should know. Alice goes over to a bar on Charles Street where she's been having a 'thing,' Eileen said, with the bartender, for ten years now."

"I've been aware of that for at least nine and a half years, Elizabeth Lamb. Remember the eggs. Good-night."

As she began to go through the contents of her clothes closet, Elizabeth stopped, staring at a gown in her hand, and thought that her granddaughter might, indeed, be better off on a large boat surrounded by people, whatever its owner was, or had been, than alone in a house with a temperamental cook. And one, moreover, who had been heard to return from the "Hibernian Sisters" obviously having had, as Otis would have said, more than "one over the eight."

Elizabeth Lamb was hanging up her dress when she heard a dash of rain against her south window, the one overlooking the little garden. She pulled the curtain aside and looked out. The bushes three stories below were glistening in the light of the street lamp on the corner of Lime Street and the brick paving was dark and wet. A cool breeze had come up. "There was an east wind, after all," she said aloud. "So much for Mr. Smarty Tibbets. Hope he got soaked, walking home, and that mean Alice, too."

As she was putting her black patent leather slippers away she remembered her sandals and radio, left in the garden. She put her dress and shoes on again and crept quietly downstairs to the little garden door in the basement. The rain had stopped and her things, protected by the tree above, were barely damp. As she started back to the house, she heard a car door shut on Lime Street and the gate of the house next door open. She pressed against the wall, hoping to hear something interesting. The car drove away and someone ran to the back door. She saw a gleam of light as it was held open.

"All right, Benno," came a voice. "Go ahead with your plans, but I forgot to tell Antonio to come back in about an hour to take Mrs. Donelli home. Would you call him before you leave? It will take us about that time to get these two letters off, wouldn't you say, my dear?"

"Is that Mr. Vincentia?" Elizabeth Lamb thought. "It must be, but his voice sounded so much lower in the daytime." Someone breathed deeply of the fresh night air. "Delicious, is it not, my dear? Stand here a moment and let all that cigar smoke out of your lungs! The dinner meeting was to our advantage, no? Now I can write and explain my plans, before we leave. By the time they decide on a course of action, the thing will be done."

Someone laughed a light, unpleasant laugh that grated on Elizabeth Lamb's nerves. "As you say, *caro,* but sometimes I think you should leave well enough alone. You have accomplished much." The voice was deep and rough, but probably a woman's, decided Elizabeth Lamb, who had an Italian classmate: "I can't see a man calling him 'dear,'" she thought.

The door quietly shut behind them. Elizabeth Lamb made sure to snap the lock on her grandmother's, hoping that Alice, unlocking it after her Charles Street celebrations, would have difficulty finding the keyhole. "I guess I'm getting vicious," she thought, as, washed and brushed, she opened *The Great American Novel.* "But I can't help hoping she'll break a leg, or something, staggering home, and then Grandmother would have to let me go on the voyage of the *Chianti.*"

• CHAPTER 4 •

Dinner on Brimmer, 2

ELIZABETH LAMB had read Mr. Roth's baseball satire for more hours than her grandmother would have condoned but she was sitting at the small breakfast table in the bay window of the dining room at eight-thirty. The night's rain had not cooled the morning air but it seemd to have soaked Alice's hair, pulled up into its customary knot with water dripping from it down into her reddened eyes. She peered through the swinging door into the kitchen and pronounced, "Huh!"

Elizabeth Lamb calculated that the dripping was not from the rain but from a cold shower, "to sober her up, I'll bet."

"Good-morning," she said nicely. "I'd like two boiled eggs this morning, please. I didn't get much chicken salad or bread *or* ice cream last night."

The red head and the red eyes disappeared and slow steps up the stairs, accompanied by subdued groans, were heard. "Hangover," thought Elizabeth Lamb, going out to the front steps for the *Boston Globe.* "Hope she spills the coffee — though not on Grandmother."

Eventually her eggs were served, along with a half-glass of orange juice and a small piece of buttered toast. "Don't fergit to make yer bed," Alice ordered. "Yer grandma had a letter from young Katie sayin' she won't be back till Friday. Somethin' about a mix-up in the planes. Why a nice gerrel wants to spend her holiday in Bermuda with all them nasty English all over the place, I do *not* know.

"And you mark me words: I've a feelin' she'll go fer a job at Jordan Marsh when she does git back. Thinks domestic service is low. Huh! She'll find her pore feet hurt worse'n ever and the wages ain't so good, neither, onct you have to pay fer yer room and meals. And it'll be me who has to train a new gerrel, before your grandma gits back from Maine, come fall.

"Now suppose you fetch yer grandma's tray fer me, like a good gerrel."

Alice cleared the table, pressing a hand to her brow frequently and grumbling about the waywardness of "young Katie," who was celebrating her forty-fifth birthday down among the nasty English. Elizabeth Lamb went glumly up to her room, haphazardly straightened her bed, put a handful of change in the pocket of her khaki skirt and wandered down to bid her grandmother good-morning.

"It's so hot," she said, after the civilities. "I wish we had an air-conditioner. Do you think Viola and I might go to the movies and get cool? I want to see *0, Lucky Man!* very badly."

Elizabeth Worthington, dressed in smock and pants, was drinking the last of her coffee. She glanced up from a sketch pad. "Absolutely not," she murmured. "Oh, why did I leave this ring for the last day! It's a special commission for Mme. Cavalle, to be done rather intricately in three colors of gold. And why does she have such fat fingers!"

"*Why* not, Grandmother? *Time* calls it 'an incandescent film, possibly a great one.' And Mme. Cavalle has very thin hands. I especially noticed them when she was over here two years ago."

"Because your mother saw it and directed that you were not to go. I can't think it would affect *you* much but, anyway, with this ill-advised rating system, you'd have to have an adult with you.

"And that was the first Mme. Cavalle. This is the second, much younger and much more, ah, robust. I'm simply going to have to charge extra; no, better not, because she'll wear it at the opening

59

and it will bring in more commissions. Why don't you go to *Paper Moon?* I read there's a sweet little girl in it. You really should concentrate more on things suited to your age, not your experiences and tastes."

"She's not so sweet. We could ask that — that houseman of Mr. Vincentia's to go with us to *Lucky Man.*"

"I said *no,* Elizabeth Lamb. Isn't there another movie? If not, you'll have to ride the swan boats, unless Viola can think of something. Take the five dollars I put by the tray."

Elizabeth Lamb sighed as she picked up the tray and the bill. "I wouldn't bet on her thinking of something. Well, I guess I won't see you until dinner, if you have to make that ring."

"That reminds me: I forgot to tell Alice that dinner is to be at seven. Mr. Vincentia wants to get an early start tomorrow, on his cruise. He'll be here at six-thirty. Would you tell her? And go out by the garden gate and lock it, please. Alice usually forgets, when she comes in late."

Elizabeth Lamb sighed again. "Well, I'll see you tonight, Grandmother — after what I guess is going to be a dismal morning."

Her grandmother smiled as she went lightly up to her studio. "You're critical this morning, dear, but then, somebody said that 'breakfast is the critical period.'"

"But he was talking about married people," happily replied Elizabeth Lamb, who seldom, with her grandmother, got in the last word.

Nor did she now. "When you are married, I think at breakfast you will not only find *la raison pour critique,* but will also *raisonner.*" Elizabeth disappeared.

"Not only find a reason to criticize, but I'll also argue," murmured Elizabeth Lamb. "Well, maybe, but I guess it depends on whom I marry. And I'm not going to marry until I'm forty, at least."

On Lime Street she encountered the old organ grinder, so old he appeared in the neighborhood less frequently than when she had first visited her grandmother and, at eight, was allowed only to throw coins from a window. He grinned and tipped his battered hat as the monkey scampered over to him with the quarter she put in its little paw. The pair followed her around to Mr. Vincentia's dark red front door. The organ churned out *Santa Lucia* as she raised the heavy brass knocker in the shape of a dolphin, noticing that just above it a small square of thick glass behind an iron grating was set in the door.

The door was quickly opened by Mr. Vincentia himself, trim in tan jodhpurs and a dark red short-sleeved shirt that almost matched the color of his door. He patted Elizabeth Lamb lightly on the shoulder as he turned to call for Viola, but it was Benno who appeared behind him. He pulled a bill from his pocket for the monkey and called, *"Bello! Bello!"* Then he smilingly put a hand over his ear and requested, *"Ma inferiore, prego!"*

The grinder evidently could not lower his volume, but, nodding and grinning ardently, he obligingly moved a little away, to the front of Mr. Vincentia's car. Antonio waited beside it, his eyes on the monkey and its master. "You look charming, Elizabeth Lamb," said Mr. Vincentia. And again he called, "Viola, your friend is here."

Viola came out, also smiling. "What's got into her?" Elizabeth Lamb thought. Aloud she said, "Good-morning. I thought Viola and I might go over to the Gardens and ride the swan boats, if that's all right. Are you going riding, Mr. Vincentia?"

He was already quickly opening the car door, before Antonio could move to do it. Benno prepared to seat himself beside the driver. "No, no, Benno," said his employer, "I want you to stay with the young ladies.

"Yes, I am going for a last run on Omerta: the last for a while, that is. *Arrivederci, ragazzas!"*

Benno reluctantly left the car, protesting forcefully in Italian. It drove away, cutting off his protests. The organ grinder ran after it until it reached Charles Street. "Come in for a minute," Viola requested. "I want to get a hat, and some money."

Benno stood sullenly as Elizabeth Lamb seated herself in a chair just inside the door. She craned her neck to look through the open double doors of a large room on the left of the hallway. Its walls were a deep red, which enriched the dark walnut panelling and picked up some of the colors in the old Oriental rugs scattered over the parquet floor. The tables and chairs were of a light fruitwood, the upholstery of the chairs a beige velvet. Many of the chairs had caned backs and some of the lamps, made from Chinese vases, had similar caned shades. The curtains on the tall windows were of cream-colored silk. There were many luminous landscapes and paintings of flowers — "real Impressionists, they look like," she thought. "Wonder if they are?"

Disregarding the sulky Benno, she got up and went to the doors. There was a large sofa covered in a pale damask that she had not seen from the hall. Above it hung the portrait of a most beautiful black-haired young woman. She wore a brown velvet dress and carried a red rose in her hand. She smiled engagingly at Elizabeth Lamb, who muttered to herself: "So much for Daddy; he says all that Italians have in the living room are pictures of President Kennedy, opera singers, and the Sacred Heart."

"Sacred Heart?" asked Viola, suddenly appearing with two large straw hats. "That's the name of the school I went to in England before Grandfather brought me over here. Put this on, because sun is bad for your complexion. Julia says so."

Elizabeth Lamb was about to refuse politely when Viola jammed a hat on her head. "Wear it!" she said, stamping her foot. Benno sniggered and opened the front door for them. "What's *ragazzas* mean?" she asked Viola. "Girls, stupid," Viola answered.

They walked slowly down Brimmer Street to Beacon, Benno behind them. He was wearing his cotton jacket although the heat was causing all the more formally dressed men they passed to carry theirs. "Who is Julia?" Elizabeth Lamb asked, determined to be civil and make the best of what promised to be a morning she well might criticize, later, to her grandmother.

"My daddy's wife. I love Julia. She's a beautiful singer. She used to sing lullabies to me, every night before she went to work. I heard her sing once on stage, and she sang better at home to me!

"She's going on the boat with us, and Paul, too. They've been over here visiting her sister down in — oh, somewhere; I can't say it — but I'll see her tomorrow. She'll bring me a nice present. I write to her and tell her everything that happens. I seal it up before Grandfather puts the stamps on so he can't read it. I love Julia because she never says I'm dumb." A tear rolled down Viola's pretty pink cheek.

Elizabeth Lamb began to feel sorry for her. "I wonder who calls her dumb?" she thought. "That Paul?" Aloud she said, "I think you're pretty smart, Viola. Who's Paul? Is he going on the *Chianti*, too?"

"Of course, stupid. He's her husband."

Elizabeth Lamb felt less sorry. "Then he's your father?"

"Of course he's not my father! My father is dead."

"But she's your step-mother?"

"No, she's not my step-mother! You really are *very* stupid."

Elizabeth Lamb was angered: "I'm not stupid at all! If she's your father's wife, how can she not be your step-mother?"

"Mrs. Donelli says you can't really have a step-mother as long as your own mother is alive. You *must* be dumb not to know that. Anyway, she's not really married. I just said that because I'm polite. You should be, too."

Elizabeth Lamb turned in confusion to Benno, who explained as he took each girl carefully by an arm and ushered them across Beacon Street. "The *padrone's* son's marriage to this one's mother was annulled when she went" — he let Elizabeth Lamb loose to tap his forehead significantly — "after bearing her. He married a woman, *Signora* Julia, and they brought up this one until a year or more ago, when the young *padrone* died. Then the *Signora* took this Paul as her *amante* and the *padrone* thought it better his granddaughter come to live with him."

"See!" said Viola. "It's easy. And if my grandfather wasn't so old and stupid, he'd have let me stay with Julia. He's old-fashioned about people being married.

"Oh, Benno! Run after that ice cream man. I want some! Quick, he's just leaving that boy on the bench!" The vendor was fast pedaling away as she spoke.

Benno stolidly shook his head. "The *padrone* say to never leave you. You eat too much ice cream, anyway."

"They never let me have the green kind! I said I want some! You run fast, Benno, you fool!"

Benno lost his stolidity, shook his head violently and burst into a stream of angry Italian. "What's he saying?" Elizabeth Lamb asked Viola, as they walked along the sidewalk to an opening in the iron fence around the Public Gardens.

"I don't know, the stupid!" Viola was bright red with fury. "I don't understand much of it. Grandfather tried to teach me, but I can't remember. He talks what he says is bird Italian when I'm around. He wants me to know a few words."

"She mean pigeon." Benno laughed loudly. They were passing the boy on the bench, who was holding three ice cream cones. He looked up, and then rose. "Well, hello there, Elizabeth Lamb," he said. "I asked that feller fer a triple dip and look what he give me!"

"Payson! What are you doing here?"

"Went over to Filene's Basement fer some new shirts. Mr. Vincentia give me some money for 'em; he said they's pants and aprons on the boat that'll fit. Want one of these?" He shyly handed the pistachio to Viola and the vanilla to Elizabeth Lamb and then, with a polite nod to Benno, sat down again and began to lick the chocolate.

"Aren't you supposed to see Viola and I don't talk to dangerous strangers?" Elizabeth Lamb teased Benno, as she and Viola joined Payson on the bench.

"I know who he is, *signorina*. He works for the *padrone* now." He lit a cigarette and glanced about, as if reminded of his duty.

"I seen you last night, too," Payson said shyly to Viola. "You peeked in."

"I do not peek at strange boys," Viola replied indignantly. "Anyway, I have a dear friend and he is better looking than you." She giggled.

Payson laughed too, as he bid them good-bye. "Got to go back 'n' git my things together. Mr. Vincentia said be at his house at eight termorrer mornin'. We're goin' to drive down to his yacht. It's anchored off the South Shore some'eres."

Viola insisted on more swan boat rides than pleased Elizabeth Lamb, and certainly more than pleased Benno. He was on the seat beside them, muttering about the heat and regarding suspiciously anyone over the age of eight who sat near them. Their money eventually ran out and he refused to supply more.

Viola was sulky on the walk home and even more sulky when Elizabeth Lamb firmly removed the hat that had been forced upon her and handed it to Benno. Elizabeth Lamb finally abandoned conversation, after her suggestion that they go up to the Athenaeum, where the air was always cool, and look at books was ignored by her companions. They parted at Mrs. Worthington's door, where Viola became civil enough to say she hoped Elizabeth Lamb could come on the boat and then, reverting to her usual self: "And your little cousin, too. Maybe she's nicer."

There was a large package with Spanish stamps on the hall table. "It's *dragees!*" Elizabeth Lamb cried in delight when she had opened it. "Look, Alice, my mother remembered how I love sugared almonds!

"When we lived in Paris, she worked till late and after school I used to sneak into every wedding and christening party I could find, because they hand out little white boxes of these to all the guests. I always got a box, sometimes more, because everybody thought I was with *another* grown-up. Sometimes on Saturday afternoons I got myself into two or three parties and everybody got lots of wine, even the children! Those were the days," she added wistfully.

"Huh! Bet they were." Alice was dusting the drawing room and was not enthusiastic. "And it might've bin the end of all yer days, goin' around free and wild and crashin' parties in Paris. Wicked, they are, them Frogs; yer patron saint must've bin watchin' fair close.

"Now, be sure to put them wrappin's in the trash," she directed. "Ever'thin's got to be spick-and-span around here, with that rich Eyetalian comin' to dinner. When I took yer grandma's lunch tray up, she said she'd make the main dish, though. Was callin' up fer some special stuff fer it. That's one blessin'; worked off me feet I am, with young Katie gallivantin' all over the seven seas.

"Ye hungry? Then make yerself some peanut butter san'wiches. I got enough to do. And mind ye don't mess up me kitchen."

The sandwiches, the radio, and a pocketful of *dragees,* along with *The Great American Novel,* occupied Elizabeth Lamb in the garden all afternoon. No sound came from the house next door. At six she went to her room to change for dinner, hoping against hope it would be her last on Brimmer Street until the autumn.

Her grandmother, shedding an apron, looked out from the kitchen as she came down the stairs. "You look nice, dear," she approved. "Pale blue is really very pretty on you."

"And so do you, Grandmother. I've never seen you look prettier."

Elizabeth Worthington's face was becomingly flushed from her cooking. Her low-necked black chiffon dress, set off by several strands of pearls, enhanced her pale, delicate features and her dark, shining hair. She had pinned one of Mr. Vincentia's roses in the V of the dress.

"I thought we'd have martinis," she said, as they inspected the preparations for drinks in the drawing room. "I feel like letting loose a little, with that difficult ring finished. I hope Mr. Vincentia drinks them. If not, he'll have to make do with Campari and soda. Continentals are fond of it, and my sister and I were not brought up to be the sort of contemporary hostess who offers a variety of liquors, as if her home were a bar-room.

"And, Elizabeth Lamb, do *not* try to wheedle a martini."

"Of course not." Elizabeth Lamb was indignant. "I wouldn't think of it. They're a very adult drink. And, besides, after that time Persis and I got so sick when we sneaked a whole pitcher of them at The Bungalow, I'll probably never be able to face one again.

"Oh, I'll get the door, Alice!"

She was there almost before the bell finished ringing. That Mr. Vincentia was smelling faintly but deliciously of some lemon scent, that he was wearing a thin dark-blue Viyella blazer, its gold buttons embossed with dolphins, a cream-colored silk shirt with its neck opening filled by a scarf of his favorite dark red, and immaculately pressed gabardine trousers that matched the shirt did not escape her notice, but her eyes focused on the huge box he carried. Its cover was striped green and white satin tied with gold ribbon, a beautiful red silk rose fastened into the ribbon's knot.

As he extended it to her, saying smilingly, "For your grandmother, and, of course, you," she saw the gold script and read it aloud with delight: "*'Ciocolatto da Vincentia!'* Oh, Mr. Vincentia, how wonderful! Please come in."

He followed her after taking a bottle from Benno, behind him, who waited until the door closed before he marched away. "Look, Grandmother, here's Mr. Vincentia and look what he brought! It must be ten pounds!"

Elizabeth was standing before the fireplace, a little to the side of the vase of roses. She offered a hand in welcome, after first making a silencing motion to her granddaughter. "I am so pleased you could come, Mr. Vincentia," she said graciously.

Mr Vincentia bowed over her hand, raising it almost to his lips, "but, properly, not quite." Elizabeth Lamb, still clutching the chocolates, thought with approval. He straightened, and staring at Elizabeth, said slowly, "It has been said that 'Boston runs to Brains as well as Beans and Brown Bread'; I never saw until now how completely it runs to Beauty."

"Who said it?" Elizabeth Lamb was burning to open the chocolates but, as ever, curious. "About Beans and Brown Bread?"

"I think it was a Texas newspaper," her grandmother answered, blushing. "About a hundred years ago," Mr. Vincentia supplemented. They laughed and he followed her to the table of drinks.

"I should have asked you to sit down," Elizabeth apologized, "but so breath-taking a compliment makes me feel the need of what my husband called 'a bit of a bracer.' I hope you drink martinis."

"I adore them," he answered simply. "The dry martini has been called America's chief contribution to civilization. Do let me mix them, Mrs. Worthington. I seldom find such a charming lady to make them for."

Elizabeth sat down, her cheeks as red as when she had left the kitchen. "Elizabeth Lamb, put those away," she said. "We'll have some after dinner." Alice came in, holding a bottle. "It comes so naturally to her she usually enters with one," Elizabeth thought with annoyance. "She's using this one to get a good look."

"This was on the hall table, ma'am," Alice said, her small eyes fastened on the guest. "It is a special chianti," he answered. Handing Elizabeth her glass, he went on, "It is a '58; a few improve with age. Ladies often find chianti too robust, but I had a feeling it would be acceptable."

He smiled at Alice. "Ah, you must be the cook Elizabeth Lamb praises so highly. I would like you sometime to tell my Rosa a few of your secrets." He took a small box from the breast pocket of his blazer. "I brought you a bribe, to advance my case."

Alice, bridling, took the box, muttering, "Thank you, sor. It ain't often a gentleman is so thoughtful." She glanced unbelievingly at Elizabeth Lamb as she went out the door.

Elizabeth Lamb, in turn, looked at Mr. Vincentia with disbelief.

67

"What a liar!" she thought. "But I guess he's just being diplomatic and Daddy says all diplomats have to be good liars."

Mr. Vincentia was standing, regarding the marble fireplace. He moved to stroke it. "This is wonderfully wrought. It must be priceless."

Elizabeth accepted the observation made by her grandmother that while it was proper to avoid discussing one's means except with intimates — although declaring to anyone that one had very few was always permissible — only the *nouveaux riches* held such awe of money that they either, one, held that to mention it was sacrilege or, two, bragged continually about the high price of their things.

"Not when my husband's grandfather obtained it for fifty cents," she replied. "Daniel Webster's house, around the corner, was being torn down when this one was being built and Mr. Worthington accosted the Irish workmen carrying the mantelpiece away. He offered a quarter but they doubled the price. It was quite a steal; I married into a family of brigands."

Mr. Vincentia sat down easily, looking about him. "I love this room," he said. "It becomes you. It is the sort of room I dreamed of having when I was a child in England and worked twelve hours a day in a factory.

"And I believe one must have had to be something of a brigand to prosper in early New England — perhaps even today, in some parts, as it often was necessary in Sicily, my birthplace."

"Do you remember much about Sicily?"

"Mostly only the hard work helping my father on his boat. He fished for tunny, off Catania. And the sunshine; that was what I missed most, in my young years in England."

"You must have had a very difficult childhood, and a disillusioning one."

"Whose childhood does not disillusion him, Elizabeth? I may call you that? You see, you remind me so much of my late wife, my beautiful Lizabetta. And I wish you would call me Vito. I am not, I hope, being too forward?"

Elizabeth, pleased despite all her innate inhibitions against quick informality, shook her head. "Of course not. The really lovely flowers you sent, and these wonderful chocolates, would qualify anyone to

68

be on a first-name basis! And we are now close neighbors."

"You have a pretty house, too, Mr. Vincentia," Elizabeth Lamb said. "Is that portrait of your wife? I saw it when I was waiting for Viola. She certainly was very beautiful."

Mr. Vincentia, refilling glasses, nodded. "I wish Viola resembled her, but she looks like her mother's family. I wish it because Viola is all I have left; her father is dead and my daughter and her family died in a tragic accident some years ago."

He sighed as he sat again, now beside Elizabeth Worthington. "Viola was much attached to her stepmother, but I insisted she come over from England to live with me, after the death of her father. Viola writes her stepmother constantly and calls her, so often that my telephone bill is enormous. But, then, like all young girls, she loves the telephone. Every time I enter the house, she is ending what seems to have been an affectionate conversation with one of her girl friends, even though she lives at her school during the week."

Elizabeth Lamb could not conceive of a schoolmate's reciprocating Viola's affection. "But then," she thought, "maybe they don't mind being called 'stupid' and Viola can't stamp her foot over the phone." She looked up at Alice, standing before her and proffering a tall glass of iced ginger ale with a whole lemon peel swirling through it.

"A horse's neck!" she said, astounded. "Why, thank you, Alice. I love them and I know how hard it is to cut the peel so carefully."

"No trouble," muttered Alice, who now had a pretty pin of gold leaves surrounding a small coral rose pinned to the white collar of her obviously just-donned best black uniform. She held before Elizabeth and Vito a plate of little golden brown objects.

"Heard you say you'd lived in England, sor," she said. "Only good thing about the English is they do know how to make tasty cheese straws. I whipped some together quick and baked 'em."

Now Elizabeth was astounded. Vito rose and bowed graciously to Alice. "But I love them!" he said. "They are one of my fondest memories of England. You are too kind!" He put one of the pastries into his mouth and beamed.

"But of course," he said to his hostess as Alice reluctantly left the room, "I have many exceedingly happy memories of England. I was there in my twenties, and I have read that one always regards with the most affection the place one lived chiefly in between twenty and thirty."

"I think that is true," Elizabeth replied slowly. "Although I was married young, here in Boston, when I was in my twenties Otis and I lived for months at a time in Paris, and I think it really is the place I love best."

"Then why did you leave England, Mr. Vincentia?" Elizabeth Lamb asked.

"Oh, many, many reasons," he answered, frowning a little. "But," turning to his hostess, "perhaps only so that one day I might end up in this room, at this hour, and be very, very happy — happier than I have been for years."

Elizabeth felt herself blushing again. She bent to pick up a cheese straw. Elizabeth Lamb, observing, thought, "Heaven help me if they begin what Eileen calls 'a thing.' Daddy, not to mention Aunt Sarah, will kill me dead. But he's such an improvement over Mr. Tibbets!"

Her grandmother went to the record-player, in a far corner of the room, murmuring, "Perhaps we might have some music." Mr. Vincentia followed her, leaving the cheese straws vulnerable to Elizabeth Lamb's quick approach. "These are so good," she thought. "Alice can't have 'whipped some together' in the few minutes after he said he'd lived in England. I bet that cook of his speaks more English than he thinks. Oh, no; now they're holding hands!"

They were not, as she saw when she hastily approached them. Vito had picked up a record and was playfully shaking his head. "Elizabeth," he said, "this Caruso aria that was conveniently on top, valuable as it must be, — you think Italians enjoy nothing but opera, no? Admit it, my dear."

"Well, Vito," Elizabeth, embarrassed, began, "perhaps—"

"She hates opera, and so do I." Elizabeth Lamb was quickly helpful.

"And so do I!" Vito was emphatic. "I enjoy nothing but chamber music — and well-played jazz. My wife used to say it was the mathematician in me."

"They're what Grandmother likes best, too!" Elizabeth Lamb exclaimed. "I'll find some Mozart, or Bach. Oh, here's a Handel."

"I do think," Elizabeth explained, as a harpsichord concerto began

70

softly, "while admitting I have no ear for it, that opera in the twentieth century is just a pretentious anachronism. Who, today, really needs it? I do believe there are sincere people who enjoy it, but more who pretend. I am not ashamed to say I prefer a good, light, contemporary musical comedy that I can relate to."

"What's a musical comedy?" Elizabeth Lamb asked.

"They were called that, in our day," Vito told her. "Now they're simply called musicals; I suppose because modern ones are not as light as the old ones were. Modern life demands some tragedy, even set to music.

"Elizabeth, I will get tickets for every one that comes to Boston next season, if you will do me the honor of being my companion for them."

"I should be delighted, but now I must leave you to finish the dinner dish. Elizabeth Lamb, do not chatter on so much that Mr. Vincentia can't hear the music."

"No need, ma'am." Alice was in the doorway. "It's on the table, nice an' hot. Best come quick. I opened the wine to let it breathe, too, like the mister always done."

"But, Alice, the pasta—"

"I done it, whilst I was heatin' the sauce slow, like you said you was goin' to. It's perfect Al Dinty." She turned to the guest and explained, "That means 'to the tooth.' It ain't too soft."

Although it was not yet dusk, Alice had lighted the candles in the heavy Georgian holders used only for the most formal occasions. As Vito pulled out Elizabeth's chair, he looked unbelievingly at the dark green pottery bowl in the shape of an enormous head of leafy cabbage that waited at her place beside three warmed plates.

"But that cannot be *pasta con radicchio!*" he exclaimed. "There is no *radicchio* to be had in Boston. Believe me, I have searched." He regarded her admiringly as he poured chianti and then sat, awaiting his portion with flattering expectancy.

Elizabeth had quickly tossed the contents of the bowl with a quantity of small leaves from another dish, spooned it on to the plates and dashed a lavish amount of grated cheese over each serving. Vito tasted his avidly and sighed with satisfaction. "Elizabeth, how did you do this? I have not had its equal since I was last at *Il Buco* in

71

Rome, three long years ago. My foolish secretary did not like it, so I ate her portion too, as well as three of my own!"

"It is as the old recipe for rabbit stew goes: 'First, catch your rabbit.' In this case, first you catch your *radicchio*, from the old man out in Wellesley who brings me firewood, in the winter. He starts the *radicchio* under glass in March. He does say, though, that spring or summer *radicchio* is not as good as that picked after the first frost. Then it has more crunch, like Belgian endive, and more of its dry, nutty aftertaste."

"But this is sublime. Little did I know, when I moved next door, what good fortune was to be mine! You will give me the man's name? And how did you make this? And the cheese is *pecorino!* From sheep's milk," he explained to Elizabeth Lamb, who was eating hungrily and appreciating the generous glass of chianti he had poured her.

"Of course I will give you Andy's number. You want the exact recipe for this, Vito?" Elizabeth was plainly pleased by his eager nod and went on: "Well, for four — and Elizabeth Lamb usually eats enough for two — you *sauté* three cups of the little inner leaves of two small heads of *radicchio* in a quarter-pound of butter with four tablespoons of chopped onion. When the onions turn pink, add six tablespoons of red wine and continue cooking for just a few minutes. I did this an hour ago and Alice heated it while she boiled a pound of *rigatoni* — one could use shells, as well, or any short pasta — and mixed in a cup of fresh cream at room temperature. Then she stirred in the sauce. You saw me put in two handfuls of uncooked leaves and add the *pecorino*.

"It's really very simple — once you catch your *radicchio*."

"I will remember," said Vito, as he ate the last bit on his plate. "Ah, I am in heaven! No, no, I will wait until Elizabeth Lamb has had more. She needs it; I had a very good lunch downtown, at the Oyster House, with my friend Eb Tibbets. He tells me he dined here last night, and I will be very hurt if he had *pasta con radicchio!*

"I know you need more," he smiled gaily at Elizabeth Lamb, "because Benno saw you in the garden eating a meager lunch of peanut butter sandwiches."

"How ever did he know what they were?" Elizabeth Lamb was

72

passing her plate to her grandmother.

"He is very observant. He judged from the difficulty you had in swallowing. I need to drink much milk with them, but he said you had none. Ah, thank you, Elizabeth."

As she served him, Elizabeth looked thoughtfully at Alice, who was holding beside Vito a platter of onion slices.

"Forgot these, I did, ma'am," she apologized. "And you told me special to bring them with the macaroni."

"It's all right, Alice. They really should be served cool. And we have you to thank for these, too, Vito," Elizabeth said. "They were baked with just a little olive oil and fresh parsley. Nothing to spoil the wonderful taste of onions. But wherever did you get so many to give us?"

"Better late than never," Vito observed jovially to Alice. "Oh," to Elizabeth, "I have a friend who has a plane. He flies in many things that are necessary to us Sicilians."

"Rather enigmatic," thought Elizabeth, who was in too happy a mood to ask him how his friend got onions through the U.S. Customs, always very particular about which fresh vegetables, or fruits or flowers, might be brought in.

"The price of onions is outrageous," she observed instead, "like the cost of most other things. But since President Nixon froze prices for sixty days last week, perhaps that will slow down inflation."

"Diesel oil is again up seven cents a gallon," mused Vito, who was eating the onions with appreciation. "I am glad it can rise no higher before my cruise. Mr. Nixon tries to exude responsibility as well as charm, but I wish he had a bit more *stile.*

"That means style," he informed Elizabeth Lamb, "just as in English. I am happy you enjoy pasta. It is so very good for you, and as Miss Loren is supposed to have said: 'Pasta never puts a pound on you except in the right places.'"

Elizabeth Worthington leaned towards him a bit, her eyes widening as she laughed with delight. "I think she's falling for him," her granddaughter thought. "Maybe I should remind her of that secretary, who calls him 'dear.'

"Could I have some more wine, Mr. Vincentia?" she asked. "Does your secretary like pasta? You said she wouldn't eat this, in Rome.

"Thank you, Grandmother. I would like more pasta."

Vito bit thoughtfully into a breadstick. He sighed. "She enjoys very few Italian dishes. She will suffer greatly on the *Chianti,* where much of the food is Sicilian-style. My cook had a French father and a Sicilian mother, making, for a gourmand like me, the best of both worlds."

"Is she going on the *Chianti* with us — with you?"

"Yes, to my driver's — Antonio's — satisfaction. He doubles as one of the crew and he and Annie have been, ah, have been seeing each other for some time. Although she will never marry another Italian, she has told him. She says" — he made a comical grimace as he again reached for the wine — "we drink too much. I tell her we drink often, but never too much!"

"She isn't Italian, then?" Elizabeth asked, looking rather more happy than when Elizabeth Lamb had mentioned the secretary.

"Annie is Irish. And she maintains the Irish are the most moderate of drinkers." He winked at Elizabeth.

"And so we are, sor!" Alice was removing the remains of the first course to the sideboard, the point at which, the times she was serving in Katie's absence, she usually joined the table conversation. Elizabeth Worthington had long since given up reproving her.

"Oh, ma'am," Alice went on, "that reminds me: the Hibernian Sisters is havin' another meetin' tonight. Is it all right if I leave after dinner?"

Elizabeth wondered how dense Alice really thought she was. "I can't quite see how the mention of drinkers could remind you of your club," she said pointedly, "since you have told me only tea is served.

"But, yes, it's all right as long as you are not out too late. Elizabeth Lamb needs breakfast at a little after seven since Mr. Vincentia has told me he wishes to leave for his boat by eight."

Elizabeth Lamb was concentrating on Vito as his dessert plate was put before him. Her relief in seeing that he knew exactly what to do with his finger bowl blocked her comprehension of what her grandmother had just said. When she realized, she jumped up to run to Elizabeth and hug her violently.

"Oh, Grandmother, I may go? Did you hear, Mr. Vincentia? I'll be going with you! And, Grandmother, what about Persis? Will you call Aunt Sarah?"

"Sit down and eat your dessert, dear." Elizabeth was cutting a bunch of grapes from the bowl Alice held beside her. "I'll call before we have coffee. I can't think Sarah would be anything but relieved; she is really beside herself with that broken leg. And you and Persis need not bother much about packing. You have clothes at The Bungalow that should still fit."

Mr. Vincentia beamed as he chose a banana. Elizabeth Lamb, as she sliced an apple, observed him sideways: her Aunt Sarah often served bananas — "just because she can be so mean," Elizabeth Lamb thought — to guests of whose social background she was not certain. Mr. Vincentia would have passed her test. He held his banana while he cut off the top with his fruit knife, then, pulling back a strip of peel with one hand, he used the other to fork up portions of the fruit.

Elizabeth Lamb smiled happily at him. "Grandmother, could I have a bit more chianti, to celebrate? I've never had it before. What kind of grapes is it made from, Mr. Vincentia?"

"It is a blend of three, Zinfandel and two others, which I forget. My son would have known. As I told you, it was his favorite." He sighed, and then brightened. "But I would choose bananas over chianti any day; they were the only fruit I had in England, as a boy, and I love them." Alice immediately secured the fruit bowl so he could choose another.

"What else did you have to eat?" Elizabeth Lamb asked curiously. "I love English sausages, especially with mashed potatoes, the way my mother and I had them in pubs for dinner, when we lived there. 'Bangers and mash' are the greatest!"

Mr. Vincentia pulled back Elizabeth's chair as she rose. "Seldom sausages. My mother and I had pasta of some sort every night, of course, but often all we had to put on it for a sauce was melted lard."

"Oh, I'm sorry! But now," Elizabeth Lamb said as she followed the two across the hall, "you have everything!"

He regarded Elizabeth as she opened the door of the cloakroom where the telephone was. "No, Elizabeth Lamb," he answered slowly, turning back to her, "I do not have everything I might want. But then" — his mood changed and he smiled merrily — "if one had everything, where, I ask you, would one put it?"

While they waited for her grandmother, Elizabeth Lamb put a Mozart selection on the record player, eyeing the box of chocolates beside it. "There will be many on the *Chianti,*" Vito assured her, and to Alice: "I will pour the coffee. You must go to your meeting. I hope to see you again, many times — the many times I hope I will dine here."

Alice smiled her way out, the bill he had handed her clutched under her apron. "Ye'll enjoy the brandy, sor. I found a whole bottle."

"Well," said Elizabeth Worthington, as she accepted a cup of coffee from Vito, "Sarah is delighted, Elizabeth Lamb. Luckily Hill is taking an early plane to Washington tomorrow and he will drop Persis here on his way to Logan. She can have breakfast with you. And, again luckily, Gus' school ends tomorrow, so Sarah will have someone with her.

"I hope," turning to Vito, "that you do not regret your kindness in letting my granddaughters go along with you. I can vouch for their manners, but you may find Elizabeth Lamb a little too observant for her age. And Persis, just a week younger, is slowly developing along her cousin's lines."

"Grandmother means she's getting bossy. But *I'm* not; not at all. But, Mr. Vincentia, how did you know Grandmother's name was Elizabeth? I've been wondering, because I know I didn't tell you."

Vito extended his left hand to her. On the little finger, he wore a wide, intricately-worked gold ring, its convolutions outlined in a white enamel that glistened with the gold only Elizabeth Worthington had been able to combine with enamels. It was studded with small rubies and emeralds. "But, as you see, I have one of her rings. When we married, I could afford only a cheap wedding ring for my wife. Years later, I asked a knowledgeable friend who made the most beautiful rings in the world? His answer was not Cartier, as I expected, but a lady in Boston, Massachusetts — Elizabeth Worthington.

"When my wife died, I kept her ring, to have something tangible of her always with me. I am surprised you did not notice it, Elizabeth."

"But I did. I have been racking my brain as to when I made it. I did remember it was for a London jeweler, some years ago, but I never knew his client's name. I hope it gave your wife pleasure."

"And you say I'm observant, Grandmother! But then, I suppose you would remember making something so lovely." Elizabeth Lamb was fingering the candy box.

"You may open it, dear. And after you've had two or three, I suggest you go up and get some clothes together." Elizabeth turned to Vito. "Eb Tibbets told me last night your yacht was rather magnificent. Will Elizabeth Lamb need many clothes? I hope they will not be too shabby; the ones that still fit her are mostly suitable for my camp in Maine, where we are very casual."

"I look forward to seeing it," said Vito. "I know it will be charming. And Elizabeth Lamb, whatever she wears, can only adorn the *Chianti!* She needs only the most simple things; perhaps a pretty dress for dinner.

"We will go slowly, to give me time — ah, to give my guests time to relax. It should take us three days, perhaps two, to Mount Desert. We'll anchor at night, so we can enjoy the coastline and the little harbors and our only formal meal."

"How fast can the *Chianti* go?" Elizabeth Lamb was making her third chocolate last and wishing the conversation to go on, so she could exceed her quota.

"She can cruise at fourteen knots, but we will, as I said, go slower."

"How big is she?"

"A hundred and sixty feet. Too large, but my son liked her lines. She was Dutch built, but I had a refit done in Italy, to my daughter-in-law's specifications, when I bought her. They used her for their wedding trip. They both loved the *Chianti.*"

He sighed and picked up his brandy glass. "I think that, perhaps, now my son is gone, I should sell her. I really use her very seldom, and the upkeep is tremendous."

"Really? How much—" Elizabeth Lamb began.

"Do you think President Nixon will resign, Vito?" her grandmother asked in a firm tone, shaking her head at Elizabeth Lamb.

He shrugged. "No, nor do I think he should. The *Globe* reprinted a *London Times* editorial the other day that called him a victim of a

Washington version of lynch laws. What he undoubtedly did, or perhaps I should say what he no doubt knew had been done, is done all the time here and in Europe by politicians, even those we call statesmen. In Europe they laugh at the furor the whole thing is causing. A Frenchman I know is calling it 'a tempest in a Puritanical teapot.' And at lunch the other day, some gentleman — that reminds me, Elizabeth, is Eb Tibbets a good friend of yours? If I may ask, my dear?"

"Not as good as he'd like to be." Elizabeth Lamb thought Vito should know he was not alone in his admiration of her grandmother.

"Don't be brash, Elizabeth Lamb." Elizabeth frowned. "And just one more piece of candy.

"I've known him for years, Vito. My husband was a partner in his firm. An old friend and a good one, and my trusted advisor, but I do deplore his economical habits."

Vito laughed happily. "*Avaro,* the good Eb is. I've told him so. When we lunch together, he puts the uneaten rolls in his briefcase!"

"But I will say for him, Vito, that he feeds them to the pigeons on the Common; he doesn't take them home and eat them. He just saves the money it would cost for the little bags of grain those old women sit there and sell.

"And he is so hide-bound! Can you believe he is very much against extending credit to married women, saying the banks and stores and credit card companies that are only now beginning to do it are going to regret it! He says only men can be trusted — and *then* he cites his long experience in handling funds sometimes of very foolish men, to prove it!

"It really is a disgrace that, until just recently, when a single woman married or a married woman is widowed or divorced, her credit was wiped out. I am so thankful my husband left his estate firmly in my own hands. Eb can only advise, but if he had control of it he'd never let me buy the expensive wine he loves to drink here!"

Vito laughed again. "You know, Elizabeth, I was forty years ahead of the times, in the matter of extending credit to women. I ran some loan agencies in England for my countrymen, and I always told my managers to make loans to hard-working women, preferably to them rather than to their husbands, if they had any."

"Because you were sorry for how hard they worked, Vito? How wonderful!"

"No," he answered ruefully, "to be honest, Elizabeth, it is because Italian women would starve themselves — even deny their children, and they love their children — rather than default on paying back a loan that had helped them. Italian men are not always so punctilious. We are handsome, we are gallant, we are *very* faithful in love, but sometimes we are *sdrucciolevale* — slippery!"

Now Elizabeth laughed. "Pour me more brandy, dear Vito — if your hands are not too slippery. Elizabeth Lamb, put down that box at once and go up and get your things ready for tomorrow. Now, dear!"

It took her less than a quarter-hour to assemble her sea-going shorts, shirts, sweaters and jeans, a bathing suit and a printed lawn dress. She put them more or less neatly into a school laundry bag, and tied the strings. Then, thinking again, she added pajamas, sneakers and her Mary Janes. By the time the bag was tied up again, she remembered her box of *dragees* and, with a sigh, the notebook in which to write "a short novel."

Finally finished, she raced downstairs. The double doors of the drawing room were closed. "Oh, no!" she thought. "*What* are they doing?" She knocked lightly.

The doors were opened by Mr. Vincentia. She gave him a hard look. "Ah," he said, "I knew you would return — for the chocolates if not for my company! But you will have both on the *Chianti,* and I must leave you now. I have some few things to arrange."

He raised his hand to his lips and blew a kiss into the drawing room. "I will call you in Paris, Elizabeth. Till we meet again, my dear." He placed a brief kiss on the top of Elizabeth Lamb's head. "And I will see *you* tomorrow at eight. Good-night."

"Grandmother!" said Elizabeth Lamb, as the street door closed behind him. "Now he's kissing us! He is charming, though, isn't he? Didn't I say so?"

Elizabeth Worthington was turning off the record player. She turned, smiling. "Yes. To both. Now, let's put out the lights. I'll be down tomorrow before you and Persis leave. I'm just going to leave a note for Alice. And I must call Maine, to tell Dora that you'll be there in a few days. Mr. Vincentia says you can call her at The Bungalow from his yacht, too. Good-night."

"Good-night, Grandmother. Didn't Mr. Vincentia enjoy himself, though! Didn't he look happy when he left? Aren't you glad you invited him? And isn't he like the man in the poem; doesn't he 'glitter when he walks'?"

"So many questions," came from the kitchen. "Run along."

"There's one more I sure could have asked," Elizabeth Lamb said to herself as she slowly climbed the stairs. "'How did Mr. Vincentia get that lipstick on his mouth?'"

• CHAPTER 5 •

Motley Crew

"ANOTHER thing," Elizabeth Lamb ended a long list of instructions to her cousin, "don't *ever* talk with your mouth full on the *Chianti*. And I hope you packed a nice dress for dinner? The *Chianti* is very elegant, according to Mr. Tibbets. *And,* Persis, I must say that is a perfectly terrible outfit you've got on."

She surveyed her pupil glumly. Persis had perched a dirty white canvas sailor's cap on her curly brown hair, matched at the other end of her body by ragged, dirty white sneakers from which her big toes protruded. A pink silk shirt shot with stripes of silver *lamé* hung loosely from her shoulders and met a baggy pair of faded khaki shorts tied with a piece of rope around her fat little middle.

Persis' blue eyes flashed above her round pink cheeks as she enunciated around a generous mouthful of pancake and bacon. "It's all I could find. Things have been horrible since Mummy broke her leg. Daddy packed all my clean clothes and he forgot to leave me anything to wear this morning, so I took a shirt of hers and a pair of Gus' old shorts.

"And you don't have to be so nasty, Elizabeth Lamb. I *never* talk with my mouth full. Mommy says you're getting insuperable, any-

81

way. So there! Oh, thank you, Alice; I would love more scrambled eggs. I haven't eaten like this for weeks. Our cook just sits in the kitchen now and reads *Ms.* and Mummy's too upset to fire her."

"Persis," Elizabeth Lamb sighed, "you've eaten enough for three meals already. Do you *want* to be fat? I have to say it; you're not just chubby anymore. You're fat."

"You leave 'er alone," Alice ordered. "She'll slim down onct she gits 'er first monthly. She's a dear little colleen, is wot I say. More sausage, Persis? And yer tea cup needs fillin'. I told ye I'd read yer leaves, now, din't I?"

"My first monthly?" Persis cried. "Am I going to get a monthly check, like Gus? Oh, that's wonderful, Alice! Did Grandmother say so? All I get now is a dollar a week and Daddy keeps forgetting to give it, with Mummy all bunged up, as the cook says.

"And could I have some maple sugar syrup, Alice?"

"Insuperable?" Elizabeth Lamb murmured, also presenting her cup for more tea. "I'm really pleased, except I bet Aunt Sarah didn't say insuperable. I'll bet she said—"

"Insufferable, probably," her grandmother observed mildly. She had come in from the kitchen, a cup and saucer in one hand and three small white boxes balanced on the other palm. She sat beside the cousins at the little breakfast table after dropping a kiss on the sleek blonde head and then the rumpled brown one.

"I'm glad you're going along, Persis. Suppose you take off that hat, though, right now. And be sure to put on your own clothes, once you get on the boat and unpack your suitcase.

"I see there's no coffee this morning, Alice. Would you give me some tea, please? And perhaps you might boil an egg. I'm going to lie down as soon as the girls leave. I was up all night in the studio and I'll never be able to sleep on the plane. I wish I were like my children; they could sleep even on the Paris Metro."

She put one of the boxes beside each of the children's plates. "Happy birthday, darling," she said to Elizabeth Lamb. "And, Persis, you may open yours at The Bungalow on *your* birthday. I have a host present for you both to give Mr. Vincentia, too. I dislike your going empty-handed to such kind hospitality."

Elizabeth Lamb was enraptured. "Oh, Grandmother! What a

beautiful gold ring! How did you ever make those tiny ivy leaves? And it's set with a pink pearl! It's my birthstone, isn't it? What does a pearl protect me from?"

"I really don't know," her grandmother answered, sipping tea. "From too much observation and forceful speech, I hope. The ivy is because I remembered Rosetti's line: 'But pluck an ivy branch for me, grown old before my time.'" She softened her words with an affectionate pat of the little ringed hand.

"Oh, then mine will have a ruby," Persis announced smugly, impeded by the large piece of bacon in her mouth. "Because I'm almost born in July. And I'll bet mine doesn't have ivy leaves."

"No, Persis," said Elizabeth, "June 29 is not July. I'll give you a hint: the other June birthstone is moonstone. And what its powers are, I don't know either."

"It stops people from talking around bacon, maybe," Elizabeth Lamb said thoughtfully.

"'Er birthday, is it?" Alice asked. "I'll start yer egg right off, ma'am. I jist have to fetch somethin' in from the yard."

There was silence for a while, broken only by happy chewing and swallowing sounds from Persis. "What did you make for Mr. Vincentia?" Elizabeth Lamb, who had been eyeing the third box, asked.

"It's a fob for his watchchain. He has a lovely old Victorian pocket watch that chimes."

"Grandmother, he wears a Cartier tank watch, on his wrist! I noticed because I've always wanted one. All I have is a cheap old Timex. Why do you think he has a pocket watch?"

"Because he took it out to let me hear how beautifully it struck, at nine," her grandmother replied calmly, accepting a scone from Alice. "You had gone upstairs.

"And the nice little Timex you have is perfectly suited to a girl of twelve, Elizabeth Lamb. Don't be — insuperable."

"What does the fob look like?" Persis asked thickly, through her scone. "Could we see? Oh, yes, Alice, I would like jam, or is there some honey? My throat's rather sore."

"No, the box is sealed so that it couldn't open accidentally. It is a gold dolphin with onyx eyes. I had noticed something on his door, so I slipped out last night to be sure of what it was. The dolphin is

83

in the shape of his door-knocker."

"Honestly! You could have been mugged, Grandmother! You certainly took a lot of trouble over him," Elizabeth Lamb said jealously.

"As he is taking trouble with you and Persis," Elizabeth answered, cutting off the top of her egg. "Alice, I wondered why there was no tea strainer, but didn't I hear you telling Persis you'd read her leaves? Won't you read Elizabeth Lamb's too, as a birthday present? And mine, as a going-away present?"

Alice was pleased. "Certainly, ma'am. I jist have to go outside fer a minute. Be right back. You all jist finish yer cups, take 'em in yer right hand by the handle, and swirl 'em around three times."

She soon bustled back, looking flushed and pompous. She sank into a chair beside Elizabeth Lamb and peered into her cup. "H'm," she pondered. "Now, wot can I tell the birthday gerrel?" She said nothing for a good two minutes. Persis chewed a third scone more quietly but no less earnestly. Elizabeth Lamb held her breath. This was the first time Alice had favored her with a reading, although she had often recounted her readings for the "Hibernian Sisters." Persis reached for more bacon, and her grandmother smiled at her, though she shook her head admonishingly.

"Well," Alice said slowly. "This here looks like a bunch o' snakes. That ain't good; that's somethin' awful bad — a real disaster." She turned the cup slightly. "Well, they're sort of goin' inter two things — one looks like them sticks th' Aussies throw. What would y' call it?"

"A boomerang," Elizabeth Lamb supplied. "What does it mean?"

"Means somebody's plottin' somethin'. And the other's a corkscrew, f' sure. That means trouble caused by bein' too nosy."

Persis giggled. "That sounds right. But isn't there anything better in her cup?"

Alice looked happier. "There's a ring; that means a marriage." She sighed. "But it's opposite the handle. Means it won't go through.

"Never mind, child. It may not go through right now, but you've got years."

"Well, thank you, Alice," Elizabeth Lamb said seriously. "What does Persis' cup say?"

Persis somewhat reluctantly handed it over. "There's a cat, for sure," said Alice. "Quarrels are comin'. And could be somebody's treacherous. And alls else is here is a bottle — that means pleasure. No, wait; there's a couple of 'em."

Now Elizabeth Lamb giggled. "It's a sign for you to stop nipping, Persis."

"No; means a sickness. Maybe you hadn't ought to have eat so much breakfast, Persis. Could be you're about to get sea-sick. And that's all I see — no, that there could be a bush. You're goin' to make new friends.

"Now yers, ma'am."

"I certainly hope Persis will make new friends, and her cousin, too," said Elizabeth, surrendering her cup. "What do you see for me?"

"A ship, very clear," Alice answered promptly. "It means—"

Both little girls interrupted with laughter. "Of course; we're going on a ship," Persis said.

Alice raised her voice. "It means a successful journey. Lots of people'll prob'ly order yer jewelry, ma'am. Also could mean you'll be thinkin' of someone at sea."

Elizabeth Lamb frowned. Her grandmother slightly blushed. "And there's a anchor, ma'am. Means business success, jist like I said. *And* it means a true love." Elizabeth Lamb frowned harder. "But there's a clock. I don't like this: there's a 7 on the face. Someone in the fam'ly is surely goin' to die; well, maybe not in *yer* fam'ly, but somebody's you're attached to."

"Oh, really, Alice." Elizabeth looked anxiously at her grand-daughters. "Couldn't you be wrong?"

"Never, ma'am. Not about what things mean," Alice said firmly. "But, well, that clock — maybe it ain't a clock after all. I could be wrong about that. Seems to be more of a basket. With flowers, I guess. That means a addition to the fam'ly."

She leaned back in her chair, looking exhausted. "And that's all I see."

Elizabeth Lamb sighed. "An addition to the family. Grandmother, if Persis can stop eating, I think we'd better go. We'll be late."

Alice left for the kitchen while Elizabeth Worthington embraced the two girls and made a few gentle pronouncements as to their

85

behavior on the *Chianti*. Persis sighed and wriggled, reaching behind her to grope for a stray sausage on the table. Elizabeth Lamb stood stiffly, staring out the bay window and thinking about snakes and boomerangs and corkscrews and clocks set at seven — and about baskets of flowers.

"Have a good time in Paris, Grandmother," she said softly, as they picked up their bags by the front door. "I heard Mr. Vincentia say he'll call you there. If he calls from the *Chianti,* maybe he'll let us talk to you."

As they turned the corner, she took Persis by the arm. "Be specially charming to Mr. Vincentia, Persis," — Persis groaned and opened her mouth to reply — "because he might end up as our step-grand-father. You heard what Alice said about the basket."

Persis' mouth opened wider. She stood still, staring at her cousin. "They were kissing last night," Elizabeth Lamb went on, "so just you—"

"*Will* you stop telling me what to do! And I can't believe Grandmother was kissing some strange Italian! I was reading in *Time* about jerry-antic sex — how old people in Florida are taking to it — but Grandmother—! Elizabeth Lamb, you're making this up. You should be ashamed."

"Hush, he's just come out his door. He's handsome, wouldn't you say, and you can't call him 'strange' after they spent all evening together. No wonder Grandmother likes him; I bet he's got air-conditioning, too. Now shake hands nicely."

Persis kicked her cousin's ankle, disregarding that her own bare toe took the brunt of the blow, and swung her suitcase hard into Elizabeth Lamb's bottom. She then smiled prettily at Mr. Vincentia, who came down his steps to greet them enthusiastically. Persis seized his gift from Elizabeth Lamb and presented it to him.

"For you, from Grandmother, because you're being so nice to us," she said winsomely.

"I will open it at dinner tonight, so everyone can see. You are as delightful a child as your cousin and I am very pleased to have you both as my guests.

"Now, the lady in the car is Mrs. Donelli, but she likes to be called Annie. Antonio will pull down these seats for you two so there will be room for Viola — if she ever readies herself to leave. Your friend Payson arrived promptly; he is as responsible as your grandmother assured me he was."

Payson grinned at them from the front seat of the limousine as Antonio was dispatched to get Viola. Benno was standing, watchful as ever, beside a small red convertible heaped high with luggage, to which he added theirs. They seated themselves opposite Mrs. Donelli and announced their names.

"I, too, am very glad you are coming with us," she said politely. "And perhaps you will distract Viola so that she doesn't interfere with my typewriter, nor anything else on my desk. I have told Vito that his granddaughter is making me think very seriously of resigning my position." Her voice was deep and somewhat harsh. She had shoulder-length black hair and grave hazel eyes. A well-shaped scarlet mouth exactly matched the scarlet of her linen dress that, in turn, nicely set off the glowing olive of her face and arms. "Although," Elizabeth Lamb thought disapprovingly, "anyone with such dark hair on her arms ought to wax them, or wear sleeves."

"My dear, dear Annie," Mr. Vincentia beseeched, although with one eye on Antonio, who came from the house shaking his head, "you must not speak of leaving. Never mention it again. Never, never, never! You know you are indispensable." He leaned into the car to look directly at her, with outright appeal, and then withdrew abruptly to run up the steps of his house and shout angrily into the open door. Benno, after a glance to locate Antonio, entered the house, muttering.

He soon appeared, pushing an angry Viola before him. Mr. Vincentia followed and got into the car. Viola was clutching to her chest a large canvas bag, from the partially-opened zipper of which a fold of white chiffon billowed. As Benno inserted her none too gently into the seat beside Annie, the chiffon snagged on the crystal vase beside the door. Viola shrieked. Annie shrugged and lit a cigarette. Benno turned to his employer, after wresting the bag, which was jostling Annie, away from Viola and placing it by Elizabeth Lamb's feet.

"*Per favore, padrone,*" he began. Mr. Vincentia looked up from a small pocket notebook he was consulting. "Speak English, Benno," he said. "The young ladies will think we are talking about them. But you should save your breath; the answer, again, is no. I told you you must stay here to supervise.

"And please start before Antonio. You must stop in Hingham to pick up — what I ordered. Put it on the boat, along with the luggage, as soon as you get to Mr. Adam's place. His gatekeeper will show you where to garage Mrs. Donelli's car, and someone will give you a lift back to Boston. Now, *pronto!*"

Benno backed slightly away. "*Padrone,*" he began again, and defiantly followed with a low, imploring speech in Italian. Elizabeth Lamb caught the word *pistolo* spoken questioningly. "*Si, si,*" Mr. Vincentia answered, pressing a button to close the window beside him and motioning Benno away. "Viola," he looked at his granddaughter, "this is Persis. Persis, my granddaughter Viola. I am sure you will enjoy each other's company." Viola shrugged and gazed down at her lap.

As soon as the red car sped by him, Antonio started his engine. Almost instantly the hot, humid air of the limousine began to cool. "Oh, it's lovely!" Persis cried. Elizabeth Lamb nodded agreement. They settled back into the grey velvet luxury of the surprisingly comfortable jump seats as the car moved smoothly forward.

"Why didn't you pack that pretty white dress, Viola?" Persis asked. "It might get dirty, on the floor."

"It's my very special dress," Viola answered sulkily. "I saved it for last." As her grandfather looked quizzically at her, she added, "It's my confirmation dress. I didn't want to forget it."

"Why," Mr. Vincentia began, "do you need your—" He sighed and turned back to his notebook, which was evidently easier to understand than his granddaughter. "Viola didn't get confirmed till last year, after she came to live in Boston," Annie informed Elizabeth Lamb, as if in answer to her unspoken question if the dress would still fit.

"I'm glad you are not letting that nasty Benno go with us on the boat, Grandfather," Viola said. "I don't see why he gets to drive Annie's car, though. She said she wouldn't ever let me drive it."

"You have no license, Viola," he replied absently, his eyes on his notebook. "You are only just sixteen. And we needed Annie's car for the luggage and to be at Mr. Adam's when we return. Annie is going to drive straight from there to Worcester, to spend some time with her mother, who is not well."

"You all certainly do a lot of travelling," Persis observed. A thoughtful smile spread over her face as she spoke. She reached into one of the capacious pockets of her shorts and surreptitiously produced a crumpled piece of paper. Alternating sly glances at the paper with triumphant looks at her cousin, she jerkily pronounced: "The use of traveling — is to regulate — imagination by reality — and instead of — thinking how things — may be — is to see them as — they are."

"What a learned child *you* are!" Mr. Vincentia looked up from his notebook with admiration. "Or did you make that up? Surely not!"

"Surely Samuel Johnson did," Elizabeth Lamb murmured. "What else," she whispered to Persis, "have you written down to impress us with?" She started in her seat, both at an elbow in her side from Persis and a buzzing from the walnut panelling behind them. Mr. Vincentia leaned forward and, sliding aside a part of the panelling, produced a grey telephone. "Vincentia," he said. He held the phone to his ear, staring out the window.

Annie sneezed violently several times and then lit a cigarette. Viola bent down to adjust her bag, from which the chiffon seemed to be emerging as if blown, although there was no perceptible draft in the car. Persis, though, rubbed the back of her neck and whispered to her cousin that she thought she was getting a stiff neck from the air-conditioning and how do you suppose it could be turned down?

"Well," Mr. Vincentia finally spoke, "there's not much we can do. It will be the better for him if he returns, or at least leaves the boat where we can find it. No, no, I don't blame you, captain. Roberto was always a bit unstable and, after all, *I* hired him although you expressed doubts. Perhaps it is for the best, except that we need to take along the Whaler.

"We should be there very shortly. Have the other guests arrived? Good. The *Chianti* can weigh anchor as soon as we board, then."

He returned the phone to the panel and turned to Annie. "Well," he said, "*this* is not so good: Captain Knudsen reports that he sent

89

Roberto with the Boston Whaler to Mr. Adam's dock over an hour ago, to pick up some last-minute supplies, and not only has he not returned, but he never went to the dock. Someone at Adam's saw the Whaler heading north, along the shore. He's jumped ship."

"You never really trusted Roberto, did you? And Antonio often said he was *stolto;* stronger than just saying he was foolish, he sometimes called him *pazzo* — really crazy." Annie began sneezing again, as soon as she had spoken. She took a handkerchief from her bag and wiped her eyes.

"No, I do not regret his leaving. We have sufficient crew without him with Antonio along. But we need the Whaler."

"But there is the *Rocca,* and the dinghy," said Annie, sneezing again.

"Knudsen left the *Rocca* at a Quincy shipyard, for repairs to her engine. There is a small, new, two-man outboard, just a toy, really, I had put aboard to entertain Viola, and the dinghy can hold six. Oh, we'll be safe enough; we have four six-man rafts and the *Chianti* is almost unsinkable, anyway.

"But I hope Knudsen locates the Whaler before we leave. This is an inconvenience, at the least."

"The *Chianti* draws only nine-and-a-half feet, though, so we can put right in to almost any harbor," Annie reassured him, through the tears now streaming from her eyes.

Mr. Vincentia looked closely at her. He pulled a huge white silk handkerchief from the breast pocket of his blazer and wiped her face. "My dear, what is it?"

"God," said Annie, sneezing violently, "I don't know. It came on so suddenly. This is what happens when I get near a cat; you know I'm allergic to them. But there are no—"

"Cioccolato," thought Elizabeth Lamb, "never misses a cue." Annie had been interrupted by a faint, smothered "Meeoww" from Viola's bag, which now writhed about on the floor.

"Viola!" Mr. Vincentia shouted. "You know what cats do to Annie! If it were not in that bag, she would have reacted within a few minutes! I wish she had!" He pressed a button and the glass between them and the front seat slid down. "Elizabeth Lamb, hand that bag to Payson, please."

As soon as she complied the glass slid up. Mr. Vincentia pressed another button and the window beside Annie opened. "Do you see what you have done, you thoughtless child?" he asked Viola angrily. "That cat was to have been left at the house. We must turn back!" He pulled the speaking tube that connected with the front seat from the wall beside him. Viola began to weep loudly, her face as wet as Annie's had been.

"No, no," said Annie, in almost a normal voice. "It will pass quickly. I'm really all right. You can raise the window again. The cat will be something to amuse Viola, on the boat, but it must be kept in her cabin, Vito. And if we turn back, we won't get the early start you wanted. You said it would be — better if we were underway before the letters we sent — you know."

"Yes," Vito said thoughtfully. "But that cat *must* stay in your cabin, Viola. I have put Elizabeth Lamb in with you, and I hope she can see that it does not get out. If I did not have the superstitious belief that it is bad luck to make two beginnings to a journey, though, we would surely return to Boston. But I have a good mind to leave that animal at the SPCA in the next town!"

"No!" Viola screamed. "I will jump overboard if you do! No! No!"

"Mr. Vincentia," Elizabeth Lamb said quietly, "I really will see that it doesn't get out of the cabin, and Viola will, too."

He relented. "Very well. But only because we are very near our destination. Stop that crying, Viola, or I may change my mind."

The rest of the drive was peaceful. Elizabeth Lamb and Persis luxuriated in the coolness although Persis rummaged through her pockets for a faded bandanna, which she tied around her neck. Viola wisely remained silent, her anxious eyes fixed on the back of Payson's head, as if Cioccolato might emerge from his bag and appear beside it. Mr. Vincentia wrote in his notebook, taking occasional sips from a glass of mineral water he poured from a bottle in the bar at his elbow. Annie smoked incessantly, looking out the window at the passing fields and villages.

From a country road they entered a narrow way marked by towering stone pillars which bore large painted signs reading "Private. Guard dogs." After a drive of over a mile there were more pillars, connected by wrought-iron gates. From a small stone house inside the high, spiked iron fence an elderly man emerged, followed by two Dobermans. He opened the gates, touching his hand to his cap as the car passed through. "It's all very futile," Persis, awed, murmured, to smiles from Annie and Elizabeth Lamb.

Antonio followed the graveled drive for almost a half-mile, swung around an enormous, Tudor-style house on the steps of which two more Dobermans lay, and stopped at a path that wound through shrubbery beyond which the sea could be seen, glinting in the sunshine. Benno was there, opening the car doors, announcing that the luggage was aboard, anxiously inquiring if the trip had been uneventful, and full of news about the missing seaman and the boat, still not recovered.

"Yes, yes," said his employer, "we know. You arranged to borrow Mr. Adam's boat for us, I gather? Good, then you can pilot us and return it here. I will call you at the house tomorrow." And as Benno assumed a plaintive expression: "*No,* you may not take Roberto's place!"

"Look at that!" Persis pointed to a long, gleaming white craft anchored in the cove a little way out from the shore. "I've never seen a boat so big!" She still stared, rubbing her neck, as Benno helped her into a motorboat, after Annie and Viola and Elizabeth Lamb had been seated. Mr. Vincentia placed Payson and the encased Cioccolato far in the stern before he and Antonio boarded.

Elizabeth Lamb opened her mouth wide and happily drew the fresh, cool salt air into her lungs, somewhat choked after more than an hour of Annie's cigarette smoke. The bright sunshine made the waters of the little cove a deep, brilliant blue that was reflected, in a lighter tone, on to the bellies and underwings of a few gulls circling lazily above it. She laughed with pleasure as the light wind caused by the skimming of the launch over the calm sea blew back her long hair, and leaned forward to give her cousin an affectionate hug.

"Oh, it's so good to be out of Boston and able to breathe again!" she exclaimed. "And," looking up at the dazzling magnificence of the yacht looming near them, "to think we're going to go to Maine in style this year! Not cramped in the dusty back of a station wagon with suitcases falling on us." Benno quickly got them to the *Chianti* and held his boat beside her while his passengers were assisted by Antonio to climb a short ladder that culminated in a small platform beside the low parapet that, interspersed with large, teak-trimmed openings, encased the after part of the roofed main deck.

As Mr. Vincentia, the first up the ladder, reached the platform, a gate in the parapet was smartly opened by a stocky, grey-haired man in a spotless white dress uniform. He removed his gold-braid-trimmed cap and held it under his left arm while he made a slight bow. "Ah, Captain," said his employer, "the *Chianti* looks marvelous, as always. We'll start at once, hey?"

Captain Knudsen inclined his head an inch or two in acknowledgment and snapped his fingers at two men in red trousers and green and white striped jerseys who were standing at attention behind him. They quickly moved to hand Annie, Elizabeth Lamb, and Persis through the gate.

"And, Pietro," Mr. Vincentia said as a tall, thin, swarthy man dressed in white duck pants and tunic, a white kerchief tied around his neck, came up to him and bowed, "I have, as I believe the captain has told you, a helper for you. Here is Payson Prouty, who will be with us as far as Mount Desert Island. Perhaps you will put him to work as soon as he changes? I'd like lunch served at twelve-thirty; the guests have all travelled this morning and would appreciate an early meal."

"One extra, sir," Captain Knudsen announced, after an anxious glance over the side to assure himself that Benno was maneuvering his boat safely away from the *Chianti*. "Stranger," he added.

"No, two, captain. I told you when I called last night that my young friend Elizabeth Lamb, here, and her cousin would be joining us."

"The Honourable Monica," Captain Knudsen, evidently a man of economical speech, replied.

"But I told you she was coming. She's been aboard before."

"Brought a young man."

"Rather, he brought her. My godson, Christopher Grenville, was invited and she managed to get him to wangle an invitation for her. But Chris is no stranger to you."

"Another young man. Named Templeton."

Mr. Vincentia frowned. "I don't know him. Miss Thornhill is a great manipulator, isn't she?

"Well, here is where I would like you to see the various passengers are lodged." He tore a page from his notebook. "I assumed Julia and her — and Mr. Cooper would take their usual cabin.

"No, wait — with this extra man, I'll have to move Viola and Elizabeth Lamb aft, to the cabin I had assigned to Mr. Grenville, and put him and this Templeton in the larger stateroom under mine. The cabin has only one bed, but the girls won't mind sharing it."

Elizabeth Lamb, gazing about her at the splendor of the *Chianti* and craning her neck around Mr. Vincentia to watch a seaman operating an electric anchor windlass, far forward in the open bow of the boat, was depressed by his words. It was bad enough to share even a cabin with Viola. "If she hogs all the blankets, I'll grab a couple and sleep up on deck," she planned silently.

Persis observed her expression and whispered, "Now you've got a kind of pain-in-the-neck, too. Gosh, but my neck hurts. But maybe the cabins aren't air-conditioned."

Mr. Vincentia, leading Annie and the girls aft, heard the last of this and assured her that they were. Now Persis became depressed, but brightened as they reached the stern of the boat. "It's like something in a magazine!" she exclaimed. "It's a greenhouse — a floating greenhouse!"

"Not quite," Elizabeth Lamb murmured, although she, too, was impressed. The stern had sweeping, curved, glassed-in, teak-framed apertures that made one feel suspended just above the water. There were two large round heavy-based tables of some white laminated wood, half-surrounded by low-backed, red-canvas-upholstered benches of a matching wood. There were several low chairs that seemed to be composed of layers of plump red-green-and-white-striped cushions. "Oh," said Persis, sinking into one, "It's heavenly! As soft as a bed. But the flowers!"

They were everywhere on the deck, in large green-lacquered baskets: colorful assortments of daisies and asters, pansies, iris, geraniums, nasturtium, little orchids and a number of flowers Persis did not recognize. Mixed with the flowering baskets were some that held tall shining-leafed plants, of not only the usual green but also of a silver-grey and of bronze. None were so tall that the magnificent view of the sea and shore and sky was obscured. This began to change as the *Chianti*, without any perceptible tremor, began to move smoothly out of the cove. More baskets, of fuschia and trailing geraniums and ivy hung from the ceiling. A seaman appeared with a brass can and began to water the flowers.

"The water will get on the deck," objected Persis, who had sea-going relatives very particular that nothing but the unavoidable dash of sea-water ever violated the teak decks of their modest crafts. "It will leak out of the baskets."

"Ah, but, no, *signorina*," said the man, putting aside some of the leaves to reveal that the potted plants on the deck were resting in bags of a heavy green plastic that lined the baskets. "Oh, good," said Persis, leaning back into her chair and yawning.

"Attend to that later, Carlo," Mr. Vincentia directed. "We are under way, and I think the captain would wish you out on deck, as you should know. Where are the other guests?"

The man pointed a finger upwards and, as he did, a pair of yellow espadrilles followed by a pair of shapely legs appeared at the top of the open mahogany spiral staircase that wound up from the deck to an oval opening in the ceiling.

"Darling Vito!" cried the owner of the legs as she appeared beside him. She dutifully kissed the air beside his cheek. "My daughter-in-law, Julia Vincentia," he said without much expression, to Elizabeth Lamb. His introduction of them to Julia included Persis, now asleep on her chair, as well as her cousin. "And," gesturing to the tall, tanned, muscular, pleasant-faced man of about fifty, with rather long blond hair shot with grey, who had descended behind Julia, "this is Mr. Cooper, Elizabeth Lamb."

"You must call me Paul," the man said engagingly, in a soft, very slight Southern accent. "It makes me feel young." His grin as he raised a hand to brush his mustache was as pleasant as his face and his voice.

Viola had raced to Julia as soon as she reached the deck. She clung to her, demanding, "What did you bring me? What I asked?"

Julia held her affectionately. She was a plump, round-faced, pretty young woman, her fairly long curly brown hair tied back with a yellow scarf. She removed the large sunglasses that had concealed earnest blue eyes and said to Viola, "How you've grown, my darling!" Her English accent was not pronounced, possibly due to association with Paul's slight Southern one. "Now come down to my cabin and tell me everything!" Her tone was girlish, despite her deep voice.

Mr. Vincentia seemed annoyed to be left with Paul. Annie had gone, after a greeting to Julia and Paul, murmuring that she needed to unpack and find her nose spray. Mr. Cooper had deprecated this, though pleasantly, assuring her that physical weaknesses were all in the mind and all her nose needed was good sea air. "And, look," he called after her, "we're out of the cove and soon sea air will be all around us."

"I've never seen anyone as healthy as you, Paul," said Vito, sitting on the edge of one of the low chairs and lighting a cigarette. "You seem never to have any sort of ailment or disability — or admit to any, could it be? But where is Monica? And the others?"

Paul moved to the staircase and called, "Hey, troops!" Turning back, he said, "They were sunning in the not-quite-altogether. They're getting themselves decent, I suppose."

"Except me and my new friend, Jake," a hearty voice announced. "We think drinking's more decent than sunning." One of the glass doors that led from the deck into the saloon lounge slid aside and the owner of the voice beamed at them over a large iced tumbler with a stalk of celery jutting from it. She was a tall, heavy woman with a gaunt, distinguished, tanned face. Above high cheekbones, her narrow dark eyes narrowed even more as she emerged into the sunlit afterdeck. Her hair was straight and silver-grey, just a little longer than Paul's and cut similarly. Her ample form was draped from below her tanned shoulders to her ankles in a sarong-like garment the same tomato-red as her drink.

"Amy, my dear," said Vito, rising to embrace her. "I am so glad to see you — and Jim, I suppose, is on the upper deck? This cruise will relax you and enable you to help with Viola's little project. But" — more softly — "I thought we agreed that — ah, nothing before noon?"

"It's only a Virgin Mary, V.V.," Amy answered cheerfully. "Jake, here, will vouch for that. Won't you, sweetie? And who are these

96

dear little girls, one of them sleeping like an angel? But no Viola? Does that" — her voice became even more cheerful — "mean she won't be with us?"

Vito assured her that Viola was aboard and Amy became perceptibly less happy. He turned to the bald little man who had followed her. He was very short and top-heavy, his broad shoulders straining a thick wool, loudly-checked jacket and his thin, bowed legs encased in tight wool gabardine trousers. His round, sorrowful eyes glistened with emotion in his little, weathered brown face as he raised himself on the toes of his tan suede shoes to embrace his host.

"Vito, me dear fren'," he beamed, "hits hever so good to see yer. Me hay fever went a'most to the minnit I clumb aboard. Yer kindness will stay in me 'eart forhever." He then grinned at Elizabeth Lamb and assured her that one butcher's 'ook at 'er 'ad convinced 'im that she would become 'is dear fren', too. After that, he drained his glass and, chewing both on the olive it had contained and a piece of ice, disappeared back into the saloon before he could be introduced formally.

"You invited Jake because of his hay fever?" Paul asked. "Really, V.V., it's all in his mind, I'm convinced. It comes and goes so conveniently."

"It has been in his mind for fifty years, then," Vito answered. "Ever since he and I started an ice business. Our wagon was horse-drawn, and horse dander, he was told some years later when he could afford a specialist and we could afford a truck, evidently triggered a number of other allergies. That to roses is one; you notice I have had my favorite roses removed for the trip.

"And I invited him, Paul, because he has been one of my best friends for all those years. I am, I suppose, entitled to invite some few people I like?"

Elizabeth Lamb thought Mr. Vincentia's tone rather sharp. So did Paul, who smiled placatingly and, murmuring that he, too, would like a drink, went into the saloon.

Feet pounded on the spiral stairs and a tall, handsome, black-haired woman, followed closely by three young men, sprang from the bottom stair to launch herself at Mr. Vincentia in a fervent embrace. Her pink sarong, similar to Amy's but requiring less yardage, slid dangerously as she did.

"Ah, Monica," he said, "I am glad Christopher brought you. You look well, my dear, tanned and happy. You were in the Caribbean with him, weren't you? And you brought a friend along, I hear? Present me, Chris."

Christopher Grenville, a slim, earnest-looking, bespectacled young person, nervously shook back his thin, sandy hair and, both lisping and stuttering slightly, introduced the man beside him as Robert Templeton. Mr. Templeton, tall and robust, pushed his sunglasses to the top of his glossy dark hair, long like Christopher's, and appeared gratified and rather smug at Mr. Vincentia's courteous reception. Below his bulging, sun-burned belly he wore a lavender and orange *pareau* that was as prone to slipping as the Honourable Monica's garment, persuaded to by the way the belly vibrated as he energetically expressed his pleasure at being aboard. His rather high voice shook with his emotion.

"He can't be for real," Elizabeth Lamb thought, regarding him incredulously. So did Amy Danniver, who had returned after a quick trip to the bar. She drank deeply of her fresh drink and looked dubiously at Robert Templeton.

The third young man, short and rotund, frowned disapprovingly at Amy. He rubbed his balding forehead and then pulled nervously at his blond hair, as if to increase its already over-sufficient length to atone for his having nothing much on top. He went to murmur strongly in her ear that she knew V.V. had told her not to drink and her new contract, as she might try to remember, could be cancelled at V.V.'s discretion if he felt she was drinking heavily. He then, even lower, reminded her that V.V. hated the practice of drinking alone, and that if she drank in her cabin, the contract was most certainly—

Amy interrupted with a cheerful, none-too-low, "Shut up, Jim," and went on to inform him that those who could, wrote, while those who couldn't, ended up as rotten little editors, who usually couldn't spell, either. "*And* as every *creative* person knows, alcohol is a stimulant to creativity," she ended and then took Elizabeth Lamb aside to engage her in what sounded to Persis, who was awake now but still drowsy, like a literary conversation.

98

Persis stretched her shoulders, shook herself a little, and then leaned again into the soft back of her chair to rub her neck and yawn. She watched Payson, crisply attired in one of his new white shirts, black trousers and a long red-white-and-green-striped apron, setting one of the tables with bright red ceramic plates and heavy cut-crystal tumblers. He winked at her, informed her that the cat had scratched his face badly while he was forcing it into Viola's cabin, and asked if she would like him to slip her some crackers. "Lunch won't be till they're finished their drinkin'," he whispered, "An' Pietro — he's the cook, my boss — says that there Lady Monica, or whatever he calls her, likes 'er hooch."

"No," she whispered back, "I don't feel so good, Payson. Do you think you could find out where my cabin is? I'd like to lie down till lunch. Tell Elizabeth Lamb I'll be back."

Payson took Persis gently by the arm and led her away, returning in a few minutes with a tray of mimosas. He circulated deftly among the guests, who had formed little conversational groups. Amy drained her (possibly) Virgin Mary and took a mimosa, after Elizabeth Lamb, who had seized the opportunity to get one for herself.

Amy smiled rather sadly at her. "My daughter loves orange juice and champagne," she said. As Payson passed her, she drank the contents of her glass quickly, put the empty glass on his tray, and took another mimosa.

"Oh, is she aboard?" Elizabeth Lamb asked. Amy looked down into her drink. "Dead," she answered briefly. "Almost two years, now. Funny, but I can't seem to grasp it. She was only fifteen." She turned away and went to press her tear-wet face against the curved glass window at the stern.

Elizabeth Lamb followed. "You *will* feel better," she said gently. "It will take a while, but you will. You won't forget her, but you'll feel better."

"If only it had been what they call an Act of God," Amy replied fiercely, "and not an act of that damned Viola. She should have been strangled at birth." Her voice had risen and several people turned to look at her. The short, fat man came over quickly, bearing a glass and several tissues.

"Amy," he said loudly, facing away from the others to frown

99

warningly, "no sense in going on about — about that poor deformed kitten of mine. It had to be done. Here, have some water. Wipe your eyes. There, there, *caro*.

"I'm Jim Darrow," he said to Elizabeth Lamb, "Mrs. Danniver's editor. V.V. spoke of you; said you're awfully clever. Well-read, too. Do you like her mysteries?"

Elizabeth Lamb was spared having to say she had never heard of them by the tall black-haired woman who came gracefully up to them. "How do you do?" she said huskily. "You're Elizabeth Lamb Worthington, I hear. I was at school in Switzerland with your Aunt Isabella a million or so years ago. I think she got most of her English accent by taking mine away from me and I got my Bostonian tones by taking them from her.

"Oh, I'm Monica Thornhill, or" — she laughed a little — "the Hon Mon, as Vito has been known to call me. I've known *him* since I was a child."

"How do you do?" Elizabeth Lamb replied. The Hon Mon was approving. "So few people realize that the only possible answer to 'How do you do?' is — 'How do you do?' I can see your manners are wonderful; wish your aunt's were!" With tactful courtesy she then introduced herself to Amy Danniver and said she simply *loved* Amy's whodunnits. "They're almost British, of the 'tea-cosy' type I adore, and very appealing."

As Amy smiled wanly, Monica went on: "And you don't fall into the pits of misinformation so many American writers, and even the British, do when writing about what Nancy Mitford termed the 'U' class. So many pseudo-posh writers call their characters' napkins 'serviettes,' for instance, when none but the most appallingly non-U people *ever* use that term. And your plots are so clever! How *do* you think of them! And your dear little sleuth; what a prodigy! Why did you come to call him Alaric C? Why not just Alaric?"

Amy brushed a hand across her eyes and responded gamely. Jim Darrow stood by, watchfully nodding.

Elizabeth Lamb bent over the semi-circular box of herbs that was placed on the deck in the curve of the stern. "Nice, ain't they?" asked the little man in the loud jacket, coming up behind her. "I'm Jake Aaronson, Vito's old pal from 'is youf. Vito's come a long w'y from wen the on'y 'erb we knoo was parsley. Likes to flavor 'is grub now, 'e does. The Hon Mon's dad taught 'im a thinger two, 'e did. Not on'y 'ow to speak an' dress an' all that lot, but habout 'igh cweezeen as well. Still grateful, 'e is; that's why 'e puts up wiv the daughter. Can be a 'andful, she can.

"Not," he went on to the fascinated Elizabeth Lamb, who had wondered how Mr. Vincentia, born so poor, had acquired all his polish, not to mention his exquisite taste, "that the lidy ain't a lidy. A charmer, too." He grinned at her as they both accepted another mimosa from Payson.

"I guess," she thought, sitting down to sip hers, "that he was born with good taste, though. You don't just acquire that, or, if you do, it shows." She smiled over at Mr. Aaronson, now in the company of the Hon Mon.

The various groups, now including Julia and Viola, were being urged by Mr. Vincentia to come to the table where Payson, in amongst his circulations with the mimosas, had placed an elaborate assortment of food. Monica was approving, murmuring in a low voice to Mr. Aaronson that, "Vito still follows Papa's dictums. 'Always serve new guests with something cold' was one of them. Do you know all these people?"

Elizabeth Lamb, putting down her empty glass and peeking around several forms at a most entrancing confection of puff pastry and glazed strawberries that was garnished with thick rosettes of whipped cream, heard a new voice. "A bit of an omnium gatherum, wouldn't you say, *caro?* Or, to be nautical, as we must be for some days, a motley crew? Two attractive kids, though; one pretty even in her sleep. Let me help you to this *pâté.*"

Elizabeth Lamb leaned around the fat body of Jim Darrow, who was obtaining a large amount of lobster salad and a bunch of cold asparagus spears tied with strips of pimento, to see who had answered Monica. Mr. Aaronson winked at her.

"Goodness," she said to him, "I *thought* you were too much of a good thing to be a real Cockney!"

"Yer not so green as yer cabbage-lookin'," he answered in his original accent and then, "if you go fetch your friend, I'll get some plates for you both. You mustn't miss out on this sumptuous buffet.

I'd be delighted to be the luncheon partner of two pretty young ladies.

"And I *am* a real Cockney, by the way; born within sound of Bow Bells. I got some polish later on, from Vito. Run along and find the little girl, and be quick. I wouldn't put it past this motley crew, myself included, to finish all the lobster before you get back."

• CHAPTER 6 •

All at Sea

ELIZABETH LAMB went through the sliding doors and found herself in a large lounge. "What they call on boats a saloon, I guess," she said aloud. "And there's the bar, where Mrs. Danniver was getting all those Bloody Marys."

The bar, against the wall on her right, was large and impressive. It was made of walnut, and rimmed around the top with padded blue leather. Several chrome stools, with seats of the same leather, lined the bar, and behind it, on glass shelves before a huge mirror etched in silver with designs of all shapes of drinking glasses, was an enormous variety of liquor. A television set hung from the ceiling, across the far end of the bar.

Blue and white striped curtains at the large windows on the port side of the saloon matched blue and white striped carpeting, and comfortable-looking chairs and sofas of blue leather were arranged in groups around low, glass-topped chrome tables. Bouquets of blue lupine and white iris were on the tables and on the upright piano against the wall across from the bar.

At the end of the room there was a floor-to-ceiling bookcase, crammed with books, beside an arched opening into the dining room. Two round glass tables were already set for dinner with blue plates, glasses and stiff linen napkins of a paler blue. Around each table were six black lacquered chairs, their arms and part of their backs composed of curvaceous dolphins carved of gold-enameled wood. Above the narrow walnut Georgian sideboard at the far wall a mirror enlarged the apparent size of the room although its entire surface was etched with leaping gold dolphins that complemented the dolphin chairs.

To either side of the sideboard was a swinging door. Elizabeth Lamb chose the one on the left, which opened into a passage with portholes showing the covered main deck and the sea beyond. There was a door to the deck and also one ahead of her that, from the smell of sizzling onions, must lead to the galley. She heard a thud on the deck and opened the first door.

The captain had been heavily descending the ladder that evidently brought him down from the pilot house at the forward end of the upper deck. He had a slip of paper in his hand and looked preoccupied. "Oh," said Elizabeth Lamb, "is the bridge up there? Could I go up sometime and look at all the equipment? There must be a lot."

"Never," he answered briefly. She followed him to the galley. "The usual," he said to the cook, who was layering two large slices of rye bread with sautéed onions and pieces of cold herring. "I know, Captain," Pietro answered. "All ready." He got two bottles of beer from the refrigerator and put them on a tray beside the sandwiches. "The new boy will take it up."

The captain nodded and started aft, along the passage. Elizabeth Lamb followed. "If Payson can go up to the pilot house, why can't I?" she asked. "I won't touch anything."

"No passengers," the captain answered firmly. "Ever. Undisciplined. The crew is warned." He paused in his stride through the small dining room to look at her. "Why are you not having lunch with the others?"

"I'm looking for my cousin, Persis. Do you know where her cabin is?"

The captain pointed to a stairway leading down, on the starboard side of the dining room, in the archway between it and the end of the bar. She had not noticed it before. "Stateroom on your right, at the bottom." He went quickly through the lounge toward the luncheon party on the afterdeck.

Elizabeth Lamb made a face at his back and, instead of descending the stairs, decided to explore beyond the swinging door at the right of the sideboard. It was a passage almost identical to the other; there was also a door to the deck and one at the end of the passage. At the middle of the passage, differing from the other, was a little vestibule, with a curved stairway going down next to a short, straight one going up. "Maybe I could sneak up while he's on deck," she thought, but decided against it; he had undoubtedly left a seaman in the pilot house. The cook suddenly opened a door in the vestibule and frowned at her from his galley.

"Those stairs go down to the two forward staterooms and the crew's quarters," he said. "And you'd better not try the others, that go to the pilot house. What are you looking for?"

"Viola's cabin," she answered on an inspiration. "I have to see if the kitten is all right. Is her cabin down there?"

"No. It's below, but aft. Go back and down the stairs by the bar. Only the *padrone's* quarters and the cabin of Mrs. Donelli and Miss Thornhill are on this deck." He disappeared back into his domain.

Elizabeth Lamb went through the door at the end and found herself next to a stateroom door. A small palm tree, in the usual green lacquered basket, was beside it. She knocked and then pushed the door open.

The stateroom was large and luxurious, sunny because of the large portholes on the port side. It was a feminine room, with sole-of-the-shoe-deep pale green carpeting, the walls and ceilings of a matching velvet. Two large beds had covers of an apricot and pale green floral chintz; the curtains beside the portholes were of the same fabric. A sofa upholstered in apricot velvet, furbished with many pillows covered in the chintz, extended around the corner of two walls and in the niche in the corner there was a shelf holding a gardenia tree. A double dressing table of a pale wood between the beds had a long velvet bench before it and a mirror surrounded with theatrical strip lighting above it. The built-in dresser drawers under the portholes were covered in the green velvet. To her right, as she stood gaping in the doorway, was a pale wood desk holding only a marble container of pencils and pens, a portable typewriter, and a bouquet of yellow roses. A similar bouquet had been placed on the low table in front of the sofa, beside a large marble ashtray.

On one of the beds there was an untidy heap of clothes and on the other only a crocodile briefcase with the initials A. D. on its massive gold clasp. "I could guess which bed was Monica's and which Annie's without the initials," she thought, eyeing herself in the mirrored doors of the wardrobe beyond the desk.

Aloud she said, "Daddy would certainly say the *Chianti* is what he calls a 'pussy palace' — he can be so vulgar. And maybe he'd say I'm vulgar, too, but in a different way, because I certainly do like comfort even when it's a bit ostentatious. That's because I'm only half a Proper Bostonian and he's the whole deal."

"Why are you standing in somebody's room talking to yourself?" Viola's voice asked. She was in the passage, holding the swinging door open.

"I'm just looking around," Elizabeth Lamb answered hastily, shutting the stateroom door. "What are you doing?"

"Nothing," said Viola, and disappeared. Elizabeth Lamb went softly along to the other door, thinking, "In for a penny, in for a pound."

This was decidedly a man's room, but that of a man who indulged his *penchant* for luxury. It was panelled in a glowing walnut, with walnut framing the white ceiling into squares and one of the squares a skylight. Drawers were built into the panelling, and cane-fronted cabinets, below several glass-doored bookcases, had marble tops with brass railings to secure what was placed on them, among which was a photograph of the portrait of Mrs. Vincentia. The lamps and the fittings for the doors and drawers were of a burnished brass. There were two pillowed burgundy velvet settees, one long enough to be made up into a bed, and the gold-tied curtains at the large portholes were of the same velvet.

A handsome antique table-desk of walnut inlaid with squares of ivory was placed in front of the smaller settee on a beautiful deep-red and gold Oriental rug. There was a small door, only about five feet high, in the forward wall that blended into the panelling, and between it and a case containing old leather-bound books there was actually a small fireplace, resting on a marble slab below which, through the cane door of a cabinet, small birch logs could be seen. Its front was of black iron ornately rimmed in brass and the wall behind it was a shining sheet of hammered brass.

A very old copy of Bowditch's *American Practical Navigator* lay on the desk beside a telephone and a gold pen and a silver tray that held a decanter of brandy and two crystal glasses. On one of the cabinet tops a small Limoges vase, white painted with rosebuds, held only one perfect pink rose whose scent perfumed the whole cabin.

As she left, Payson suddenly came into the passage through a door at its far forward end she had not observed. "What's in there?" she asked.

"The storeroom. They needed another cheese. And the cook's got a little cabin offn it. There's a stairs down to the crew's place, too. What's *chèvre* mean? Where's Persis? Still asleep?"

"It means it's goat cheese. And I'm going down right now to check on her. I was just exploring."

At the foot of the stairs between the dining room and bar there was a yellow-carpeted lobby with three doors, two to her left. A painting of a brook running amongst large ferns was on the wall and beside each door there was a fern in a green basket, each fern of a different variety. The small lobby was brightened by white wallpaper with a design of green ferns and by a mirror on the outside of each door, along with inset ceiling lights under which the ferns seemed to be flourishing.

She opened the door across the lobby. The cabin was less luxurious than the two on the main deck but, even in semi-darkness, was cheerful with its light wood walls and furniture and pink-and-green patterned bedspreads and chairs. Persis was sitting on the edge of one of the beds, on which the spread had been neatly folded down. She looked flushed with sleep.

"I feel as though I'm drifting, Elizabeth Lamb," she said. "Sort of light, all over, and bewildered. I feel like Mummy must feel when she says she's 'all at sea.'"

"We're *all* at sea. And it seems to me we're going a lot faster, too." She walked to a porthole and pulled aside the pink curtain.

"We should be able to see land, because we're on the port side and Mr. Vincentia said we'd sail sort of close to shore, but there isn't any. That's funny.

"Want to go up and have some lunch? Wait till you see it; it's like something you'd be served in a palace, I bet. If it isn't all gone by now, that is. And I've been looking at the staterooms upstairs. They're just magnificent."

"Grandmother says it's low to go around snooping into people's rooms. Honestly, Elizabeth Lamb! And I bet they aren't more magnificent than my bathroom. All the walls are mirrors, and the ceiling, too, and even in the shower they're a shiny metal that looks just like a mirror. Somebody unpacked all my clothes while I was asleep; imagine that!

"That tall lady in a red sarong is in here with me. She came down to get some cigarettes a while ago. She straightened my bed and took me into the bathroom and washed my face with cold water. She said she hoped I didn't have a fever. I like her, but I wonder why Mr. Vincentia didn't put you here with me and her with Viola?"

"It's because she did something bad to Mrs. Danniver's daughter. She's dead, and Mrs. Danniver can't stand Viola. She even said she should have been strangled at birth." Elizabeth Lamb was leading Persis up the stairs.

The luncheon party was still in merry progress when they reached the afterdeck. Payson was rushing about refilling glasses with white wine, removing used plates and presenting the guests with new ones that held bunches of black grapes attractively frosted with some white substance. Pietro, carrying a large tray of biscuits and cheeses, followed in his wake. Elizabeth Lamb was relieved to see, as she and Persis accepted their portions of lobster and asparagus from Jake Aaronson, that the strawberry dessert was as yet untouched. They seated themselves beside him on the bench around one of the tables. Viola was opposite, staring moodily out to sea. Elizabeth Lamb averted her eyes from the grape seeds Viola was absently spitting on to the deck.

"Glad to see you've come for a bite of lunch," Jim Darrow observed affably, passing them with a plate heaped high with what looked like a sample of every type of cheese Pietro was offering. Elizabeth

Lamb smiled politely, thinking he was indeed the sort of person who said "bite of lunch" and sympathizing with Mrs. Danniver, whose prose he undoubtedly tried to influence.

Mr. Vincentia was being pursued by the earnest Robert Templeton. He seemed amused by what he was hearing, although the guest's solemnly-quivering jowls and ponderous tone did not indicate he meant to amuse. Nodding politely but dismissively at Mr. Templeton, he paused beside the children and patted Persis on her damply disheveled head.

"Why are we so far out in the ocean, Mr. Vincentia?" Elizabeth Lamb asked.

"The captain brought down a radiotelephone message for me. I must be in Canada sooner than I thought, so I am having him take a direct northeast course across the Gulf of Maine. We will put in at Matinicus tonight and be at Mount Desert by tomorrow evening," he explained, his eyes directed not at her but at Persis.

He touched Mr. Aaronson on the shoulder. "Jake, you had some medical training. Look at this child. Her face and arms are covered with faint but very definite flat, raised pinkish spots."

"Migawd," said Mr. Aaronson, turning from a conversation with Amy Danniver and rising to regard Persis. "I'd say it might be German measles. Does the back of your neck hurt?" Persis, who was pushing lobster and *pâté en croute* about her plate between sips of *Bianco di Verona,* nodded.

"And a friend of mine had German measles awhile ago," she answered. "But I really don't feel very bad, now that I had a nap. Am I contemptuous, though?"

Amy got up decisively. "She ought to go to her cabin. I've had them, so I don't mind being in with her. I think she should have a bath, with baking soda, first, though, if we may use your tub, Vito? And then," she eyed Persis' *lamé* shirt, "she can have a change of clothes, I hope."

She looked around. "Has anyone here not had German measles?"

"I haven't," said Julia, shortly. "And neither have you, Viola — why, where is Viola? She was right near you a minute ago, Jake, I thought. And, Jake, shouldn't the little girl stay apart from everyone?"

"She's not too contagious now," he answered. "But, certainly, any dishes and silver she uses should be sterilized. And she shouldn't be in the close proximity of you and Viola. I gather you're the only ones who should avoid her?"

Mr. Templeton admitted that he, too, had never had German measles, adding proudly, although obviously no one cared, that he had never had any of the usual childhood diseases. He and Julia immediately moved as far away from Persis as possible, Julia anxiously murmuring that she had no idea what had become of Viola who had, Elizabeth Lamb had noticed, left the deck almost as soon as she and Persis had arrived.

As soon as Mr. Aaronson finished instructing Payson as to the handling of Persis' eating utensils, Mr. Vincentia handed Payson a tray on which he had placed a selection of the luncheon foods. "Mrs. Donelli is on the upper deck," he directed. "She wished to be in fresh air for a while, and perhaps she has fallen asleep. And get a small pot of coffee for her; she does not drink wine at lunch."

He turned as Viola appeared, entering from the starboard deck. "Ah, there you are, my dear. Go to Julia, she wishes to give you some instructions."

Payson apprehensively eyed the circular staircase as he cautiously approached it with the laden tray. He stopped, with an expression of relief, as Annie Donelli pushed abruptly through the saloon doors. "Viola," she asked angrily, "have you seen my nose spray? I put it on a shelf in my bathroom and now it's disappeared."

Viola, smirking and avoiding Elizabeth Lamb's eye, announced brightly that she had been nowhere near Annie's cabin, from the moment she had boarded. Annie exhaled irritably and turned to her employer.

"Really, Vito," she said, "the thing didn't just walk away. And Viola has played tricks on me before. I really need that spray, after that reaction I had on the drive down. I told you that just one more—"

"Annie, *caro*," he answered quickly, "when we arrive at Matinicus tonight, I will send the Whaler over to Rockland and get your prescription refilled." He then frowned as Annie raised her brows and he obviously remembered the Whaler was not available. "You will be all right," he went on soothingly. "Jake can concoct something, and the fresh salt air will work almost as well as a spray.

"But," he regarded his guests, "there are keys to every cabin inside their wall safes and I beg that you all use them. That would avert these little — ah, mishaps."

Several people began to talk at once. Mr. Aaronson announced that it was medicine he had studied at Luke's, not pharmacy, and he wouldn't dare mix up anything for use by a human being, although he had, in his time, doctored horses. Mrs. Danniver murmured thoughtfully that there was a famous Christie death plot involving a nose spray — she subsided and drank wine defiantly as Jim Darrow came over to mutter at her. Paul asked, rather peevishly, why they were making for Matinicus tonight and not the Isles of Shoals? Monica observed that Papa always said it was very non-U to lock one's cabin door and she would never forget his rage, one time on the *Queen Mary,* when she had locked—

Mr. Templeton interrupted to declare that locks might not be upper-class, but he, for one, was all for them. Looking at Amy Danniver, he asked loudly why anyone would want, in such a congenial group, to connect nose sprays with death. Looking at him, Amy asked loudly why his "friend, Miss Sayers," hadn't told him about the subject. Mr. Templeton, offended and puzzled, sought solace in a large piece of the strawberry tart while muttering to Elizabeth Lamb that, for goodness sake, he certainly hoped she would not grow up to be the sort of offensive old lady who drank too much; why, his sainted mother never touched a drop of anything.

Julia, murmuring, "Clean air," and casting an angry look at Persis, who was obliviously consuming a piece of the tart Elizabeth Lamb had obtained for her from under the large nose of Mr. Templeton, put her arm around Viola and urged her up the ladder to the open deck. As they went she admonished Viola to avoid that spotted child because young girls were so delicate and vulnerable— They vanished.

Mr. Vincentia took Annie away, saying he had letters to get off at Matinicus and informing his guests that tea would be served in the saloon at four. He carried Annie's luncheon tray as they left. Amy announced that Persis should rest in their cabin, after a bath, while she got off some notes for a chapter that the excellent luncheon wine — she looked sardonically at her editor — had suggested to her *creative* mind.

Those remaining drank the espresso Payson served while they chatted politely. From him Elizabeth Lamb learned that her cabin was reached from the middle door on the lower deck, beside Persis' and Amy's, and that Julia Vincentia's and Paul's cabin was on the starboard side, opposite hers.

"I always remember that port is the left side of the boat because 'port' and 'left' each have four letters," she confided to Payson.

"I use that, too," said Monica, overhearing. "And it helps at night, even more, when a boat has its red port light lit on its left side, because port wine is red, too. Aren't I clever?"

"I think Graham Greene's 'Aunt Augusta' thought of that, *caro,*" Christopher Grenville suggested.

"Can't help that," the Hon Mon replied. "I thought of it first, I'm sure. Maybe I met him somewhere and he copped it from me.

"You know," she went on to Jim Darrow, who was eyeing her with the same somewhat-adoring look which he had earlier, Elizabeth Lamb had noticed with wonder, directed at Viola, "writers do the damndest things. Papa told me Willie Maugham was always recounting anecdotes from his books to people in the Far East and infuriating them because *they'd* usually told *him* the anecdotes! They — writers, I mean — just can't help using everything they see or hear. Sooner or later, they sell out everyone they know, or have even met."

"I know about writers," Jim answered gloomily. "Trouble with them is, they're in two places at once: in the world with us and in their fictional world. That's why what they do and say doesn't make sense half the time, and why they're so damned hard to get along with. Especially when they drink," he added, more gloomily.

"All writers drink," Monica informed him. "I hear it's their greatest occupational hazard. So would you drink, after a day, or even an hour, of dredging up words from your very soul while being sure that at least one critic — and usually more — will tear them apart. Papa always said that before a critic should be allowed to review, say a play, he should be required to have written a play that had been performed; before reviewing a book of poetry, he should have written one that was published, and so on."

112

"You need only apply the seat of the pants to the seat of the chair, to be a writer," Robert Templeton informed them solemnly. "That's what Hemingway said, and he should know."

"A woman writer said it first," the Hon Mon replied brusquely. "I forget her name, but he copped it from her."

"Well, she, whoever she was, copped it herself," Paul Cooper began, "from Flaubert, or was it—"

Elizabeth Lamb did not wait for any more learned revelations about writing, especially since the only writer aboard was not present. She had, unhappily, been reminded of the "short novel" hanging over her head and so she found her cabin, got a bathing suit and a white linen sun hat from the drawers where someone had put them, and looked for her notebook. Through the holes of a basket covered with a tray weighted down with a large pot of daffodils, placed atop the dressing table, one green eye had surveyed her balefully from the moment she had entered.

The cabin, similar to Persis' but even more cheerful with its yellow and white floral fabrics and white-painted furniture, was not large, but it took her a long time to find the notebook. After examining every drawer, except those that obviously held Viola's things, even those in the (like Persis') mirrored bathroom, and turning inside-out the empty laundry bag she had used as a suitcase, now folded neatly on the floor of the wardrobe, she dragged a chair over to the wardrobe and stretched to run a hand over its top.

She knocked down not only the notebook but also the box of *dragees* that had been in the top of the bag with it. A piercing "Meeooww" came from the basket when they hit the floor. "Poor Cioccolato," she said, "I'll let you out when I go. Somebody put a sand box for you in the bathroom and you'd better use it, too."

Remembering that she had put the pretty box in which her grandmother had presented her birthday ring into the bag beside the *dragees,* when they were saying their good-byes that morning, she pulled herself up by grasping the wardrobe so she could peer at its top. Nothing more was there, not even dust.

"Darn," she said aloud, "and that box was beautiful. The paper on it looked just like white satin. I'd like to keep it, or maybe use it to hold a present in for Dora." Then, thinking that she was becoming like her Worthington relatives who tore the fronts off Christmas cards they received and used them as gift tags on the gifts they gave, she laughed as she put the *dragees* in a drawer. The box was much lighter than it had been. She opened it to find that less than half its contents remained. "Viola?" she wondered. "It would be like her to steal my candy and then hide the rest, and hide a notebook, or anything else she felt like hiding, along with it, to be mean. But there must be lots of candy aboard, so why would she? Maybe the sailor who unpacked — or maybe it was the cook — likes *dragees*."

She sat at the little writing desk to print "CAT LOOSE. OPEN CAREFULLY." on a piece of paper which she taped to the outside of the cabin door. She took Cioccolato out of the basket and placed him in the bathroom next to his box of sand, as soon as she had changed into the swim suit. Then, clutching her notebook, pen and hat and seizing a shirt from the wardrobe, she rushed out of the cabin before he could follow.

Everyone except Persis, Amy, Annie, and Mr. Vincentia was enjoying the sun on the upper deck. Julia and Viola, who was chewing gum noisily as she, as usual, stared out to sea, wore large sun hats similar to Elizabeth Lamb's. Monica wore only the bottom half of her bikini and displayed large, firm breasts as brown as the rest of her body. Elizabeth Lamb, as she found a desk chair, noticed, of course, the reaction of the men present to the display of the Hon Mon. Chris Grenville, reading, and writing in a notebook, was obviously immune, possibly from long association. So was Paul Cooper, also reading. But Jim Darrow, face redder than the sun's rays could have made it, was openly appreciative, in contrast to Robert Templeton, also red-faced, whose glance went everywhere except towards the oblivious Monica. She, luxuriating like a cat in the warmth, was, with closed eyes, desultorily talking to Jake. He sat beside her, despite the bright sunshine still wearing his thick tweed jacket, and worked on a crossword puzzle. Payson, opening a locker against the rear of the pilot house to obtain water for the bucket he carried from the tap within, had cast one quick look back along the considerable length of the deck, blushed, and bent again to his bucket.

She watched as he came astern, passing davits amidships, two of which were empty, a small motorboat slung in the third and a large fiberglass dinghy in the fourth, to wash tables and chairs on the deck still some distance away from the party lounging around the wet bar in the far stern. Since watching him was, really, not a profitable occupation, she sighed and opened her notebook.

After some moments of uninspired staring at the page headed *Title: A Case,* she moved her deck chair so that it was just behind Mr. Aaronson and Miss Thornhill. "Maybe I'll hear something that will give me an idea," she thought. "Goodness, if Mr. Vincentia really was in the Mafia — or is — and Mr. Aaronson's a long-time friend of his, could be he'll say something to Monica about old times. I could maybe make up a case about it — and solve it myself, of course. At least on paper."

At first their talk was disappointing. "What do you suppose 'Literary man who is the opposite of dull' is? Four letters."

"Poet?" Monica suggested. "But why 'opposite of dull'?"

"No, has to begin with 'b.' I've got it — 'bard.' Must be, because backwards — opposite — it's 'drab.' Ha!"

"How in the world can anyone possibly do those *London Times* brain-bogglers?" Monica asked crossly. "They're so damned maddening, with all those double-edged clues. Give me another; might as well try to sharpen my very dull wits. I'm rather bored." She yawned lustily.

"This is easy: 'Hidden to make the greyhound race.' Begins with the 'd' of 'bard.' In five. Got it?"

"Dog, obviously. No — you said five letters, *caro?*"

"It's 'doggo,' of course. Remember the 'hidden' in the clue. When you lie doggo, you're hidden.

"And speaking of hidden" — he dropped his voice — "we may have something of a spy aboard. An FBI agent hiding as an innocent guest. You, my dear?" Jake chuckled.

"What can you be talking about? Are you making this up?" This was more like it; Elizabeth Lamb listened intently.

"No, indeed. Vito spoke of it on a little trip we took last month. Said that the last time he'd seen that lawyer of his — Winthrop, the one who was killed in the car crash — Winthrop told him he'd heard from one of his sources that an agent was slated to get on the *Chianti* next time Vito used her. And this is the next time. I can't imagine what gen they'd be after, though. Not these days.

"Winthrop had amazing contacts. He was worth every cent Vito paid him. Vito still supports the widow, probably will for years. There's a young daughter, too. Nice girl, very horsey, but pretty. Met her once at Myopia when Vito was invited by one of his Baked Bean friends. He took me along, knowing my interests."

Mr. Aaronson sighed. "Funny about Winthrop's death, too. Brakes failed on practically a new car."

"That may be why Vito supports the widow," Monica replied slowly. "Do you actually suppose, though, Jake, that—"

"I suppose nothing. Nor should you, *caro*. But it might be amusing, though certainly a waste of his time, if there *were* a spy among us."

Elizabeth Lamb gasped with excitement. Anne, who taught Viola riding, was named Winthrop. "I wonder if her father's death wasn't accidental," she thought, moving her chair closer. "I could make a plot about a young girl whose father was killed."

"An agent might be a woman, these days," Monica said. "Maybe she's wasting 'her' time." Smiling, she turned around to Elizabeth Lamb, whose gasp and movement forward had not escaped her sharp notice. "You, little one? Vito told me he'd heard from friends in Maine that you are something of a detective. And daring runs in your family; your Aunt Isabella would delight in being an FBI agent — all those handsome men around, that sort of thing. Except" — she grew pensive —"I do think they require an agent to have at least a modicum of brains."

Elizabeth Lamb gulped. Evidently Mr. Vincentia knew everything about everybody. Probably he even knew who the agent was, if there really was one on board.

"No, ma'am, not me," she answered fervently. "Mr. Vincentia especially invited me, and my cousin, too. He seemed awfully anxious to have us."

Monica laughed. "You've certainly got good manners, as well as charm; I approve of children addressing their elders as 'sir' and 'ma'am.' Quite British; quite Royal Fam.

"I'm awfully glad you're here and I know Vito is. But he was, initially, anxious to get you so as to avoid there being nine at table. The number nine he considers unlucky though to most Sicilians it is seventeen. His wife died on September ninth, quite suddenly, and his daughter and her family were all killed in an accident on the same day a year later. And his son, Danilo, choked to death at dinner when there were nine at table."

"I didn't realize that," Jake said. "Of course, I knew the facts but not that Vito was so superstitious about nine."

"Oh, yes; you know he's superstitious about lots of things. That's why I leaped at Robert Templeton. There he was, hanging about the bar down the street from our hotel in Guadeloupe, trying his best to pick up lovely young birds of all colors and having no success whatever. We knew there were to be only nine aboard if you couldn't make it — and Vito said he wasn't sure of you till you showed up.

"And Robert, boring and dull as he is, was sharp enough to jump at the chance, probably hoping he'd have more success on a yacht than in a bar. Little did I know," she finished, "how impossibly boring and pompous he is. *No* brains, it seems. Oh, well.

"Look, Jake, one of the o's-and-ah's has come up to man the bar. Who is it — oh, the newest one, Paulo. Roberto used to tend it but I hear he's jumped ship. Hope we don't have engine trouble; he was a genius with engines. That's why Vito hired him, although Captain Knudsen didn't like him."

"How do you know that, *caro?*" Jake asked absently, eyes on his crossword.

"Knudsen told me, of course."

"Knudsen? He never speaks!"

The Hon Mon giggled. "He does off duty. I happened to meet up with him on a flight to Sweden last summer. And I've been aboard before, remember. He gets quite loquacious late at night when we're having" — she turned to look at Elizabeth Lamb, listening avidly — "ah, when we're having a schnapps or two.

"Maybe Roberto was your agent, Jake, and got off because he felt he was suspected. Or maybe the new man is. I think I'll go sample his wares and give him one of my complete — inspections."

Elizabeth Lamb felt quite dizzied by all the possible plots being

117

suggested to her. "Or maybe I'm getting seasick," she said aloud. "Ginger ale's good for that." She followed Monica to the bar, where Paulo was mixing orange juice with champagne for her.

Before Elizabeth Lamb could make her request, Robert Templeton had handed her a tall plastic glass with a lemon peel swirling through its contents. "How did you know what I wanted?" she asked him as he leaned on the bar sipping the same drink as hers.

"Heard you," he answered. "Besides, that's what my little sister likes."

"He may be dull but he certainly has good ears," she thought. "Wonder if he heard what Miss Thornhill was saying about him. He wasn't far away."

Monica Thornhill turned to him. "What's that hanging around your neck, Bob?" Elizabeth Lamb looked. A small blue canvas pouch printed with a golden sun holding a fish in its mouth hung from a gold cord that reached just to Mr. Templeton's fat stomach. "It's got a Club Med insignia," she said. "What's in it?" Then she blushed, thinking she might have denigrated the Hon Mon's opinion of her good manners.

But Monica too was curious. "You don't smoke, Bob, so it can't be cigarettes. A small revolver, perhaps?"

Mr. Templeton, still not looking at Monica's upper torso, nevertheless turned red. "My cabin key," he said with dignity. "Mr. Vincentia said we should lock our doors so Chris and I each took one of the keys in our safe. Right, Chris?"

"Y-y-yes," Christopher Grenville agreed. "It s-s-seemed wise. Not — not that we have any v-valuables. In fact, I've got only a pound or two to my n-name, after Guadeloupe. But" — he looked over his shoulder at Viola, still seated beside Julia and manipulating her chewing gum — "once when I w-was aboard — o-once before —" He subsided, giggling with embarrassment, and carried his drink back to his chair and the notebook in which he had been writing.

"There's more than a key in there, Robert Templeton," said Monica teasingly. "Show!"

Mr. Templeton, clutching his pouch with one hand, backed away, holding his glass in front of him with the other. His manner suggested he almost might dash its contents at her. He turned

118

and made a quick run back to the chair beside Grenville. Paul Cooper looked up in annoyance as Templeton's rush caused him to stumble over Paul's feet and dash ginger ale on his book. Shaking his head, Paul rose and went to the bar.

"Sure you don't want a spot of something, Jake?" asked Monica, rejoining him with Elizabeth Lamb close behind. "You don't look awfully fit."

Aaronson had turned up the collar of his tweed jacket and was holding a handkerchief to his nose. "Feel a bit King Billy," he answered. "Yes, luv, would you h'ask the feller fer a blanket? Vito h'always kep' 'is travelin' rugs in a case be'ind the bar. 'm so cold me mince pies is waterin', as well as me old cloes." He then wiped his eyes and nose and sneezed loudly.

"You're going all sound-of-Bow-Bells again," Elizabeth Lamb giggled. Her giggle was duplicated by Paul, who had taken the rug from Paulo and tucked it competently around Jake. "You're a most observant young lady," he said in his soft Southern voice. He smiled kindly at her. "Vito said nothing much gets past you. He's told me about things you've — found out, once or twice." He left for the bar again, making a wide detour around Templeton who still held his glass and had pulled on a bright orange canvas shirt that now concealed his blue pouch.

Elizabeth Lamb watched Paul go, wondering where Mr. Vincentia got all his information. "Maybe from Anne's father — and now he's dead, poor man." She smiled sadly and Templeton, coming up, thought her smile was for him.

He also was approving of Elizabeth Lamb. "Can't be too observant," he said ponderously. "Good training for when you grow up. In my field — I'm a real estate consultant — you have to notice everything." He beamed at her and carried his drink to one of the tables Payson had now finished washing.

"What d'you think of him, Monica?" Mr. Aaronson asked in a low voice.

"Told you; he's a pompous ass, but quite harmless."

"No, I mean Cooper. He seems much more light-hearted than the last time I saw him, in London a year or so ago. Used to sigh a lot. Gloomy, I thought. Now he's all light-wines-and-dancing.

Don't you think he's changed? Maybe it's his new job; he's with a travel agency in London now, Julia said, and making a bundle. Or maybe he's fallen in love." He looked doubtful. "But with Julia?"

"I wouldn't have an opinion," Monica answered. "I never even met the man till this morning and heard little of him before that."

Mr. Aaronson was surprised. "Oh, but you must have. Chris said his agency booked your Caribbean trip. And how, knowing Vito and Julia and all the rest of them so long, could you not—"

"Jake!" Monica raised her brows. "You heard what I said."

"But, my dear, people of a certain — ah, set, class, all over the world, either know each other or know intimately people who know everyone they know. Why, you know Elizabeth Lamb's aunt, you said—"

"Jake," Monica was definite, "I – never – met – the – man – before. Of course I had heard something of him, from Vito. And I believe my poor cousin Portia knew him." She drank deeply of her mimosa, with a decisive air of ending the conversation.

"I never knew anyone named Portia," Elizabeth Lamb offered quickly, before Mr. Aaronson could further annoy the Hon Mon. "I never heard the name, except in *The Merchant of Venice*. Was she named after the character?"

Monica smiled at her. "Everyone in her family had a Shakespearean name; mad about W.S., they were. A great-uncle of hers had something to do with starting the festival at Stratford, I think. That's where Danilo, Vito's son, met her, at a performance of *Twelfth Night*. A sad, sad day for her, that was, and for me, too. We were inseparable, like sisters, but even more devoted than sisters, and now she's—" She turned away as her voice broke.

"Then she was Viola's mother!" Elizabeth Lamb exclaimed, before she thought. This did not seem to be a conversation that would please Monica, either.

But Monica was not angry, at least not at her. "And if that brat had never been born, Portia wouldn't have gone out of her mind. The pregnancy did it; oh, the doctors had a lot to say about hormone imbalance and all that rot but I firmly believe it was the utter evil of that child that put her mother where she is. That may not stand up medically, but 'there are more things in heaven and earth,

Horatio, than are dreamed of in your books' — or something like that. I'm not the Shakespeare expert Portia was."

"Who's Horatio?" Viola was behind them now, snapping her gum. "Is he nicer than you?"

"I think Julia wants you, Viola," Jake said quickly, through a sneeze.

Viola grinned and ambled down the deck to where Robert Templeton was sitting, avoiding her step-mother, who was now at the bar talking to Jim Darrow.

"I did hear Viola's mother was in a — place." Elizabeth Lamb was too curious to be tactful. "But Viola's father married Julia. I thought Catholics couldn't get a divorce?"

"Oh, they can," Monica answered. "Well, not a divorce — an annulment. If it can be proved, as Danilo proved, that your wife can't sustain a marital relationship. Which, naturally, Portia couldn't," she ended bitterly, "being in the bin from very shortly after the birth.

"Daddy always said," she looked out to sea, "that Portia would recover her mind when Viola died and her utter evil was removed from this earth. Daddy firmly believed in the existence of evil as a force."

"*Caro,*" Jake said gently, "Viola is only a child, although I do think that her — her lack is aging Vito too fast. I do resent that." His mouth set in a grim line and his eyes hardened. "He is so conscientious, such a real, a good person." He turned to Elizabeth Lamb and smiled slightly, although his eyes were still cold. "What we Jews call a *mensch.*"

"A *mensch?*" Elizabeth Lamb was delighted. "I like that word; I'll remember it. Do you know any other *mensches?*"

Jake regarded her seriously. "Well, I'd say you might be one. As is Monica, here. And Mrs. Danniver — she's another."

"And Viola pushed *her* daughter down a well!" Monica burst out. "And then didn't tell Vito" — she turned to Elizabeth Lamb — "it was at his old house, in Boston; there was a well in the back garden, until it was too late. The girl drowned.

"I never met Mrs. Danniver before today, but she seems a woman of character, as you say, Jake. I wonder she can stand to be near that brat!"

121

"She must live, *caro,*" Jake answered. "Hard as it is to be alone, 'better alone and alive than alone and dead,' as my mum used to say. And since Viola owns her father's half of Placido Press, Vito must consider her wishes, even though she's still a minor. Her present wish is to write a children's book, about a kitten, I think, and Vito has asked Mrs. Danniver to help her. With that feller Darrow to act as a buffer, it would seem.

"And what else can the woman do, if she's to live? Her royalties from *Placido* are larger than any other house would pay, and she knows it."

"I thought Danilo had left his half to you," Monica said, in surprise. "Vito always said he meant to. I know he was obligated to you, for a few things."

Jake smiled. "Oh, he remembered his obligations — somewhat. He left almost everything to Viola, with the provision that Julia will inherit only if Viola dies before she, Viola, marries. And as long as Viola lives *and* if Julia does not re-marry, Julia gets a tidy little sum each month. Since it seems very unlikely anyone would want to marry Viola, heiress though she is — and she'll get a lot from Vito, too, when he dies, plus a substantial amount from him when she's 21 or married — it's very much in our dear Julia's interest to keep Viola in good health as well as devoted to her, and certainly not to re-marry, Paul or anyone else, herself.

"Danilo had it all set up, in a most complicated trust. You can do things with trusts you can't do with wills, you know. And Vito, now that all his heirs but Viola are dead, set up the same."

"Well," Monica said slowly, "this is all very nice for Viola, and Julia, too, but what's it got to do with Danilo's 'somewhat' remembering his obligations to you?"

Jake blew his nose loudly and sneezed again. "Wandering, that's what I am. It's this bloody cold. Forgot to say that Julia doesn't inherit everything if Viola dies: I get Danilo's half of Placido." He laughed. "But somehow I don't think I'll live to see the day; years do count and I've got many on Viola."

"But, Jake," Monica was still surprised, "I thought you were relying on your dividends from the Press. Don't tell me you still have to make a living from the horses?"

122

"Of course, and not a bad one. Just had a good thing on Secretariat for the Belmont, and before that for the Kentucky Derby and the Preakness. I'm doing all right, and Vito is very kind, very often, for old times' sake.

"And I've got my health. Although I must admit that money can buy health but health can't buy money." He laughed, and sneezed again.

"You don't look very healthy at the moment, Mr. Aaronson," Elizabeth Lamb offered. "Don't you take something for that cold?"

"All of us English look unhealthy," observed Julia, coming over to them. "It's those quantities of boiled sweets we consume. You and Vito ate too many, as boys, Jake. Almost time for tea, though; a good cuppa will buck you up, *caro*." She smiled pleasantly at them all and went to join Paul, who was leaning on the rail across the deck. They walked arm-in-arm to the spiral stairs and disappeared.

"She smells so good." Elizabeth Lamb sniffed the perfumed air Julia had left behind her.

"Can't smell a thing," said Mr. Aaronson. "This cold's a bad one; usually I can tell Julia's coming before she turns the bloomin' corner. Elizabeth Lamb, what about asking the o-and-ah behind the bar for a brandy and soda? Might clear my nose a bit."

When she returned, she informed Jake: "I've just figured out why Miss Thornhill calls the crew the o's-and-ah's. All their names end in 'o' and whenever you speak to them, they say, 'Ah, *signor*,' or 'Ah, *signorina*.' That one just did."

"You *are* clever," said Jim Darrow, who had followed her from the bar. "Awfully clever people aboard, clever as well as nice. See you all at tea; I'm going down to find Amy, see if she needs anything."

He sighed heavily. "Or that she's okay. You never know." He brightened. "Mrs. Vincentia and Viola — Miss Vincentia, I mean — are certainly okay. Awfully nice. I do like them."

"Is he bonkers?" Monica asked angrily as he left. "Viola and Julia *nice?*"

Monica's voice had risen so loud that Robert Templeton, far down the deck, had glanced up from his magazine. Paulo, behind the bar, giggled nervously. Quickly, Elizabeth Lamb sought to divert

123

her. "Was your cousin Portia an actress, a Shakespearean actress, maybe?" she asked.

"No, a singer. Beautiful voice, too," Monica answered sadly.

"I guess Viola's father liked singers." Elizabeth Lamb was remembering Viola's saying that her stepmother used to sing her to sleep and "sang better than she did on stage."

"*And* actresses, *and* shopgirls, *and* birds — all the pretty little 'birds of Britain,'" said Monica sourly. "Unlike his father, Danilo was scarcely the faithful type.

"Oh, well." She rose. "It was long ago — and in another country. I'd better put something on for tea." She glided away, smiling radiantly at Templeton as she passed him. He rose, as if mesmerized, and followed.

"Why does Mr. Vincentia have all those Italian o's-and-ah's for his crew but the captain is some sort of Scandinavian?" Elizabeth Lamb wondered.

"Because I like the *atmosfera* of having Italians about me — but I was on the last voyage of the *Andrea Doria,*" said the voice of Mr. Vincentia, who had come up as Elizabeth Lamb watched the Hon Mon's graceful departure. "I'll let you puzzle that out.

"Now, come, let us go down to the saloon. Almost everyone is already there."

"You and Annie been turning old pounds into new, Vito?" Mr. Aaronson asked as they descended the spiral stairs.

"Or new dollars into old, perhaps," Mr. Vincentia laughed. He became serious as Viola, barefoot, arrived on the lower deck just behind him. "Viola, you know I like shoes worn under a roof." He frowned as she giggled, taking his arm and pulling him into the saloon.

Elizabeth Lamb looked down contritely at her own bare feet. "Is it that he thinks bare feet are unsanitary, or something?" she asked Jake Aaronson quietly.

"It's a Sicilian superstition: bare feet are supposed to presage death," he answered. "Vito is very superstitious, as you have heard. But don't worry; he'll get over it. Probably the men are barefoot, too."

They were not. Everyone was shod except Viola and her, as she saw when she and Jake joined the group around the tea table. She quickly ran to the staircase beyond the bar, rushed down to her cabin and seized a pair of sandals from the wardrobe. She was careful to open and shut the cabin door quickly, to avoid Cioccolato's rush, which did not come. "Probably in the bathroom," she thought, running upstairs.

Amy Danniver had finished pouring for the company, which had formed little conversational groups as Payson served cucumber sandwiches. As Elizabeth Lamb approached, she saw Amy's hand slide quickly into her capacious bosom, produce a small chrome flask, and dash some of its contents into the cup before her.

Amy's face was flushed and her eyes bright. She served Elizabeth Lamb and took a deep draught from her own cup. "Is Persis still asleep?" Elizabeth Lamb asked, thinking, "Oh, I hope Mrs. Danniver hasn't been drinking all this time, and Mr. Vincentia doesn't want her drinking alone in her cabin, either, Jim told her."

"She had a wonderful warm bath in Vito's tub and she's just resting and reading now. How providential the designer of this boat planned a tub in the master suite!"

"If—if it could only be set up to allow a bath in sea water," said Christopher Grenville, who had come over for a refill. "The w—way the old C—Cunard liners did." He giggled deprecatingly. "Then we'd all b—borrow your t—tub, V.V."

"I've thought of it, Chris," answered Mr. Vincentia, reaching for a slice of cake from the 3-tiered small round mahogany stand beside his chair. "Perhaps someday."

"Oh, you have a 'curate's friend!'" Elizabeth Lamb said, going over to him. "It looks very old. It is certainly handsome!" She accepted cake from the plate he held for her.

"What?" asked Viola, who was sullenly munching a sandwich, her bare feet brazenly straight out before her as she sat on the floor beside her grandfather. "Whose friend?"

"That little stand," Elizabeth Lamb explained. "They're called that because they were always put beside the chair of the poor young curate when the kind ladies of the parish had him to tea. Which they did often, because the curates didn't get paid as much as the rectors, and were always hungry, and this way they could keep helping themselves to food!"

Mr. Vincentia laughed with delight. "What a lot you know, *caro!* Well, today I am the poor—" He ended in almost a scream and leaped to his feet, clawing at Cioccolato, who had appeared from nowhere and sprung into his lap. Monica rushed to pull the kitten off and pushed it at Paul Cooper, the nearest person to her, while she attempted with the other hand to retrieve the dropped tea-cup.

"Take it out of here at once!" she commanded. Paul quickly retreated to the back of the sofa where Amy sat, staring at Vincentia and pouring tea into an already-overflowing cup. "Cats hate me!" he said loudly. "It would scratch my eyes out!" Annie, entering the room from the main deck, cried out and closed the glass door with a crash as she leapt back behind it.

Elizabeth Lamb seized Cioccolato and ran with him to her cabin. When she got back Mr. Vincentia was sitting, white-faced, sipping a glass of *Grappa* as Christopher held a broken ampule to his nose.

"Enough, Chris," Mr. Vincentia said, patting his arm as he pushed it away. "But you are indeed my good godson! Think of your always carrying amyl nitrate capsules in case I need one!"

"Actually, V.V.," said Chris, who seemed to have lost both his lisp and his stutter somewhere in the excitement, "they're always in the pockets of all my clothes because sometimes Papa needs one. But I'm glad it helped." He went back to the tea table. Annie came in and joined him, looking with suspicion at Viola, still seated on the floor, calmly munching away,

"Aren't you supposed to take digitalis, Vito — those heart pills?" Julia asked. "Yes, the heart pills," Paul echoed. "Hadn't you better take one now, V.V.? Are they in your cabin? I'll get—" He broke off to sneeze. "Damn," he said to Jake. "I hope I'm not getting your cold."

"Darling," Julia assured him, "you know you never have colds. It's the tension. But, Vito, surely—"

"No, no," Mr. Vincentia said firmly. "Not now, with *Grappa.* Later."

"Oh," said Monica, "that reminds me; time for one of my antis. One at breakfast and one at tea, the only meals at which I don't drink." She giggled as she took something from the pocket of her white linen shift and popped it into her mouth, following with a sip from Mr. Vincentia's almost-emptied cup, which she still held. Payson produced a cloth to wipe up the spilled tea at his employer's feet.

"Your *Auntie's* medicine?" Paul asked irritably, sneezing again. "Isn't taking someone else's prescription rather dangerous?"

"Antibiotics, *caro?*" Aaronson asked, coming up to her. "P'raps I'd better cadge one."

"No, anti-neurotics; that's what *I* call them," Monica answered gaily. "They're my happiness pills. Sometimes I need two at night to make me go to sleep, as well as the ones I take at tea and breakfast. If there's nothing else to make me go to sleep happy, that is." She looked provocatively at Jim Darrow, who blushed, and then at Chris Grenville, who didn't.

Payson was interrogated by Mr. Vincentia, as he accepted bread-and-butter sandwiches from the tray Payson held. "No, sir, I never," Payson was heard to say firmly. "Didn't go atall near that cabin since I put 'im 'n his box there, this forenoon. Maybe one of them sailors went in to do somethin' and let 'im out." Mr. Vincentia shook his head and then turned to speak civilly to Templeton, who had managed to stand impassively, looking both watchful and thunderstruck, throughout the whole incident.

Monica joined Amy on a sofa. Elizabeth Lamb hastened to sit on Amy's other side. "Maybe she won't put any more liquor in her cup, if she's surrounded," she thought. "And maybe I'd better tell Persis to stop her, or try to, if she drinks in the cabin. Mr. Darrow seemed sure she'd be fired if she did."

"Yes, he's Vito's godson," Monica was saying to Amy. "Chris is of an old Catholic family, relatives of ours. Papa introduced Chris' people to Vito, years ago, and they got on with him. And they never gambled, either! That's how Papa got friendly with Vito, you know: he'd run up staggering debts in Vito's club and absolutely couldn't pay. But unlike all those stories you hear of unlucky gamblers getting their knees nailed to the floor, all that happened was that Vito asked Papa to work off the debt by teaching him all the things he didn't know.

"Well, Papa was delighted, of course. And they grew to be really great friends. Oh, that's right; you were asking about Chris. We were children together, but he was always very religious; he was going to be a priest but he gave up the idea just before he took his vows."

"What changed his mind?" Amy asked. "Surely not women; he's 'one of the boys,' as we used to say, if I ever saw one." She drank again. Elizabeth Lamb wondered how she could get her cup away from her.

"Oh, I think not," Monica answered Amy coldly, raising her brows.

"I'm never wrong." Amy was being much too brash, Elizabeth Lamb thought. "Maybe he hasn't come out of the closet yet." She drank again.

Monica suddenly smiled. "Oh, perhaps," she said more politely. "And, considering all who have, I really never dreamed a closet could be so big. What is that," she smiled again, "that makes your tea smell so delicious? Could you spare a drop for mine? Daren't have more than a drop."

Amy laughed raucously. Mr. Vincentia frowned as he looked over at her. Before Amy could say anything more, or reach for her flask, Elizabeth Lamb thought she would introduce something the ladies could agree on besides whiskey in tea.

Nodding at Julia, who was at the piano softly playing a selection from *Cabaret* while Jim, Paul and Chris stood admiringly beside her, she asked Monica, "Did you ever hear Mrs. Vincentia sing on stage?"

Monica looked surprised, probably at the swift switch from closets and whiskey to Julia. "Once, at a fête in our village. She sang some *lieder*." She giggled maliciously. "It was hardly a *fait accompli!*"

Amy laughed louder. Mr. Vincentia frowned again. Annie came over to Amy, urgently requesting the loan of some typing paper. "If you have some to spare?" she asked politely. "I'll come down to your cabin with you. I don't know why I didn't make sure I had enough on board."

She casually took Amy's arm as they left, as if she herself were in need of support and not, as Elizabeth Lamb suspected, Mrs. Danniver. "Annie likes her, too," Elizabeth Lamb thought. "And she's trying to protect her. I wonder if Annie was there when Viola pushed the daughter into the well?"

She wandered about the room for a time, listening to Julia's playing and to the several varied conversations, and then decided to check on Persis. She first went out quietly to the rear deck, to see if land were in sight. Annie, holding a package of white paper, was standing beside Antonio over on the port side. They leaned into one of the large glass windows, their heads close together and their backs to her as they talked very softly.

Elizabeth Lamb had excellent hearing. She stood quite still. "But where did you find my spray?" Annie was saying. "Oh, I am so pleased, Antonio!"

"That little *bestia* had hidden it in the fronds of the *felce* outside her cabin door," he answered. "I know her tricks. *Caro,* I see she causes you much trouble, but you would not leave the *padrone* because of her? Tell me you would not!"

"I think I may," Annie answered slowly. "She is getting worse, and she hates me. She could do something quite vicious, quite dangerous."

"But, no! You must not go! And I know the *padrone* would get rid of her rather than lose you. You are necessary to him; he trusts you. Tell me, you would stay if — if the girl went?"

Annie laughed, a sad little laugh. "Do you know the saying 'blood is thicker than water'? The *padrone* would never send her away. I would hate to leave you, *caro,* but—" Annie shrugged and turned away from the window. Elizabeth Lamb quickly walked toward them, nodding and smiling with innocent politeness as she passed and turned to enter the deck running forward on the port side. She strolled along it until she reached the door where she could go into the dining room and cross it to the stairs.

"I wonder if there's a plot in that I could use?" she thought. "I'm certainly getting a lot of ideas. Maybe too many." She decided to take her before-dinner shower and think them out under its soothing warmth. As she entered her cabin Cioccolato turned, purring, from a large dish of herring put beside a bowl of cream that had been placed on a mat in the corner.

"Well, you're happy now," she told him. "I wish you could talk

129

so I'd know who let you out. It could have just been Viola, being careless. Or I wonder if it was somebody who knew Mr. Vincentia hates cats and wanted to give him a scare? That could have been dangerous, with his heart . . ."

• CHAPTER 7 •

A Whole New Can of Peas

WHEN SHE came out of the bathroom, wearing only printed cotton briefs, after a thorough inspection of her chest in the mirrored walls and an expressed hope that she would never need a brassiere — "and even if I do, I won't! It must be like strangling" — Viola was seated at the dressing table. She was pulling a comb through her curly hair and applying a pale pink lipstick that matched her puff-sleeved silk dress. "You look very nice, Viola," Elizabeth Lamb said politely. "I'm sorry I was so long in the shower. Did you want to use it? Just see how sweet Cioccolato looks when he's sleeping!"

"I took a bath in my grandfather's tub," Viola answered, ignoring the kitten. "Julia says baths get you cleaner than showers. I don't think you're as clean as me. Look what she brought me!" She rose and held up her hands, fingers spread wide. On the index finger of each hand she wore a wide chased silver ring.

"I wanted gold!" Viola stamped her feet. "Gold was what I told her! I guess she didn't have enough money; gold costs more than silver, you know. When I get my own money, I'm going to be good to Julia because she's sweet to me. You're not!" She stamped

131

her foot again, giggling, and left the cabin.

There was a large green velvet box on the dressing table with *A. Russell, Hamilton, Bermuda* inside its open lid. "I guess I misjudged her," Elizabeth Lamb thought, brushing her hair. "She wouldn't have taken my ring box when she had a handsome velvet one of her own."

She quickly put on her smocked lawn dress, short white socks and black slippers and crossed the yellow-carpeted foyer to knock on Persis' door. Persis opened it, dressed similarly to her cousin. "Are you better?" Elizabeth Lamb asked. "You don't have spots any more, only sort of a flush all over your face. Do you feel all right now?"

"Much better," Persis answered, standing aside so she could enter. "Wait till I get a sweater. I'm still kind of cold." Amy Danniver was examining her face critically in the mirror of the dressing table and drinking from a large glass. A half-empty bottle of brandy was at her elbow. "I *should* have told Persis about that instead of planning my novel in the shower," Elizabeth Lamb thought. "Maybe she couldn't have done anything, though. But if Mr. Vincentia should come in—"

The door, which Persis had not completely closed, opened and Viola appeared, holding the package of typing paper. "Annie sent this down to you," she said, looking back and forth from Mrs. Danniver to the brandy bottle. "She won't need it because she got a call about her mother and she's leaving right now." With a final triumphant look at the bottle, she abruptly left.

Amy held her bowed head in her hands and wailed loudly. She got up unsteadily and walked to the bathroom. "Come, Persis," Elizabeth Lamb said, taking her hand, "let's go say goodbye to Mrs. Donelli. I think we should leave Mrs. Danniver alone."

Annie, with Mr. Vincentia, was standing beside the opening in the parapet on the main deck. Paulo waited nearby to hand her down the ladder. "It will be all right, *caro,*" Mr. Vincentia was saying in a low tone as the children came up to them. "But the plans for — you know, my dear — must be postponed—" He turned with a welcoming smile to Elizabeth Lamb and Persis.

"We received a radiotelephone message from Annie's home," he explained. "Her mother is much worse and she must go there at once." Annie nodded politely to them and descended the ladder to the small motorboat Antonio held beside the *Chianti*. The boat sped away, skirted a headland, and disappeared.

"We're anchored!" Elizabeth Lamb realized. "I never even knew we'd stopped!" She looked toward the shore. They were in a small cove, several houses visible on the cliff above it. "Is this Matinicus?"

"Yes," Mr. Vincentia answered. "Antonio is taking Annie to the harbor, where she will catch the mail boat to Rockland. I have arranged for a man to meet her and drive her to the airport. It appears her mother's condition is critical.

"Dinner will be in half-an-hour," he informed them, and, raising a hand in farewell, went lithely along the starboard side to the open deck, where he mounted a ladder far forward. "I guess he's going up to see the captain," Persis said. "Mrs. Danniver told me a sailor told her the captain almost never leaves his place up there; she talks to everybody, she says, because someday she'll use the material. The captain has a little cabin behind the steering place and he even eats up there. He won't eat with the passengers, ever. He just refuses."

"Really?" said Elizabeth Lamb, who wondered why Mr. Vincentia had not made Captain Knudsen his tenth person at table. "The Honourable Monica said he drinks with them, though. Sometimes, anyway."

"I don't know about that. But the cook is strange, too. He belongs to some church — I forget; the Seventy Day Adventurers or the Harry Kerchners or something like that — and he won't speak or even be near anybody from ten o'clock at night till breakfast time. He goes into his cabin and locks the door and prays all night; once they had some kind of accident and he still wouldn't come out.

"He wouldn't sign off, the sailor said, unless Mr. Vincentia agreed to that. In writing," Persis added solemnly.

"Persis, you can't believe all you hear. And you mean 'sign on' not 'off.' He's not a radio station. And it's *Hari*—"

"Oh, Elizabeth Lamb, you're being insuperable again. Let's go see if we can help Payson. I'm getting hungry."

Payson was lighting the two tall, five-branched candelabra placed in the middle of the dining tables. Each candelabrum stood in the open center of a shallow round crystal bowl shaped like a wreath.

"What do you put in those?" Persis wondered. "Water, in case the candles fall over?"

Payson opened a box of *Vincentia* chocolates he had taken from the sideboard. "Jest taste one. They're awful good. The cook said I could take a box to Mumma, too. He's got more'n a mite of temper when he's cookin' but he's real good-hearted.

"They's to go in them glass circles," he directed. "Put 'em in artistic-like, could you, Persis? You got a more delicate touch than me."

"Oh," said Persis, swallowing her second, "they're like Heaven!" She took another. "But maybe Elizabeth Lamb should fix the candy dishes in case I'm still contemptuous."

As they stood admiring her arrangement, the others began to arrive, some from the stairs beside the bar, some from the door to the passage that opened on the port deck, and Mr. Vincentia and Monica from the door that led forward on the starboard side. "There are place-cards," their smiling host said. "I like to control the seating." He beamed jovially at Amy as he held the chair facing his for her. Viola grinned and cast her eyes demurely down as she observed him. Her pink dress stood out against the dark silk gowns of the other women and the navy blue blazers the men wore.

Elizabeth Lamb found that she was to his right hand, and Persis to his left. Chris Grenville's card was between Persis and Amy and Jake Aaronson's between Elizabeth Lamb and Amy. The other table was headed by Viola, who had Jim to her right and Paul to her left. Robert Templeton faced her and Monica was between him and Paul. Julia was left to sit sulkily between Templeton and Jim.

"There will be a few moments while Pietro toasts the bread for our *cozza* soup," Mr. Vincentia said, motioning for Payson to offer a tray holding ten small glasses of a rosy liquid. "I did not think you and Persis would like Campari *secco*," he said to Elizabeth Lamb, who was disappointed. Amy noticed her wistful look as Payson passed her by. "Have mine, dear," she said, and, more loudly: "I really am cutting down." There was a malicious giggle from the other table.

"Is it just soup for dinner?" Persis asked. "No," Mr. Vincentia answered, "but we Italians love to start with soup. We call a dinner that begins with the main course a 'dry' dinner." Persis poked with her spoon one of the opened shells in the large shallow plate Payson had placed before her. "Oh, good," she said; "it's mussels. I didn't terribly much like the sound of *cozza*."

"And olive oil and tomato sauce mixed into the mussel broth, and garlic and red pepper and — what's the herb; oh, oregano — and thick slices of good bread in the bottom. Delicious!" said Amy. "Vito you know more about food than anyone else I've ever met." She sounded to Elizabeth Lamb more than a bit sycophantic. Viola giggled again.

Mr. Vincentia looked appreciatively at Amy as he poured white wine for his table and motioned to Payson to do the same for the other. "And a good, a suitably good, *Frascati* to go with it. We will have a great wine for the next course."

"Do you have mussels on board, Vito?" Julia asked. "They're most perishable."

"No, but Antonio knows I love them. He stopped on his way back from the harbor to gather some, the tide being right. Oh," — he looked around at his guests — "Annie took the mail boat from the harbor. Her mother is very sick."

Murmurs of polite regret ended when Payson put before Mr. Vincentia an enormous crusted leg of lamb, redolent of garlic and rosemary. He deftly carved two large platters of it and handed one to Pietro to take to the other table while Payson served the guests small roasted potatoes and peas.

Jake cautiously tasted the red wine he had been poured. "*Clos Vougeout!*" he exclaimed. "Now, that's a bit of all right, Vito. Can't smell the aroma I know's there, but it tastes loverly. Loverly plonk!"

"It's wonderful, but *Clos Vougeout* accompanying tinned peas, Vito?" Julia protested. "I think that's a bit off-limits."

"I adore tinned peas; one cannot call them a vegetable perhaps, not like *radicchio*" — he winked at Elizabeth Lamb — "or *melanzana*, or *carota*, but I had them as a child only on special feast days and I have a nostalgic fondness for them." He beamed as he helped himself lavishly to peas from the bowl Payson held at his left elbow.

"You know," said Jake, who was eating and drinking with relish, slowed down only by frequent delicate applications of a dazzling white handkerchief to his eyes and nose, "that American general, Wainright — 'Skinny Wainright' the Yanks called him — felt the same way. When he finally got back to San Francisco, just released from the Jap prison camp he'd been in since Corregidor fell, one of the posh restaurants there wanted to put on a dinner for him. They were famous for their steaks, and he approved of steak, with potatoes, and they suggested their special salad, with their own secret dressing, that was pretty famous.

"But the general turned it down; said all the years he was imprisoned he'd dreamed over and over of canned peas. So that was that, and everybody else had to go along with it."

Mr. Vincentia laughed and poured him more wine. "Did you ever meet him, Jake?" Monica asked. "You were in the Far East all during the war, weren't you?"

Mr. Aaronson regretfully shook his head. "Only ever met one high-ranking Yank officer. Admired General Wainwright; wish I had met him."

"W-was that the Marine colonel who taught you jujitsu?" Chris asked.

"No, I learned that in Singapore. He did teach me one or two special blows, though, some time afterward."

"I heard about that," Monica observed. "Danilo said you learned to touch an opponent just above the waist, somewhere — and there's another spot, too, around the collarbone — so that he couldn't move. Said you used it on a couple of rough Teddy boys you and he encountered once in Liverpool.

"And he suspected, he said, that you knew that blow they call the Black Death, that blinds in two hours and kills in two days, but you wouldn't admit it."

Mr. Aaronson merely looked enigmatic and drank his wine. "There can't possibly be such a thing," Paul said.

Robert Templeton differed. "Oh, yes, there can. I've heard of it. Heard stories from people I trust. Who was the colonel, Mr. Aaronson?"

"He's dead now." Robert looked disappointed. "Can't remember his name, either. Something that ended in 'el.' Maybe it was Tappel, or Scrapple. Or Lydel; Biddle, maybe."

136

"He must have been from Philadelphia," Jim said genially. "There's a story about an old English lady back from an American visit who said she'd especially enjoyed Philadelphia, where she was lavishly entertained by a large and wealthy family named Scrapple and introduced to a delicious dish called biddle."

Everyone laughed except Viola, chewing unnecessarily loudly on her peas. "Were you in the English army in the Pacific during the war, Mr. Aaronson?" Elizabeth Lamb asked, happily accepting more meat from Mr. Vincentia and hopefully extending her empty wine glass to him.

"Never was. I'd been in Singapore on some business of — some business and didn't leave soon enough after Pearl Harbor. The Japs came in shortly afterwards and I was lucky to get out in a fishing boat. Made it to Sumatra and sat out the war on one little island or another. I met up with some Aussie coast-watchers and helped them out a bit."

"My goodness," Persis said. "It must have been very scary. Did you see any enemy people? I'm not sure," she added apologetically, "which war this was."

"World War Two, my dear. No, not one Jap, not after Singapore. Saw their agents, though, or, rather, saw some of their work. Once the Yanks got P.T. boats operating and had them based on little islands and atolls, the Japs were pretty busy trying to put them out of commission. A favorite trick was getting harmless-looking natives to hang about and put paraffin into the 50-gallon fuel drums that supplied the P.T.s.

"A very ingenious trick. Sometimes the engines would conk out when the boats were scarcely away from shore; sometimes farther out, right in the middle of one of their hit-and-run actions. My mates and I often managed a rescue of the crew, in the second instance, if it happened close enough to shore."

"Why were they P.T. 'boats' and not 'ships'?" Elizabeth Lamb asked. "They weren't really tiny, were they?"

"A boat is something that will fit on a ship," Julia told her. "My father was a naval officer and very particular about the difference."

Payson had been clearing the tables and enjoying the conversation. Now he produced two large glass bowls of a salad of mixed greens and placed one before Amy, along with six beautiful *faience* plates shaped like big leaves, and the same in front of Monica. They served the others as he removed the wineglasses, poured water, and placed butter, cheeses, crackers and slices of Italian bread on each table.

"So like you to insist on Bath Oliver Biscuits and not ordinary Carr's or the like, Vito," Monica said with appreciation. "They have a distinctive taste and I adore the darling profile of the good doctor on each one. You really know — and have — everything valuable there is. The epitome of civilization, you are!"

"Here, here!" Templeton said solemnly, lifting his water goblet to his host.

Mr. Vincentia was enjoying his salad. "Civilization has not got to do with *things, caro,* like good food, Handel, Georgian silver and the like, but with the invisible *ties* that join one *thing* to another. What is valuable is a certain *ordering* of things."

"How profound!" said Amy, who had been flatteringly concentrating on him all through dinner, as well as concentrating on drinking very little. "And how beautiful!"

Mr. Vincentia grinned. "Antoine Saint-Exupéry said it, not I." He began to talk to Elizabeth Lamb, and Amy to Chris. Persis leaned across the table to Jake.

"I love quotations," she confided. "They make me feel so smart. I copied down some about travel at home last night. Do you think I should say one, or would it be too show-offish?"

Jake smiled kindly at her. "Tell me one quietly, would you, please?"

"'It is better to travel than to arrive' is one. It's certainly 'better' to travel on this boat than almost anything!" She helped herself to several chocolates from the centerpiece, ignoring her salad. "Of course, I know it means something deeper than just travel."

"You are certainly a clever little girl. But, you know, you ought to wait till dinner is finished to eat sweets. And there will be a box of *Cioccolato da Vincentia* in your cabin, too. The crewman who turns down the beds leaves one every night."

"Really! That's wonderful! Wait till Elizabeth Lamb hears. Oh, I wish we were going to be aboard for a week so we could get seven boxes.

"But how can the man get in? Mrs. Danniver said we were supposed to lock our cabins. She has one key and she got the other for me, out of the safe in our room." She reached into the skirt pocket of her dress and displayed it.

"The captain has a master key. He gives it out to the crew when they need it and then locks it up again. I wouldn't worry about getting your box tonight.

"And tell you what: you and your cousin come down to my cabin after dinner and take mine, too. I don't eat many sweets any more, just desserts." He smiled a little. *"Just* desserts." He turned to Amy.

"Want my salad, Elizabeth Lamb?" Persis asked. She deftly reached across Mr. Vincentia, who had turned to speak to Pietro, and switched their plates.

"Oh, Persis, I really can't eat any more—" She stopped, staring at Persis' hand. "Why are you wearing that moonstone ring? Now you *know* Grandmother said not to open your birthday present till next week!"

"Well, I didn't, so there! The box was in the drawer beside my bed when I woke up before lunch but the ring was sitting right on top of the table when I went down afterwards. And the box isn't anywhere. I know they unpack for you but I think it was a bit much to throw my box away."

"The whole thing's far-out, Persis," Elizabeth Lamb said thoughtfully. Mr. Vincentia stood up, tapping his water glass with a fork:

"Pietro is bringing champagne so you can drink a toast to my friend, Elizabeth Lamb. It is her twelfth birthday." He unclasped his wristwatch and handed it to her with a little bow. "I found out only this morning, from her grandmother's cook, who also told of something she would like to have."

"Oh!" Elizabeth Lamb was overcome. "I never thought I'd have a Cartier tank watch! Oh, thank you, Mr. Vincentia." As, beaming, he helped her adjust the black lizard strap and fasten it on her wrist, she thought: "Alice has either got religion or is going out of her mind. Maybe I'd better call when I get to The Bungalow and be sure she hasn't burned the house down, or something."

"And," he went on, "she and Persis have given me a present, for my pocket watch. I could not resist opening it," he confided in an

139

aside to Elizabeth Lamb as he took out the fob from his breast pocket and held it up as the company murmured in admiration. With a caressing gesture, he attached it to his watch chain.

"To Elizabeth Lamb!" he said, raising his glass. "May she have many more birthdays aboard the *Chianti*." The others followed his example, except Viola, who remained seated, glaring at her grandfather. "All the women have deep voices and all the men high ones!" Persis murmured to Elizabeth Lamb across the table, as the chorus of congratulations died down.

Finger bowls resting on crocheted lace doilies placed on gold-rimmed, deep red dessert plates had been placed before the guests. "Oh, look, there's a nasturtium in my bowl." Persis looked around the table. "And Elizabeth Lamb has a violet and Mrs. Danniver a tiny lily.

"But," she turned to Aaronson, "you and the other men only have slices of lemon. That's not fair. What's your favorite flower?"

"Oh," he answered, "life is not fair at all. I love roses but I have not been near enough to a rose to admire it for some years. You see——"

He was interrupted by loud applause. Payson was marching around the tables to display a cake he carried on a round silver platter. It was pale yellow, in the shape of a large inverted bowl, decorated with a delicate design of candied violets. Lavender candles blazed on its top and shiny green leaves made a border around the edge of the plate that held it. It was put before Elizabeth Lamb, who took in a mighty breath. She blew out the twelve candles and then began to slice the cake. When she finished, Payson took it first to the other table.

"Good heavens, Vito," Julia said as the platter was held beside her so she could serve herself a slice, "laurel leaves are poisonous, I think!"

"I know, my dear," he answered smoothly, "and so does Pietro; those are fresh bay leaves. In honor of Elizabeth Lamb's victory in arriving at the great age of twelve."

"Oh, this cake is divine," Monica called. "Did Pietro make it? I've never had anything like it."

"It is *cassata alla Siciliana* — a Sicilian cream cake made only with *ricotta* and sugar, vanilla and *crème de cacao*. And bits of chocolate

140

and candied fruit, as you can see. One lines a bowl with slices of *pan di Spagna,* a rich sponge cake, pours in the cream mixture and then chills it for some hours.

"I had Benno pick it up," Mr. Vincentia went on, "this morning, in Hingham, on his way down. There is an old woman there who makes it as no one else can. Pietro turned it out on its plate a little while ago and added the violets; he is very fond of using them for decoration on desserts."

"I don't like it, Grandfather," Viola said, waving in front of her face the pansy from her finger bowl. "I want ice cream." Her grandfather sighed and nodded to Payson.

"Would you like Viola and me to begin on her book tomorrow?" Amy asked him. "The sooner begun, the sooner done."

"Maybe it will never get written, Grandfather," said Viola, speaking indistinctly through a mouthful of pistachio ice cream. "Or maybe she won't be able to help me." She grinned maliciously and licked the corners of her mouth.

Mr. Vincentia had shown pleased surprise at the enthusiasm with which Amy had asked her question. Ignoring Viola, he answered Amy: "Why, yes, my dear. You know, it might turn out quite well and I will be very grateful to you. Viola needs something to give her assurance, a sense of having done something important."

"I can do it all by myself," Viola said rudely. "I don't need her." Her grandfather made no answer. Amy, smiling pleasantly, and everyone else began to make light conversation.

"The-the first book one does is o-often the b-best," Grenville put in. He had been quiet during the meal, eating with appreciation. "It-it's the o-one that you w-want so badly to write. Viola's could be a suc-success."

"Is that really so?" Elizabeth Lamb asked him, thinking her "short novel" might be her first but that it was certainly not one she wanted badly to write. She smiled at him and he smiled back, shyly. "I like him," she thought, "and I don't know why Mrs. Danniver was making cracks to Monica about him. It was probably that she'd been drinking; she probably has no opinions at all about him or, if she has, doesn't care one way or another. Daddy says that's why there are so many fights in bars: people drink and rant on about

141

anything, whether they care about it or not, just to be provocative and get themselves noticed."

"So I-I've heard," Grenville answered her question. "I'm-I'm writing a b-book of poetry," he added confidingly. "Vito says he may p-publish it. It's h-happy poetry. Placido P-P-Press only p-publishes p-p-pleasant things. He says there's-there's enough unpleasant things p-published." He blushed and bent his head to concentrate on his cake.

Viola had heard, although he had spoken softly. "Well, *I* have to like it, too, and I don't think I will. I looked in your notebook and the ends of the lines don't match. I like it when one line says 'hat' and the next 'cat.' That makes a song. I don't like the stuff you write."

Grenville blushed redder. "Viola," said her grandfather, "it is not necessary for you to approve things you know nothing about and—" He stopped at a loud scream from Viola.

"Take your hand off my leg!" she shouted at Jim Darrow. "You've been running it up and down all the time! He is a *villano*, Grandfather, and I don't want him around anymore!"

Darrow put both his hands on the table, looking both guilty and indignant. His face was a brick red. "That's not so, Miss Vincentia," he said, turning not toward her but to Mr. Vincentia, who regarded him with distaste.

"Now he says I'm a liar. He *is* a bad *villano!*"

Everyone was looking at Darrow, except Elizabeth Lamb, who was observing the others' faces. Some were amused, some shocked, some perplexed and one, very strangely, showed more distaste than Mr. Vincentia's — almost anger. "That's funny," she thought.

"Be quiet, please, Viola," directed her grandfather, though he still regarded Jim sternly. He rose. "I think we will have our coffee in the saloon."

Elizabeth Lamb and Persis followed the adults, keeping well away from Viola. Mr. Vincentia took Jim Darrow's arm and guided him to the passage that led to the master stateroom. The others gratefully took the coffee Payson poured from the espresso machine behind the bar, and some helped themselves to the bottle of cognac he had put out, along with large-bowled stemmed glasses. When he had served everyone except Elizabeth Lamb and Persis, they asked if he could get them glasses of milk. They wandered separately about the lounge, listening to the various conversations. Persis was beginning to feel tired; Elizabeth Lamb was experiencing a vague feeling of puzzlement. "But what about?" she thought.

"Liquor destroys brain cells," Persis observed to Jake and Chris who were talking beside one of the large windows, their snifters warming in their cupped hands. "Elizabeth Lamb and I are having milk."

They laughed. "After forty, I hear you lose 10,000 brain cells a year, liquor or not," Jake said. "Better hurry up with your poetry, Chris."

"I've read that the number of cells in the human brain is equal to the number of stars in the universe," Chris, too earnest to stutter, told them. "That's a lot of cells, Persis."

"But what happens to the stars when we lose our cells?" Persis worried. Jake laughed again. "You are a *most* intelligent child," he told the pleased Persis. "And the prettiest little girl I have ever seen!" He made an apologetic face at Elizabeth Lamb, who had come up to listen.

She handed Persis her milk and took hers over behind the sofa where Julia and Viola, heads close together, were sitting. Viola had tucked her pansy behind her ear. "Ah, *caro*," Julia was saying, "in every love affair there is one who loves and one who is loved. And the French say, 'We choose our first love to make us weep.' But he will say nice things to you someday; do not worry so. But when will you tell your Julia who—" She broke off as she noticed Elizabeth Lamb.

"That pansy matches your eyes, Viola," Elizabeth Lamb said as she wandered off.

"I know somebody who thinks my eyes are *just* like pansies. So there! *Your* eyes are ugly. Green — ugh!" Viola was exhibiting her usual charm.

Jim Darrow came in, face redder than it had been at the table. He joined Amy and Monica. Vincentia entered behind him, poured himself cognac and went over to Paul who was sitting alone, sipping his cognac with closed eyes and an expression of content. "What do

143

they think in London about this Watergate affair, Cooper?" he asked, with more of an air of wishing to be a courteous host than a desire for information.

"I don't hear much, in my circles," Paul answered. "My friends aren't interested in politics, even British politics. They talk about Anne's engagement; it's just been announced, you know. Great relief at Buck House, I hear. Now they'll have to match up her brother and he's 'bi,' of course."

"Really, Paul!" Mr. Vincentia responded, frowning.

"Fact. They had to rush a young clergyman out of the country recently." Elizabeth Lamb wondered if Mr. Cooper had had too much to drink and, like Mrs. Danniver, was being unnecessarily provocative.

"Paul, I detest that sort of talk." Mr. Vincentia turned to Jake, who had come over to them. "We were speaking of the Watergate affair."

"There's a new feller named Attorney General, whatever that is," said Jake. "That's all I know about it. Maybe he'll stop it."

"Yes, Richardson. When he was Attorney General of Massachusetts, a paper said that 'he'd put his own mother in jail if he had to.' Smart man; was one of the editors of the *Law Review* when he was at Harvard. Think he was arrested for drunk driving when he was there; seems to me someone dredged that up the other day. Oh, the Democrats are having a happy time."

"All I know," Persis had followed Mr. Aaronson, "is my daddy says the Democrats don't have to be so happy. He says nobody drowned at Watergate."

"Sit down here," Monica was saying to Jim as Elizabeth Lamb went over to their group. "You're safe beside me."

Jim was almost tearful. "He was awfully terse, Amy," he said in an undertone. "Said if I ever get near Viola again I'll be instantly dismissed. He called her 'an innocent child' and said I should be ashamed twice over because she also has a 'lack.' Her only lack is that she's vicious!

"God, on a boat this size, how can I avoid her? And I need my job."

"You seemed to admire her greatly, this afternoon," Monica observed.

"I was mistaken," Jim said with dignity. "I'm just not very smart about women. Maybe I sort of just touched her knee when she was eating her ice cream; she looked so cute, with that little flower face. Just like a kitten."

Elizabeth Lamb raised her eyes to Heaven, as did Monica, who replied, "Yes, well, she's more like a saber-toothed tiger. She'll lie any time she thinks it will get her some attention, so just keep your distance. I do wonder," she became thoughtful, "why she made such an extravagant scene, though? To make Vito angry — jealous? Maybe he was giving Elizabeth Lamb too much attention. Strange, in any case." Jake, who had joined them, shook his head and sighed.

"Jim," Amy said, "we'll protect you. Perhaps the brat will fall overboard, and all our worries will be over. Now, let's talk about something more pleasant:

"This morning I opened the mail I brought along. Just look at this clever rhyme from a fan. Oh," she said to Monica, "my newest Alaric C. book is set in Japan, you see. That's the reference in the rhyme."

"Why Japan?" Elizabeth Lamb asked.

"Well, his father — he has no mother — is an engineer who travels around the world and, of course, Alaric C. encounters murder wherever he goes. Somehow, sending them to Japan took my fancy." She sighed. "You might as well ask why I have the little monster live between trips in France, although he's American. Writers do strange things and then have to live with them: didn't Mrs. Christie say she wished she'd never invented a Belgian sleuth?"

"Well, Belgian or not, all sleuths should be professional," Monica observed. "It's tasking the reader's imagination to have an amateur run into crime everywhere he goes. Of course," she added hastily, "little Alaric C. is just so very entertaining that one can't quibble about his numerous encounters with murder."

Amy sighed again. "Well, you're right, of course." She looked downcast.

"What's the letter — the rhyme — say?" Jim asked quickly. He had finished the cup of coffee Amy had barely touched and looked calmer.

Amy beamed and recited:

"Alaric C. with precocious ease
Speaks French, and now speaks Japanese.
He snoops, concludes, eaves-drop-of-a-hat
Till readers scream, 'Will you *smack* that brat!'
And yet, we say, there's no one we'd rather be
Alone on an isle with than clever Alaric C."

She went to get more coffee. "You see," she said to Elizabeth Lamb, "he's quite an insufferable child. And don't ask me why; he just turned out that way. Characters, I do assure you, take over. I read that statement by an author years ago and thought the man was just being eccentric. Then I started to write and found he was absolutely correct."

"Really," said Elizabeth Lamb gloomily. "That'll be discouraging," she thought, "if I ever *get* any characters."

"I like children in mysteries as long as they're seen and not hurt and your charming Alaric C. is my favorite detective," Monica assured Amy cheerfully. "Don't you want that milk you're holding, Elizabeth Lamb?"

"Well, would you like it? I can get another."

Monica took the glass, brought out two capsules from her small satin evening bag, dropped them in the milk and drank it off at a draught.

"I thought you took your 'antis' at tea," Amy said.

"Oh, these are sleeping pills; they go well in milk. I never sleep the first night alone in a strange bed." She seemed to consider a provocative look at Cooper, who had come over, but changed her mind. Instead, she rose, telling Amy, "I do like your dress."

Amy was pleased. "I didn't know," she murmured, "if a little black dress would be all right."

"Except yours is rather a big black dress, dear," Monica answered, then patted Amy's shoulder with affection. "I'm rude only to people I like," she explained. "Well, I'm off to the luxury of my stateroom, all mine now that Mrs. Donelli's gone. See you tomorrow."

"She's a one, she is," Jake said. "You should hear the things she says to me, Mrs. D., all because she 'likes' me."

He beckoned to Persis. "Your cousin and you," he said to Elizabeth Lamb, "have been promised my chocs but you've got to come down

146

and get them." They went in single file down the curved staircase beyond the dining room. "Oooh, me plates o' meat is too big fer these twistin' apples 'n' pears!" Mr. Aaronson declaimed, to Persis' delight.

Jim Darrow was his cabin-mate, he told them, "and Chris and the Templeton feller are across the hall." The room was small and sans portholes but was comfortable and even luxurious with its walls of light paneled wood, brass lamps and lighting fixtures and two softly upholstered arm chairs placed beside a low, square game table that held packs of cards and a chess board. The chairs were of a striped beige-and-white velvet that matched the fitted covers of the twin beds that were now folded neatly over blanket stands. Carpeting in squares of yellow and dark orange was complemented by the large sheaf of yellow and orange silk lilies placed in a bronze vase on a table in a corner.

"What a dear little bathroom," said Persis, who had thoroughly inspected the entirety of the small premises. "Oh, but Mr. Vincentia's is just wonderful! You go in through a little door in the panelling — he must have to bend his head — and there it is, all dark red and gold with a big, big bathtub of pure marble!"

"I've seen it," Mr. Aaronson assured her. "You two run along to your bunks. I'm barely able to keep my eyes open, what with all I've eaten and drunk today and no exercise. What say the three of us do something strenuous tomorrow like a spot of walking around the deck once or twice?"

"If your cold's better, we will," promised Persis, outmaneuvering her cousin as she reached for the box of chocolates. "I'd better keep these, because Elizabeth Lamb has to share a cabin with Viola, and she might eat them all up."

They smiled "Goodnights" at Jim, Chris, and Robert, who were waiting at the top of the stairs for them to reach it. They were involved in a spirited discussion of women in literature, and Templeton seemed to be defending the character of Becky Sharp against criticism from the other two. As they crossed to the stairs to the aft cabins they saw Mrs. Danniver and Mr. Vincentia deep in conversation. They were in a far corner of the saloon lounge and he was talking earnestly while she, head bent, seemed to be trying to

147

interrupt. From a stool at the bar Viola watched, grinning unpleasantly. Paul was behind the bar, mixing a drink for Julia, who turned, smiling, and waved at the cousins.

"I bet Viola ratted about Mrs. Danniver's drinking," Elizabeth Lamb told Persis, who was laboriously unlocking her cabin door. "I can't think he's going to fire her because of that little sneak, but try to stop her if she starts again, Persis." Persis promised and Elizabeth Lamb crossed to her own cabin, which she had not troubled to lock, "since there's no sense locking the stable door after the horse is stolen *or* if the thief sleeps inside!" she murmured.

Viola came in as Elizabeth Lamb was donning her pajamas. She pulled off her pink dress and threw it on the bed. She tossed all the contents of a drawer on the floor so she could find a nightdress among them. "I'm going to sleep in Julia's room," she announced. "She's got a bigger bed and there's another for Paul. Just you don't snoop around in my things."

"Viola," Elizabeth Lamb called before the cabin door could be shut with a crash, as Viola's violent opening of it suggested it would be, "what do we do about breakfast tomorrow? I mean, do they bring it here, or what?"

Viola turned. "Oh, you *are* a pig. You can't be hungry again! The cook or the boy puts coffee and fruit on the bar. There won't be much else and you'd better not complain, either!" The door banged.

Elizabeth Lamb crammed Viola's clothes back into the drawer and hung up the dress, thinking she would rather throw them all out the porthole. Brushing her teeth, she remembered that she had not brushed them all day, not even after breakfast, in all the excitement. "And all the food I've eaten today!" she thought. And then she frowned. "What's bothering me?" she said aloud. "What should I remember, besides to brush my teeth?"

Lying in bed, she stared at the full moon visible through the porthole, the curtains of which she had opened although they had been shut by whoever had turned down her bed. She closed her eyes and tried not to think: "The way you do when you don't know where you've put something and if you just let your mind go blank, sometimes you walk straight to where it is."

148

She sat upright, drawing in her breath with a gasp. What she had seen and heard in the Brimmer Street garden, at her grandmother's house, in the car, at lunch, in the cabin and at tea and dinner all came together. "Yes, and Julia's—" she said — "and that look of — oh, I *must* be right. But how could it ever happen?" And then she remembered something Monica had said. "Of course; that's how!" she exclaimed loudly. From Cioccolato's basket came an indignant little noise before he settled again into a herring-and-cream slumber.

She lay back, worried. Then she smiled, a sad, tight little smile, and sighed. "Well, as Daddy would say in that terribly dated slang he uses: 'This is a whole new can of peas.'" She went to sleep, murmuring to herself Miss Scarlett O'Hara's famous line.

• CHAPTER 8 •

Better to Travel

ELIZABETH LAMB woke early. She looked out the porthole and saw that the *Chianti* was still anchored. The sky was grey and the sea reflected its sullen cast. Cioccolato rose and stretched, his rear end high in the air, and walked leisurely to his sandbox in the bathroom.

When he had returned to his cream, she splashed water on her face and brushed her teeth before she pulled on jeans, shirt, and a sweater. "And it's cold, probably: I'd better wear socks with my sneakers," she told the kitten who received the information calmly, yawned, and returned to his basket.

She went slowly up to the lounge, thinking that some hot coffee with milk might help her decide whether to reveal her conclusion of the night before. The certainty of action that often appears at night after copious food and even more copious drink had melted away in the cold reality of daylight. "I'm not really, really sure and I could cause terrible trouble," she thought despondently.

There were Pyrex jugs of black coffee and hot milk on the bar, along with large cups, and a bowl of tan sugar. Payson was lighting the squat warming candles in the brass rings on which the jugs rested. There was a platter of sliced bread spread with *ricotta* and a bowl of peeled oranges and one of pieces of fresh pineapple skewered with toothpicks. Jake Aaronson came in, Darrow following him, and looked first at the bar and then sorrowfully at Payson.

"Think you could scrounge me up some eggs and potatoes all scrambled together with lots of chopped onion, son?" he asked plaintively. "That's my own private cure for the kind of cold I've got." Payson looked both dubious and apprehensive as he left for the galley.

Amy Danniver was sitting on a sofa, drinking coffee and frowning with concentration as she wrote in a spiral-bound notebook. She looked wan and worried but glanced up with a polite smile as Jake carried his coffee over to her. "'Scribble, scribble, scribble,eh,' Mrs. D.?" he said. "You're at work early. Can you think to write, though, with all of us milling about?"

"I write better with people around," she answered. "Writing's an awfully lonely trade, you know. And I didn't want to disturb Persis; she's still asleep. I thought I'd better get started outlining this damned — this story Viola wants to write. She wants it to be about a kitten all alone on a little island, Vito says, and though I half-tried to tell him that's been done, all things considered," — she sighed — "I thought I'd better get on with it.

"Oh, there you are, Persis. You locked the cabin, I hope? I left a manuscript of my own I'm working on in a drawer of the desk. Jim, maybe I'd better give it to you, though. You're up forward, away from — up forward, that is."

Jim was abstractedly eating slices of orange. "Better not. Neither Jake nor I could find our keys this morning. With him not feeling so great and with me still a little — upset last night, we must've laid them down somewhere in the cabin, under something, or stuck them deep in pockets.

"Oh, well, probably the fellow who straightens up will find them. But I think you'd better keep your stuff in your room, till the keys turn up, I mean." He smiled his thanks as Persis poured coffee for him.

"Not eating anything?" he asked her. "You can't live on coffee, young lady."

151

"I'm stuffed, from last night," she answered. "Me, too," said Elizabeth Lamb, although she reached for pineapple to accompany her coffee. Julia arrived, looking tired and irritable. She moved to the end of the bar farthest from Persis. "I bet Viola either talked all night or kicked her in her sleep, or both," Elizabeth Lamb thought.

"Where's that boy with my eggs?" Jake wondered. "In spite of so much eating and drinking last night I'm feeling peckish."

"Really, Jake," Julia protested, "with a heavy cold, one shouldn't eat a great deal. 'If you feed a cold, you'll have to starve a fever,' you know. But I just saw the boy on deck. Paul and I walked around a few times and Paul's up there now watching them lower that little motorboat."

Payson put his head around the edge of the archway. "Pietro's cookin' yer egg thing, sir. He'll bring it because the boss wants me t' go over t' the haabaa 'n' git somethin'." He disappeared. Curious, Persis and Elizabeth followed him to the deck. Julia, cup in hand, went languidly after them, keeping well away from Persis.

"Bring at least twenty pounds." Mr. Vincentia handed Payson several bills. "What's he going after?" Persis asked. "Can I go with him? I've never seen Matinicus harbor and the boat has two seats."

"Or we could toss to go," Elizabeth Lamb said quickly. "I've never been there either."

"Vito, let the smaller child go," Julia suggested. "The air would do her a world of good." Elizabeth Lamb thought resentfully that Julia was really too frightened of German measles.

Mr. Vincentia hesitated. "Well, yes, you may go along, Persis," he said finally. "Payson is very knowledgeable about boats, the Captain has observed. But I want you both to put on the life jackets that are under the seats.

"He is going for salt cod," he told Julia. "I thought to get some when we arrived at Mount Desert this evening, or perhaps it will be tomorrow morning, but now I have decided we will stop there only to let the children and Payson off. Then we'll drop you and Paul in Seal Harbor, as you wished.

"I'm afraid," he turned to Elizabeth Lamb, "that I find I cannot stay a day or two in your cove, as I planned. The rest of us will not

152

even go ashore but will head straight for Montreal since — Payson!" he shouted over the side, "be more careful! I thought you were going to knock Persis into the water when you stumbled on the ladder!"

He shook his head as the little motorboat moved slowly but evenly away. "I hope I do not regret letting her go with him," he told Elizabeth Lamb. "Do you think dear Elizabeth, if she were here, would have permitted it?"

"Who in the world is 'dear Elizabeth'?" Julia was annoyed. Mr. Vincentia merely smiled faintly as he held the door to the dining room open for them. Elizabeth Lamb quickly assured him, "Oh, she would. She always says: 'Never refuse new experiences.'" He smiled more widely as they joined the others in the saloon.

"Sit down with Jake and me on this dear little *canapé*," Monica invited Elizabeth Lamb warmly. "I talked the cook out of some sweet biscuits. They're crammed with vanilla, and vanilla has a good deal of reviving alcohol, you know." She patted the seat of the small sofa invitingly.

"Did you say 'can of peas'?" Elizabeth Lamb was startled.

"No, I said 'vanilla' — oh, yes, I said '*canapé*.' But I thought you knew French?"

"Oh, yes, of course. I was thinking of something else." She sat down beside Monica and took a biscuit, thoughtful again.

Jake was eating heartily, crouched over the plate on the low table before him. "There's nothing like eggs scrambled up with slices of cooked potato, and onion," he confided to Elizabeth Lamb. "The rich don't know what they're missing, my mum always said. We had it sometimes for high tea when I was a nipper. First time she made it for Vito, he took on 's if it was caviare!"

Mr. Vincentia laughed. "We got our taste for caviare much later, Jake. But, yes, I agree with you: there are few things so good. The *'gliotta* we are to have for lunch will not compare, although I think you will like it."

"What's that?" Mr. Aaronson asked suspiciously, signalling to Jim, pouring coffee for Julia, that he would like some, too. "Not that gamy, tough old goat you Eyties like so much, I hope?"

Jim looked nervously at Mr. Vincentia as he delivered Jake's cup. Jake saw the look: "Vito and I're used to insulting each other, son.

He's called me a block-headed Limey often enough.

"Vito, tell me this stuff won't be castrated goat!"

"No, not *castrato,* although Sicilians are the only 'Eyties' who appreciate it. *'Gliotta* is salt cod cooked with broccoli and sprigs of fennel. I like dishes seasoned with fennel; it is the symbol of success, you know." He smiled. "I sent the cabin boy ashore for the cod. As soon as he returns, we will get underway and make straight to Mount Desert."

"Vito, I've been thinking." Julia came over to him, speaking most winsomely. "Paul and I don't have to go to the Uphreys in Seal Harbor tonight, or even tomorrow. Our invitation was very loose. We can just as well be left there on your return from Canada. I love being with you and Viola, you know."

"No, my dear, I really think you should not put your hosts off. As much as I will miss you — and Paul, of course — perhaps Viola can concentrate better on her book without your pleasant self to distract her."

"I want Julia to stay!" Viola, in a loose lavender angora sweater and white jeans, came in from the afterdeck. She stamped her foot. "I do!"

"Enough, Viola," her grandfather said, rising. "I will see you all here at lunch, about one. You, *caro,*" to Viola, "I expect to work with Mrs. Danniver till then."

Viola tore apart a slice of the *ricotta*-spread bread and crammed the pieces into her mouth. She looked at Mrs. Danniver unpleasantly. "Don't you want some fruit?" Chris asked politely, proffering the bowl of pineapple. Viola angrily pushed it away and followed her grandfather into the passage to his stateroom. Her arguments could be heard in the saloon, even through the closed passage door.

"I was reading," Elizabeth Lamb spoke a pitch or two above her normal voice, afraid that Viola's carrying tones would pronounce something that would hurt Mrs. Danniver, or Jim Darrow, or both, "that in the Middle Ages, the English serfs only got onions for supper, Mr. Aaronson."

"That's — that's right," Chris Grenville also spoke loudly. "And y-yet they sur-survived — and h-here we are!" Elizabeth Lamb thought again how much she liked him.

"It's so true," Amy also raised her voice, although Viola could not now be heard, "that the forebears of most of us were serfs, and yet our vanity somehow always makes us feel they had few descendants and that only the nobles are responsible for the present population. There just weren't enough nobles, in any country, for that to be so!"

"No, indeed," Robert Templeton said heavily. "You're absolutely right, ma'am." As usual, as Elizabeth Lamb had noticed, when the solemn Templeton spoke people dispersed in hope of finding lighter conversation elsewhere. Julia, no longer looking winsome, left, murmuring she must see if Paul wanted coffee — "he never comes in for breakfast unless he is urged." Jake began to discuss London with Monica. Chris and Jim turned on the television above the bar and settled themselves on stools, gazing up at an earnest, plump female weather forecaster. Elizabeth Lamb went over to Amy Danniver.

"Mr. Vincentia doesn't seem too mad at you," she ventured. "I heard what Mr. Darrow said to you yesterday and when Viola came into your cabin last night and saw — and saw that brandy, I was worried."

"Oh," Amy said sadly, "he's not angry enough to cancel my contract although he could, as Jim says. But he reduced my royalty rate five percent on the Alaric C. that's just come out; he's got the right to do that, too."

"That's awful! I thought authors got at least ten percent of sales. I met a lady in Bar Harbor last year who writes children's books, and that's what she said."

"Oh, I still will. Because of a — a sort of obligation to me, he's been giving me a very, very lavish twenty-two percent on my books. He doesn't need the money his publishing house makes, so he can afford to be generous. And he's spending a lot to advertise them; that's important, you know. I'll still get seventeen percent, more than the usual.

"I had — I had a bad time a few years ago and was drinking too much and writing badly and being very belligerent, so he put in that clause about drinking in a new contract in which he raised my royalty rate. And gave me Jim as a sort of guardian angel, or warder, perhaps." She smiled wryly at Jim as she caught his eye. "But if that little beast tells on me again, he'll reduce the rate by another five percent. And I can't afford it. My father is very old and in an expensive nursing home."

"Don't give her the chance." Elizabeth Lamb was very earnest. "If you don't drink — I mean—"

"We know what you mean." Jim had come over to them. "Terrible reception on that channel," he said to Amy, "and it's the only one we seem able to get. But, Elizabeth Lamb, Miss Vincentia can just make things up, as you know; it doesn't matter if they are true or not. I wish this voyage was over!"

Templeton had disappeared in the direction of the galley. Now he returned, looking gratified. "I just found that boy and asked if I could have an omelette. I require a substantial breakfast, always have. Break down and can't think clearly if I don't get one.

"Better the eggs break than me: you can't make an omelette without breaking eggs, you know. Ha!"

"What a very original, not to say witty, thought!" Monica observed, with a perfectly straight face. "I do congratulate you."

Mr. Templeton was pleased. "My mother always said I had a dry wit."

"Any drier and we'll all drown," Amy muttered. "Elizabeth Lamb, could you go find Viola and tell her — no, speak to V.V., that would be better. Ask him to send her in here. We should begin this epic of hers and damned if I'm going to do it all. They're in his stateroom, probably."

Payson was in the dining room as she crossed it, getting a knife and fork from the sideboard for the plate of bacon and eggs he carried. "That's not an omelette," she told him. "You've been a long time ashore, too. You look awfully down, Payson."

"Pietro don't feel like makin' omelettes," he said heavily. "I'm okay; jest got mad waitin' fer Persis to make up her mind what she was goin' to buy in the store. Wanted a present fer somebody. Then she didn't hev any money and I'd spent all I was give fer the fish and when she said her pa would send them a check, they didn't go fer it. Then she jest moseyed along real slow to the boat pickin' flowers along the way."

"Honestly, Payson. That child! Where is she now?"

"I dunno. Her cabin, maybe."

Her knock at Mr. Vincentia's stateroom was answered by a request to come in. He was sitting on one of the red velvet settees, Viola beside him and leaning affectionately on him. "Viola loves the story of Tom Kitten," he said. "She would not let me read my book until I read it to her again." He closed the small volume and patted Viola's curly red head lovingly.

"What was the book *you* were reading?" Elizabeth Lamb asked, as always curious.

"Walton's *The Compleat Angler*. I read it often. My friend David, Monica's father, gave me a list of a thousand books years ago. He said that until I read them, I would never understand the world and the world would never understand me! This is perhaps my favorite of the thousand."

"That's why he knows so much; he's in here reading a lot," Elizabeth Lamb thought as she delivered Mrs. Danniver's message. He firmly ushered Viola out, instructing her to go to the saloon and be civil to everyone, "especially Mrs. Danniver, *caro*. She wants to help you." He asked Elizabeth Lamb if she would like to call her grandmother's camp from his room to advise the housekeeper that she and Persis would probably arrive that night or possibly early the following morning.

"And perhaps she will tell Payson's people to expect him. We are under way now and heading at almost full power for the Deer Island Thorofare."

Elizabeth Lamb produced her "society smile." Coaxingly, she asked, "Oh, couldn't I go up to the pilot house and call?" She smiled again. "If you were with me, then the captain couldn't say a thing about passengers being 'undisciplined.'"

He also smiled as he pulled on a heavy dark red sweater. "I wish my granddaughter had your charm.

"Very well; you find Persis and I will meet you both on the bridge. She would like to see it, I am sure."

Persis' door was locked. Through it she announced that she was waiting for a seaman to bring her some things she needed and, no, Elizabeth Lamb could not come in. "That would spoil the surprise, wouldn't it?"

"Well, if it's a birthday surprise for me, my birthday was yesterday, anyway, so what's the big secret?"

Persis said maybe it wasn't for her and to go away. "You always try to boss me every time I do something."

Elizabeth Lamb gave up and crossed to her cabin for her notebook. "I can write down what the pilot house is like and maybe use it somewhere. Persis says Mrs. Danniver uses almost everything she sees or hears," she murmured. Her cabin door was also locked.

"Viola, are you in there? I've got to get something."

She was again answered through a closed door. "Go away. I'm thinking."

"I thought I heard you talking to someone. But I'll only be a minute."

"Go away, I said." The inevitable foot-stamping. "You can just get it later."

"I certainly am unwanted, on all sides," she thought as she ran up to the top deck. Mr. Vincentia courteously explained the workings of the communications panel, the radar equipment, the loran — a navigational aide — and the autopilot and depth sounder. He showed her how to put her call through on the Sailor VHF radiotelephone. No one answered at The Bungalow. "Dora may be in one of the other buildings; Grandmother only had a phone installed in her studio. Gee, nobody seems to want to talk to me."

Captain Knudsen, who had been watching her every move, advised her to go below and find another passenger to speak with. She lingered a moment, observing a large sailing schooner approaching them. "That's one of those ships from Camden that takes paying passengers," she informed Mr. Vincentia, to postpone leaving a little longer. "They come into our cove sometimes and anchor. Grandmother's caretaker calls them 'cattleboats' but I think they could be fun. Gosh, it's so foggy you can barely see the island behind her!" He agreed, smiling. The captain firmly ushered her out.

It had begun to rain. She ran along the deck and down the spiral ladder to the fantail lounge. Mrs. Danniver was there, patiently explaining to Viola that the story in the book she was holding, *The Little Island,* could not, absolutely not, be used by them. "Viola, it's copyrighted. That means you — we — have to think of a whole new story. We can still use a kitten, but he'd better be born on the island and grow up there with his mother. And we have to think of new, different things to happen to him.

"Now, take this notepad and pen and write down things you think could happen. And write what he looks like. I'll start thinking of some conflict, action, in the story. Does he run away from his mother and get lost? That's one idea. Write what you think he would feel like if he were lost — Viola, you need not put out your tongue at Elizabeth Lamb. She's going away." She motioned Elizabeth Lamb toward the saloon.

Viola withdrew her tongue long enough to announce she was an owner, too, and Mrs. Danniver's boss, too, and she could stick out her tongue if she wanted to, too. She proceeded to do so.

Everyone in the saloon but Persis was reading or glancing out the portholes at the gloomy sea and sky as Elizabeth Lamb went through it and down for her notebook. The door to Julia's and Paul's cabin was opened and Payson came out with an armful of soiled sheets and towels. He frowned at her as he carefully locked the door behind him.

"Why do you look so down, Payson?" she asked again. "I really think you do."

"Oh, they got me fixin' up cabins because the captain wants all the crew up topside. The fog's gettin' worse. Antonio says we'll hev to slow down a mite.

"And," he ended gloomily, "it ain't 'sif I ain't got enough to do helpin' Pietro, neither."

"Cheer up; we'll get to Mount Desert soon. Don't you want to see your mother?"

Payson sighed mightily as he went up the stairs behind her. "Don't see why they didn't make a passage through the engine room so's a person wouldn't hev to run up 'n' then down," he complained as he left her to carry his burden forward and down the stairs to the crew's quarters where the laundry equipment was.

Monica was behind the bar, whistling light-heartedly as she poured white wine for herself, Julia and Paul. "You seem happy," Paul remarked.

"Had a great zizz. Nothing like my special sleeping pills to knock

159

you out and then morning comes instantly, it seems, and you feel wonderful. I even got up at seven and walked around the deck. Glad I got some exercise before this filthy weather set in." Everyone settled down to read or chat or yawn the morning away.

Viola and Amy came in, Viola putting out her tongue again at Elizabeth Lamb as she wandered through the saloon and disappeared. Amy sank into a chair, put her long, grey-flannel-clad legs on the table in front of it and requested somebody — anybody — "some angel" to make her a drink. "A mild Bloody, please.

"Really, I wonder who gets that child's Placido stock if she should fall overboard in the fog," she mused. "Whoever it is, he — she would be bound to be easier to get along with. She's driving me up the wall. Not only can she not think, she can barely write. Or, I should say, print."

Jim handed her what Elizabeth Lamb had observed was a very, very mild Bloody Mary. "Maugham said that a good rule for writers is not to complain overmuch," he advised.

"That was *explain,* you dolt," Amy retorted, drinking deeply. "Oh, liquor is wonderful; how it lifts the spirits! And what mystery writers would do if it had never been invented, I do not know. Whenever you want a pause in the story — time to have something significant happen — you have the characters go out for a drink, or mix one, or whatever."

"Really?" said Elizabeth Lamb, opening her notebook to write "have them drink a lot" and wondering what her English teacher, a stern elderly man reported to be a member of A.A., would think. Payson and Persis were putting napkins, silver, and plates in neat piles on one of the dining room tables. She went in to help. "Are we having lunch in here?" she asked.

"Pietro says it's to be that help-yourself style. They kin git their food here 'n' carry it to the lounge.

"He don't let nobody into the kitchen so s'pose you two stand over here by the door 'n' take the glasses 'n' wine 'n' stuff I hand out and set it on the tables. It'll go faster; the boss wanted lunch at one 'n' it's most that now."

The food came last, and it was less elaborate than luncheon the day before: a large pottery dish of the salt cod and broccoli, a bowl of dressed greens — "them's 'aroog somethin' — oh, I can't say it in Eyetalian but they call 'em 'rocket,' too" — that were dotted with nasturtium flowers, crusty round loaves of bread on boards, bowls of sweet butter, a platter of cheeses. A deep tray held sherbet glasses of grainy, coffee-colored ices placed in a bed of crushed ice.

Mr. Vincentia and Viola joined the appreciative company. Viola refused to take anything except bread she cut and spread thickly with butter, waving a long knife around dangerously as she sliced. Not only Jim but everyone else avoided getting near her as they served themselves.

"Oh, this fish is good!" Persis had seated herself beside Jake Aaronson. "What's that you're drinking? Don't you want a glass of the white wine? I'll go get you one."

"No, thanks, dear," he answered. "I'd better stick to Pimms Number One. This is my fourth, I'm ashamed to say. Rain and fog always make me both sleepy and dreadfully thirsty. Should I live in the desert, do you think?"

Persis giggled. "But," he went on, "you could fetch me a bit more of this *'gliotta, caro.* 'm so tired that it's an effort to get up. Rain and fog have that effect on you?"

"It's probably that Pimms stuff," Persis told him, complying. Mr. Vincentia received many compliments as his guests finished their portions and went back for seconds and thirds. "And *granita* is just the perfect finishing touch, Vito," Julia assured him, again winsome.

Mr. Aaronson sighed with content and patted his stomach. "You are *abbufato,* my dear Jake," said Mr. Vincentia. "That means 'eating one's bellyful,'" he informed his friend.

Mr. Aaronson replied that if it meant "boa-constrictor" he wouldn't be surprised, because that's what he felt like. "Darrow," he added, "if you want anything from the cabin, could you get it now? Because in about two minutes I'm going to stumble down, kick off my shoes and fall on my bed, like a boa-constrictor that's just swallowed a goat."

Persis giggled again and said snakes didn't have to take off their shoes. She then told Elizabeth Lamb, *sotto voce,* that she loved, just loved Mr. Aaronson and that he would just love his surprise, too.

Elizabeth Lamb, finishing her ice and picking up her notebook to write "have someone say he feels just like a b.c.," nodded vague agreement. Jim Darrow settled himself beside her, also with a notebook, and said he'd stay where he was for a couple of hours. "I've got to draft some letters, been putting them off because I just plain hate to write letters though I find I do it better when it's raining."

Amy, also carrying a notebook, took a cup of espresso from Payson and moved to a corner of the lounge, telling Jim as she passed him: "Noel Coward said he was bored by writers who could write only when it was raining." Jim told her Coward was a crank, as everybody said who had known him.

"There are very few writers who aren't cranks in some way," Monica said cheerfully, softening her remark with a grin at Amy as she selected a book from the case, and, carrying her coffee, announced she was going out to the fantail to read and doze till tea. Jake, yawning, got up and said if he slept through tea, would someone wake him for dinner? "You, Jim?" Jim nodded, writing away.

"We will probably not anchor for dinner," Mr. Vincentia told them as he finished his coffee. "We'll keep going in case the fog becomes worse later. The Captain plans to be at your cove," he said to Elizabeth Lamb and Persis, "before nine. And then we may proceed around M.D.I. to Seal Harbor, or we may stay the night, depending on the weather.

"I will miss you both," he added, and turned to Payson, "and you have been a great help. Perhaps we may stop to see you girls on our way back from Canada, with your permission." He smiled and left, followed by Viola, leaving Payson, Elizabeth Lamb, and Persis looking both gratified and sad.

"Well," said Julia, who was holding two packs of cards, "what about some bridge? Paul, I know you want a game. Chris? You, Robert? We can play in our cabin so as not to disturb the writers."

There was agreement, although as they moved to the stairs Christopher Grenville suggested they might play at one of the dining room tables. "No," Julia said, "I find those dolphin chairs most unpleasant. Danilo always said they were *spagnuoleggiante*, a Sicilian term of derision for something too garish, calling it 'Spanish.' I

162

believe," she giggled, "Viola's mother selected them. No taste." The four disappeared.

Amy looked up from her work. "I do *not* like that woman. She might as well have been Viola's mother: she's nasty enough. I'll bet she let that kitten loose to annoy V.V. You know," she told Elizabeth Lamb, who had found a copy of *Jonathan Livingston Seagull* and had come to sit near her, "V.V. is the most generous of people. He sent Jim and me to Majorca last month to get some local color for the next Alaric C. and I'm sure I saw that boyfriend of hers living it up there, probably on V.V.'s money. *Which* they wouldn't be enjoying if she hadn't nabbed that son of his, and if V.V. weren't so kind.

"Don't you remember seeing him, Jim? He's quite distinctive-looking. And I swear I saw Monica, too. Doesn't she look familiar? Maybe I didn't see her there but I've seen her somewhere before."

"Don't remember seeing either of 'em." Jim was frowning as he labored over his letters.

"Oh, you must have. In a *café*, maybe? You went everywhere I went; certainly you tagged along to every *café*! I've got a great memory for faces. I don't remember seeing nasty Julia, though."

She got up and stretched. "I think I'll write in my cabin. Some of my notes are there."

"Could I come down, too?" Persis asked. "I'm getting sleepy. If it wouldn't bother you to have me around?" Amy assured her she would be no trouble.

Elizabeth Lamb read for a while, only half-concentrating on her book because she was wondering why Julia might have tried to upset her father-in-law. "You know," Jim said suddenly, as if reading her thoughts, "it was Viola who let that cat out yesterday. I had gone down to check on — to find Amy, but she had already left to come up here for tea. Viola came out of the next cabin holding the kitten and jumped back in when she saw me. She must have let it out when I went back upstairs.

"I didn't know," he sounded worried, "how strongly V.V. feels about cats. When all the commotion started, I didn't like to say anything, then. And last night, after she — well, after what she said about me I felt I just shouldn't. It would have sounded as if I made it up to get back at her."

"No," Elizabeth Lamb said thoughtfully, "I see you couldn't. Well, there wasn't any serious harm done. I'd just forget it."

Reassured, he went back to writing. She read for a time and then went out to the fantail to see if she could observe a seagull who might look like Jonathan. Monica was not there. She went up to the open deck and stared out into the fog.

No seagulls were in sight but Monica soon ambled along from the direction of the pilot house. "It's too cold up here," she said. "Come on down. Are you looking for land? We just picked up the buoy on Hay Ledge, whatever that might mean. I couldn't see a thing, myself."

"I'm looking for a seagull." Elizabeth Lamb wondered if Monica and the captain had been "having a schnapps" as she had said they did sometimes at night. Paulo, appearing behind Monica, laughed and pointed. A gull was riding on the sea astern of the *Chianti*. He dipped his bill into the water and then rose on long, graceful wings to circle the boat before he vanished into the fog.

"Ah, he was wetting his beak, *signorina,*" the seaman said, laughing louder. He stopped in confusion and walked quickly back toward the bow as Mr. Vincentia's head appeared at the top of the spiral ladder. He only nodded curtly to them before he followed Paulo.

"What did that mean?" Elizabeth Lamb asked as she and Monica descended.

"Oh, it's sort of *Mafioso* slang for getting a piece of the action, or the profits, or something," Monica answered carelessly. "And Vito hates being reminded — ah, hates being *surrounded* by fog. It makes him tense."

She went to the bar and poured a glass of wine. "Well, I'm off to a hot shower. It's awfully dank on a boat in weather like this. See you at tea."

Elizabeth Lamb returned to *J. L. S.* After a while she ventured a remark or two to the engrossed Darrow and was answered only with polite grunts. "I wonder if Persis feels like playing cards, or something," she thought.

Payson, carrying a bulging leather-handled canvas bag, came out of the door that led to the passage forward as she made for the stairs to the aft cabins. "Don't you get any time off, just to read or rest on your bunk?" she asked. "What's that? Is the cook still making you work?"

"Pietro's havin' a nap," he answered, carrying the bag to the galley door. "So I got to do things."

She followed. "What's in that? What in the world are all those candles for? Can I see the kitchen, if Pietro's not in there?"

"Honest, Elizabeth Lamb! You always got to know everythin'. I had to git them in case the power goes out. And, no, you can't 'cause Pietro don't allow nobody—" As he pushed the door open, they saw Viola, leaning against a stove and noisily drinking a glass of milk. "Miss!" Payson said nervously. "Not any passengers kin be in here. Please!"

Elizabeth Lamb hastily retreated, wishing the best for Payson as much as she was reluctant to attend any more of Viola's temper tantrums. Persis was not amenable to a game of cards. "Mrs. Danniver is helping me write a story," she said importantly.

"Yes; can you imagine that Persis has been assigned to write a short story over the summer!" Amy exclaimed. "She must be in a very advanced English class. Now, Persis, here I think you should say—"

Elizabeth Lamb retreated again, murmuring gloomily, "Well, *my* class has to write a *novel*." She lay on her bed, feeling unwanted, and watched Cioccolato attacking a fresh bowl of herring. She wondered if she might go into Julia's cabin to watch the bridge game, but decided against it. She fell asleep.

When she woke, the cabin was very dark. Cioccolato was sleeping, making cheerful little cat noises. She drew the curtains at the porthole and turned on a lamp. "If he thinks it's night, he'll sleep now and then meow for hours when I go to bed," she thought. "Oh, I hope Viola stays in Julia's cabin again tonight," she said aloud, and then — "oh, but we'll probably be at The Bungalow tonight! At least Dora will talk to me there, and Persis, too." She brushed her teeth, feeling more cheerful.

Chris and Paul were still playing cards in the cabin across the hall, now some sort of two-handed game; Julia and Templeton were not in evidence. When she got to the lounge, everyone else except Mr. Aaronson, Mr. Vincentia and Viola was there and tea was almost over. "Where have you been? I saved all the cakes I could for you, and some bread-and-butter," Persis said, leading her to a chair with a plate of food beside it. She lowered her voice: "The Captain eats an awful lot; look, he actually came down! He said he'd been too busy up in the steering place to eat any lunch and then when that sailor broke his leg—"

"*What!*" She wondered if Mr. Vincentia, angry at Paulo's remark, had done something to him. "Who, the new one, Paulo?"

"Yes, it was," Monica answered for Persis. She handed Elizabeth Lamb a cup of tea. "He was running along the deck up forward a little while ago and just slipped. Damndest thing!"

"Did anyone — like — push him?" Elizabeth Lamb asked.

Monica raised her brows. "Of course not. I saw it, actually. I'd just woken up after a nap and was looking out a porthole to see if the fog had cleared. Someone on the top deck, Antonio, I believe, called down to him and as he looked up, he turned his ankle, skidded, and fell.

"Antonio saw it too, of course. You may, as Vito says, be quite a detective, little one, but you mustn't imagine plots where there are none."

Reproved, and feeling ashamed of her suspicion of Mr. Vincentia, Elizabeth Lamb buried her face in her cup. "I'll get you more," Persis offered. "We're waiting on ourselves because the Captain sent Payson up to be with Antonio while he's down here. The fog's bad and Pietro had told the Captain Payson can see in the dark. The other sailor's down in the engine room, I guess, or something."

"Why don't we just anchor somewhere," Elizabeth Lamb questioned, "if the fog's so thick?"

"Oh," Jim said reassuringly, offering her the remains of a plate of smoked salmon sandwiches, "we've got all sorts of equipment, they say — radar and things. And, besides, they want to get that man to a hospital. They figure it will be quickest to head to your grandmother's place and call the hospital in Bar Harbor and get an ambulance sent over. Quicker than calling the Coast Guard."

"It won't be long now," Robert Templeton told them solemnly. "When the Captain came down, he said he'd waited till we passed something — Flye Ledge, I think. We're heading up Blue Hill Bay

166

now. They've given the man a painkiller and he's in his bunk; all they could do. We're going at full speed, too."

"Really?" Julia asked. "It seems to me that in the last minute or two we've been going very slowly." She glanced over to the Captain, who had put down his cup, frowning. He rose to his feet just as Antonio ran in.

"Captain," he said urgently. "Would you come? We were having a power slow-down and now we've lost almost all—" The Captain rushed out after him.

"I'm frightened," Persis said loudly. "What's the matter? Will we sink?"

"Well, of *course* not." Amy was heartily reassuring. "I'm going to carry these tea things out to the cook. Anyone want to help? Action's good in a crisis.

"Not that there really is one," she added hastily. "Persis, why don't you get a tray and put some of these plates and cups on it?"

"Well," Persis answered slowly, "I thought I'd maybe take some tea to Mr. Aaronson. And he'll want to know what's happening, too. Elizabeth Lamb could come with me and bring him some cakes — if the Captain left any, that is."

"Persis," Elizabeth Lamb was emphatic. "He said he wanted to sleep."

"Well, he's slept a long time. Come on; get a plate."

Elizabeth Lamb opened her mouth to argue but Amy Danniver firmly shook her head. "Yes, you children do that," Julia agreed. "And, Monica, let's take a couple of cups down to Paul and Chris. They'd like a break and then you and I can persuade them into another game. There's not much else we can do. I wouldn't even suggest the Coast Guard to Vito; he'd think calling them was an insult to his *virilità!*"

Templeton looked a little downcast at not being invited to play again. "And perhaps I should take some to the injured sailor. Somebody should think of him. Better not give him liquor, I believe."

Amy put a cup and saucer and a teapot on a tray. "There's a plate of biscuits out there on the sideboard no one thought to bring in," she told him. "Do you know how to get to the crew's quarters?"

Templeton assured her he always made a point of learning the layout everywhere he went. "In case of fire," he said heavily. He preceded Elizabeth Lamb and Persis down the forward stairs and went through a swinging door at the end of the hall, beyond the doors of the two passenger cabins.

Mr. Aaronson did not answer their knock. They knocked again harder and heard only a soft groan. "We'd better go in," Persis said. "Oh, I hope he hasn't broken his leg, too!"

They timidly opened the door. The cabin was pitch black. "Where's the light switch, I wonder?" Elizabeth Lamb said. "Mr. Aaronson, where are you? Are you all right?"

"The switch's to your left," a thick voice answered. "Migawd, what's happened to me? I can't see!"

He was lying on his bed, fully dressed except for his shoes. His face was a livid red and his eyes were swollen shut. His hands were feebly waving in the air. The scent of wild roses was overpowering in the small cabin. Persis went to him and touched his shoulder. "It's me and Elizabeth Lamb," she said. "Why are you so sick?"

Elizabeth Lamb was shocked into speechlessness as she stared around the room. There were large glass vases of pink, red, and white wild roses massed everywhere — beside each bed, on the game table and the chest of drawers; on the floor, several in every corner. She picked up two and ran with them to the passage. "Bring the rest out here, Persis! Quick! He's allergic to roses!" She ran back for more.

"He's what?" asked Persis, stumbling as she obeyed. "But he said he loved them!"

"Roses?" came from the blind form on the bed. It struggled painfully to a sitting position. "What roses?"

Elizabeth Lamb continued removing the vases as Persis sat down on the floor and began to cry. "They were a surprise for you," she sobbed. "You were so nice to me — you said such polite things — and you said you hadn't been near a rose for years — I wanted to surprise you! I picked them when I went ashore with Payson. Oh, I've made you blind! I didn't know; I didn't know." She ended in a wail, hiccuping loudly.

"There were about a million of them in here, Mr. Aaronson,"

Elizabeth Lamb said quietly. "Didn't you see them? Didn't you smell them?"

"I was so tired that I just came in and made for my bed," he answered in the same thick voice. "Didn't put a light on and there are no portholes. And I haven't been able to smell a thing since yesterday.

"It's all right, Persis. You couldn't have known what roses do to me, my dear. But could you two help me get this jacket off? My back is hurting badly."

"Persis should have known," Elizabeth Lamb said sternly. "Right after we came aboard, Mr. Vincentia was saying he'd had all the roses taken away because you were allergic — oh, that's right, she was asleep on a chair.

"I'm sorry, Persis, but stop crying and help me."

They carefully removed his jacket. He unbuttoned his shirt slowly and they eased it off. His back was like a side of raw meat. Persis began to cry again. "What can we do?" Elizabeth Lamb asked. "Is there any medicine you can take? Will your eyes open? Oh, Persis, I wish you hadn't tried to be so nice! I wish you'd told me what you were going to do!"

"Now, now," he said. "Leave off Persis, dear. Just you lead me to a chair — put a soft towel on the back of it first. And wet a face flannel with warm water. There's a bottle of stuff in the medicine chest; it's all right, you can't make a mistake. There's only one bottle there.

"Put four drops of it in a glass of water and hand it to me, please. Now, Elizabeth Lamb, suppose you straight-off get rid of those roses, wherever you put them. Have that cabin boy throw them over the side. And find a basin I can keep wetting this cloth in.

"This will pass, but it'll be hours before I'll be able to see normally again, so maybe you'd best stay for a bit, Persis, and chat with me. That would buck me up, dear."

Persis began to feel better. She found a pajama jacket and helped him into it. "Elizabeth Lamb will have to throw the roses overboard herself because Payson's busy." She told him of the engine trouble and Paulo's broken leg by the time Elizabeth Lamb returned with a silver bowl.

"This is all I could find," she said. "It was in the dining room. Persis will stay with you but I'd better go tell Mr. Vincentia how you are. And then I'll come back. Persis, put on some lamps and turn off that overhead light. If his eyes start to open a bit, that strong light could hurt them."

As she entered the passage to Mr. Vincentia's stateroom, he ran out of it, Payson behind him. They brushed past her and raced up the stairs to the upper deck. "Where are you going?" she cried. "Mr. Aaronson's cabin is down the other stairs." She went up after them.

The deck lights were on but beyond the *Chianti*'s rail she could see nothing but blackness. She stumbled over a bucket lying on the deck and fell. She picked herself up as Antonio, running towards them, stopped: "The Captain says to try to help Carlo, *padrone*. If only we had that Roberto in the engine room—" She arrived at the pilot house just behind Mr. Vincentia and discreetly went only as far as the open door.

"What the hell is going on, Captain?" His voice was loud and anxious. "Payson says the radar shows an island dead ahead where there is none on the chart? Just a ledge? And you couldn't call me because the phones are out? What happened? This is insanity!"

The Captain gestured helplessly. "I don't know how it happened, sir, but the communications panel is drenched with water. Nothing works. It is completely dead. Try it yourself. I found out only a minute ago when I tried to call you. I've had no reason to use it in the last hour or so.

"And the boy says he sees a light ahead, as well as the radar blip. If we are approaching something where there are people, we had better put in and call for help. We are making almost no headway and Carlo cannot determine the trouble."

Mr. Vincentia peered through the glass above the wheel. "I see nothing." He glanced at the chart. "Payson said we should be just between Hardwood and Long Island. And Hardwood is uninhabited? And we are south of Long?"

"There's a light dead ahead fer sure, sir," Payson put in. "Mebbe five hundred yards now. Think we should try fer it, if we cain't git over to Schooner Cove? Dunno what it could be — Elizabeth Lamb!

It's that cousin of yours! Got to be; Mumma said he'd had barges goin' out to that ledge he laid claim to ever since last summer, with rocks 'n' earth 'n' bags 'n' bags of concrete. Must've built it up 'n' now he's—"

"Yes! It's got to be Crazy Cousin Curtis!" Elizabeth Lamb almost shouted. The two men turned to stare at her. "It's a cousin of Grandmother's. My daddy says he's absolutely out of his mind, has been for years. That's what he calls him. His wife finally left him and he's been saying he was going to build his very own island — he's awfully rich — and get out of the world and write his book—"

The Captain had turned away from her in bewilderment: "There is a light!" Mr. Vincentia continued to regard her in amazement. "You know this man, this cousin?" he asked. "He lives here; does he have a phone? He seems to have electricity, so he may have run a cable from Mount Desert or Blue Hill."

"I guess he lives here, if his house is built. I guess he has a phone, but he's absolutely crazy, so you never know. There's two men he found in Norway who've worked for him for years, my daddy says, and he says they're crazy too—"

With a shudder, the almost imperceptible movement of the *Chianti* ceased. Captain Knudsen turned quickly, seized the microphone on the communications panel and revolved a knob and then cursed as he threw down the useless instrument. "Boy, run like hell to the engine room and tell Antonio to drop anchor! Quick!"

The light was now plainly visible. It was on a post on the seaward end of a stone jetty and its glow revealed a small harbor in which there was one mooring buoy. Another light suddenly flashed on at the land end and two figures in dark clothes were visible walking along the jetty. Antonio dropped the anchor, and the *Chianti* swung evenly around so that her bow pointed landward.

One of the figures waved a rifle as he advanced. As they reached the end of the jetty he shouted something in a loud, deep voice. "What is he saying, Captain?" Mr. Vincentia asked. "It's not English, is it? Can you ask if they have a telephone?" The other man began to shout.

"I don't understand all the words," the Captain said slowly. "I think it's Norwegian; it's something Scandinavian. I'll try Swedish."

He picked up a bullhorn and pushed aside a small pane of the window in front of the control panel. What he said to the men on the jetty was not acceptable to them. They yelled and angrily waved their arms.

"What did you say? What are they saying?" Mr. Vincentia was rigid with anxiety. Payson, frowning, reappeared behind him.

"I told them we have an injured man aboard and want to come ashore to call for help. They said, as far as I could understand, that their boss is not here and they won't let anyone on the island. They say, sir, we have five minutes to leave. I think they said five minutes."

"Tell them again someone *must* come ashore. Tell them our engines have failed and we cannot leave. Tell them we have no working radiotelephone."

The Captain shouted again. The two men replied, one after the other, even more emphatically.

"They say they have orders, sir, orders to shoot any trespasser. They sound sincere to me."

"They're crazy, I said." Elizabeth Lamb was almost jumping up and down. "One of them shot a man who just stopped for directions at Cousin Curtis' house, when he lived outside Boston. He got away with it, too."

A vein stood out in Mr. Vincentia's forehead. "They didn't say they don't have a phone, did they? Tell them I, the owner, am coming ashore. Make it clear I am coming. I'll take this boy with me." Payson frowned harder.

The Captain spoke again. The man with the rifle raised it and fired a shot. The other pulled a revolver from a pocket and aimed it at the bridge of the *Chianti*.

"They shot across the bow! Next time they might shoot us!" The Captain reached for a switch and the lights in the pilot house went out. He shouted again through the bullhorn, at some length, controlling his voice although he was clearly enraged. He closed the window, pulled another switch and the deck lights went out.

"I told them we will leave as soon as our engines are repaired and that it may take some time. I hope to God they understood me. I am going to the engine room to try one last thing. If it fails, sir, someone will have to go for help; God knows how or where.

"The rest of us must stay out of sight and be prepared if they try anything."

The *Chianti* had now swung so that her port side was turned away from the jetty. Crouching, he made for the ladder on that side. His head was just above the deck when he spoke again: "Boy, you come after me, and warn Pietro, and the two of you get all the curtains pulled. Sir, you had best take the girl back along the deck, keeping low, and assemble the passengers."

"This is worse than the 'Cosa Nostra pirates' Mr. Tibbets was babbling about," Elizabeth Lamb thought, scuttling along, Mr. Vincentia keeping himself between her and the starboard side. He gestured her to go down the stairs first, swearing under his breath. He glanced into the saloon where Payson and Pietro were swiftly pulling the curtains over the portholes.

"Good, you've turned off all but one lamp," he said to them. "Now draw the curtains over those glass doors to the afterdeck. You two," to Amy and Templeton, who were sitting in astonishment beside their reading lamps that had been switched off, "do not go out on deck and keep away from the portholes. I will be back to explain." He turned toward the forward passage.

"Your stateroom and Miss Thornhill's are secure, *padrone*," Pietro called to him. "Miss Thornhill was not in hers, though."

"Good. Then you and I," he put a hand on Elizabeth Lamb's shoulder, "will attend to the staterooms below and get the passengers up here. You, Pietro, can go back to your galley."

"I'll take care of the rear cabins," Elizabeth Lamb told him, "but you ought to see Mr. Aaronson. Persis is with him but he's awfully sick. It's too long for me to explain, but they will."

Julia, Paul, and Chris, putting their cards away, were surprised when she knocked and informed them Mr. Vincentia wanted to be sure their portholes were covered and that they should stay away from them. "And he'd like you to come up to the saloon, but don't go out on deck. He said absolutely not."

"What's going on?" Paul asked. "I thought I heard an explosion."

"I felt us stop a little while ago," Julia added. "Are we at your grandmother's place? Monica went up to see."

Elizabeth Lamb ran to the deck above without answering. Monica

173

was there, calmly mixing a martini at the bar. "Oh, good!" Elizabeth Lamb said. "I was worried. I thought you might be on deck."

"I was." Monica raised a brow. "What's your trouble? There was nothing to see but a mooring and a light. Where are we? I couldn't find Vito so I came in here and Amy and Bob said to stay. The boy said someone was shooting at us? I can't wait to know the plot, but, meanwhile, this gin may destroy a few of my brain cells so I can't comprehend the horror of it." She laughed merrily.

Elizabeth Lamb went down again and shut Persis' curtains. She left a lamp on. "They should have locked the door when they went up to tea," she thought, "but I guess Viola is the least of our troubles now."

The least of their troubles was in her cabin, patting Cioccolato and talking to him. "Go away," she said. Elizabeth Lamb sighed. The portholes were covered as she had left them.

"Your grandfather wants you to stay inside and go up to the saloon," she told Viola. "Now, please don't argue. Just do it." As she left, Payson appeared. He was surprised to see her. "I thought you was in the saloon jest now, Elizabeth Lamb," he said, frowning. "Miss Vincentia, I cain't git what you wanted, but mebbe if you'd come up with me, Pietro might give me a few cakes for you, before he starts heavy cookin'."

Viola informed him coldly she had something to do first. Elizabeth Lamb went to check on Persis and Mr. Aaronson. "I hope Jim's with them," she thought. "I haven't seen him." Payson was behind her, as far as the dining room, and, to her question, said he hadn't seen Darrow anywhere.

Jake Aaronson seemed a good deal better. His face was less flushed and his voice not so hoarse. "I can see just a glimmer, too," he said. "Persis can go back with you; she's been shut up in here a long time. Maybe she'll get me more warm water, first?" Persis took the bowl with a competent air. "My back hurts like hell, though," he went on. "Perhaps I'll lie on my stomach for a while."

"Vito," he glanced at his friend who was slumped in an armchair, frowning at the unlighted cigarette he held, "told me what's been going on. I don't suppose you have any idea what could've happened to the communication panel, young lady?"

174

"Jake," Mr. Vincentia laughed slightly, "how could she? She's far too intelligent to have been playing around with a bucket of water in the pilot house and not to tell us if she'd seen anyone else doing it. And some member of the crew was always there, anyway; the Captain or Antonio."

"Bucket," Elizabeth Lamb thought. "There was a bucket on the upper deck, right in the middle, as if someone had thrown it down in a hurry. And Antonio did leave at least once, to get the Captain, at tea. And he was alone there, too, before the Captain sent Payson up. Maybe he put the auto-pilot on and went out for something. Maybe somebody could have got in and doused the panel. But why?"

She pursed her lips thoughtfully. "Could it have been the rain?" she asked. "Couldn't some have got in, if the door was open? Because I certainly don't see why anyone would have a reason to do it deliberately."

"No," Mr. Vincentia agreed, although he, too, became thoughtful.

"Do they know what's wrong with the engines yet, Mr. Vincentia?" she went on. "Maybe water got into the fuel tanks, too. That would stop an engine. Sometimes there's moisture in the gas line in our car in winter, and it freezes, and the car won't go."

"We have centrifuges that would throw the water out, if that had happened," he answered. "Though there is absolutely no way any water could get in. Except deliberately," he added heavily, "but I can see no reason for that. And, as I said, it wouldn't work in any case."

"Well," he rose, "I must go up to the saloon. You'll be all right alone, Jake, for a while? I'll have a tray sent down later.

"Elizabeth Lamb, did you find all the others and tell them to go up and to avoid the outer decks?"

"Oh, my goodness, I never did find Jim!" She ran ahead of Persis and Mr. Vincentia.

Jim was in the saloon along with all the other passengers except Viola. Monica was acting as bartender. "Where is Viola?" her grandfather asked. "I told her to come here and not to go out on deck; she was going to do something but she'll be up in a minute," Elizabeth Lamb answered.

A chorus of questions was directed at Mr. Vincentia. He held up his hand, smiling pleasantly, and picked up the glass of *Grappa* Monica had poured for him before he spoke.

"My friends," he began, seating himself on a bar stool, "we are in a slight predicament." He paused to turn questioningly to the Captain, who came in quietly to stand beside him. "No, sir," said Captain Knudsen, "there is no way. I have tried everything.

"Antonio and Carlo are washing up and then I told them to go to the cook and get something for themselves and Paulo to eat. Then they are to post themselves on deck, in case—" He shrugged and drank moderately from the glass of iced whiskey Monica provided.

"So," Mr. Vincentia said. He took in a deep breath. "We have an injured man on board; we have no capacity to move; we cannot call for help because our communication systems are out and" — he paused — "and I must tell you that we have arrived at a small island inhabited by what are certainly madmen who say they will shoot if we go ashore and, indeed, may attempt to do us some harm even if we do not."

He took a sip of *Grappa*. "Has anyone any suggestions?"

Everyone stared at him in bewildered silence. Except Persis: "Well," she said slowly, "it certainly *does* seem to be better to travel than to arrive!"

• CHAPTER 9 •

Under Siege

THERE WAS general laughter, and it somewhat dissipated the tension hanging over the company. Paul got up, stretching, and suggested he assist Monica. "Drinks all 'round, just one apiece, may help us to think a little clearer. There's got to be some way out of this."

Elizabeth Lamb had seated herself beside Christopher Grenville when Mr. Vincentia had begun to speak. "Have you seen Viola at all?" she asked him quietly. "She's supposed to be up here. Her grandfather had me tell her that."

"Oh," he answered, rising to join the others, "I w-wouldn't w-worry. I saw her p-peek in just a little while ago. It was w-when V.V. w-was talking."

Elizabeth Lamb went to their cabin. No one was there except Cioccolato, now stretched arrogantly on the bed, where Viola had been stroking him and whispering in his ear. He eyed her coldly. "She might have gone to the kitchen," she thought. "Payson said something about cakes to her."

As she cautiously opened the door to the galley, Antonio, cramming the last of a sandwich into his mouth, was leaving by the other door, to the passage that opened on to the port deck. He shook his head warningly, pointing to Pietro, chopping violently. Pietro glanced up and saw her. "Out!" he said firmly. "Now! And send that boy in here. He should be helping me."

She closed the door and ran through the vestibule, after Antonio. He was nowhere in sight. "Probably went to the upper deck, to keep watch," she said aloud. "But *where* is Viola? He might have seen her."

She hesitated, wondering if Viola had been so foolish as to go out on deck. "I'd better walk around and look," she thought. "And if I get shot — well, I won't think about that." She moved cautiously along the open deck, towards the stern. Somewhere above her there was a loud thud, accompanied by a sound of breaking glass. Someone ran heavily along the upper deck. At the same time there were two shots from the shore.

The *Chianti*'s port side was still turned away from the jetty. Thinking only, "If that spoiled brat is up there being shot at, somebody's got to get her down," she ran lightly to a ladder at the stern and cautiously mounted it. A thin beam from a flashlight was being directed at something lying in front of the wet bar on the top deck.

"Viola?" she whispered, crawling across the deck. Antonio swung the flashlight toward her and then quickly back again. "Be quiet," he said softly. "Didn't you hear those *villanos* shooting?" She crawled toward him, stifling an exclamation as something sharp pierced her knee. "What are you doing? Have you seen Viola? Oh—"

The flashlight revealed a curly red-blonde head jammed face-down sideways across the brass rail at the bottom of the bar. It moved a little to show Viola's darkly-clad form lying crumpled on the deck in a puddle of liquid dotted with shards of broken glass. "Get below," Antonio said, "and ask someone to help me. I don't dare move her alone. And then *stay* below!"

"Is she shot?" she asked, although she turned to obey his order. Before she could crawl to the spiral ladder down to the fantail lounge, Captain Knudsen's head appeared at the top of it. Someone came running along from the bow; Payson emerged from the semi-darkness.

"Here, Captain," Antonio hissed. "*Signorina* Vincentia is hurt. Her neck might be broken." Elizabeth Lamb retreated to one side of the bar to watch as the Captain, followed by Robert Templeton, both crouching, came over to it.

Templeton moved quickly in front of the Captain to kneel and gently run his hands over Viola's upper torso, feeling the back of her neck, then the front and then her shoulders. He pressed lightly along her backbone, lifting up her dark sweater. "I was a medic in 'Nam," he said as he worked. "Didn't mean to be pushy, Captain, but from the way her neck is turned, it could have been broken. I don't think it is, but her right shoulder and arm sure as hell are, I'd say. I could be wrong, but I think we'd better carry her below while she's still out. The pain will be terrible when she comes to."

"You *could* be wrong, you say." Knudsen was terse. "Suppose you are, and we move her and kill her; sever her spinal cord?"

"We can't leave her here. I'll turn her over, and you hold her head while I do. Then keep supporting it while I put my hands under her armpits and the boy lifts her by the knees. Help me move her right arm so her body supports it. Getting her down that ladder will be tricky, but I've moved people under worse conditions.

"But could your man get a deck light on back here? It's worth risking it, for a few minutes."

Paul's head showed above the staircase. "What the hell is going on? V.V. wants to know. Did you find out what that noise was? And the shots?"

"Get out of the way, you," the Captain ordered. "We're coming down." Paul disappeared.

A light came on beside the bar. The three moved cautiously across the deck with their burden. Elizabeth Lamb painfully got up to follow. Her knee hurt badly; when she touched it her hand became stickily wet. "Don't tell me I'm shot!" she said aloud. The Captain, still half above deck as he guided Viola's head while Robert and Payson eased her body down the spiral ladder, turned.

"Dammit!" he said hoarsely. "What do you think you're doing? Get below! And bring whatever that is beside you."

She had noticed nothing before, in the dark, but there was something large and white and soft beside the bar. "It's my laundry bag," she said. "How in the world—?" As she picked it up, a large piece of green glass with the remnant of a Mumm's *Cordon Rouge* label, unmistakable even though the remnant was small and the light dim, fell off it. The bag was heavy; she grasped it and pulled it along behind her as she slowly followed them down the staircase. She sat for a moment on the bottom stair and pulled aside the torn leg of her jeans to look at her knee.

There was a wide gash that was still oozing blood. A few very small fragments of green glass were wedged in the cut. She rummaged in her pockets for a handkerchief or a tissue, found none, and took a fold of the bag to try to ease the glass out. Unable to dislodge the pieces, she got up and hobbled after the others.

Paul had held the saloon door open for them; after she went in he closed it and pulled the curtains across again. Breathing hard, the men had stopped just inside the saloon to adjust their hold on Viola. The people in the room turned and rose, their faces white in the lamp's glow.

Mr. Vincentia ran over. "What—" he said, "what — is she dead?" He put his hand to his chest and bent forward breathing in shallow gasps. "Take her to my cabin at once—" he bent still further and sagged to the floor.

Monica screamed and ran to kneel beside him. "He's had an attack; he had one like this once before; I saw it," she said, running all her words together. "Chris, help me get him to his bed. The girl, you must" — she looked up at the Captain, "take to *her* cabin. What is the matter with her—" she turned again to Vincentia.

Templeton was still in charge. "Just let's keep going," he said. "We've come this far, we can certainly make it down to the lower deck.

"You," to Chris and Jim, "do as Monica says. She probably knows what to do. I'll be up in a minute." He and his helpers started across the saloon. Julia, looking dazed, followed, murmuring little piteous cries. Paul, equally dazed, went behind her.

"What," Amy shrieked, "has happened to you, Elizabeth Lamb? This place is becoming a casualty ward! You've got blood all down your jeans, child. What the hell is going on?" She took Elizabeth Lamb's arm as Persis picked up the bag. "Here," Amy said, "we'll go down and get those pants off you and assess the damage." They went down the stairs behind Julia, still murmuring, and Paul, still in a shocked silence. He went into his cabin and firmly shut the door.

"Scream if you want to," Amy said a few minutes later as she probed with an eyebrow tweezer at Elizabeth Lamb's knee. Elizabeth Lamb complied, once or twice, less because of pain than of frustration at being pinned by Amy to Persis' bed, with Persis holding her hand in damp sympathy and wincing mightily at each thrust of the instrument, while who-knew-what was going on with Viola and her grandfather.

"There!" Amy finally said. "I don't have any iodine or rubbing alcohol so let's just pour a little brandy on the cut." This time Elizabeth Lamb screamed ardently. "At least there were Band-Aids in the bathroom," Amy went on. "I'll put a few of the biggest on this. Try not to bend your knee when you walk. I wonder if Persis could get into your cabin for some clean pants?"

Persis soon returned with them and with the information that Payson had brought sheets and they were being torn in strips so Viola could be tied to the bed. "Because she's waking up, a little, and she'll try to move and she could hurt herself."

"She has enough people tending her," Amy decided, "whatever's the matter with her, so we'll just go back to the lounge. I'm worried about V.V. *And* I'm worried about getting off the *Chianti* in one piece. Talk about a ship of fools; this is a ship of fatalities!"

Elizabeth Lamb lingered by Viola's closed door. Everyone in the cabin except Viola seemed to be talking. Templeton came out and started upstairs. "What happened to Viola?" she asked, limping after him. "Was she shot someplace?"

"No," he answered quietly, "but she had a bad fall. It knocked her out, but she's coming to and I don't think there's a concussion. Her arm is broken and her shoulder, if not broken, is at least dislocated. But the worst thing is, her throat was badly bruised by falling on that railing and her larynx is crushed, I think. There's a long narrow mark across her throat and she's not able to talk, so that's what must've happened. She's crying, tears running down her face, poor kid, but she's not making a sound. Her stepmother is giving her aspirin but, God, we've got to get her to a hospital."

He pushed open the door to the passage that led to the master stateroom. "You'd better not come in here; go into the saloon with the others."

"He sounds different, more reasonable and not so — what's the word? — heavy, stagy?" she thought. Antonio ran in from the deck. "The Captain?" he asked excitedly.

"Here," said Knudsen, who was coming up the stairs, Payson behind him. "What now?"

"Captain, the little motorboat has been lowered! I just noticed it. Something seemed wrong up topside so I flashed a light for a second on the davits and the boat was gone."

"What! How the hell could those maniacs ashore have stolen it? I sent you and Carlo to watch the decks!"

"No, no; it's beside us, still secured to the ropes. Carlo took food to Paulo and then he came up to be with me and by that time you had got the *signorina* so he went back to take a jar to Paulo because he can't get to the head but he came back up — Captain, no one *could* have got aboard; no one could have touched that boat—" he stopped, looking at Payson. The Captain turned quickly and angrily regarded him.

"Pietro was looking for you, a long time ago," Antonio said slowly to Payson. "And you came astern on the top deck when the *signorina* was hurt. What were you doing up there, and coming from where the boat was slung? What's your game, boy?"

The Captain took Payson roughly by the arm. "You'd better tell us."

Payson's face was white and his eyes tearful. "Somebody had t' git help," he said. "I seen this mornin' how to lower the boat. I bin over ever' part of this bay. I could git over to Mount Desert. I only wanted—" he gulped and began to weep.

"There's no need to take on so," the Captain said, less angrily. "Stop that blubbering. But your lowering the boat may have provoked them to shoot and that's probably what made Miss Vincentia fall. She's badly hurt, and if you—"

"No, I never!" Payson sobbed. "I never did nuthin' to cause her t' git hurt. They was jest shootin', mebbe because they seen her up there; mebbe jest because they're plain crazy. But that's what give me the idea: when they shot, I thought I'd try to git the boat down, 'cause the sooner somebody gits here to help us, the better."

"That doesn't quite explain why you were up there in the first place," the Captain said slowly, "but—"

Robert Templeton had come quickly from the passage to Vincentia's stateroom. "He's in a bad way, Captain," he said. "Miss Thornhill and Grenville have given him his stuff and he's sitting up, but he shouldn't move. Who could go for help, and how? I'm a good swimmer, but I don't know what the hell to swim to."

"Just what we were talking about," Knudsen said. "A motorboat is lowered, on the port side. This boy knows how to run it and he has good night vision and he's familiar with this area. But I need someone to go with him; he's only a boy. You?"

"Let's go!" said Templeton. "Just wait till I grab a sweater and a slicker. And I've got a flashlight with a compass on it."

"Be quick, before we swing around and they see the boat. They're apt to shoot at it, thinking we're coming ashore. We'll put a ladder over, and you and Payson be damned quiet going down it. Antonio will hand oars down to you; use them until you're out of gunshot range and then go like hell."

"Payson needs warm clothes, too," Elizabeth Lamb told him.

"You again," said the Captain. "But you're right; Antonio, see to it. Get another flashlight and flares for them, and you, girl, go into the lounge and stay there. They don't need a *bon voyage* party."

"Good luck Payson," she whispered, taking his arm. "Payson, stop crying. Don't feel so bad; it's all right. You'll make it and you'll bring help for Viola and Mr. Vincentia and Paulo and you'll be a hero!"

Payson rubbed a hand across his face. "It ain't all right," he said finally. "It's all ruint. I never thought—" He shut his eyes and stood, swaying a little.

"Come on. Right now, fast and quietly," the Captain ordered, pushing a dark quilted nylon jacket at Payson. "I'll stay here; only you and Antonio and Mr. Templeton go out. The fewer on deck, the better. And good luck."

Elizabeth Lamb sat quietly in the lounge. Amy was holding Persis to her, patting her soothingly. Paul came in and slumped into a chair. Jim and Chris arrived just after him. "I went to tell V.V.

that Viola's all right," Paul said somberly. "I made her sound better than she is, I guess, though I haven't seen her."

"Mr. Vincentia's quiet now and breathing better," Jim informed them. "Chris and I thought we might be in the way and Monica said she'll stay and talk to him. He's determined to go down and see his granddaughter but Monica's persuading him it wouldn't do her any good and might be very bad for him. Where'd Templeton go?"

As Knudsen explained, Antonio looked in. "They're gone," he said. "They were out of sight when I heard the motor start and it was so faint, through the fog, that I'm sure they didn't hear it on shore. I'll go back topside now, sir. Carlo is there, too."

"Why would those men on shore care, if they heard the motor?" Elizabeth Lamb asked. "They want us to go away."

"They might think we've abandoned ship and try to board," the Captain said. "They'd probably figure they could find useful things to carry off, like petrol and — petrol! Antonio!" he shouted after the sailor. "Did you give them extra petrol? The tank on that boat doesn't hold much!"

"Captain, oh," Antonio was red and stammering, "oh, I didn't! I never thought of it! I was trying to get them and the oars down the ladder so fast — *Dio,* I never thought!"

The Captain sighed. "My fault. Get on deck." He rose wearily. "I'd better tell the owner we've made an attempt to get help. But if they run out of gas, God knows when they'll reach shore. If they're drifting, they won't be seen till daylight, either."

"Let's turn on the television," Elizabeth Lamb said, to break the gloomy silence that followed the Captain's departure. "Or will we be able to get enough electricity for it, since the engines aren't going?"

"There's a generator aboard," Paul said, going over to the set. "How do you think yachts have lights, and power to cook and so on when they're anchored? Really, for a young person who's supposed to be so knowledgeable, sometimes you're extremely ignorant!"

Elizabeth Lamb flushed with anger, but, realizing he was worried and upset, made no reply. "I thought we could have a power shortage, though," she murmured to herself. "I thought somebody said we

184

might." She sat quietly, looking at the television.

"I'm hungry," Persis announced, as the blank screen materialized into a picture of a large, powerful woman showing large, powerful teeth as she powerfully beat at a large bowl of batter. "Elizabeth Lamb, let's go see if the cook would like some help."

Elizabeth Lamb thought it doubtful, but she was hungry too, and even rebuff from Pietro was preferable to the depression of the dimly lit saloon with its silent people and its hyperactive television personality. She limped after Persis.

Pietro did not rebuff them. "Yes, set the tables for me. I don't know how many will be eating; you find out. I'm about to put a *frittata* in to bake and you can arrange this *prosciutto* and melon on two platters and put them on the tables for the first course."

He propped open the galley door so Elizabeth Lamb could carry out plates and glasses from a small pantry just inside it. Curious about his domain, she opened a door next to the pantry and found behind it a small lavatory. "This boat is so luxurious," she thought. "A special lavatory for the cook and his helper and, at home, Payson and his family only have an outhouse, and wash in the kitchen sink."

Reminded of Payson, and his distress, she felt sad as she put the crystal circles in the center of each table and filled them with Vincentia chocolates. "I'm like the band playing as the *Titanic* went down, with these chocolates," she thought. When she had placed the candelabra inside the circles, she went out to Pietro:

"I guess we should have candles, because they're cheerful, but the ones in the holders are burnt almost down. I looked for new ones but there are only some sad-looking grey ones in the sideboard. Where're the others?"

"I don't have time to go to the storeroom. Use the grey. And put these bottles of wine on the tables, to go with the ham. They'll stay cold enough. You can call the guests soon; I'll tell you when."

"But Payson brought a whole big bag of candles in here—"

"Out," he said firmly. "Take the wine. That boy is *folle* — *pazzo*, I think. God knows where he put them."

Chris was surveying the tables in the dining room. He took the bottles from her and opened them. "Don't set a place for me," he said. "I'm not hungry. I'm on the way to V.V.'s room to stay with him so Monica can have a break."

Elizabeth Lamb went to the saloon to ask Paul, somewhat stiffly, if Julia were going to eat. He was back in his usual polite mood; he smiled charmingly at her and offered to go find out. "Probably not," he said, brushing back his mustache, "unless Viola is asleep. She's very worried."

"We'll go down." Monica appeared, along with Chris. "Look, I brought my sleeping pills. Two will put Viola out till morning, by which time, Knudsen says, the Coast Guard, bringing a doctor, should be here. He wants to stay with V.V. a while, so Chris says he'll take over for Julia so she can have dinner.

"Would you make me a g-and-t, Paul? Be up in a minute." She and Chris went to the stairs. "Oh, Elizabeth Lamb," she called, "tell Pietro we'll wait on ourselves so he can take a tray to V.V. and the Captain. Just some soup for V.V., but Knudsen's going to be up all night, so he needs everything."

"A tray!" Persis stopped her artistic arrangement of slices of *prosciutto* and cantaloupe wedges. "Mr. Vincentia said he'd send Mr. Aaronson down a tray; Elizabeth Lamb, we forgot all about him!" She ran to the forward stairs. Elizabeth Lamb gave Monica's message to Pietro, who nodded approvingly, and then continued placing the silverware, counting people on her fingers. She came up with eight diners, "if Mr. Aaronson is well enough to eat up here."

Evidently he was. As Persis led him, now wearing a loose silk shirt, proudly in to the dining room, he announced that he was ready not only for some grub, but for a drink or two beforehand. "I can't see but a bit, just enough so that I can go down and take a look at Viola after dinner. Then I can give Vito my semi-professional opinion that she's on the mend and that he's to stay put. Persis says help's been sent for, too. She's filled me in on all I've been missing, snoozing away."

Persis guided him to the bar. He requested a Pimms #1 from Paul, who frowned but complied. "I can't see why you're so chipper, Jake," he said. "We're hardly out of the woods yet. If the Coast Guard doesn't get here soon, V.V. might get worse, and as for poor little Viola—" He turned his back and, facing the mirror, bent his head and rubbed his eyes with both hands.

"There's also Paulo," Persis reminded him. "We should worry about him, too. Could I have a ginger ale, Mr. Cooper?"

"Job's Comforter, that's what you are," Jake told her. "Come over, Mrs. D., if you're up here among the non-casualties, and join us.

"Monica, is that you? Thought I heard your elfin step. Now, with a lovely lady on each side, I'm the piece of tough old ham between two slices of delicate bread. Julia, dear, have a nip of something. Buck you up."

By the time everyone had a drink or two Elizabeth Lamb had lit the candles and called them to dinner. Persis sat beside Jake, and Monica and Amy joined them. At the other table Elizabeth Lamb served the first course to Julia and Paul and Jim. As the guests ate silently, drinking rather more than eating, Elizabeth Lamb suddenly thought of her laundry bag, now in Amy's and Persis' room: "I've *got* to see what's in it. How could it have got to the top deck? Viola must have taken it, but why?"

She and Persis removed the plates while Jim and Paul went to the sideboard for a large baked omelette, loaves of bread, and bowls of butter. "I'll get some chianti from the bar," Monica offered. "We haven't had it once and it goes so well with a rustic *frittata* like this. I love peasant food; Vito always said I'm a *contadino* at heart."

"I'm one by birth," Jim assured her. Everyone laughed. Wine and food were having their usual effect, Elizabeth Lamb thought. Pietro came in with a tray and got a large helping of the *frittata*, bread and butter, and a glass of the chianti. "And you," to Persis, "put some of the ham and melon on a plate for the Captain."

"What's Mr. Vincentia having?" Persis asked. Pietro told her tersely not to worry; he had made the *padrone* one of his favorite soups. "And take him a small glass of wine," Jake suggested. "He may not drink it but it will have a psychological effect."

Dessert was halved pears poached in rum, their centers filled with a cream tasting of vanilla and lemon. Julia moodily pushed her portion about her plate, as did Paul. "I've always loved these," she said, "though I do *not* see how Pietro can make something so delicious with Vito and Viola so badly off. I just can't eat them."

Pietro had been about to leave the dining room. He turned, and with more than a touch of insolence said, "Because the *padrone* pays me well to cook for his guests. And I, for one, *signora,* cannot take his money without giving something in return."

Julia turned an angry red. So did Paul. They excused themselves and went to the bar, where Pietro had placed espresso. They talked softly, heads together.

"Well, well," Jake said, "that was a marvelous dinner, Pietro. Now, let's go down and take a dekko at Viola. No, no; you have your coffee, Monica. The girls can guide me."

Except for a light by a chair in which Grenville sat writing in his notebook, Viola's cabin was dark. Cioccolato slept in his basket on a table by the bed and Viola looked half-asleep. "Now, dear, you'll be fine," Jake said. "I just want to look at you. Grenville, would you put on another light?"

Viola's eyes became terrified, her mouth tremulous. She was covered to the chin with a blanket on the sides of which the strips of sheeting holding her torso and right arm to the bed could be seen. Jake turned the blanket down and, peering closely at her, gently touched her throat and shoulder. "I don't think she should have these pillows," he said. "I'd like her head flat."

He carefully removed them and handed them to Elizabeth Lamb. "Put them in Persis' cabin," he directed. "You'll probably be sleeping there tonight." Elizabeth Lamb took them and, in the cabin, limped over to the laundry bag at once. She untied the cords, emptied out the contents on a bed and examined each article.

Evidently Viola had appropriated her bag and packed it with her own things: a nightdress, a Liberty dressing gown of rose-printed Viyella, a pair of pink satin scuffs, underwear, two pairs of jeans and two sweaters, sneakers, white kid low-heeled pumps, her confirmation dress, a pair of shorts and two shirts. In amongst the clothes was another bottle of Mumm's *Cordon Rouge* and, Elizabeth Lamb saw with rage, her and Persis' ring boxes crammed full of her *dragees.*

An oiled-silk cosmetic case held lipsticks, a powder compact, a comb and brush, shampoo and hair conditioner, a wallet with about fifty dollars in bills and a stiff white manila envelope. In this was a birth certificate that stated Viola Portia Vincentia had been born in Boston, Massachusetts on February 21, 1957, to Danilo Vittorio Vincentia and Portia Agnes Vincentia (*née* Thornhill), British citizens.

"Well," Elizabeth Lamb said aloud, "it looks as if she were planning a trip — out of the country, maybe, or else why the birth certificate? And with *my* laundry bag and *my dragees!*" As she repacked the bag and put it in Persis' closet, she thought: "But why was she hiding it all behind the wet bar? Because it sure looks as if that's why she was up there. And she was going to Canada anyway — do you need a birth certificate to get into Canada? The whole thing is just crazy, but that senseless, spoiled girl would just do anything she felt like doing, reasonable or not."

Mr. Aaronson was stroking Viola's forehead. "You'll do, dear," he said. "The cabin boy and Mr. Templeton have gone to get help. A doctor will be here soon. And you mustn't try to move; just try to sleep, hard as it is." He turned to Chris: "What have they given her?"

Chris' speech was slow but calm, with no stutter. Elizabeth Lamb remembered she hadn't heard him stutter since all the calamities began. "I hope he's cured," she thought.

"Julia gave her aspirin and Monica brought down sleeping pills, but we didn't know if she should have them," Chris said. Jake pondered. "Well, she's only had a few aspirin," he said, "and Vito told me they gave all the morphine tablets the Captain had to Paulo. I don't think Monica's stuff would hurt her, on top of aspirin, but why don't you read me what's on the label?"

As Chris did, Amy came in. Monica was with her, carrying a large flat cake pan. "What's that for?" Persis asked.

"Well, really, dear, what would you think? We've got a girl here who's tied down so she can't hurt herself and that means she can't go to the bathroom, doesn't it? You'd think that pea-brained Julia would have thought of that." She laughed. "Freudian slip, hey?

"Now, suppose you all scoot and Mrs. Danniver and I will do what we can. Get me a pair of her pajama bottoms, if you can find some, Amy, for after we ease her jeans off. And I'll stay, Chris. Wouldn't you like something to eat, by now?"

Chris admitted he was hungry. Mr. Aaronson directed Monica

to give Viola two sleeping tablets and then Persis and Elizabeth Lamb led him up to the lounge, in the wake of Chris. The Captain was there, issuing information and directions.

"Mr. Vincentia is napping," he said. "I'd like someone to volunteer to stay in his cabin tonight. There are extra blankets and it is possible to rest, though not, I'd say, to sleep very well, on the settee there. You, Mr. Grenville? Good.

"I'm going to be on the bridge. Maybe I can do something with the radiotelephone when it's dried out some. Carlo has an hour off to rest, then he'll relieve Antonio on deck for an hour. After that they'll both be on watch, since I believe that if those on shore try anything, it won't be till midnight and by that time three of us will be up there. I have Mr. Vincentia's pistol although I hope I won't need it.

"Now, I'd like one of you men to be here in the saloon all night where we can get him quickly if we have any trouble." A hand was raised. "Thanks, Mr. Darrow. The rest of you can stay in your cabins, since Pietro has agreed to watch Paulo." He went out briskly.

Amy arrived. "I'm ready for some brandy. Monica will be up soon. She wants to know if you'll stay with Viola tonight, Jake." Jake nodded.

"Can't sleep anyway, so I'll be glad to oblige. I'll put some blankets on the floor and stretch out on my stomach. My back won't take much more of my sitting up."

"That's good of you," Amy said. "Monica's played out. Let's hope we have a peaceful night and that they bring somebody back soon — what in the world are you doing?"

Carlo had appeared with a watering can. "Ah, *signora,* the *padrone* always say his *fiore* must be wet down each day and I didn't get a chance before." He went out to the plants on the afterdeck, cautiously opening the glass doors by which Julia and Paul had been sitting quietly with their coffee, talking softly. He quickly slid through, closing the doors after him.

There was an exclamation from Julia. She stood up, dashing the contents of her cup in Paul's face. "I don't believe you!" she cried. "Liar! What can you mean by saying such a thing? You're out of your mind!"

190

Paul glanced at the others. He wiped the coffee from his face with a handkerchief and slowly, staring at Julia appealingly, put it back in his pocket. "We don't need to talk about it now, my dear," he said with dignity. "Not here. Too many — please be calm."

"Be calm!" Julia laughed loudly. "You tell me you and Viola were planning to marry in Canada and you tell me to be calm! You've gone completely bonkers! She's a child. V.V. would never permit it."

"I agree," Paul said wryly. "If he knew. And now that everyone has heard, he will. I only told you out of consideration for you, so that you would be prepared. We planned how it was to be done. Julia — I love her. She loves me. You don't, my dear, and I doubt you ever did. And she needs me; she needs a man who is older and who can care for her. She's different with me, more responsive, more reasonable, more mature."

"My God," Julia said dully. "To think that all these years, behind my back — and every time we've visited—" She sat down heavily, looking at the company, standing or sitting frozen, in shocked silence. A spasm of pain passed over her face. She began to weep like a child, noisily, tears running down her face. She pressed her hands tightly together, rubbing the palms back and forth in an agony of frustrated rage.

She got up unsteadily. "Well, it won't work. I'll tell V.V. as soon as he's better, and if he doesn't forbid it — well, *I'll* just see it *doesn't* happen. Just be warned. I'll do what I have to. And don't you ever, ever come within a foot of me again!" She swept out and ran down the stairs to her cabin.

Still no one spoke. Everyone looked at Paul. "But it can't be," Elizabeth Lamb thought. "And yet — Mr. Aaronson said he was different, as if maybe he was in love, even. But Viola and — Paul? I don't believe it."

"Well," Amy's voice compensated for its uneasiness by its volume, "how about a touch of whisky for everyone? Elizabeth Lamb, if the cook's left the kitchen, perhaps you might dare to go in and get some milk for you and Persis? It will make you sleep. And then we had better turn in."

Paul stood up and went to the bar. He poured brandy and held

191

it, thoughtfully looking around at the faces which had turned instantly to him.

"Mrs. Danniver," he spoke hesitantly, "I think someone should stay with Julia tonight. Would you? I'll sleep up here, or try to. If *you* don't mind?" He turned courteously to Jim.

"I really feel the children should have me with them," Amy said coldly. "I'm afraid not."

Paul looked slowly around again. "Then what about Elizabeth Lamb? I'm frankly afraid to leave Julia alone. She might try to hurt — herself."

"Or Viola, maybe?" Persis said helpfully. Elizabeth Lamb kicked her.

Paul was embarrassed. "Well," he said, "anything is possible. I can't believe she would, but—" He turned to Elizabeth Lamb. "I have both cabin keys," he told her. "The cabin has what I think they call a dead lock; it was used by Viola's mother and she wanted it that way. Sometimes," he sighed, "she was irrational, unreasonable. If you locked the door from inside and kept both keys on this chain around your neck, it could only be opened from either side with a key, and then we'd be sure—" He broke off, even more embarrassed.

"You'd be sure Mrs. Vincentia didn't get out," Amy finished for him. "But, really, I don't think a child should be put in any danger — have so much responsibility, I mean. What about Monica?"

"Julia doesn't like her, to be frank," Paul answered. "Really, there'd be no danger. I rather think Julia will have taken something to calm herself; she'll probably just sleep till morning, when help should come."

"And *you'll* have to face Mr. Vincentia, probably," Elizabeth Lamb thought. Aloud she said, "I can do it. My grandmother always says not to refuse new experiences. I'm not afraid of Mrs. Vincentia."

While arguments broke out, some people agreeing with Paul, some disputing his suggestion, Carlo, who had been standing stiffly for some time just inside the door to the fantail lounge, passed unnoticed through the saloon and dining room and entered the passage to Monica's and Vincentia's cabins. He reappeared a few minutes later and lightly touched Mrs. Danniver's arm.

"Ah, *signora,*" he said quietly, "the *padrone* wishes to see you and the little blonde *signorina.*" He beckoned Elizabeth Lamb to follow them.

Mr. Vincentia was lying on his bed, his head and shoulders raised by several pillows. His face was pale above the dark red silk dressing gown he wore, but his voice was strong and steady. "Carlo has told me," he said. "He knows I am to hear at once of everything that concerns me. You have heard what those two said. Do you believe it? I ask you because I know you both — I say 'both' even though Elizabeth Lamb is very young — possess a great deal of insight."

"Vito, it was very convincing," Amy said slowly. "But there is no reason for you to get upset—" He motioned her to silence. "And you, *caro?*"

"I don't know, Mr. Vincentia. *Some* things make me believe it, some things I heard, some things that Viola packed — but it doesn't matter, does it? You can stop it."

"But I cannot rest until I *know,*" he said fiercely. "I have always been like that: I must *know* of deception. If this is some trick—. I want you both to go to Viola and ask *her.* And now."

"But, Vito, she can't speak," Amy began. "She shouldn't even nod her—"

"I know that. And I know she will soon be asleep. But if you ask her if she planned to marry; if you ask her that, assuring her that I am not angry; if you hand her this" — he picked up the gold pen and a pad of paper from the table in front of the bed — "and ask her, for me, just to make a mark if the answer is 'yes,' then I can rest. And whether it is 'yes' or 'no,' I will know what to do," he ended grimly.

"Vito, her arm is broken—"

"Her right arm. But she is left-handed."

"But, Vito, I don't think Elizabeth Lamb and I should judge—"

Again he interrupted: "Amy, *I* will be the judge. *Caro,* you are used to noticing things; that shows in your work. You could not write if little *sottile* things in people's actions and looks escaped you. I can see you believe what Paul said, but I would like you to watch Viola when you ask her, so that you can form an opinion even if she will not write.

"And this little one notices everything. She has seen the truth in things that have puzzled her elders. But I am asking neither of you to judge, only to get an answer from Viola. If I could move, I would go down, but the pain in my chest and arm comes back when I try to stand. Uncertainty will only make me worse; I must *know*. Do this for me, my friend. Do as I ask. You, Elizabeth Lamb, please go with her. Carlo, stay here."

Doubtfully Amy took the paper and pen and left, Elizabeth Lamb close behind. They started in silence down the aft stairs. Paul looked up from his glass, frowned and followed. He remained in the hall, half behind the fern by the open door of Viola's cabin, as they entered to stand quietly by the bed.

"Is she asleep?" Amy asked Monica, who lounged, yawning, in a chair across the room. "Not quite," Monica answered, "but she will be very soon. And so will I; the pills I took are beginning to work on me. Jake coming down?"

"Yes," Elizabeth Lamb answered absently. "In a minute or so." She gently touched Viola's cheek. The beautiful violet eyes opened, calmer now.

"Viola," Amy cleared her throat, "Viola, dear, your grandfather wants us to ask you something. He is not able — that is, he is busy upstairs. He wants us to tell you first that he loves you and is not angry, but he must know something. He must know if it is true that you planned to get married when you got off the boat?"

Viola's eyes, frightened now, opened wider. "Viola," Amy said more loudly, "he is *not* angry, neither at you or, or your friend. He just wants to know so he can — so he can help. He understands. Please just take this pen and make a mark if it is true. Would you do that?"

Viola's eyes went to Paul, who had moved away from the fern and now stood tensely directly under the light in the hallway. She smiled, a little triumphant smile. Her left hand took the pen Amy offered and she made a scrawled dash on the pad of paper Amy held for her. Then she drew a heart under it and smiled again. In the heart she slowly printed a capital P. She dropped the pen on the bed and closed her eyes.

"Take this back to V.V.," Amy told Elizabeth Lamb. "Monica,

you'd better get to bed. I'll stay here till Jake comes.

"Elizabeth Lamb, you and Persis come down with Mr. Aaronson and then I think Persis had better go to bed, too. And maybe you should ask Mr. Vincentia what he thinks about Paul's asking you to stay with Julia."

Paul had gone ahead of her back to the saloon. She passed Carlo on the stairs coming down with his watering can. Chris was with Mr. Vincentia, putting blankets and a pillow on the settee in the stateroom. She silently handed over the pad. Mr. Vincentia sighed and sadly shook his head.

"Mr. Cooper wants me to stay in Mrs. Vincentia's cabin tonight," she said. "He wants me to lock the door and keep the key. I guess you know what he's thinking."

"Why not Monica?" he asked. "Julia is, of course, distraught and so she might be better off with an adult to talk with. She would not hurt you, *caro,* nor," he sounded bitter, "is she likely to do any harm to herself. And I really doubt she would harm Viola, angry as she must be. But I think Monica would be more suitable."

"Oh, I really don't mind. Monica took her pills and is awfully sleepy. I don't think she'd be much good talking to Mrs. Vincentia. And *she* probably took something, too, Mr. Cooper says. She'll just sleep, he thinks, and besides, there's a bed for me there. In Mrs. Danniver's cabin, I'd have to sleep with Persis. And Persis kicks terribly *and* talks in her sleep," she finished gloomily.

He smiled. "But you could have Monica's stateroom — oh, very well. I suppose Monica would balk at being confined with Julia, asleep or awake. I don't see any need for locking poor Julia up, but I'm really too tired to dispute that *villano's* — Mr. Cooper's — thinking. And before I sleep, I've got some thinking to do.

"Good night, my dear. I will remember your kindness and concern. By morning, some of our troubles should be over."

"Or we'll have new ones," Elizabeth Lamb thought, proceeding slowly to get Persis and Mr. Aaronson. "And I hope that one of them isn't that I get blood poisoning; gosh, it hurts worse." Jim was lying on a sofa in the saloon lounge, smoking and gazing at the ceiling. He wished them a "good night. And let's hope it's good, good *and* quiet."

"I'll go down with you," Paul said. "Just to knock and tell Julia that — oh, that V.V. wants you to sleep there. I gather you got his approval."

As Elizabeth Lamb and Persis guided Jake out, Monica left the bar, carrying a glass of mineral water and bidding them a peaceful night. "She's left her sleeping pills on the bar," Elizabeth Lamb observed. "Should I take them to her? She might want them later."

"No need," Jake decided. "She doesn't need any more tonight. And I noticed them, too; 'blimey, my eyes are getting better!" He settled himself in the chair Monica had been using, after Persis put two soft towels down the back. "There should be a couple of blankets on the wardrobe shelf. Just put them over in the corner, would you?" he directed Persis. "My back isn't coming along as fast as my eyes. It's mighty sore and I may have to lie on my stomach for a while."

Viola was sleeping peacefully. Persis gently patted her hand before she went to her cabin. Elizabeth Lamb brushed her teeth, found a pair of pajamas, wished Mr. Aaronson a pleasant night and went out to where Paul was impatiently standing by Julia's door. "Here, Elizabeth Lamb," said Amy, coming over with a handkerchief just as Paul, tensing his mouth, had raised his hand to knock, "tie this over the Band-Aids on your knee so they don't slip off."

She tucked the handkerchief in the breast pocket of her pajamas as Paul, now angry as well as apprehensive, finally knocked firmly on the door. "Julia," he said loudly, "Elizabeth Lamb is staying with you tonight. V.V. wants it that way." He quickly ran up the stairs.

Elizabeth Lamb slowly opened the door. Julia, wearing a tan wool robe, was lying on her bed. In the light from the bedside lamp, her face was red and her eyes closed. She opened them and raised her head. "Hello, Elizabeth Lamb. I really don't need anyone but I suppose you haven't a place to sleep. At least they didn't send that child with measles to guard me. That bed is all turned down."

Elizabeth Lamb smiled and nodded politely, unsure of what to say. She lost no time in changing into the pajamas, wincing as she slid the leg of her jeans down over the injured knee. "I guess I'd better make sure the door is shut," she said casually. She pulled out

196

the long key chain from under her pajama top and locked the door. She slid the chain and the two keys back before she turned. Julia, eyes closed again, appeared not to have noticed. "Turn out the light, would you?" she said.

Elizabeth Lamb lay tensely in the dark. Julia began to sob quietly after a while, then she sighed deeply and there was silence except for her heavy, even breathing. Elizabeth Lamb went to sleep.

She woke almost at once, it seemed to her. She sat up and looked around. The portholes were light through the curtains. "It's morning!" she said aloud. She went to a porthole, her knee still hurting but not as badly. A large boat was approaching the *Chianti*. It bore the Coast Guard insignia.

"Mrs. Vincentia," she said, "the Coast Guard's come!" Julia made no response. Elizabeth Lamb pulled the blanket gently up to her shoulders and unlocked the cabin door. She crossed the hall to stand by the partially-open door of Viola's cabin. "Mr. Aaronson," she whispered, "they've come."

There was no answer except the sound of the shower from the bathroom. She went in and opened the porthole curtain before she crossed, smiling, to the bed.

Viola still lay quietly as she had the night before, tied as she was, but her head was turned slightly to one side. Her ear showed rosily pink above the blanket. Her cheek showed a slight pinkish-purple mottling, instead of its previous pallor, and her hair was plastered damply to her forehead.

Elizabeth Lamb touched her cheek. It was cool, although the cabin was very warm and she lay under a blanket. "Viola?" she said uncertainly. "Viola? Wake up, Viola! Are you all right?" She picked up the limp wrist. She could feel no pulse. She put her ear gently on Viola's chest, pushing the blanket down. She could hear nothing. "Oh, no!" she cried. She ran to the bathroom door, which was open a wide crack.

"Mr. Aaronson!" she screamed. "Are you in there?" The water was turned off. "Well, of course I am," he called. "Did you think it was a dolphin? You're up bright and early. Or maybe it isn't so early; I've been running this blessed water on my poor back for a half hour, at least. What time *is* it?"

197

"Mr. Aaronson, come out! Something's happened to Viola!" She went slowly back to the bed. She roughly patted Viola's cheek. There was no response. "Oh, no, no!" she said dully. She brushed the lank hair back from Viola's forehead. There was a smudge of dirt under the hair; she took the handkerchief from her pajama pocket and gently wiped it away. She felt suddenly dizzy and sank to the floor beside the bed.

Mr. Aaronson had quickly dried off and wrapped a large bath towel around him. "What's the matter, Elizabeth Lamb?" he asked, blinking but walking fairly quickly and steadily toward her. "What is it?"

"Can't you see? Look at Viola!"

He leaned over the still form on the bed, squinting. He, too, felt for a pulse. He bent his head to her chest and then put his hand on her forehead. Mouth open in bewilderment, he turned slowly to Elizabeth Lamb. "My God," he said weakly. "She's dead. She's dead."

• CHAPTER 10 •

J. Aaronson Quotes A. Hitler

JAKE SAT DOWN heavily in the chair by the bed. Elizabeth Lamb's face felt as if it were on fire but her feet were very cold; she absently rubbed them. Her hand came away damp and, in the irrelevant way one's mind sometimes behaves in a crisis, she thought that Mr. Aaronson should have known to shut the shower stall door tightly so that water would not have spilled out on to the bathroom floor. They sat silently for what seemed to them a long time but was really only a minute or two.

Jake cleared his throat. "Vito mustn't know right away. And how and when can we tell him, after his seizure last night? God, it's so true that a belly blow is always followed by a right to the jaw!"

"We've got to tell somebody!" She leaped up and ran for the stairs. Jim Darrow was just leaving by the door to the port deck, where there was a commotion as the Coast Guard vessel was made fast to the *Chianti*. Paul Cooper's back disappeared into the galley as she ran after Darrow. She was suddenly nauseated; she rushed into the galley after Cooper. The door of the washroom in the galley was locked. She hit it violently with her hand and screamed, "Let me in! I'm going to be sick!"

The door opened at once and Paul smiled wanly at her. He sneezed and rubbed his nose. His eyes were red and watering. "Has he heard?" she thought, swallowing hard. Obviously he had not: "Just washing my hands before I squeeze more oranges. I'm getting a damned cold. Orange juice's what's kept me going all night. Would you like some?"

She pushed him aside and had barely shut the door behind her when the vomit rose in her throat. She knelt on the floor in front of the toilet and was very sick for some minutes. She finally rose, trembling all over, and unsteadily dashed cold water from the wash-basin over her face and arms. She leaned against the wall and breathed through her mouth, a trick learned from her father, a prodigious drinker, which he said controlled the nausea when he'd "had one over the six."

Pietro's voice sounded in the galley. "Out, and *pronto!* I will bring you juice when I have fixed a tray for the *padrone*. I have much to do, and by myself, and no one, *no one* is to make confusion and dirt in my kitchen! Out!" Paul's placating tones ended when Pietro slammed the galley door upon them.

She glanced around to see if she had made any disarray in the lavatory that would turn Pietro's anger upon her. The floor and the walls and the mirror above the basin were spotted from her heedless splashing of water. Still breathing through her mouth, she took a towel from the stack on a shelf and wiped everything dry. There was water even on the floor behind the toilet; as she knelt and reached to wipe it she encountered a heavy plastic bag tossed there, along with one of the striped aprons Payson wore.

Muttering about the carelessness of boys she retrieved both items and crammed them and the now sodden towel into the laundry bag for soiled kitchen linen that hung on a hook in the corner before she emerged to face Pietro. "Hello," she said nervously. "I had to go in there because I felt sick all of a sudden. I've cleaned everything up. Can't Payson help you make breakfast?" And then she thought: "Why am I babbling like this? Viola's dead and I'm talking about breakfast!"

Pietro turned from the stove to glare at her. "That worthless boy did not come back on the *marinaio* boat. Now *you* get out!"

Paul was crouched on a bar stool, blowing his nose, his head resting on one hand. He did not raise it to look at her. His blue linen shirt, so neatly tucked in the night before, sagged in loose folds around his narrow hips. She was standing indecisively, wondering whether she should tell him about Viola when Monica came out of the passage to her stateroom. She wore a bright red sweater above white canvas pants rolled up above her slim ankles and bare feet. Her face looked drawn under her tan.

"You're up early," she said. "I feel like hell; I hardly slept at all, for some reason. Wandered around half the night. And then just as I managed to pass out, I heard a boatload of lovely young male voices, and who could sleep then?"

"Monica," Elizabeth Lamb said quietly, "come down below with me a minute. Please." Monica was protesting that she wanted to go on deck and check out the prospects as Elizabeth Lamb took her warm hand into her own cold one and firmly led her down the stairs.

Jake was still slumped beside Viola's body. He stared vacantly at them as they entered. There was a piteous "Meeow" as Cioccolato crept cautiously from under the bed; he darted to the door and escaped. "I forgot all about him," Elizabeth Lamb exclaimed, "and now he's loose!"

"It's all right. Vito will stay in his stateroom for breakfast," Monica assured her. "We'll get the cat before he comes out." She walked casually to the bed. "Viola's sleeping soundly, I see.

"What did you want, *caro?* And how are you, Jake? You look a bit under the weather this morning, I must say."

"Viola's not asleep," Jake said heavily. "She's dead."

Monica's eyes and mouth opened wide. She made a strangled sound and her tanned face turned the color of putty. "It's almost too perfect," Elizabeth Lamb thought. "She looks like any Academy-Award-winning actress who's bucking for another Oscar." And then she felt ashamed of herself.

"But how? When?" Monica cried. "She was all right around two this morning when I brought brandy down to you. What could have happened? Are you sure?" She picked up Viola's lax wrist and held it while she stared at the dead face. Then she put it gently down on the blanket. "Yes," she said, "she's dead."

"I don't understand it," Jake said in the same dull, heavy tone. "Darrow brought me down some coffee after that and Cooper some orange juice a bit later and then Mrs. Danniver glanced in to see if I needed anything. They were each here only a minute or so but they all looked at her.

"And she was fine at daybreak, breathing evenly. I had dozed off for a bit but I checked her when I woke up. And then I just sat here, wide-awake, till I went in to shower. And that was about an hour ago — maybe less, maybe more.

"Oh, God, Vito will never forgive me!"

"Jake, how can you say that? It's not your fault. It must have been a blood clot, an embolism or something, from falling on her throat, maybe. Or maybe her heart just stopped, from the trauma of the fall. There wasn't a thing you could have done. Not a thing.

"Look, I'm going up to make sure Vito stays away. I don't know how we're going to tell him. I've got to think."

"What is it that's wrong with his heart?" Elizabeth Lamb asked.

"Well," Jake answered, "up to now it hasn't been too serious: he's had occasional spells of what a layman would call heart flutters. But I learned last night that he's had one or two angina pectoris attacks — that's when the heart isn't getting enough blood, oxygen. Chris said he had nitroglycerine capsules and told him to put one under his tongue."

"And it was the last one!" Monica said. "His doctor told him to be sure to always carry a supply! He thinks he's indestructible, or something. I'll tell Chris and Paul about Viola, and anyone else who's around, and I'll see if a doctor came on that boat. He can't do anything about Viola but he might have some nitroglycerine and, anyway, we'd better tell him about her—" She ran out.

"You go tell Mrs. Danniver, Elizabeth Lamb," Jake said. Still clutching the large towel around him, he rose and pulled the blanket up over Viola's face, paler now and peaceful in death. "I'll get dressed and we'd better all go up to the saloon. I'll lock the cabin door and we'll have to find that kitten and shut him up someplace else. Persis could do that."

Persis' efforts were not required since, as Elizabeth Lamb knocked and then quietly opened the door of Amy's cabin, Cioccolato suddenly appeared beside her and ran to climb into Amy's lap. She was fully dressed and sitting at the desk, a pad of paper and a pen at the ready although she was doing nothing but staring at the porthole. Unlike Monica she received the news impassively, except that a look of strain appeared in her eyes.

"I don't know what to say," she sighed. "It's just so hard to believe that she's dead too, like my Jane, so young and so suddenly. I'll tell Persis when she gets out of the shower. We've been awake for hours; she woke up when I came back from seeing Jake and we've just been sitting here, both of us trying to write in the hope it would make us sleepy.

"We'll keep the kitten in here; maybe you'd go get his box and food bowls? And has anyone told Viola's stepmother?"

Monica and a young Coast Guardsman were in Viola's cabin. He was ill-at-ease, anxiously explaining that he was not a doctor but something termed an Emergency Medical Technician. "They don't usually send out anybody but one of us and all the man who called the base said was wrong was that somebody'd broken his leg and a girl had a bad fall. He told us where to pick him up and he never said anything on the way here about a death, only that you had engine trouble and no communications.

"Gee, ma'am, if he'd said—"

"Well," Monica told him, "she wasn't dead then. And now that you've got Paulo comfortable on your boat, I guess that's all you can do. The girl's grandfather was taken ill after her accident but I don't think *you* could do anything for him so I guess we'd better let him eat his breakfast and rest." She smiled graciously and patted the boy's arm, to soften her statement.

"They're attaching tow lines," she told Jake, "and we should be over at Elizabeth Lamb's grandmother's place in an hour or so, Vito says. He asked the Coast Guard Captain to take us there.

"And I must," she turned to the technician, "insist that you come up with me and have some good strong Italian coffee. I bet your service doesn't provide that." She leaned heavily on his arm as, blushing, he escorted her out.

Jake, now dressed, locked the door and took Cioccolato's things to Amy's cabin. Elizabeth Lamb hesitatingly went to Julia's and, before she put on her clothes of the night before, spoke softly in Julia's ear. "Could you wake up, Mrs. Vincentia? Viola — Viola's had — had an accident and I think you should."

Julia only burrowed her face deeper into the pillows. "No," she said groggily, "I want to sleep. Please leave me alone. I'm not well. Go away."

Everyone except Mr. Vincentia and Amy and Persis was drinking coffee in the saloon, and everyone except Robert Templeton appeared sick as well as shaken. Jim Darrow rubbed inflamed eyes and cleared his throat frequently. "I'm too old," he muttered hoarsely to Elizabeth Lamb, blowing his nose, "to sit up smoking all night." He blushed as she discreetly indicated the zipper in his once-white flannel trousers was down. Chris Grenville's face was a sickly white and he had developed a hacking cough. His camels'-hair cardigan sweater was crookedly buttoned and his shirt hung down below it. Paul Cooper's eyes were redder than Jim's and he frequently applied a handkerchief to them and to his nose. Monica returned and almost fell into a chair, wiping her face with what looked like a towel from the galley and using it to push back her damp hair. Jake got up, almost tottering, and carried a cup of coffee to her.

Templeton, seemingly not at all tired from his night excursion, was announcing that Payson had decided he should stay at — "what did he call it, The Bungalow?" — to get things ready in case any of the guests wished to spend a night ashore, "because we figured the Coast Guard would tow the *Chianti* there.

"When we finally reached the place around four this morning, after running out of gas and having to row, it was wide open but the housekeeper Payson thought would be there, wasn't. She'd left a note saying she was going to her daughter in Machias for the weekend and would be back by the time Elizabeth Lamb and her cousin arrived. Guess she didn't expect them so soon. Lucky for us she'd had the phone turned on; when we ran out of gas, Payson said it was the nearest place where there'd be one and I honestly don't think we'd have been able to row any farther!" He drank coffee and produced his usual jovial smile. "Nice morning, isn't it?"

The sick, silent company looked at him dully. "Mr. Templeton," Elizabeth Lamb asked, "don't you know about Viola?"

204

"I just came in after helping them move Paulo. What about her? Is she worse?" He looked questioningly around.

"She's dead," Cooper said baldly. He buried his face in his hands and sobbed unashamedly. A fit of sneezing interrupted the sobs and he got up unsteadily and walked out to the fantail lounge.

Templeton was as astonished as Monica had been. He opened his mouth to speak, frowned, and closed it. Finally he announced that he had better see her and then her grandfather.

"No!" Monica, Jake, Chris and Elizabeth Lamb all shouted at once. "Bob," Monica said wearily, "we haven't told him. We think we'd better wait till we get to shore and have a doctor aboard because he might have another seizure and I gave him the last of his medicine last night."

"Then I've got to make a call," Templeton replied calmly. "I'll go aboard the Coast Guard ship before they get under way."

"Our dog-and-bone is working now." Jake spoke as tiredly as Monica had. "The Captain was in here before you and said he'd got it going just as the Coast Guard hove into view. He's already called for a doctor to meet us on shore.

"And so who have *you* got to call so urgently, if I may ask?"

"You may," Templeton replied pleasantly, leaving the bridge. Those left looked at each other with as much surprise as their depleted emotions could muster. Paul came in from the fantail.

"Where's Julia?" he asked Elizabeth Lamb. "I didn't — didn't tell her, Mr. Cooper," she answered. "She doesn't feel well."

"Then I'd better go," he decided. "She must be told; she — she loved Viola." Wiping his eyes and nose, he left, his step firm but the tenseness of his shoulders revealing his apprehension.

The tow lines had been secured; the *Chianti* began to move slowly away from the shore. Elizabeth Lamb and Monica trudged to a porthole for a last look at Crazy Cousin Curtis' bare little island. A small, weathered-grey clapboard house that had been concealed in the darkness last night was the main feature of its landscape. Two figures on the jetty, surrounded by a gaggle of squawking geese, watched the *Chianti*'s departure.

"There were *geese*!" Elizabeth Lamb exclaimed. "I guess they were shut up last night. It's a good thing Mr. Vincentia and Payson didn't

205

try to go ashore because geese can be worse than guard dogs! I might have known Cousin Curtis would have geese because he had them all around his house near Boston."

"You mean you *know* that maniac?" Monica cried. "*I* might have realized he'd be some relation of your Aunt Isabella's!"

Elizabeth Lamb went into an explanation of the life and times of Cousin Curtis, such as she knew of them. Everyone welcomed her story as a distraction from their worries. "And he made that island for a place to write his book of world history," she finished. "Daddy told me he's said he's interested in people, has always studied them and their behavior, and people make history so that's why he thinks he'll make a great historian."

"Nonsense," said Amy, leading in a flushed, sniffling Persis. "A man interested in people writes novels or becomes a psychiatrist or a policeman, not a historian." And Monica snorted: "*He's* interested in studying *people?* I should think people who were *psychiatrists* would have a great time studying *him!*"

"Studying who?" Julia asked listlessly. She came in, followed by Paul, who kept a respectful distance behind her. Her face was white, taut, and sans makeup and her hair was pulled back into a disheveled knot. She took coffee and sat down, staring at the rug and plucking at a fold of her cotton skirt. "Studying who?" she asked again, looking up with not much interest.

Elizabeth Lamb began courteously to explain, but Julia closed her eyes and appeared not to listen. "Isn't there any breakfast? Just coffee?" Amy asked. "These children should eat, even if no one else feels like it."

Paul, somewhat back to his pleasant, obliging self, rose instantly. "I'll see what I can get, if the cook's not in the kitchen." He had barely moved towards the galley when Antonio came in with a large tray of bread, butter, cheese and peeled oranges.

"The *padrone* feels much better," he offered, going among them with his tray. "He took a good breakfast. He is dressing now. How is *Signorina* Viola?"

"Oh, my God!" Monica shrieked. "You don't know — no one told you? Antonio, she died during the night and we don't want to tell her grandfather till we get to shore. You must quietly let

206

Pietro know and — who is it? — yes, and Carlo, and say they are not to speak of it. I'm going to go to the *padrone* and try to detain him." She put down her almost-untouched plate and went quickly out.

Antonio had been perfectly still as she spoke. Now he swayed a little and dropped the tray. Oranges rolled everywhere. Persis and Paul moved to retrieve the food from the carpet as Jim and Chris took hold of Antonio and put him into a chair. He accepted the coffee Amy poured him and swallowed a little. *"Dio,"* he muttered, "I never thought — I never thought—"

Paul carried the tray of debris to the galley. Elizabeth Lamb ran after him with a few oranges that had lodged under a sofa. Pietro was grim as Paul pushed open the door: "I told you to keep out." He looked at the broken china. "What now? That clumsy Antonio!"

Paul explained tersely. Pietro leaned against the sink and looked as if he were going to faint. "Go out and sit down," Paul suggested. "Stretch out your legs. I'll get some more food together." Pietro merely seized his shoulder and pushed him out of the galley, muttering in Italian.

Antonio had somewhat recovered. He put his cup down with a shaking hand. "I will tell the Captain," he said, rising. Elizabeth Lamb was about to say that he would have been told by Robert Templeton and before that by the others but desisted, thinking, "What does it matter? Let him do something to feel better. And I wish I could just go to sleep and wake up to find this was a crazy dream; that's the only thing that would make *me* feel better. I'm getting so tired I can't think."

"This will kill the *padrone,* when he hears," Antonio said as he left. Julia looked up: "He must be told, and now." She stared accusingly around. "You are all afraid to tell him but it will be worse if he goes on believing the child is all right. He is more resilient than you think and he will never forgive me for keeping it from him. He must *always* know everything that happens. I'll do it, this minute."

Amy grasped her arm and began to argue with her. Templeton returned. "I've called for the local police to meet us when we arrive. Is there anything to eat? We'll be at the cove in about half an hour, at the rate we're going, Knudsen says, and we won't get much chance to eat then. I can function without sleep, but not food."

"Why did you do that, Bob?" Grenville demanded. "V.V. will see the police and — oh, God, it's going to be terrible! Maybe we *should* tell him first. I can do it. But I think you took a lot on yourself, making that call. It isn't as if somebody killed Viola!"

"I had instructions," Templeton replied coolly, making for the fresh tray of food Pietro carried in. "Even if I didn't, the police should be informed of any sudden death."

"What do you mean, 'instructions'?" Jim Darrow demanded.

Templeton turned, regretfully relinquishing the slice of bread he had buttered. He pulled out the blue pouch from under his shirt and took from it a small black leather fold. He opened it and displayed it first to Jim and then to Chris.

Jim's jaw dropped. He reached for the fold. "You're FBI?" he asked dazedly. "You're an FBI agent? And your name isn't Templeton? It's Redford? But your first name is still Robert?"

Robert withdrew the fold from Jim's reach. "Sorry," he said. "I'm not supposed to hand it over." He replaced it in the pouch and took a deep breath.

"My real surname is Redford, yes," he answered. "But when I'm off duty, I don't use it, because it causes too much comment, attracts attention — the actor, you know. I was vacationing when I met Chris and Monica and so I went by the name I use at those times. My chief suggested it."

"I knew there was something strange about you," Amy cried. "Your boss must be a Sayers fan: 'Robert Templeton' was the name of her character Harriet Vane's sleuth! Of course, he may just have chanced on it but, somehow, it made me suspicious of you. It seemed like sort of an 'in' joke."

"So that's why you said something once about my 'friend, Miss Sayers'? I wondered."

"You remember that?" Amy was impressed. "I was just sort of talking, for talk's sake, really."

"We're trained to remember everything, ma'am," Redford-Templeton answered, pouring himself coffee.

Jake Aaronson had been sitting apart from the group, eating and drinking nothing and frowning into space. Now he regarded Robert with distaste. "You haven't been trained to remember to introduce yourself correctly when you accept hospitality," he remarked. "Or was there a reason for concealing you're an agent?"

Robert was unfazed. "No, sir," he answered earnestly. "No reason at all. As I said, I was vacationing — 'on holiday,' as you British would say — when I met Monica and Chris and they invited me to come along here with them. I don't remember I'd ever before even heard of Mr. Vincentia."

"Then your memory training must be extremely faulty," Jake responded rudely. "He's quite well known — in some circles. But, of course, I'm sure you're also trained to lie well, when you have to."

Robert was pleasant. "Oh, no, sir. Never." He looked at the rest of the company, pointedly not at Jake. "If you all think our host is going to be upset by seeing police when we arrive, perhaps the news of Miss Vincentia's death should be calmly broken to him now. A sudden shock is not beneficial to someone with angina. I could handle it, without emotion."

"*And* you know he has angina," Jake said thoughtfully. "I only just realized it. Your briefing must have been very thorough, and for merely going on a pleasure cruise with someone you'd never heard of, invited by people with whom you just *happened* to strike up an acquaintance."

"I have some medical training. I could tell." Robert was not at all offended, seemingly, by Jake's sardonic tone. "Well, what do you all say?"

Julia moved away from Amy and sat down. "I think he's right," she said, breaking the silence in the saloon. "It would be just terrible for V.V. to have police coming aboard and demanding, 'Wot's all this?' Or whatever they say here in the States. It would be just too much. And I think Robert could do it more easily than I." She eyed him warily. "He appears to be what you Yanks call a smooth operator.

"And I think something else: I think that little girl" — she pointed at Persis — "should go with him. V.V. loves children" — her voice shook and she clenched her hands tightly together — "and he'd keep outward control in front of her. And controlling yourself

209

outwardly helps you control yourself inwardly. I *know,*" she finished sadly.

Everyone looked at Persis. "I don't want to," she said simply. "I'd cry, and he'd feel worse. I already cried, when I stood outside Viola's door and said a prayer this morning. Elizabeth Lamb is tougher than I am. She'd be good."

Everyone looked at Elizabeth Lamb. "I don't want to go either," she said. She sighed. "But I will. I found her, so I guess I should." She got up resolutely, breathing through her mouth again as Robert took her arm and they walked slowly to Vincentia's stateroom.

Monica met them at the door. "He's dressed," she whispered, "and determined to go down to Viola. I — I just said she was resting quietly, when he pressed me, and he said his looking at her wouldn't disturb her. He's in good spirits and seems fine; listen, you can hear him humming even though the loo door's closed. What shall we do?"

Mr. Vincentia ducked his head as he came through the low bathroom doorway, still vigorously applying two military-type brushes to his thick black hair. His eyes were bright and his color good, the tinge of red on his high, tanned cheekbones picking up the tone of his shirt. He smiled pleasantly and then, observing the strain on his visitors' faces and the fright on Monica's, slowly put the brushes down on the top of one of the low, caned cabinets.

"What is it?" he asked. "Something is wrong?"

Robert cleared his throat. He produced his black leather fold and opened it for Vincentia's observation. "This is who I am," he said. "I have to tell you something although who I am really hasn't anything to do with it. Would you sit down, sir? Please."

Mr. Vincentia still smiled slightly. "But of course I thought you might be an agent. Not that there is any reason for one to be aboard, but, well, let us say only that the way you of the Bureau carry yourselves is unmistakable to one who has, ah, had some few opportunities to observe them." He smiled more widely. "Even though you made some attempts to be, perhaps, less acute, more ingenuous, than you really are." Elizabeth Lamb was not surprised at his perception; she had thought more than once that he seemed to know everything about everybody.

He sat down. "Now, what is it? You have observed something about the *Chianti,* or something about someone aboard her, that interests you? I really doubt that there is anything to warrant your interest." He smiled again. "At least, not on this voyage. But tell me. If," he added with an affectionate look at Elizabeth Lamb, "it is suitable for those young and innocent ears to hear?"

Robert sat, facing him across the inlaid desk. Elizabeth Lamb moved to sit on the settee beside Mr. Vincentia. She put her hand gently on his bare forearm, swallowing hard. He reached across with his other hand and patted it lightly. "You look too serious, *caro,*" he said. "Is it that you are worried about — about the message, the news you brought me last night? Do not be; it will be all right. I know what to do."

Elizabeth Lamb swallowed again. "Mr. Vincentia," she said, "you mustn't be upset; of course, you will be, but you must be as calm as you can. Think of good things: I always think of my grandmother when I'm worried—" Her voice broke and she buried her face in his shoulder.

He frowned in bewilderment, and then smiled again. "But I *have* been thinking of dear Elizabeth. We will soon be at her cottage. And Payson decided to stay there to make us feel comfortable if we go ashore, which we well may do, while we wait for the engine repairs." He frowned more deeply: "That boy has much initiative, as much as I did at his age, but perhaps that was not a bad thing for me and will not be for him.

"I am distracting you; what is this news you have?" His face and tone changed, hardening. "It is Viola. She is worse. Tell me!"

"Mr. Vincentia, she is dead." Her face still against his shoulder, she grasped his arm tightly and felt his muscles tense. He shuddered a little and for a moment said nothing. Then he leaned his head against the back of the settee and a terrible rough cry came from his throat: "*Sangue mio! Sangue mio!* My own blood! My own blood!"

Monica had been standing rigidly against the cabin door, ever since Robert had first spoken. Now she ran to Vincentia and grasped his hand in both of hers: "Vito, Vito, I know how you feel. She was all you had left and you loved her. But, Vito, please, please remember your faith; she is at peace now, in a good place. Vito,

211

life would have been hard for her; you know that. It may sound harsh to you now but you must, you *must* understand what I am trying to say: that she will never be old and alone, never be frightened of anything. She will never have to face the hard things in life that you *do* know she was born not really able to face. Oh, Vito, please!"

He straightened and sat quietly for some time, his eyes closed, breathing in little gasps, while the three watched him anxiously. He sighed deeply then pulled his shoulders back before he rose. He clasped Elizabeth Lamb to him and held her. With great calm, he said, "This has been hard for you, *caro*. Now I want you to go and tell Mr. Aaronson to meet me at Viola's cabin. I must be with her for a time.

"Do not be frightened; I am *bene*." He kissed her lightly on the forehead. They walked steadily out and he as steadily descended the aft stairs while she went into the saloon and gave Jake his message.

The others looked uneasily at her. "V.V. took it well?" Paul asked. She only nodded and went out to the fantail, followed by Persis. Paul turned to Monica and Robert who had come in and collapsed into chairs. "He's all right?" he persisted. "It must have been terrible for him." They, also, merely nodded.

"I could use a drink," Julia said to no one in particular and no one except Paul responded. "So could I. A Screwdriver, maybe? I'd like one. There's ice and vodka at the bar, Grenville. I'll get some orange juice from the kitchen."

Chris moved reluctantly to the bar and was soon joined by an embarrassed Paul. "That cook's temper is worse than usual," he said. "I couldn't get anything out of him; hoped he'd be on deck. There's tomato juice here, Julia; what about a Bloody?"

"Oh, all right," Julia answered wearily. She looked at Paul. "Thank you. It's very kind of you." She managed to smile at him. He ducked his head, embarrassed again. "Not at all, my dear. One for you, Mrs. Danniver?"

"No, thanks," Amy answered coldly. She went out to the fantail where Persis was sitting shivering and sniffling, enduring a lecture from her cousin.

"Really, Persis," Elizabeth Lamb was remonstrating, "no wonder you're getting a cold! You're not even over German measles yet and you've stayed awake half the night and why aren't you wearing sneakers? And your socks are wet! Honestly! Don't you remember that Alice said she saw a sickness, in your tea leaves? You ought to be more careful!"

"Well, I got a sickness, didn't I? That was the German measles, wasn't it? So why should I expect another?" Persis answered thickly. "And I broke both my sneaker laces this morning and I didn't know my socks were wet but I *do* know I just want to get into my bunk at The Bungalow and go to sleep. I hope Dora's there because I'm sick, all right; I'm sick of being bossed and I'm sick of this damned boat!"

"Persis!"

"Well, I don't care. And Mrs. Danniver and I didn't feel like sleeping so shoot us, why don't you? At least we just sat there writing and not going around bossing people!"

Amy concealed a smile. "I think it's a good idea for you to stay ashore, Persis. It will be a lot more peaceful there, because they've called a boatyard for people to come and take the engines apart — the Captain and the engineer on the Coast Guard boat think there's something wrong with the fuel injectors, I think they called them. They've got to be taken out, anyway, and sent over to the boatyard to be rebuilt or else new ones ordered.

"And the police will be here, asking questions, and the doctor, too, maybe; oh, you'd be much better off at your grandmother's cottage."

"Police," Elizabeth Lamb said thoughtfully. She got up, giving Persis a conciliatory pat and went into the saloon. Jake had come back. "Vito's just sitting down there," he was saying. "He's pretty much in good shape. One thing I did: I convinced him to ask for an autopsy. Even if the doctor doesn't think one's indicated, Vito can request one, I believe. The next of kin can in England, and probably here, too."

"What!" Monica was outraged. "He's going to have them — have them cut Viola up? Oh, Jake, what's the matter with you? Why did you tell him that? And why on earth did he agree?"

Julia was also appalled. "I can't believe it," she cried. "That you would do that! It's horrible! And why? Why, if the doctor doesn't want one?"

213

"Because," Jake answered stolidly, "I was alone with Viola all night and in the morning she was dead. But Vito isn't dead and I don't want him wondering for the rest of his life, not to mention mine, if I did something or didn't do something that cost him his granddaughter.

"And he agreed, Monica, because he and I have always done each other favors. This was a hard one for him to grant, but I've granted harder ones to him, over the years. He owed me."

Julia angrily put down her glass and left, announcing her head was pounding and she was going to lie down. Paul, shaking his head, went out to the fantail. Jim got up slowly, saying a walk around the decks might get him ready for the police. "Come on, Chris. Do you good. Salt air might clear your nose." Monica merely sat, regarding Jake with compressed lips.

Elizabeth Lamb also looked at him. "Mr. Aaronson," she said, "I know a state detective. I know him very well. They don't send them unless the doctor thinks a death is suspicious, but suppose he does? The man I know is awfully smart and if we could get him sent, he'd get to the bottom of it, which is what you want, isn't it?"

"Get to the bottom of *what?*" Now Monica was angry with her.

"Well, probably not of anything. But what I'm trying to say is that *if* they're going to send one, what about if I call my friend first and see if it could be him — he, I mean. It might save time. And even if they weren't going to send one, if he came over on his own, if he's not busy with something else, and sort of looked into it, you'd feel much better, wouldn't you, Mr. Aaronson, to positively *know* that there was nothing you did, or didn't do?"

"We're going to have more time than we need, without having to save any, if we have to sit here while they get new engine parts," Monica said bitterly. "But," thoughtfully, "maybe if it was *certain* everything was on the up-and-up, we could leave the *Chianti*. I think a spot of peaceful old England is what I need."

"If they think there's something funny, they won't let us go. But," Elizabeth Lamb spoke shrewdly, "my friend could find there *wasn't* faster than the sheriff, or a deputy, who are the police here, could."

"But," Monica argued, "if the doctor issues a death certificate *and*

214

this damned autopsy shows nothing suspicious, they'd let us go anyway — oh, I'm too tired to argue. I suppose," she again was thoughtful, "Vito would feel much, much better if he knew he'd looked into everything; had questions asked and all that."

Robert spoke up. He had been sitting a little apart, listening carefully to everyone. "It's a decision the police will make," he said. "For you to call a state detective now would be both premature and a bit out of line."

"I don't see why, if he agrees and his superiors let him," Jake said. "It would be what you might call an heroic decision, for us to decide to do it, but I know Vito would appreciate our concern. And I know he has a high regard for your judgment, Elizabeth Lamb. He thinks you're no fool, young as you are.

"What was it Hitler said?" he went on. "Something about 'just as a hundred fools don't make one wise man, so an heroic decision doesn't come from a hundred cowards.' Let's not be cowards. Let's be bold and get it over with."

"Jake!" Monica cried. "How can anyone quote that maniac? And you, of all people, a Jew!"

"Well, my dear, I'd say he was *worse* than a maniac; he was evil personified. But just as it's agreed the devil can quote Scripture for his own purposes, so I give credit to Hitler for having a lot of knowledge of the dark side of human nature, if 'credit' is the proper word. And that's why I quote him. What else did he say that I've always remembered — oh, that people 'believe a big lie rather than a small one.' Evil as he was, he was shrewd."

"Then I should call my friend Buzzie?" Elizabeth Lamb was impatient and really not too sure who this person Hitler was.

Robert's expression was thoughtful. "I'll make the call for you. The Captain might not agree to your doing it, but Europeans are very respectful of authority and he knows who I am, of course." He consulted his watch. "Let's go now, because we're almost at your cove and he'll soon be concerned with getting loose from the tow. He's pretty tired and only running on nerves."

"Look!" Elizabeth Lamb exclaimed as they walked quickly along the upper deck. "We're around Bartlett's Island! You can see The Bungalow. There are people on the float."

215

Captain Knudsen, rigid at the wheel, agreed to Robert's request. "Ask for Lieutenant Alfred Higgins," Elizabeth Lamb directed. "Oh, darn, I don't know the number of the State Police in Orono. How long will it take to get through?"

"But *I* know it," Robert replied calmly, placing the call. He was quickly connected. "On leave?" He spoke resignedly. "And going on a three weeks' vacation out of the country? Do you know if he's left yet? I see. Thank you."

"Try his home!" Elizabeth Lamb was jittering with tension. "Oh, I forgot the number; no, I remember!" She supplied it and there was an agonizing wait. Finally, Robert spoke again: "Lieutenant Higgins? I have a young lady here who'd like to speak to you." He beckoned her over.

"Buzzie!" she screamed. "It's me, Elizabeth Lamb. I'm on a boat; there's a girl dead; we're just coming into Schooner Cove. Can you come over here? There's police coming but I wish you would, too. You know how to do things." She listened.

"No, of course I don't *know* that it's murder! It was just — funny. Wouldn't they let you come over and ask questions? Well, when *are* you going to Paris? Buzzie, I am *not* getting excited. No, I am not *either* imagining plots where there aren't any! It was just, well, funny. It was sudden and for no reason and there's people who would like to know *why*." She listened again.

"Couldn't you get permission? I know you're packing but if you're not leaving till the day after tomorrow—. Look, there's an FBI man here with me. Yes, that's what I said. He'll talk to you."

She handed the instrument to Robert and turned away to stare out a window, her whole body damp with sweat. Knudsen turned once to give her a cold look. Robert spoke lucidly for a time, with a tinge of persuasion. He hung up and smiled at her.

"He's coming; be here in about fifteen minutes, he says. He lives nearby, I guess? He's just going to clear it. I told him Mr. Vincentia was a pretty important person." He smiled wryly. "I figured I perhaps owed him something, for, well, imposing on him without explaining who I was.

"So I told Higgins to tell his chief the Bureau would appreciate

216

any cooperation. And he said — he said *he* 'owed' *you* 'a few.' What's that mean?"

She only smiled with relief. "Although," she thought, "maybe Buzzie was right. Maybe I am getting too excited about nothing. But if it makes poor Mr. Aaronson feel better, I don't care if Buzzie thinks I'm foolish."

They told Jake and Monica that the detective was coming and then Robert said he was going to pack. "I think Mr. Vincentia won't be sorry to see me leave, and my, my vacation's about over. Got to get back to work."

"Of course you do," Jake agreed sarcastically. "We all know you've not been working. Although I hope you don't get paid on a commission basis because if you *had* been on a job, you wouldn't get any payment for this little trip, would you?"

"But can you just *go,* Bob?" Monica asked. "With the police coming? Don't you have to answer questions, too?"

"They'll know where to find me. And I wasn't here last night so, even if I weren't, as an agent, somewhat above suspicion, there isn't much I could tell them about what went on here, then or early this morning. Or didn't. I'll speak to the man in charge when he gets here, of course." He offered a polite hand to Jake, who withheld his, shaking his head.

"Nothing personal," he said. "I just don't like coppers. I'll be up in a bit, Monica, after I change into some clean clothes. I feel as if I've been in these for a week."

"I really hope to see you again, Monica," Robert said earnestly. "Under different circumstances, we might hit it off."

"We might," she agreed. "And it's a small world. *Ciao,* Bob." She kissed his cheek. "One for the road, till we meet again somewhere along it."

Amy, passing through the saloon with Persis, announced, "We're going to pack Persis' things. I'll stay ashore with her till the housekeeper comes, if she hasn't already."

"Elizabeth Lamb made a call to a detective she knows," Monica told her. "He'll probably want to ask you questions."

"Then you can tell him where I am," Amy answered cheerfully. "If I'm not still here when he arrives, that is. But since Persis and

217

I were together from the time I came back from looking in on Jake and Viola — and she was very much alive then, as Jake can tell you — until Elizabeth Lamb came in this morning with the news, Persis and I have what my dear little Alaric C. would term 'mutual alibis.' Unless this detective thinks we two conspired to strangle Viola, or poison her, or something."

"I bet it's Buzzie who's coming!" Persis exclaimed. "He knows me," she assured Mrs. Danniver, "and he knows I tell the truth and don't fall asleep like a baby and don't strangle people either, so he'll know we certainly do have muted alley bins!"

Monica and Elizabeth Lamb collapsed into chairs, laughing loudly. Persis was beginning an angry comment when there were voices on deck, the almost imperceptible motion of the *Chianti* stopped, and Jim and Chris came running in.

"We're there!" Jim said. "Antonio and Carlo have dropped the anchors and they're casting off the Coast Guard boat."

"We're anchored near the shore," Chris told them. "I heard the Captain say this cove's very deep. Come on out on deck; it's a lovely place. I had no idea Maine was so beautiful, having only seen it in fog and rain yesterday.

"And there are people getting in a rowboat. Come look."

Elizabeth Lamb raced out, followed by Monica, and Amy and Persis went more slowly after them. Jake appeared, and Julia, with Paul walking a little behind her. Several of the Coast Guard crew waved as their vessel moved out of the cove.

"Well, at least Paulo is free of this," Monica remarked. "The poor man probably can't wait to get into hospital and have some proper care. I wish Vito had been able to say goodbye to him because he must be awfully anxious, getting sent off alone to a strange place, although that medical technician did tell me it's only a few miles across the island."

"Oh, he'll be all right." Paul was cheerful. "V.V. will call him and he'll rent a car, if it's possible, so Knudsen can go over to see him. Maybe he will be released by the time the engines are repaired."

He was staring at The Bungalow float. "Who's that woman? She looks familiar — my God, it's Annie!"

Elizabeth Lamb had been looking, with relief and happy nostalgia, at the wooded shores of Schooner Cove and the weathered grey-shingled main building on the top of the rise above the bridge to the float. Then she had watched the small boat with four men in it being slowly rowed toward the *Chianti.* Now she shifted her eyes to follow Paul's.

"It *is* Mrs. Donelli!" she agreed. "Her mother must be better, but how did she get here so fast? I guess they couldn't get five into the skiff and the doctor and the police had to come first."

No one answered her. They were all anxiously inspecting the men in the boat, now beside them. Antonio removed the gate in the deck railing and went down the ladder to hold the boat as three of the men climbed on to the little platform that folded down from the base of the ladder. The fourth, Payson, glanced briefly up at her as he maneuvered the skiff away. His face was pale and tense and his shoulders shook as he bent to the oars.

"He shouldn't have to do that," she thought. "He's been up all night and rowed half across the bay, besides. He looks sick, too." The first man had reached the deck. "Buzzie!" She darted around Paul to grasp him and rise on her toes to press her face into his chest.

He hugged her tightly. He was tall and thin, wearing faded jeans and a short-sleeved blue denim shirt, his brown hair close-cropped under a duck-billed cap. His face was tanned, his muscled arms a deeper tan and his eyes, behind horn-rimmed spectacles, were very shrewd. Still holding her, he appraised the rest of the group with a steady regard.

He put his hand under Elizabeth Lamb's chin and tilted up her face. "Now then, dear, what's all this?"

Julia began to laugh, loudly and with more than a hint of hysteria. "They do say it!" she gasped. "They really do!" She choked on her last words and, pressing a hand to her mouth, ran inside.

"I didn't mean to upset the lady," Buzzie said. "I'm Lieutenant Alfred Higgins and this is Deputy Sheriff Little." The deputy was a short, fat, red-faced man of middle age, also clad in jeans. A badge was pinned to his checked gingham shirt. Under one arm he had a large, rolled bag of a heavy grey material that displayed a long zipper among its folds. He nodded solemnly at the group.

A third man with somewhat the same features and carriage as

Buzzie had stepped off the ladder. He carried the usual black physician's bag. "And this is Dr. Hinton. He's a Medical Examiner, too; just got named one, and—" He broke off as loud sobs sounded through the open portholes of the saloon. "Is that lady all right?"

"No, she's far from all right," Paul informed him stiffly. "She's — she was the dead girl's stepmother. She raised her from a baby. I'll see what I can do." He left.

Persis pressed forward. "Hello, Buzzie," she said. "I'm here, too, so you can hug me and not just Elizabeth Lamb! The girl who's dead is Viola Vincentia and I can take the doctor down to where she is.

"Is that bag the man has what people get put in when they're dead? I certainly hope she *is,* because—" Elizabeth Lamb put her hand roughly over Persis' mouth. Monica, eyes widening in horror, angrily left the gathering. Chris followed her, and Jake hastily beckoned the three men to follow him.

Amy took hold of Persis before Elizabeth Lamb could reprove her further and led her down the deck. Jim went with them. The shore breeze carried Persis' voice back: "Well, I'm sorry, but all I meant was that if she wasn't *really* dead then she would smother in that thing. I mean, suppose a person really isn't and they don't know and they put him—"

Antonio had run down the ladder to hand Annie Donelli out of the returned skiff. Elizabeth Lamb put her head over the railing. Antonio was asking Payson if he would stay to make up the cabins and help with lunch. Payson's reply was an exhausted mumble as he again wearily headed back to shore.

"Better he not come aboard and work. He should rest." Antonio and Annie were standing in an embrace on the little platform. "It has been terrible, *caro*; better, maybe, you were not here. I will tell you. And you know the *signorina* has died?"

"I know. Those men spoke of it. Antonio, my dear, you must tell me: you did not — you did not—"

"Of course I did not!" He looked up and saw Elizabeth Lamb as he and Annie mounted the ladder. "Hush, *caro*; I did nothing."

"I'm glad you're back, Annie," she said politely. "Mr. Vincentia is pretty sad and you'll make him feel better. Is your mother all right? How did you get here?"

Annie looked almost as exhausted as Payson. "My mother was very much better when I got to her, and my sister had arrived. I tried to phone last night, to see if Vito wanted anything brought back, until two or three this morning. I finally called the Coast Guard and heard something of what happened. They said you were being towed, so I got a friend of Vito's to fly me to a little airport nearby — his plane was almost too big to land there — and we rented cars; two, because he thought he and his crew would stay a few days in Bar Harbor. And so here I am.

"With a few stops for directions," she added. "This place is lovely, but so hard to find! I'm awfully tired. After I wash and lie down for an hour, I'll be ready to help Vito." She touched Elizabeth Lamb's cheek and was off, directing Antonio to give the large canvas bag he was carrying to Pietro: "Mr. Moselli said he shot those pigeons on Vito's land in Sicily only two days ago." Antonio began to talk to her again, his head close to hers, as soon as they were inside.

Elizabeth Lamb felt lonely: everyone had a companion except her. "And I wish *I* could change my clothes and lie down," she thought. "But I can't for a while, not till they take poor Viola away." She decided to see if Pietro might want help with lunch. "At least, he might *talk* to me."

In the passage she encountered Jim Darrow, hastily leaving the galley. "I wouldn't go in there," he advised. "He's in a bad mood. Looks rotten and is losing his voice, too. I was trying to get some ice cream for Persis — Amy says she's a little feverish — and he about killed me. Well, don't say I didn't warn you."

Pietro was on a stool by the stove, listlessly stirring a large copper pot of bubbling tomato sauce. "Now you," he said, his voice cracking. "My God, my kitchen might be a Saint Catherine's wheel, with everyone spinning around on it."

"Pietro," she began, "I could help—" He turned his head sharply away from her as the other kitchen door was cautiously pushed open. He threw down his spoon and advanced menacingly upon Paul Cooper. "And now *you!* The fourth in four minutes! When the fifth comes in, I will take a knife to him! Get out!"

Paul backed away. "I only want some aspirin for Mrs. Vincentia.

Her head's bad. I saw some in your w.c. this morning. I'll just be a minute."

"She can go down to her cabin and get her aspirin and stay there!" Pietro's voice got more hoarse with each word. "And I am locking both my doors from now on, when I am in here and when I am not, beginning the moment you leave."

"She doesn't want to go down." Paul was standing his ground. "She's afraid of meeting them on the stairs, carrying Viola." He made another attempt to enter. "My good man, you might re-member— "

"I am nobody's 'good man'! And I *swear,* by the Blessed Virgin and all the saints, if you take one more step I will cut out your heart!" Paul disappeared. Elizabeth Lamb began another offer of help. Pietro merely shook his head and pointed emphatically to the door, still swinging from Paul's departure.

Julia, eyes closed, lay on a sofa in the saloon. Paul was bending deferentially over her. "I couldn't get it," he was saying. "He is more than a trifle insane, I think. He threatened me."

Julia was disgusted. "He is only a servant, you fool. I am going to tell V.V. to dismiss him! If you had any guts at all—"

Elizabeth Lamb had come quietly down to them. "I'll go see if Mrs. Danniver has some aspirin," she began. Julia opened her eyes and sprang up. "You startled me!" she gasped. "I will go mad if I don't get off this boat. Insolent servants — creeping children — yokel police—" She almost ran to the stairs. Paul sat down in her place. "And Viola dead," he muttered. "And my Viola dead."

Elizabeth Lamb backed away from him. "I don't know why," she thought, "I don't just go to Persis' cabin and take a shower and put something of hers on, if her stuff isn't all packed yet. And lie on her bed and get away from all these jumpy people for a while."

She met Buzzie and Robert and Mr. Vincentia on the stairs. The last was grim but controlled. "I want you to go to the saloon and stay there," he said. "I would like everyone to stay there; if people come in, please tell them. I must arrange for the dinghy so Mr. Redford can leave and they can — can take Viola away.

"And then we must eat something because, well, because we must. Then Lieutenant Higgins wants to speak to everybody."

With a nod to her and a handshake for Buzzie, Robert, who was carrying two small suitcases, followed Vincentia to the deck. From below there came the voices of men talking as a door was opened. "Gently; here, I'll go first," one said. "Right behind you," another answered.

"Elizabeth Lamb," Buzzie said quietly, "take me to this saloon he talked about. That it, the big room aft there where the feller is? And you just keep looking at the portholes or back over the stern." The Captain came down the spiral stairs in the fantail lounge as she was showing Buzzie the flowers. He nodded to Buzzie's request that he round up the passengers and send them in. "The owner wants it that way," Buzzie explained.

Monica and Chris had descended the stairs just after Knudsen, Monica subdued and tense and Chris shivering and coughing. "I *told* Chris people with a cold should stay out of the sun," she said plaintively, making for the bar. "It makes them worse, not better. Chris, I want you to drink this whiskey I'll mix with lemon in hot water."

"Good luck on the hot water," Paul told her. "The cook is threatening to knife anyone who goes into his damned kitchen. Anyway, you can't get in because he's locked the doors." Monica merely smiled, handed a pitcher to Knudsen, who was ushering in Jake and Julia, and sweetly made her request. Amy and Jim appeared, Jim carrying Persis on his back and staggering a little as he tried to hold on to her with one hand and blow his nose with the other.

"For heaven's sake, put that heavy child down," Monica directed him. "You look awful." Persis glared, Elizabeth Lamb giggled, and Jim sneezed as he complied. He gratefully accepted the hot whiskey and water she offered him. Everyone ignored the sad little procession that had come up the stairs and through the dining room to the outer deck. Mr. Vincentia joined the group in the saloon after a short time, during which Monica filled drink orders. Buzzie refused refreshment and watched the others.

Mr. Vincentia seated himself on a bar stool. "You have all met Lieutenant Higgins, I think," he said in a colorless tone. "He would like to ask some questions. He has a a list of all your names but please identify yourself when you answer. Pietro will give you lunch shortly and I have invited the Lieutenant to join us. And then, after lunch, we will continue to tell you—" he looked at Buzzie— "what you want to know."

"Why's Buzzie asking questions?" Persis demanded. "Did somebody kill Viola?" Elizabeth Lamb groaned inwardly while Julia did so loudly.

Mr. Vincentia's face turned pale, but he answered with composure. "I think now Lieutenant Higgins should do the talking. I'm rather tired, Persis." He accepted the glass of *Grappa* Monica poured for him.

Buzzie leaned against the bar beside him. He opened a small notebook and took a pen from his shirt pocket. "Well," he began, "I know you've all been through a lot, even before Miss Vincentia's unfortunate death, so we'll make this as brief as we can, and I'm really not going to ask a lot of questions. Your experience at Mr. Worthington's island shouldn't ever have happened and Deputy Little is going to find out just who has jurisdiction there. Could be Mount Desert, could be Blue Hill, could be Tremont. Anyway, the situation will be dealt with; we can't have people getting shot at.

"Now, I'm not going to ask you anything about what happened before this morning, because I guess I can get that all filled in later. My friend, Elizabeth Lamb, here, has an awfully good memory." Everyone looked nervously at Elizabeth Lamb, who blushed.

"What happened to your engines and communications, for instance," he went on, "which may or may not have had anything to do with Miss Vincentia's death, would be awfully involved to get into right now."

"Did that FBI fellow have anything to do with either, do you think?" Jake interrupted. "God knows why he would, but we don't know what was on his mind. And I guess we never will, unless" — he looked appraisingly at Buzzie — "he confided in you?"

"He says not," Buzzie answered, "and I believe him, because — well, let's just say I believe him. I *do* know what was on his mind, but it isn't any longer, so we can forget him."

"Why isn't that sheriff asking the questions?" Amy inquired, in a professional manner. "What did the M. E. say? *Was* there something strange about the death?"

"Dr. Hinton is young and new at the game," Buzzie answered. "He's a good man, though," he added quickly. "He thought death was caused by an embolism from the fall." Monica looked triumphantly at Jake and Elizabeth Lamb. "That's just what I told *them!*" she exclaimed.

"*But,*" Buzzie went on, "both Little and I noticed something we thought needed explanation. We persuaded him to order an autopsy." Mr. Vincentia, looking suddenly sick, announced he would rejoin them for lunch. Everyone was more at ease after his departure.

"Was it that Viola's face was sort of pink and, like, mottled?" Elizabeth Lamb asked. "Buzzie, that could have been because she was catching Persis' German measles!"

Buzzie was surprised. "But it wasn't; she was very pale." He considered her thoughtfully. "You found her, I know. I'll talk to you later, by yourself. Well—"

Amy interrupted. "Lieutenant, Persis hasn't recovered yet, really, and she's getting a bad cold. She wants to go ashore and stay at her grandmother's cottage and I think that's wise. I'll go with her, if the housekeeper's not back."

"She's back," Buzzie said. "Okay, just a question or two, Persis, and then maybe one of you men can find someone to row her ashore. The boat will be back soon, as soon as the transport for the body to Bangor gets to the cottage."

"God," Monica muttered, "Viola was no flower child — I always called her a weed child! — but to hear that she's now just a 'body' —"

Paul stirred. "That's enough of your snide remarks, Monica. Let's get on with it. And I hope we're finished before lunch; I'd like to eat in peace." Julia glanced at him contemptuously.

"Well, Persis," said Buzzie, "what did you do this morning and what did you see or hear anyone else doing? Anything strike you as unusual?"

Persis had been leaning against Amy. Now she sat up with an air of importance. "Well," she said hoarsely, "I woke up awfully early. Mrs. Danniver and I share a cabin and when she came back from going next door to see Mr. Aaronson, she made noise, I guess. It was just four o'clock, because I looked at my watch."

"That's right," Amy confirmed. "I hadn't slept well and so I thought I'd walk over to see how Jake was." She looked contrite. "And, of course, Viola. Just for something to do."

"And I couldn't go back to sleep," Persis went on. "So we just started writing the story I have to do for school. And I kept looking at my watch, hoping it would soon be time for everybody else to wake up, so I know I didn't fall asleep again. So Mrs. Danniver is very in the clear," she finished quaintly, "because we both stayed right there until Elizabeth Lamb came in and said Viola was dead. I had just gone into the shower but I heard her. So there!"

Buzzie smiled at her. "And then what?"

"Well, I got dressed — Mrs. Danniver had got dressed while we were writing — and we came up here. And we stayed here, and there were other people around, talking, and then you came and then Mrs. Danniver and Mr. Darrow and I walked around the deck and he felt sick but he tried to get me some ice cream but he couldn't and then we all went down and packed my suitcase and brought it up and put it in the dining room and then we went up on deck again to look at the cove and then the Captain said to come in here. Mr. Darrow carried me because I really feel just terrible and I'm not," she glared at Monica, "very heavy, either!

"And if anybody did or said anything that would make me think they hurt Viola, well, I wouldn't even have noticed it because I feel too sick."

"Well," Buzzie said, looking up from his notes to smile at her again, "that's clear, Persis. You can go. I'll stop in at The Bungalow, on my way home, to see you. Maybe you'd want something I could get you."

"The boat's back," Elizabeth Lamb told him. "I just saw Antonio walk by, on the deck."

Amy and Persis got up thankfully. Persis went over to Buzzie and leaned up to kiss him affectionately, one smug eye on Elizabeth Lamb. Paul, always obliging, rose, too. "I'll get Antonio," he said. "Best you get to Bedfordshire and out of this, Persis. And why can't the other little girl go along? Better for both of them."

"No," Elizabeth Lamb told him, "I want to stay. And" — she looked to see that Persis was picking up her bag, out of earshot, but she lowered her voice, anyway — "Persis is awfully mean when she's sick. It wouldn't be a bit better for *me*.

"Besides, I've got to write something for school, too. I might get some ideas. And I don't think we should all, well, desert Mr. Vincentia. He's been so kind. I'll row over and see Persis later, though."

Monica poured more drinks. Paul came back and, a little later, Amy. "Well," she asked, "shall I go next?" Buzzie nodded agreement.

"I'm Amy Danniver," she told him. "I guess by now you've been told by V.V. who we all are and why we're aboard." Buzzie nodded again. "Well," she went on, "you've heard me say I was restless, couldn't sleep. It was just a little before four when I put on a robe and went over to Viola's cabin. Jake was awake, said several people had been kind enough to be concerned about him — brought him brandy, coffee, orange juice. None of which he drank, by the way; they were untouched, I noticed, so it isn't possible that someone had given him anything to make him sleepy."

Monica, Jim and Paul all looked at her, first with anger and then, realizing what she had really said, with some relief. "Although," Paul asked, "were they still all untouched this morning, Lieutenant? Because maybe they should be analyzed?"

Now Monica and Jim looked angrily at him. "Mr. Aaronson said he hadn't drunk from any of them," Buzzie answered calmly, "but we've sent the contents to a lab."

Amy continued. "So, since Jake was all right and Viola sleeping, I went back and put on another light so I could see to pour myself a drink — ah, a drink of water — and Persis woke up. Then, as she said, we wrote, about five pages and, if *you* know anything about writing," — a pause for a sigh and a glance of derision at Jim — "you know that took time. Then Elizabeth Lamb came running in, barefoot and in her pajamas, and told us about Viola. The cat came in with her, and we kept him—"

"So that's where that damned animal is!" Paul exclaimed. "Mr. Vincentia's terrified of cats," he told Buzzie, "and his secretary's allergic to them. I was afraid it was running loose and we'd have another *contretemps*."

"Well," Amy assured him, "it's gone with Persis. She thought

227

of it as she was getting into the boat so I went down and put it in a little airline bag of mine. It'll be happier ashore and company for her.

"Where was I? Well, Persis came up here with me, as she said, as soon as she'd dressed and, really, she reported everything correctly and since I was with her the whole morning, do I have to go through it again?"

"Did you notice that anyone seemed unduly upset — or not upset enough?" Buzzie asked. "Or seemed excited, or said or did or wore or drank or ate anything that would have been unusual for him? Or her?"

"No, I didn't notice anything unusual, on the part of anyone. Well, Mr. Cooper was, of course, very upset. He and Viola had planned to marry. And Mrs. Vincentia, Viola's stepmother, felt bad, naturally. It would have been unusual if they *hadn't* reacted the way they did. And, to be honest, some of us didn't like Viola very much, so although we were disturbed, and regretful that she had died, there wasn't a lot of grief. That's natural, too.

"And, really, Jim and Mr. Grenville and Mr. Cooper were almost too sick, from not being able to sleep properly last night and coming down with colds as a result, to exhibit what you might call normal reactions. Mr. Aaronson *was* terribly upset, since Viola had died when he was watching her. He hadn't had but a nap or two, either. And Monica — oh, with what we've all been through, how can our reactions in any way be judged?"

"Maybe they can't, ma'am," Buzzie answered, writing busily. "And, you know, you mustn't all be apprehensive, or suspicious of each other, or resent what someone else says you did or said, just because an autopsy was ordered. It well may show nothing. Now, this lady?" He looked at Monica.

"Wait a minute," Jim said thickly. "In Amy's books, it doesn't go like this. I mean, it isn't certain that the girl's death was suspicious, yet we've got a state detective asking us questions. Why don't you wait till you learn if she was murdered? Why this official inquisition?"

"Well," Buzzie said, "I'm putting you through this because, not only will it save time if the autopsy indicates the death was suspicious, but because Mr. Vincentia asked me to, in the hope you would cooperate. He told me that he 'always has to know' and my feeling is this is helping him, in his grief.

"Now, at this point, you can refuse to answer. You can also refuse to have your fingerprints taken, which I'd like to do before I go. Just another time-saver. I'm on leave, although I have permission to be here, so in no way is this little 'inquisition' official. The one thing you can't do, until we determine things one way or another, is leave the area."

"Fingerprints? My God! Look—" Jim began.

"Shut up, Jim," said Amy. "If you read my books — although it is my belief that you really *cannot* read — you'd remember that the one who makes the most fuss is the one whodunnit." She laughed. "Now, that *isn't* true at all; I'm just talking to annoy my editor. But go on, Monica."

"I'm Monica Thornhill, The Honourable," she responded. Buzzie was puzzled. "And," she continued, "*I* didn't sleep well, either. Too much excitement before I went to bed, I suppose, though I'd taken my usual pills. Around one or two in the morning, I guess it was, I got up, put on a raincoat and my comforting woolly slippers — oh, the coat was a Burberry and the slippers Morlands; are we supposed to tell these details? — and went out on deck, against orders, of course, to see what might be up.

"Nothing much was. Antonio was walking back and forth, on the starboard side of this deck, and he said Carlo was over on the other. The Captain, he said, was on the bridge. I suppose he was, though I didn't quite dare go to the upper deck. Vito's told you about that, of course.

"I came in here. Paul was lying on a sofa. Jim was just coming from the galley with coffee. I drank some with them and then I wandered back to my stateroom, retrieving my bottle of sleeping pills from the bar on the way. Oh, I might add that none were missing. I noticed there were twelve left after Jake gave two to Viola and I'd taken two, and there were still twelve in the bottle. I've got them, if you want to send them to the lab, but you'll have to get a doctor to give me some more."

Buzzie regarded Jake thoughtfully. "We won't need them,

ma'am, unless the contents of the stomach— Go on."

"Well, I read in bed for maybe a half-hour. Then, wearing same old raincoat and slippers, I went to the bar and poured a glass of brandy for Jake. Jim came in as I did; he said he'd been sneaking a look at that damned island. He didn't put it quite that way; he just said he'd been looking around. Paul came out of the galley with a pitcher of orange juice. I took the brandy down, and Jake was wide-awake. He said his back hurt so badly he'd been walking around the cabin for hours. Viola was all right, breathing well, not trying to thrash around, or anything.

"Then I tried to sleep again. I know I was still awake around three-thirty. I fell asleep soon after and woke up at exactly five-thirty, when I heard the Coast Guard boat. I dressed, omitting shoes, and came out and found Elizabeth Lamb standing in the dining room. She had only pajamas on, which I thought strange, that and that she was up so early, but she seemed all right. Paul was sitting at the bar, head down, looking exhausted, at least from the back. I didn't see Jim. Elizabeth Lamb asked me to go below with her; I did, and found Viola was dead."

"Monica," Julia put in, "you know how V.V. feels about bare feet. You'd better get shoes before he comes back." She explained to Buzzie: "He has a Sicilian superstition about them — thinks they indicate a death."

"You all knew that?" Buzzie asked her.

"Well, I did. I don't know who else did. Does it matter?"

"Anyway," Monica said impatiently, "I've already attended to shoes, Julia." She bent below the bar and came up waving a tan suede, fleece-lined slipper. "My feet were awfully cold so I nipped back to my room for my good old woollies and I've had them on ever since. Nobody noticed? Well, Lieutenant, if they didn't notice I was running around all morning in my bedroom slippers, I'm not sure what you can expect they *did* observe!

"Well, Jake was more stunned than anything else, I'd say. He also was blaming himself. I went looking for a doctor from the Coast Guard boat — took a few seconds here to get my slippers — found there was only a Medical Technician and took him down to Viola."

"Why?" Buzzie asked.

"Well, I thought *somebody* official should look at her. Maybe I wasn't thinking too clearly, but what else should I have done? Then I took him to the galley for coffee and Pietro was in his usual state but I just ignored him."

Julia nodded, looking at Paul reprovingly. "Quite right; we *all* should ignore him. He's much too arrogant."

"I certainly did. I went into the loo in the galley and washed off my face and smoothed my hair, even though he tried to stop me. When I came out, Jake and everybody else was in here and Jake had evidently told them about Viola. Everybody except Vito, Mrs. Danniver, Persis and Julia, I mean. They were all shaken, of course, but why wouldn't they be? Nothing unusual about that and nobody was saying or doing or wearing or eating anything unusual, either.

"We talked about nothing much and a seaman, Antonio, came in with a tray of breakfast and dropped it when he heard about Viola. I'd say *he* was extremely upset, more upset than I was, to be honest. He said Vito had eaten breakfast and was going to go see Viola so I ran to Vito's cabin to try to dissuade him. After a while Bob Templeton — or whatever his name is — and Elizabeth Lamb came in and told him about Viola. He took it better than I thought he would. He went down to her cabin and Bob and I came in here and—" She stopped. "You know, I'm getting so tired I'm almost dizzy. No sleep, and trying to remember—. Have I told you enough, Lieutenant? I just can't think of anything at all that seemed suspicious."

"I've got something of a picture," Buzzie answered. "You feel that no one was acting out of character or doing or saying anything unusual?"

"That's right. Although Julia and Paul started speaking again. I was in Vito's room last night when they had some sort of argument in here, but Vito told me the gist of it. But it would be perfectly natural for them to make up, after the death. I mean, why stay angry? None of us were showing much anger, or any other emotion, tired as we were and probably getting annoyed by every little thing. I know little things bothered me, but I was too tired to show it, or even, now, to remember what they were."

"You showed some anger when Jake said he'd convinced V.V. to

231

ask for an autopsy even if the doctor didn't think one was required," Paul reminded her, with his pleasant smile.

"And so did Julia!" Monica spoke sharply.

"Yes, I did." Julia's voice was weak with exhaustion. "I'm Julia Vincentia, Lieutenant, and Viola was my late husband's daughter. I had cared for her since she was two until last year when she came to live with her grandfather. She was a pretty child, then a beautiful girl, and I thought it horrible to — to deface her."

She lit a cigarette and inhaled deeply. "You might as well know, Lieutenant, that Mr. Cooper and I became close, very close, a few years ago. He was kind to me when I was suddenly widowed. I had grown to depend on him. Last night he told me that he and Viola — that he and Viola—" — she drew again on the cigarette — "were to be married. I was distraught. But, whether you believe it or not, by the time I woke up this morning, I was completely resigned to it. I felt sick, and shaken, and, of course, betrayed, but I *was* resigned. But I wouldn't be honest if I said I would agree to attend the wedding!

"And then he came in and told me Viola was dead and though you may disbelieve this, too, my first reaction was grief for the child I had loved, and my second, grief for him." She looked at Paul. "I can never feel again for him what I had felt; I cannot say I ever want to see him again after we leave this boat, but I am not capable of staying angry with anyone for very long. Life is too short." She sighed and her eyes filled with tears.

Buzzie spoke with compassion. "You don't have to go on now, Mrs. Vincentia." He looked at his watch. "You may feel better after some lunch; you could tell me the rest later; what you noticed, and so on."

"No, I'd rather do it now though I can't say I noticed very much. Elizabeth Lamb tried to wake me this morning — I don't know what time that was — but I couldn't get up. Then, after Paul told me about Viola, I dressed and came up here. I did think Viola's grandfather should be told before the police came, and I thought it my responsibility to do it. I began to argue, and we were all getting excited, although I'd say no one was *unduly* disturbed. Then that man Chris and Monica invited on the voyage announced he was from

232

the FBI. He said *he* could tell V.V., and I agreed. And we were right, because V.V. has taken it well; better, I think, than if we had waited until the police appeared."

She rubbed her forehead. "I have such a headache! Well, V.V. was told, as you've heard. When Jake came back from going down to Viola's cabin with V.V., he told us about an autopsy. I was really angry, then. I went to my cabin and lay on the bed. When I felt the boat stop, I came up, the others were there, and you came aboard.

"I honestly didn't notice anything strange about anyone. I am certain Viola died naturally and I can't wait to be allowed to go back to England and just be alone and peaceful. I've had it, as the Americans say!"

"But what you have not had, my dear, is luncheon," said Mr. Vincentia. He had been standing in the doorway as she spoke. "You will feel the better for it. Come, everyone."

The tables had been set so quietly that the preoccupied guests had not noticed. Pietro was at the sideboard, poised to fill the plates that Carlo, beside him, stood ready to serve. Mr. Vincentia indicated that Buzzie was to sit at his right and Elizabeth Lamb at his left and that the remaining places at his table were to be taken by Amy, Jake and Chris. Then, frowning at Paul who was standing by the other table, he asked Amy to move to it and put Julia in her chair. Monica and Jim sat with Amy and Paul.

"Oh, good; there's ten of us eating," Elizabeth Lamb said cheerfully. "I thought there might only be nine and I know you don't like that." Mr. Vincentia looked thoughtfully around at his guests, his gaze remaining on Jake, who was still wearing the flat, tweed golf cap in which he had appeared, along with a jacket of a matching soft tweed, when he had come up on deck to see the arrival of the police. "Does that hat help your allergy, Mr. Aaronson?" Elizabeth Lamb asked curiously.

Jake snatched it off. "Bless me, with all this upset, I forgot I had it on! Or maybe it's a high holy day and the outside of my head remembered it but the inside didn't! I'm afraid I'm not as religious as my mum brought me up to be."

Mr. Vincentia almost laughed. "You were *a coppola,* my dear friend. Just like the dish Pietro has for us. I think it was your stomach that was aware, not your head."

Carlo was placing before them deep plates of spaghetti covered with a tomato sauce smelling strongly of basil that was topped with slices of fried eggplant. "See, Jake, spaghetti *alla coppola:* 'with a cap on'! Your head matched," Vincentia smiled.

"And none for me, Vito? The only Italian dish I like!" Annie, speaking with mock chagrin, was beside him.

"My dear! Jake told me you had returned. I am so glad! I thought you would rest a while longer. Pietro, set a place for Mrs. Donelli and get some bottles of that special chianti she likes. Take these away" — he indicated the straw-encased bottles on the tables — "and use them for cooking. Mrs. Donelli and Lieutenant Higgins must have the best."

Annie graciously received the friendly greetings of the others. "We have you to thank for being saved from that *château cheapeau,*" Monica muttered to her. "But I'd be glad to see you, anyway! We need a cool brain around here. I think the rest of us are going bonkers from tension."

Mr. Vincentia, pouring wine, regarded his guests gravely. "Now, like the unsurpassable Mr. Nero Wolfe, I must prohibit all talk of — of business matters while we eat. We must all speak of something other than what concerns us."

After some moments of silence, Jim offered: "I see they've got Ozawa to lead the Boston Symphony, starting next fall. Wonder what the Bostonians will make of a Jap conductor?"

"Oh, he'll have critics, no doubt," Julia replied, sipping chianti. "Even though he's supposed to be very talented."

"Yes," Amy sighed, "in music, as in painting or writing, 'Everybody's a critic!' But Boston's worse than the average city. Didn't Twain write that 'in every Boston audience, there are 4000 critics'? Something like that."

There was silence again. Monica turned to Paul, who was eating heartily. "You know, one shouldn't eat much, with a cold. You'll get worse."

"Oh," replied Paul, who was looking much healthier, "I feel a good deal better. Anger" — he glared at Pietro, who glared back at him before he left for the galley — "always makes me hungry.

Grief, too." He put down his fork, a little abashed. "I mean—" He drank wine, sighing.

"This pasta is awfully good," remarked Chris, who had eaten little of it. He coughed as he spoke. "It's that *di Nola* brand, isn't it, V.V.?"

"I will use no other," his host replied, although he pushed away his hardly-touched plate. "It is the best." He got up to pour himself and the others more chianti. Jim, who had also eaten little, thirstily drank from his replenished glass, so earnestly that he spilled some wine on the pink linen tablecloth. He blushed, embarrassed, although no one appeared to notice.

Silence again. "What is this book you said you're writing, Elizabeth Lamb?" Monica finally spoke. "I hope we aren't going to be characters in it."

"Have to be careful about that, you know," Jim admonished. "Wasn't it Marquand, Amy, who was sued by his relatives after some book of his was published? They said he'd depicted them—" He broke off to sneeze, then blushed, embarrassed again.

"Being sued isn't the worst hazard a writer faces," Amy replied. "Editors are. I thought of a good plot the other day: you send in a manuscript you know is bad to an editor you don't like, and you poison the flap of the return envelope you include with it. One editor less in the world! And you'd never be caught," she finished happily.

"But suppose his secretary licks the envelope?" Elizabeth Lamb worried. "And you kill an innocent person?"

"Let's not talk about things like that, Elizabeth Lamb," Jake told her sternly, one eye on Vincentia. "How's your knee? Persis told me it was badly hurt when you fell last night."

Elizabeth Lamb had been cleaning up her plate. She indicated to Carlo that she would like some more pasta. "Oh," she said, surprised, "you know, I forgot all about it. It doesn't hurt any more."

"Good," Mr. Vincentia said, smiling at her. "We don't want another 'Wounded Knee' fiasco, as they had out West in April, with a Federal Marshal dead. Dead," he repeated throatily. He drank wine.

"Well, *caro,* I'm very happy your knee has healed. But I have been thinking about you, and not just your knee. Would you not like to join Persis at Elizabeth's cottage? You could come aboard and see us often, while we are here. It will be several days, at least. The men from the boatyard found the fuel injectors clogged with some — with something, and have removed them. New ones will have to be ordered.

"I do enjoy having you with us," he ended, somewhat wistfully, "but I must think of your welfare and, also, what your grandmother might wish."

"Oh, no, Mr. Vincentia! It would be very boring at The Bungalow, till Persis feels better. I am perfectly safe aboard the *Chianti;* what could happen to me? And Grandmother knows how I love new experiences and being on this lovely boat certainly is one. I've got the rest of the summer to be at The Bungalow."

"Well, then," he said slowly, "very well. I will have your things moved into Mrs. Danniver's cabin, if you agree, Amy?" He signaled to Carlo to remove the plates and got up. "I wish to speak to Pietro about the dessert."

The company sat silent again. "Mr. Vincentia has such style," Elizabeth Lamb whispered to Buzzie, who had eaten appreciatively while watching the guests closely. "My English teacher said Hemingway said style was grace under pressure and that's what he has." Amy, who had heard, said, "You know, I was just thinking that very thing. He is so gracious, so thoughtful of us, in spite of what he must be feeling. I do admire him."

"So do we all," Monica told her. "Although I would think he'd like to be free to wash his hands of the lot of us and just step away, into the Fourth Dimension, or something."

"I never really understood what the Fourth Dimension is supposed to be," Elizabeth Lamb said thoughtfully. "Does anyone? I don't see how it could be time, but I'm really awfully bad at scientific stuff. They say at school that some people are factual and some are verbal, and I guess I'm verbal."

"I would agree that you are," Julia told her, a bit sarcastically. Chris Grenville spoke kindly: "The Fourth Dimension is what we and the universe can be, Elizabeth Lamb." He was more hoarse than Vincentia, who smiled a little at him as he seated himself again.

236

"And the Fifth Dimension is what we and the universe must *not* be. "

Elizabeth Lamb thought this over, with such concentration that she at first did not notice that it was Payson who had placed a large platter of *cannoli* in the middle of the table and turned to put the same on the other. "Payson!" she said. "You're back — I'm so glad!" His face above his clean white shirt and striped apron was grey with fatigue.

"Yes," he said despondently, "there's a lot to do, cabins cleaned 'n' all. Figgered I'm still gettin' paid so I'd best work fer my pay. Nuthin' else to do now." He staggered a little as he went to the sideboard for dessert plates.

Mr. Vincentia served the *cannoli*. "No, Payson, you are to get some rest before dinner. Carlo can attend to the cabins. Just bring coffee to the saloon first."

"I love *cannoli*," Jake Aaronson observed although he was only pushing the crisp, cream-filled tubes about his plate. "Remember when your mum used to make it for us to sell from our ice truck, Vito? And how we'd eat almost as much as we sold? Never thought then that we'd someday be eating it in style, on your own posh yacht, did you, now?"

"No," Vincentia said grimly. "I never thought of half the things that have happened to me." He stood up. "If you have all finished, Lieutenant Higgins can get on with his inquiry."

Buzzie refused the coffee Payson offered and opened his notebook. "Well, I guess maybe you — Mr. Aaronson, is it? — could tell me anything you noticed. I think Mrs. Vincentia's told us all she can."

Elizabeth Lamb waved her hand to attract his attention. "Buzzie, there's one thing Mrs. Vincentia didn't tell you and it's because she didn't know. I was in her cabin last night, to sleep, and Mr. Cooper gave me the keys. He was sleeping in the saloon because they'd had, well, you know, a fight, sort of. She told you.

"Anyway, he was worried about her. I mean, we *are* on a boat and she might have gone out on deck, I guess he thought, and ju — and fallen off. So he gave me the two keys and told me to lock the door from the inside. So I did, and kept the chain around my neck, under my pajamas. We were both locked in all night and although I could have got out, she couldn't." She pulled the chain

237

off her neck and timidly took it over to Julia.

Julia showed anger as well as surprise. "Thank you, Elizabeth Lamb," she said, taking the keys and giving Paul Cooper a venemous look. "Well," Buzzie said quickly, "back to Mr. Aaronson. Thank you for telling us that, Elizabeth Lamb."

Jake had put his cap on again and was shivering even in his tweed jacket. "You know that I was with Viola all night," he said slowly. "Monica brought me brandy; she told you that. Later, I don't know how much later, Darrow came down with coffee. I take it white — with cream, as you say here — and there wasn't any in it, so although I'd've liked some, I didn't drink it. Didn't want to send the lad back up for cream, because he didn't look well. Looked about as I feel now," he added wryly.

"Then Cooper showed up with some juice. Said he'd been squeezing oranges all night and it seemed to him he'd been doing it for years. Viola was sleeping without stirring, through all these visits. They all looked at her — didn't go right up and lean over her but if she was — dead, I think they'd have noticed. There's a look," he added wearily. "I've seen it a few times too many."

"She was okay, Jake," Jim said. "When I was there, anyway."

"When I was, too," Monica agreed; "I've told you, Lieutenant." Paul also nodded agreement: "She looked fine when I glanced at her. Well, as fine as possible under the circs."

Jake went on: "I may have dozed off once or twice, but I was awake from the time Mrs. Danniver came in until I went into the shower. She's said she came in around four, and that's my guess, too." He looked over at Elizabeth Lamb. "Would you pour me more coffee, dear?"

"And you had never met Mrs. Danniver before you came aboard, when was it, day before yesterday?" Buzzie asked, evenly.

Jake's surprise turned to obvious anger but he answered as evenly: "No, I had not. To" — he turned to Mrs. Danniver and suddenly smiled — "my everlasting regret."

Mrs. Danniver's thin, tanned face turned red, either from his gallantry or the anger she did not control as well as Jake. "No, he certainly had not, Lieutenant!"

"I just wondered," Buzzie murmured. "Go on, sir."

"It was daylight when I suddenly realized that running water on my sore back might ease it a bit; don't know why I hadn't thought of it before, but I just hadn't. Anyway, I was under the shower, oh, maybe half-an-hour, just standing under the warm water. It felt so good. Then I heard Elizabeth Lamb calling."

He raised his head and looked sadly at Vincentia. "That's all I know, Vito. All this morning, I guess I was a bit dazed. I can't say I noticed anything at all about anyone. I can only say I wish it had happened to me and not Viola."

Everyone was silent. Finally Buzzie asked, "Who would like to be next?"

Chris sighed loudly. "I'm Christopher Grenville," he said. "I'm V.V.'s godson, though not the only one. There must be a dozen of us. I've known Viola since she was born—"

Buzzie, with a polite smile, interrupted him. "Just what you noticed late last night or early this morning, Mr. Grenville."

"I can't say there was much. I was asked to stay — someone was asked, and I volunteered — to stay with V.V. last night, because he'd had a bad turn when Viola had that accident on the upper deck. I was sleeping, more or less, and really less, on the smaller settee in his stateroom. It's too short for me so I was fairly uncomfortable. I went out briefly to the deck a couple of times, just to see if those men on the island were lying doggo or trying something on. I saw no one at all, neither seaman, though I heard someone walking around above me, several times."

"How long would you say you were on deck, each time?" Buzzie asked.

"Oh, just a minute or two. V.V. was sleeping but I was afraid he'd wake and, well, get worse, so I didn't stay out long. I looked through the door at the end of the passage once but I couldn't see or hear either Cooper or Darrow back here in the saloon. I was cold but I didn't dare take the time to go down for warmer clothes. Monica looked in this morning. She seemed nervous and later I realized why, but she didn't tell us then about Viola, of course. V.V. said he felt well and Antonio came in with some breakfast for him so I went to my cabin, washed up somewhat, got a sweater, came up here and heard the — the sad news.

"And my mind is utterly blank as to anything unusual, the things you've asked if we noticed. I felt too rotten to take in much of anything. After you've finished, I just want to go to bed." He searched through his pockets for a rumpled handkerchief and applied it gingerly to his reddened nose.

"It won't be much longer," Buzzie assured him. He turned to Paul. "You are Mr. Cooper, I believe."

"Paul Cooper, yes. I was here in the saloon all night, with Darrow. Monica's told you she came in. She seemed completely normal to me, though I did wonder why she was up and about, since she's said she always takes pills at bedtime that knock her out." He smiled appealingly at Monica. "Sorry, my dear, but he did say to give our observations."

"You are speaking entirely according to what *I* have observed of your character, Paul," Monica said sweetly. "And that is: in a most dependable and trustworthy manner. Carry on."

Paul colored a trifle. "Neither Darrow nor I got much sleep though we stretched out on the sofas now and then. He left once or twice to make coffee and, as Jake said, took some down to him. He went out on deck a couple of times and so did I. I saw both seamen, a little distance from me, each time. I don't know if they noticed me.

"I made sandwiches for us from the ham we'd had at dinner and at least two pitchers of orange juice. I'm afraid I left the ham out and the oranges all around and the cook's fairly angry with me. But, then, he's angry most of the time." He looked indignantly at Vincentia: "He actually threatened to knife me a while ago, if you can believe it, V.V.!"

"Yes, Mr. Cooper," Buzzie said patiently. "But about this morning?"

"Well, I'd dozed off for a bit, I suppose. Darrow was asleep, too. Anyway, I woke suddenly, sat bolt upright. I felt sick, grubby, as if I'd been out on the tiles all night is the best way to describe it. My throat was sore and I started for the galley for more juice. All at once I felt terrible, dizzy, ears ringing — I'd 'come over all queer,' as my old nurse would've said. I was just standing there when Darrow ran past me, saying something about a boat, I thought. I made it to the w.c. in the galley, was washing and feeling much better when Elizabeth Lamb banged on the door and said she had to use it. Then the cook showed up and started his usual tantrum, so I left.

"I felt too tired to go out on deck with Darrow, though I realized the Coast Guard had come, so I just sat here. Darrow came back; then Jake, looking like death, came in and told us about Viola." He seemed to choke, and rubbed his hand roughly across his eyes.

"The others have told you what was said and done after that. I can't add anything to it. Nobody's actions or speech or dress was in any way unusual; certainly not suspicious, though I can't say I was in any condition to observe closely. Although," his voice strengthened with anger, "I hope you are looking into the actions of Pietro, that damned cook, and Antonio, too, because when Antonio heard, he almost fainted. He had to sit down.

"I took the tray he'd dropped to the galley and when I told Pietro, he looked about the same. I really think *their* responses were most peculiar and I think you should find out why!"

"And," Jim added explosively, "I hope you take their fingerprints as well as ours!"

"Yes, of course. That'll be attended to," Buzzie assured them. "Nothing else, Mr. Cooper?"

"Nothing else," he said dully. "Nothing else."

"I guess I'm the last," Jim said. "Unless you want to say something, V.V.?"

"I have already spoken to the Lieutenant," Mr. Vincentia answered coolly.

"Well, then, I'm Jim Darrow. As you know by now, I guess. Cooper's told you what we both did here last night. He forgot to say we turned on the t.v. for a while, but we did. He dozed off a couple of times — I could hear him snoring right across the room — but I couldn't. I went down once to Miss Vincentia's cabin, as enough people have mentioned by now. She was all right at the time, and *I've* mentioned that. I know I was still awake at 4:40, the last time I looked at my watch. Then I dropped off, I suppose, and came to when I thought I heard, or, I guess, felt, a bump. Cooper wasn't around.

"There seemed to be voices amidships, if that's the term, on the

241

left side, port side. I went through the dining room and Cooper was in the vestibule as he's said, just standing there. He certainly looked sick, had his arms sort of clutched across his stomach. I told him I thought the Coast Guard boat had come and went on out to the port deck.

"The cook, Pietro, was standing just inside the door to the deck, looking at the boat. He was mumbling to himself in Italian, sort of angrily, which I thought strange, but he probably hadn't had any more sleep than the rest of us. He was watching the man with the broken leg, you know, all night.

"I went out and watched them lashing on to us, and so on, for a few minutes and then I thought I'd get more coffee but I heard the cook and Cooper having an argument so I just came in here and lay on a sofa. Cooper was at the bar, just sitting there, and after a while he went over to another sofa. Then Mr. Aaronson came in and told us and then the others sort of trickled in, I guess. When that FBI guy was told of Miss Vincentia's death by — who was it? oh, Elizabeth Lamb, *he* didn't show much emotion at all.

"But then, I guess in his trade, one doesn't. Anyway, I have to say, like Grenville and Cooper, that nobody else seemed strange. Everyone reacted as you'd expect, except maybe the two crewmen were a little excited. Although maybe they would behave that way, being Italians—" He stopped short, face a bright red, and looked nervously at his employer. He gulped. "And that's all I know," he finished weakly.

Buzzie hastily turned to Annie. "And you, Mrs. Donelli, weren't here," he observed. "You'd had a message the first night out that your mother was sick, so you left then?" Annie nodded. "How did you get the message?"

"Why, Mr. Vincentia brought it to me," she answered, frowning a little.

"I was on the bridge when the call came in," Mr. Vincentia informed Buzzie pleasantly. "The Captain had gone into his cabin behind the pilot house for a few minutes, leaving the auto-pilot on, but I assure you the call was made." He raised his brows.

"Of course, sir," Buzzie agreed. "Well—"

"You aren't going to ask Elizabeth Lamb anything?" Julia

questioned. "You did the other little girl, and Mrs. Danniver said she was with her all the time, up to when they heard of Viola's death. Not of course that I ever thought that play *The Bad Seed* made any sense at all. But the rest of us have answered."

"I do *not* like that woman," Amy muttered quite audibly to Jim. "I've told you that."

"I'll speak to Elizabeth Lamb later, ma'am, as I've said," Buzzie told Julia stiffly. "Unlike the rest of you, she's been known to me a long time. I know she observes an awful lot, too much to have you all sit here while she goes through it.

"But, just for an example: Elizabeth Lamb, tell us what you noticed about — oh, say, about people's clothes this morning. Make it brief, because after I take fingerprints and speak to the crewmen, I've got to go ashore to make some calls and do some other things."

Elizabeth Lamb cleared her throat. "Monica's feet were bare when I first saw her, but she's said that, so maybe it doesn't count? I did notice that later she had on those slippers, but my grandmother brought me the same kind from England last year, so maybe that's why I did but nobody else did. And Persis didn't have her sneakers on and her socks were wet and Mrs. Danniver was only wearing one of those little gold hoop earrings she always wears, the left one."

Amy put her hand to her right ear. "Oh, no! It must have fallen out. Well, it can't have gone far. We'll find it." Elizabeth Lamb went on. "And Mr. Vincentia has on the same red shirt I saw him wearing in Boston; it's been washed and ironed but the third button down is cracked, just as it was in Boston." Vincentia looked down at his shirt and smiled. "I need a wife," he told her, almost gaily.

"And Mr. Darrow's fly was open this morning but I told him about it" — Jim blushed — "and Mrs. Vincentia's skirt zipper was, too, and still is. And Mr. Grenville's sweater was buttoned crooked but he's fixed it and Mr. Cooper's shirt is all wrinkled and hanging out but it was all neat and tucked in last night." Paul raised his eyes to Heaven: "I slept in it, child."

"And Mr. Aaronson put his shirt on wrong side out this morning and it stayed that way till he went down and changed." Jake nodded: "I knew, a little later, but it's supposed to be bad luck to alter clothing you've put on wrong." He laughed hollowly: "Bad luck! Ha."

"Nobody else mentioned it," Buzzie observed. "Anything more, Elizabeth Lamb? Well, I'd say that proves my point. Now, I'm going to get my equipment and I'll take your prints. Then I'll leave you alone for a while.

"The autopsy is getting special attention, so I'm sure I'll have the report in a couple of hours and then your minds, I'm sure, will all be relieved." He smiled around, politely. "And I thank you for your patience and cooperation, as I know Mr. Vincentia does."

As they waited for Buzzie to assemble his equipment, Jake Aaronson leaned over and whispered to Elizabeth Lamb: "And I wonder which, if any, one of us has told Hitler's 'big lie'?"

• CHAPTER 11 •

A Trout in the Milk

THE FINGERPRINTING of the passengers and crew completed, Buzzie had left the *Chianti*. Mr. Vincentia had gone with him, telling Elizabeth Lamb he felt a walk in the woods and the *atmosfera* of "dear Elizabeth's cottage" was what he most needed. "And Lieutenant Higgins is to call me there; I thought it best."

Waiting for Buzzie to finish speaking to the crew in the galley, she and Vincentia had leaned on the railing above the ladder, gazing at the bright blue waters of Schooner Cove and the three cottages visible amongst the trees above the granite shores. "So peaceful," Vincentia had sighed, "and so beautiful. When you are married, perhaps it will be from here. Would you like that?"

"I won't be married till I'm quite old," she had answered. "I can't imagine wanting to have children, either, so I think I'll wait until I'm at least fifty." He had laughed a little, then sobered. "I wonder why people do want children? To satisfy their egos, I suppose, or perhaps it is in the hope of immortality? Then they grow up, and marry and leave you. Although I *had* looked forward, a little, to someday handing out boxes of *confetti* at Viola's marriage. But it would have been a marriage to a man *I* chose."

"Confetti?" she had asked. "But you throw that. It's paper."

"No, no; *confetti* is what we call the sugared almonds, some silver, some white, that we give to the wedding guests in little white boxes. It is an Italian custom."

"Oh, just like the French," she had answered thoughtfully, and then turned to give Buzzie a farewell hug.

She went slowly down to her new quarters, passing Payson on the stairs, carrying linen and obviously disregarding his instructions to rest. Carlo, muttering to himself in Italian, was watering the ferns in the little lobby outside the cabin doors. He regarded her sternly and told her to leave the plants alone. "I don't touch growing things," she told him coldly and he mumbled that then the other little *ragazza* played tricks. "If somebody's broken them, you ought to ask Vi—" she started to say. "Good heavens," she thought as she stood under the shower, "I'm so tired I almost forgot Viola's dead. My mind must be going."

Clean, and in fresh jeans and shirt, she felt much better. Amy had come down for her notebook while she was dressing, observing that "a real pro writes after a death as well as when it's not raining," and now Elizabeth Lamb decided she would take her own notebook up and join her. "I can sleep tonight," she thought.

The saloon presented a scene of what Disraeli, that great aphorist, would have termed masterly inactivity. Jim slouched in a chair, legs stretched out and eyes closed. Annie had curled up in a corner of a sofa, staring at her folded hands that rested on an opened magazine in her lap. Paul was crouched on a bar stool, looking into the empty glass he held. Amy sat near the door to the fantail lounge, her notebook on a table in front of her, gazing out at the water visible over the stern while she tapped a pencil slowly against her cheek.

"Where's everybody?" Elizabeth Lamb asked. "Why, everybody who *is* anybody's right here," Paul replied with a smile. "But I think I'll go down and straighten out my things; V.V.'s had them put in Grenville's cabin." Annie got up, too. "I should get some letters typed, the ones I didn't finish before I left." Only a loud snore came from Jim.

"Jim!" Amy said sharply. "For God's sake, go to your cabin and sleep there. I'm going mad trying to get Alaric C.'s clues in order

246

and you're not helping." Jim managed to rise and shamble out.

"I guess I'll write my novel," Elizabeth Lamb told Amy. "I guess I'll make it a mystery, because maybe you could tell me how to begin? It's hard to write, isn't it? I just realized it. I don't know how you ever start."

Amy laughed hollowly. "You start about two years before. You go around writing down ideas and inventing or borrowing scraps of conversation and jot down descriptions of people and places, all these on little pieces of paper you manage to misplace or lose completely because you're too disorganized to remember to take your pocket notebook everywhere with you. That is, if you're like me. Then the terrible time comes when you have to put it all together so it makes sense and then you start to write it — remember, now you're also probably correcting proofs on a previous book, or maybe even just finishing one.

"Then you finally *do* it and it's published — maybe — and then the critics tear it apart. Critics are people who can't write so that means they're able to say how others should. So then you start another, and that takes two years, too.

"Yes, writing *is* so hard and some critics so petty that I don't think there's ever been an author — that's a *published* writer — who feared going to hell. He's had it here."

"Then why do you do it?"

"God knows. Well, I guess most so-called 'serious writers' feel they have something to say the world would be better for hearing. In my case, I just want to entertain people, get their minds off their own miseries for a while. I know a lot about misery, and that almost everyone has some." She sighed heavily.

"Aren't you a 'serious writer'?"

"No, because I try to be humorous. I take pokes at people and classes and institutions. Although murder is a serious subject, my books try to be more than just a puzzle; I try to entertain. You know, E. B. White — you've read his *Charlotte's Web,* I'm sure — said the world appreciates humor but doesn't value it. Something like that. He said any writer who wants to be taken seriously must deal with serious subjects, and not try to be funny. If I wrote tragic stories about poor people instead of murder mysteries that occur mostly in what you might call the 'upper classes,' I'd be thought a much better writer than I'm considered now."

"Yes; well, look, I have to begin somewhere and I don't have two years to get material so why don't I write about what's happened to us, here on the *Chianti?* Even if nobody killed Viola, it's still a mystery what happened to the engines and why the radio-telephone didn't work. How would I start figuring that? And I could use us, us real people, because this isn't going to be published so they can't sue me like they did that man Jim was talking about at lunch."

"That's an idea! And I'll be your collaborator." She brightened. "Anything to get away from that damned Alaric C. for a while. Open your notebook. Now, I don't do it this way but I read some books by a woman — she was a rotten writer, too; no clues. All of a sudden the murderer confessed, or her lady detective saw him trying to knock off someone else, or he tried to kill her. But she had the detective do something I thought was good, except I'm just too disorganized to have Alaric C. do it. And it wouldn't be in character for a child to be so methodical. *And* the little brat would probably refuse, anyway," she ended gloomily.

Elizabeth Lamb thought that a bit fanciful. "So what did she do? What should *I* do?"

"Well, she listed all the people and where they were, or weren't. And what motives they had. If you're going to start about the engines and the communications, you write down where everybody was and what they were doing when these things happened, or you think they did. Then you eliminate those who couldn't have done it. You might develop it further, bringing in when Viola died, or we think she did, because you want this to be a mystery, whether she was murdered or not, don't you?

"And it *could* be; make it that one of us murdered her even if she *wasn't* murdered, if he or she could have. This is fiction, after all. Only don't let V.V. see it. It would be really bad taste to capitalize on his tragedy, if you see what I mean. And," she added thoughtfully, "don't let anyone else see it, either, because maybe one of us *is* a murderer. My God, that's a terrible thought. And it could be dangerous for you. Are you sure you won't go ashore with Persis?"

"Oh, my goodness, nobody's going to know what I'm doing.

248

But, as for Mr. Vincentia, I heard Monica say that a good writer sells out everyone he knows or has even met, sooner or later. She said they just can't help using everything they see or hear. It was the first day out, after lunch, and you had gone down to get Persis a bath, but I remember."

"I think you remember *everything* you hear," Amy said slowly. "Ever think of really being a detective? They're using women now a lot, in agencies."

"No, although I've — oh, it doesn't matter. Let's get started, before anyone else comes in. *You're* the only one who couldn't have murdered Viola, you know, because Persis was with you till I came in and told you. And you couldn't have done anything to the engines or the phones, either. At lunch, the engines were fine, we were travelling fast, and then you and I and Jim and Persis were right here and then you and Persis were writing in your cabin, together.

"Then you both came up to tea. I was late, but some others were here. And it was then the engines slowed down and it was just after that that they found the communications panel didn't work, was all wet. And you were here in the saloon all that time; you were still here, with Mr. Templeton, when I came down from the bridge after we got to Cousin Curtis' island.

"So I'm not even going to list you because you aren't only 'very clear,' as Persis says, just about Viola, but about the engines and the phones, too. So let's get going."

"Thank God for Persis, my 'alley bin' all through this," Amy murmured. "Okay, about the engines and phones: let's list where everybody was after lunch and till we got to that island."

"I'll think and you write, would you, Mrs. Danniver? And you'll remember if I forget something. Well, let's see: Monica. She went out to the fantail after lunch and later I saw her on the top deck. Then she went to her cabin. She was here at tea when I came in and later she and Mrs. Vincentia took tea down to Mr. Grenville and Mr. Cooper and the four of them were together in Mrs. Vincentia's cabin.

"So I guess we put that Monica could have wrecked the engines, between lunch and tea, but the communications went out later, the Captain said, so I think she's clear there. Even though she said she'd talked to the Captain on the bridge, but that was much earlier, before she left for her cabin. And I can't see she could have put water into the panel with the Captain right there. *And* I can't see any reason for her doing either one.

"Mrs. Vincentia. She was playing cards with Mr. Grenville, Mr. Templeton and Mr. Cooper from right after lunch. I don't know when she came up for tea?"

"She came out of her cabin, with Templeton, just as Persis and I came out of ours and we four came up here together. Then she was here in the saloon and, as you said, she and Monica went down together with tea for Chris and Cooper. She would seem to be clear of both incidents of sabotage."

"Sabotage. That's a good word. I just learned in school it comes from when striking French workers threw their wooden *sabots* into the machinery. But I guess you knew that. Now, we're letting Mr. Templeton out. Except he was certainly all over the boat, knew all about the crew's quarters, for instance. Just as if he were looking for something, do you think?"

"Perhaps. We'll never know. But if he had seen anyone on this deck putting something into the fuel tanks — and we heard V.V. say the fuel injectors were clogged with something — he'd certainly have mentioned it. Same thing if he'd seen someone going to the bridge, any time on his travels around the boat. But he was playing cards, or at tea, at the times we're concerned about, so he couldn't have. Now Jake."

"He's certainly out of both. He went to his cabin right after lunch and he's so allergic to roses — honestly, that Persis! How could she? — that he'd have been affected right away, wouldn't he?"

"I think so," Amy agreed. "I know a little about allergies, had to read up on them because dear little Alaric C. has hay fever. I have to have him sneeze at times, when he's hiding from the murderer. Adds to the damned tension Jim always demands I put in. An attack will come on fast but subside fairly quickly if the sufferer doesn't spend much time around the irritant.

"But Jake was so badly affected that I'm sure he stayed right in the cabin till you and Persis went down. He couldn't have faked that severe reaction and we know he went straight to his cabin after lunch. He really seemed awfully sleepy, just as he said he was."

"Unless he's a good actor," Elizabeth Lamb remarked.

"Unless who's a good actor?" Jake's voice asked. They started guiltily. Their heads bent over the notebook, they had not heard him descending the spiral stairs in the fantail.

"Oh — oh — that actor Redford, the one with the same name as the FBI man," Amy said quickly. "Elizabeth Lamb thinks he isn't very good but I think he's wonderful."

"Well, that's what makes horse-racing," he replied jovially, pouring a glass of mineral water at the bar.

"*What* makes horse-racing?" Elizabeth Lamb demanded.

"Difference of opinion. Get it? Well, I'm off to my comfortable bed. Fell asleep on the upper deck and woke with a stiff neck. Where's Darrow?"

"He's in the cabin, too. Probably asleep," Amy said.

"Then I won't turn on the light and wake him. Unless," he beamed at Elizabeth Lamb, "Persis put more flowers there to cheer me up? No? Then I'll see you at dinner, ladies."

"Wow," said Elizabeth Lamb. "That was close. Let's sit on the sofa way over in the corner, where the porthole's closed. We can see everybody who comes in. Who's next? How about Mr. Grenville?"

"Playing cards all the time, first with Templeton, Cooper and Julia, then just Cooper. I suppose he and Paul *could* have done the communications thing together, when the other two left to come up here, but I just can't see them in cahoots."

"Well, let's clear him, at least about the engines; probably about the phones, too. We could always ask them if they stayed together, but if they were guilty, they'd lie."

"Better not go about asking questions," Amy advised. "This is only a mental exercise, remember, for your book. Now Paul Cooper."

"Like Chris, he was with Mr. Templeton and Mrs. Vincentia when the engine thing must have been done. They can't all *four* have done it together. And since we believe he and Chris went right on playing when the other two went to tea, I would certainly say he's clear for both. Jim?"

"He was still writing letters here when Persis and I left," Amy said. "But you were still here. How long did he stay?"

"I don't know, because after I came down from looking for seagulls, I went to my cabin. I talked to Payson a minute, and I saw Viola in the galley, then I just went and took a nap. He was still here then; was he here when you and Persis came up to tea?"

"He was, but he could have left for a while, in the meantime. But, *Jim?* Why would he want to wreck the engines? When Viola pulled that scene with him at dinner the night before, all he was thinking of was how he could avoid her for the rest of the trip, so why would he want to prolong it? But, you're right; he also probably had time to dowse the communications panel, but why?"

"Well, he's the only one who appears to have had time alone to do both," Elizabeth Lamb answered. "And I couldn't find him any- where, later, after we got to the island."

"It's all what you call circumstantial evidence," Amy told her despondently. "But, as Thoreau said, 'Some circumstantial evidence is very strong, as when you find a trout in the milk.'"

"What's that mean?"

"Why, that someone had watered the milk before he sold it. Elizabeth Lamb, I would have thought you could figure that out! But I still can't believe Jim — well, who's next?"

Elizabeth Lamb was apologetic. "I guess I'm not as sharp as I should be. I *should* have figured that out. First I was tired and now I'm getting hungry, though. Maybe that's it. Well, all we've got left is Mr. Vincentia and the sailors, because Persis was with you and she wouldn't have played tricks, anyway. And I certainly didn't."

"There's also Viola," Amy reminded her. "Though I don't think she would've had the brains to know where the fuel fitting is. I only know because I was on the *Chianti,* with Jim and some others from Placido Press, a few years ago, and saw them refueling. And so did Jim," she finished slowly. "More trout."

"Yes, Viola." Elizabeth Lamb was frowning. "We don't know where she was, at all, except, as I said, I saw her drinking milk in the galley just before I went down to sleep, before tea. She left here after lunch with her grandfather but she obviously wasn't with him all the time. Neither one of them came in for tea and I never saw her again till I went to my cabin, to pull the curtains as Mr.

252

Vincentia told me, and she was there talking to Cioccolato. Then, the last time, she had fallen on the top deck, and you know all about that."

"What was in that laundry bag she had?" Amy asked curiously. "Persis brought it to our cabin when we all went to fix your knee. I noticed it still there when Persis was showering this morning but then with all the excitement — ah, I should say, what with the tragedy — I didn't look into it."

"It was stuff of hers she'd packed. And, Mrs. Danniver, why would anyone pack a fancy white dress and white slippers, a bottle of champagne, a birth certificate and a couple of boxes of sugared almonds?"

"Why, for a wedding, of course," Amy answered promptly. "I don't hang around with Alaric C. for nothing. And she was planning to be secretly married in Canada. The girl wasn't very bright and so she packed her things ahead of time and was hiding them on the top deck. Maybe she thought you'd see them and ask why. The bottle you cut your knee on was champagne, too, Antonio — or maybe it was Carlo — said. She was probably trying to get a second bottle to pack, which was why she was at the wet bar up there."

"Yes, that's what I thought, after Mr. Cooper told Mrs. Vincentia he and Viola were going to get married. But, still, why so—"

"Well, now," Amy interrupted, "what about V.V.? Do we include him? It seems to me he could have done both pieces of sabotage, but why? If he wanted the boat to stop or slow down or put into this cove, he had only to give the order. And why cut the *Chianti*'s communications?"

"He's going to Canada for something," Elizabeth Lamb said slowly. "I don't know what. Maybe he *wanted* to be unreachable for a while. But, then, he said yesterday that he wasn't even planning to stay here, after Persis and I got off. He said he had to get to Canada faster than he'd thought. Why would he lie?"

"I don't know." Amy spoke as slowly. "But I've never yet been able to figure him out and I've known him a long time, though only in a business relationship, except for trips on the *Chianti*. Well, now only the crew are left."

"And Paulo broke his leg before the engines slowed, a couple of hours before, from what Monica said at tea. And I think, from what the Captain said, that the phones were still working when he fell. I can't see why he'd want to do either thing, but he's the newest sailor. Maybe he was up to something."

"I'm sure V.V. screens new crewmen very carefully, and I don't see how Paulo could have managed either action; not enough time. Leave him out. The cook? The other two: Antonio and Carlo?"

"Pietro; well, I don't know. We're never going to know where he was. His cabin's off the storeroom, Payson told me, up forward, so he isn't around the rest of the crew very much. Carlo? I don't see how we could figure out where he was at these certain times, either. He was all around the boat.

"But there *is* Antonio. The Captain had left him on the bridge when he came down to tea so he *could* have done the water thing — no, Payson was with him. Payson wasn't waiting on us at tea and Persis said the Captain sent him up because the visibility was bad and 'Payson can see in the dark.' He can, too; he could see a light ahead on Cousin Curtis' island when Mr. Vincentia and the Captain and I certainly couldn't."

"But Antonio could have sabotaged the engines at any time and how can we say where he was, most of the day?" Amy pondered. "Or why he'd want to? Now, what about Payson? You've known him for some time, I take it. Do you think he'd pull those tricks?"

"Well, I don't see *why*. He was awfully anxious to get up to Maine; talked my grandmother into having Mr. Vincentia bring him along. He didn't want to fly or take the bus. He's saving all his money for getting married to his girl, I guess. And he's awfully conscientious about working for his money; I can't see a person who'd wreck anything being like that. I suppose he *could* have; he was here and there, all over, doing his work, but why would he?

"You know, Mrs. Danniver, I'm starving. If Pietro's in the galley, I'm going to beg for some tea and sandwiches. Wouldn't you like some?"

"Yes, I would. Before we get on to cudgeling our brains as to who could have murdered Viola and why, I think we need to be fortified. See if you can get toast with anchovy paste; fish is brain food, so they say. But he probably won't oblige. He's been in an unusually foul mood."

254

"If the door's unlocked and he's not there, I'll just run in and make tea fast and grab some cake or whatever's around."

The door was locked. She thought of going out to the passage and trying the other galley door but she heard a murmur of voices inside. She timidly knocked. The voices stopped and Pietro opened the door. He frowned and made as if to shut it.

"Pietro, please; I'm so hungry," she said rapidly, "and so is Mrs. Danniver. Oh, we would so much like something to eat. I know you're tired but I could make it and I wouldn't dirty your kitchen. You can watch me." She produced her "society smile."

He opened the door wide and beckoned her in, almost smiling himself as he said, "*Signora* Danniver needs food, eh? But of course, she always does. A big woman requires much food and big women I admire! And she put me in one of her books: me, Pietro Noyelle, a cook! It was one where the little boy found out about a killing in a restaurant and she got the *sfondo* — background, yes? — from me. She even used my name; I was a chef, in the book. It made much excitement in my village, with those who could read it!

"What would she like? And, you" — Payson was slumped on a stool — "as I have just said, are to sleep until I need you for dinner. That is an order!" He opened the lavatory door and removed the bag of soiled laundry, hanging on its hook the clean bag he snatched from Payson. "Yes, you may take the dirty things, but you are not to do any laundry, no matter what Carlo told you. I am your boss and I say you are to rest now. The dinner tonight must be *par excellence,* to cheer the *padrone* and to show that *flic* a thing or two. Now go, and to bed!"

Payson took the bag and more or less staggered out without even a glance at her. "You feel better, Pietro?" she asked, as he began to boil water and assemble a tray of cups and plates.

"I am better. I had an hour to meditate, as I could not do last night. I am refreshed. I must always meditate or my spirit becomes *bouleversé.* Now, what would the *signora* like me to bring you?"

"Well, she said she'd especially like anchovy toast. And anything else you could give us. Writing has made us really hungry. She's helping me — I mean, I'm helping her — with one of her books. Yes, one of her books."

"Ah, you too will be a lady *autore*? *Bien!*"

"You speak French as well as Italian and English, don't you? But Mr. Vincentia said your mother was Sicilian and your father French. I wish I could speak those languages as well as you. I just know a word or two of Italian." Society smile again. "He also said there were very few cooks in the world as good as you."

He beamed. "I think you know how to — what is it? — use the butter, *signorina*. That cop should have more of your *grazia*. Asking *me* if I made *marmellata*, like an old peasant woman! I tell him I have no time for that, with the fine *cuisine* I am called on to prepare. We buy it!"

"What's *marmellata*?"

He took a jar from a shelf, opened it and spooned some of its contents into a glass dish which he put on the tea tray. "Oh, *jam*," she said. "And blackberry! I love that. But why would he ask you if you made it?"

"The old women seal the jars with *cera*, when they make it. He thought there would be some in my kitchen."

"What's *cera*? Why did he care if there was any?"

He turned from the refrigerator and rapidly began to peel a cucumber. "They think that was what some *villano* put into the fuel tank that made the fuel not go into the engines. You know the boat could not travel."

"But what *is* it?" He gestured helplessly: "I forget the English word."

"Oh, I know!" she exclaimed. "Wax! That's right; they put it on top of jelly jars. Paraffin wax. I guess that certainly would clog up the line." She stood thinking, looking out a porthole, her mind working furiously. He gently took her by the shoulder.

"You go out," he said. "I wish to lock the door. I always lock it now. I promise you tea in fifteen minutes." He was better than his word; in ten minutes he placed before them a tray with not only a large pot of tea and the requested anchovy toast, but also cucumber sandwiches, a little basket of peeled hard-cooked eggs, still warm and rolled in coarse pepper, biscuits spread with butter and the jam beside them, and a plate of thin almond cookies.

"Oh, thank you, Pietro!" Amy exclaimed. "How wonderful! But

256

it's almost too much for us. Would you mind if we shared it, if anyone else comes in?" She also, Elizabeth Lamb noticed, could produce a "society smile."

"As you wish, *madame*. But," with a glare at Paul Cooper, who had appeared to stand beside the bar, "I have too much to do to make tea today for anyone but you. I will now lock my kitchen doors and rest for a time. Perhaps the *signorina* would put the tray in the dining room when you have finished?"

"Would you like some, Mr. Cooper?" Elizabeth Lamb asked when Pietro had gone. "I would indeed," he answered, pulling over a chair. "Though I only came to see if I could possibly get some hot tea for Grenville. He started a fit of coughing just as I was falling asleep and thought tea might help."

They rapidly disposed of most of the food. Paul, still eating a sandwich, poured a cup of tea for Chris and left them, saying he was going to sleep till dinner, with a pillow on top of his head. Elizabeth Lamb removed the tray and picked up the notebook again. "Now I can think! Let's see; since it seems we've decided only Jim could have done all the sabotage, we can get on and see if there's anyone who could have killed Viola, or wanted to."

"If she really was killed," Amy reminded her. "Let's not get carried away. And, you know, it isn't really certain that Jim's the only one who could have done the engines and phones. V.V. could have, Viola, the sailors, the Captain — Elizabeth Lamb, we forgot him!"

"Well, I just remembered that. But he could have done both the easiest, and isn't the obvious suspect the one who's always innocent? It's that way in books. And why should he, anyway?"

"Well, we haven't figured why any of them would. Maybe if we knew why, we'd know who, although the maxim is: If you know *how,* you know who. And I don't see how we'll ever know *why,* unless we get a brainstorm or somebody confesses. So let's start on Viola's death.

"You know," Amy's voice had saddened, "when I said maybe she'd fall overboard, I never really thought anything would actually happen to her. I do feel guilty, though."

"Well, don't," Elizabeth Lamb answered. "That's silly; really,

Mrs. Danniver, it is. Now, who would have wanted to murder her and could have? How about starting with Jim?"

"Poor Jim. You know, Elizabeth Lamb, you ought to realize that I might have been in collusion with Jim. We both disliked Viola. Perhaps you don't remember, but I told you the first day out that she caused my daughter Jane's death; well, knowing you, I'm sure you remember but until you have a child you can't realize what a bitter loss that was. She got my royalties reduced, too, as I've said, and her constant snooping about my drinking could have caused V.V. to cancel my contracts. That wasn't likely, but it was possible. And Jim, for his part, might have lost his job if she told any more tales about him, true or not.

"He could have committed the sabotage, we've decided, and maybe he and I working together could have killed Viola. Mystery writers are always thinking up new ways of killing people; wasn't it Sayers who said how very necessary and yet how very difficult that was? Maybe it was Christie. Anyway, when we find out why Viola died, if it was murder I'll have to go back on the suspect list."

"I don't think you're tricky enough," Elizabeth Lamb replied, after only a little hesitation, "to set yourself up to make me think you couldn't be guilty because you say you could be. And I don't think Jim had reason enough to kill Viola, with or without your help."

"Well, you know, if I lost my contracts, even if he didn't lose his job, his next assignment mightn't be so pleasant. He has other work to do, other authors, but he gets to travel around a lot with me and we have a generous expense account."

"I just don't think that's enough reason, either. But he certainly did have the *chance* to because Mr. Cooper and he weren't together all last night. They both said they went to the deck and the galley and Viola's cabin by themselves. So let's just write that Jim could have but didn't have a strong motive. Now, Chris."

"Okay; you're the author. Chris. Well, he could have gone to Viola's cabin while V.V. was sleeping, though he says he didn't. But why? She was announcing, in that dreadfully smug manner she had, that she had to approve of his poetry before V.V. published it, but, really, I don't think V.V. was at all controlled by her. He's not controlled by anyone, so far."

"But maybe Chris thought he was," Elizabeth Lamb suggested. "And he'd known Viola for years; maybe she'd done something bad to him or to somebody he loved. We can't know that, but if she *was* murdered, Buzzie, or whoever takes over when he leaves, will go into everything and everybody, starting way back. And Chris seems to love his godfather; if he were sort of crazy, he might think Mr. Vincentia would be happier with Viola dead.

"I know that sounds weak, Mrs. Danniver, but let's put that Chris could have done it, and might have had, or thought he had, a reason. Now Mrs. Vincentia. She certainly had a reason to kill the person who took Mr. Cooper away from her, even though she says she wasn't all that angry. But unless somebody used the Captain's master key to let her out — hey, you know we'd forgotten about his key! — I absolutely don't see how she got out of her cabin to do it.

"And though she wouldn't have inherited her husband's money if Viola married, I can't see how you could bring yourself to kill someone you'd raised from a baby, for money. *And* with Viola dead, she wouldn't get the big monthly allowance Mr. Aaronson said she lives on. So though she might have had a motive, she had two motives — if motives work both ways, in books; do they? — *not* to kill Viola. But the big thing is that I don't see she had any opportunity to do it. So I'd say she's clear. Who'll we do next — Mrs. Danniver, somebody's coming down the stairs in the fantail!"

They had closed the notebook and picked up magazines by the time Monica came through the glass doors. She wore a loose yellow eyelet-embroidered shirt over her bikini bottom and although she had taken the trouble to don sandals, the eyelets in the shirt revealed she had compensated by omitting her bikini top. She removed her sunglasses and smiled happily at them.

"Everybody's disappeared except thee and me?" she said. "Marvelous sun you have here, Elizabeth Lamb. Not too blinding. No tea? I could do with some."

"There's some left in the pot out there on the sideboard," Elizabeth Lamb told her. "Pietro gave us lots of cups too, out of habit, I guess. I'll pour you some, but it's probably cold."

259

"So it is," Monica agreed, tasting it. "But, oh, rapture; Pietro's made his wonderful eggs." She rapidly ate one. "I was planning a quick hot soak in Vito's tub before he gets back. My feet have been frozen ever since they got so cold and wet this morning. And I'm taking the rest of these along for a tub picnic! I adore them."

"You'd better not use his towels," Amy called. "I did that once and got hell."

"Well, of course not. I'll stop for my own." She pushed the basket of eggs up under her shirt. "What are you doing?" Elizabeth Lamb asked.

"Annie'll see me and she can't resist them even though she's terribly allergic to eggs, except, for some unknown reason, when they're baked in cakes. She'll eat just a bite and then be sick for hours. I've seen it before and I have to share a room with her." She settled the basket under her ample breasts and put one arm below to support it. She raised the other in a graceful wave of farewell. Elizabeth Lamb stared after her.

"Now, what about Monica?" Amy asked. "She admits she was wandering around half the night. She had a chance to kill Viola except I can't see why." She sighed. "I just can't see how *anybody* could've done it!"

"Well, we've said that about a million times. But as to why: Mrs. Danniver, her cousin Portia is Viola's mother and Monica loved her, said they were closer than sisters. Portia's been in some special home since right after Viola was born and Monica said her father, Monica's father, thought Portia would recover her right mind if Viola was 'removed from this earth,' because it was Viola's 'evil' that made her mother go crazy."

"Monica's father sounds a touch crazy himself," Amy observed. "Wonder if Monica inherited any of it? I suppose she believes him, but strongly enough to kill? Although it is strange that those pills didn't take effect and why did she leave the bottle on the bar? She knows Chris. Was it for him, so he could somehow give an overdose to Viola? She could be lying about the number that were left in the bottle. But how could he do it, with Jake there?"

"Let's say she could have murdered Viola. But until we know

how, the way you say, Mrs. Danniver, we can't say she did. We can't say *who.* Mr. Aaronson next?"

"Let's leave him for a minute," Amy replied slowly. "I'm thinking about him. Now, there's Paul. Like Jim, he was going around by himself at times. He could have done it as well as Jim could. But why kill an heiress you're going to marry before you marry her? After, yes, if you're inclined that way, but not before."

"Well, let's say he could have, as much as Jim could have, or even the others, but no motive. Now Mr. Aaronson?"

"Wait a bit, for him. Well, we can definitely leave out your friend Payson and the sailor, Antonio, because they weren't on board. And I would say Captain Knudsen wouldn't have decided to kill her; if she'd annoyed him, she'd been doing it for years. I suppose there is just a chance that he and Julia were in it together, and he let her out of her cabin, but I think it's an awfully slim one.

"But there *is* V.V. He certainly seemed to love her, though how he could I'll never understand. But maybe years of coping with her got to him. And she was getting older and harder to manage. And suppose she married somebody completely unsuitable and caused him more headaches?"

Elizabeth Lamb pursed her lips: "Well, she *was* going to. I mean, Mr. Vincentia certainly wouldn't have wanted someone so much older for her, who'd been living with his daughter-in-law, besides. But I don't think he did it, because you should have heard him when I told him she was dead. He just sort of terribly yelled out in Italian: 'My own blood,' it was. 'My own blood.' And that's why he loved her, awful as she was.

"But, you know, as for Antonio, he was scared Viola was going to cause Annie to quit her job, and he loves her and is trying to get her to marry him. Could he have done something before he went for help? He was right beside her when I found her lying up on deck. Maybe she didn't fall. Maybe he hurt her so that she just died later?"

"Again," Amy sighed, "we won't know till we hear about the autopsy. I suppose there is something that could kill one much later and that's what's been bothering me about Jake:

"You heard Monica saying at dinner that he might know that

261

jujitsu blow, 'The Black Death,' that kills some time later. Two days, I think she said, but she could have been wrong about the time. And Jake wouldn't answer. Suppose he used it on Viola last night? I can't put it out of my mind, because I really like him." Her face reddened slightly.

"But there couldn't possibly be such a thing, Mrs. Danniver."

"Yes, there could. About twenty years ago, some woman wrote a biography of her father, a Drexel or a Biddle, or of some other old Philadelphia family. I forget, exactly. I read it and it was very good as well as quite popular, was first made into a Broadway play and then a movie. He was a millionaire, a sportsman — and a jujitsu expert. She mentioned the 'Black Death,' said there were rumors he'd known that blow though he would never exactly admit it. Just like Jake. *And* he was an officer in the Marines and Jake said 'some Yank officer' had taught him some blows."

Elizabeth Lamb was silent for a time. "I can't believe it, that Mr. Aaronson would kill a sleeping girl," she said finally. "But I suppose he had the best chance to."

"Do you know any reason why he'd want to?"

She answered reluctantly. "I know he'd get her stock in the publishing house if she died. He said that himself, to me and Monica. And I know he has a great feeling for Mr. Vincentia and thinks Viola wore him down, sort of."

"Oh, dear. Those are two very good motives. Well, I've had it, for the time being. I'm going up to get some sun while I brood over this. I think Maine is beautiful but a bit too chilly for my taste. My feet are as cold as Monica's must have been this morning.

"Why don't you start writing this up? The way to begin is to begin, I tell myself all the time. Only don't try to prove whodunnit because of a similarity in names, or something weak like that. I've read two mysteries lately and all the sleuth, in the first, had to go on was that a woman's name had a diphthong and years later her assumed name did, too, so that made him suspicious of her. And that was the only clue!

"And in the second, somebody's name in German meant the same as somebody else's in English, so that proved they were connected and one of them committed the murder to protect the other. Honestly!" She went out to the lounge and up the spiral stairs, her shoulders drooping a little.

Elizabeth Lamb closed the notebook and shut her eyes. "Monica's feet," she thought. "They were cold and wet and mine were cold and wet and Persis' were, too. And what else bothers me about Monica? What did she say just now when she was here? Or *was* it something she said?

"And Pietro. He said someone put wax into the fuel intake. You seal jelly with wax but you make candles out of it, too. Payson was carrying a big bag of candles yesterday and I couldn't find it afterwards. But Payson couldn't have killed Viola, no way."

Feet pounded down the spiral staircase. She opened her eyes. Antonio ran into the saloon. "Just as he did yesterday," she thought. *"Just as he did yesterday.* He ran in here to get the Captain and that left Payson alone on the bridge. It was Payson who was alone there, not Antonio. And there's a water tap right there, behind the pilot house. Payson was using it when he washed the upper deck furniture the first day out."

She stared blankly at Antonio. "I'm sorry; what did you say? I was thinking."

"I already say it twice! I say the *padrone* want to see you in his stateroom, *pronto.* I have been looking all over for you, ever since we got back."

"Well, you didn't look in here," she replied mildly, following him to the passage. He answered something, irritably, but she hardly heard. She walked heavily, thinking: "Payson. It was Payson who ruined the engines and the communications panel. It had to be Payson."

Mr. Vincentia was sitting at his desk, his head in his hands. He raised it to look at her. "He seems old, suddenly," she thought. "Stay outside the door, Antonio," he ordered. "No one comes in. Elizabeth Lamb, sit down."

She sat beside him. He took her hand in his and said gently, *"Caro,* you must leave the *Chianti.* You must pack and Antonio will row you ashore. I will miss you more than you know, because I so love to have you with me. You, as well as your grandmother, remind

263

me of my Lizabetta. She was beautiful, like you, and brave, and intelligent, like you—" His voice faltered.

He steadied it and went on: "But both Lieutenant Higgins and I want you ashore, in The Bungalow."

She regarded him levelly. "Then Viola *was* killed. How was she killed? Tell me."

He removed his hand, raising his brows. "I do not take orders, child."

"Like you, Mr. Vincentia, I always have to know," she answered quietly. "What did Buzzie say when he called? Please."

Still looking at her, he lit one of his brown cigarettes. After a moment, he said, "There are strong indications she was smothered, as she slept. As she slept," he repeated bitterly. "Higgins and the other policeman noticed her ear lobes were a bright pink. They had seen that in another case of suffocation. The autopsy shows a raised level of carbon monoxide in the bloodstream and the little blood vessels in her eyes were broken. Her eyes. She had such beautiful eyes and they had to—"

He cleared his throat. "But the thing is, it is not *certain*. It is strongly indicated, but *not* certain. There is no foreign matter in the windpipe or lungs and her throat shows no sign of strangulation, only the faint narrow bruise from falling on the bar railing."

With unsteady hands, he filled a glass from the brandy decanter before him. "We may never prove how it happened. And how could anyone have smothered Viola with Jake right there in the room? Jake. *Jake.*" His voice was bitter again. "I am almost forced to believe that Jake—"

She interrupted. "Mr. Vincentia, it is absolutely certain she was dead before they put her in that plastic bag and took her away? Persis isn't always very smart but she did say, when she saw the deputy carrying it, how you could smother in it if you weren't really dead."

"*Caro,* that *is* certain. I was with her for a long time, and I know. I have seen death. And the doctor confirmed it. How, who, and how Higgins can prove it is not certain, but that—"

She had stopped listening to him. "Of course! That *must* be it!"

she was thinking. "And if it is, that's why I remembered when Monica—"

She reached for his glass and took a substantial swallow before he could remove it from her hand. "Mr. Vincentia! I have to ask somebody something. If the answer is 'yes,' maybe we *can* prove it!"

"No!" He stood up. "You are to do nothing! Antonio is to be with you every second until you leave the boat. Don't you realize that Higgins and I believe someone murdered Viola? Proving it may be another thing, but we do not need to get proof by having someone murder you. Listen to me!"

She stood up, too, and angrily demanded: "Don't you want to *know?* Antonio can come with me; he can ask; he can be right beside me, but when I come back with the answer — if I get the right one, that is — then I want you to listen to *me!* I mean it!"

He sat down, leaning back and smiling a little. "You could be Lizabetta, child: the way you speak, the way your eyes flash, the way you defy me. Few dare.

"Go, ask your question and come back." He raised his voice: "Antonio!" Antonio opened the door. "You are to stay beside the *signorina* and do as she says. Then bring her back here."

Outside the stateroom, she said quickly, "Antonio, we must find Carlo. I want you to ask him—" The door to Monica's and Annie's stateroom had opened and Annie looked out. Elizabeth Lamb raised on her toes and whispered in Antonio's ear. "What?" he asked. She repeated the whisper. As they passed Annie, she murmured something heard by neither Antonio in his puzzlement nor Elizabeth Lamb in her excitement.

Carlo was tending the plants in the fantail lounge. Elizabeth Lamb stopped in the middle of the saloon. "I'll stay right here," she said. "You can keep turning to see I do. He may not answer if I ask or if I am with you. And ask him *quietly.*"

Frowning and glancing back over his shoulder, Antonio went quickly to the fantail, and as quickly he was back. "He say 'yes,'" he reported. "And I say why do you want to know?" She only shook her head. He remained outside Vincentia's cabin as she entered.

He still sat at his desk, staring down at it, ignoring his brandy. She drew in a deep breath. "I know how Viola was killed," she said, "and I know who did it. And I know how we can prove it, with no circumstantial evidence, either: with no trout in the milk. We can prove it because Payson's very, very tired."

His look had changed from one of despair to bewilderment. "What trout?" he asked. "Payson? You said *Payson?*"

"No, no; he didn't do it. But you must get Payson here, because I want to tell you a story and I know he'll back me up. I know he'll tell the truth now. And the story has a lot to do with who murdered Viola. And why."

"Who was it?" he demanded fiercely. "Before Antonio brings Payson, you must tell me! Who?"

She told him.

• Chapter 12 •

Judgment

VINCENTIA had directed Antonio to have coffee for three brought to the stateroom and to wait outside the door on his return. By the time he came back with Payson, Pietro had already deposited on the desk a tray with not only the cups and a silver coffee pot but also a plate of little cream-filled pastries and slices of sponge cake. A surprised, still-sleepy Payson was told to sit down as Vincentia handed him a cup of coffee and Elizabeth Lamb held the plate before him.

Mr. Vincentia spoke without emotion although his hands were clenched tightly together on the desk and his eyes glittered like black ice. "Payson, I wish you to listen to Elizabeth Lamb, as I shall. I will tell you now that we think Viola was killed deliberately—" Payson sprang up, his empty cup and his saucer falling to the rug.

"Who done it?" he cried. "Who?"

"Sit down and be quiet. We must listen to her. She is sure about the beast who did it but we need some information from you. Although she is confident she is correct, I, too, must be absolutely sure. Then if we can prove it—"

"Whoever done it, hangin's too good fer 'im! You'll prove it and

267

then they'll let 'im out after a few years! They don't execute murderers in Maine now, sir — oh, tell me who it was? I'll kill 'im myself and my father'll help me!"

Elizabeth Lamb spoke quietly. "Varner probably would help you, Payson. He was going to be her father-in-law, wasn't he?"

Payson's face became a sickly white. His mouth opened and his head turned apprehensively toward Mr. Vincentia. "You're jest crazy, Elizabeth Lamb," he muttered.

Vincentia's face showed first astonishment and then a kind of comprehension. "Suppose you tell your story, Elizabeth Lamb. We have time. Higgins cannot get here until early this evening, possibly not until after dinner."

She put down her cup. "Well, it was the first night at dinner, when Viola said Jim Darrow was feeling her leg, or something. I looked at people's faces and Payson was the only one who was angry. I wondered why. I was thinking before I went to bed and I started remembering things: way back, at tea in your garden, Viola said you'd 'like to anchor in a pretty cove' and that then she could see my 'grandmother's place.' Now, after Viola came in to tea, *nobody* had said anything about my grandmother's having a place in Maine nor anything about what it was like. Somebody had told her. Something bothered me, when I was walking home that day, but I didn't realize then what it was.

"And then Payson showed up at Grandmother's, trying to get her to help him get to Maine. I realize now he knew you had fired the cabin boy; Viola had told him. He wangled a place on the *Chianti* through Grandmother because Viola had called him and told him Persis and I might be going with her. He knew Cioccolato's name and he knew he was a kitten and he said he knew because he'd heard somebody next door calling his name and 'kitty, kitty.' But you say that when you're calling a cat as well as a kitten. And somebody at Viola's school, 'the dear one,' she said, had given him to her. You thought it was a teacher but she never said that.

"And Payson told us he had a girl, 'Pansy,' and he put a pansy in Viola's finger bowl at dinner and after dinner she was holding it and she said someone thought her eyes were 'like pansies.' It was at dinner that Monica was talking about Bath Oliver biscuits, saying she 'loved the profile of the good doctor' on them and I remembered that Payson had spoken of working for a 'Doc Oliver.' That's the name of the man who runs the Exceptional School, where Viola went, isn't it, Mr. Vincentia? They met at the school and they fell in love."

Vincentia turned to look at Payson, who put his head down and stared at the rug. "That all don't mean much, Elizabeth Lamb," he mumbled.

She went on. "Mr. Vincentia, you told me Viola would eat fruits and vegetables only if they were given her by 'someone she loves and who loves her.' Payson passed her grapes at lunch, the first day out, and she ate them. She ate cucumber sandwiches he was handing around at tea, and peas at dinner. She never ate any fruit or vegetable anyone else suggested. He got a pistachio ice cream cone for her, when he saw us coming across the Public Gardens, and he got pistachio ice cream for her at dinner here. He knew she liked it and she said 'they never give me the green kind.'

"She brought her white confirmation dress along, to be married in, and her birth certificate, and she got a bottle of champagne, probably from the bar in the saloon. She looked in there last night, and we were all there, so she went up to get a second from the wet bar. She took little white boxes Persis and I had and filled them with my *dragees* — what you call *confetti* — to give out at the wedding.

"Don't you realize that, after Payson heard you saying at Matinicus that you were only going to stop here to let Persis and me off, — and he stumbled and nearly knocked Persis off the ladder when he heard — he poured water in the communications panel so you couldn't call ashore and head him and Viola off, *and* he put candles in the fuel tank, to stop the engines. He was listening at that first dinner when Mr. Aaronson mentioned how the Japanese put paraffin in P.T. boat fuel and I guess he learned in school, just as I did, both that paraffin is a wax and you make candles from wax.

"You see, when he heard you wouldn't be stopping here so Viola wouldn't have a chance to get off, he had to do those things. He knew how to run the little motorboat and he was going to lower it when the engines stopped and he and she were going to take off. That's why she was out on deck with her bag of clothes; it was just bad luck that she went up to the top deck to get that champagne. He'd come into our cabin just before that and was talking to her. I bet he'd even called his mother from Boston, at the factory where she packs sardines, and told her he'd be showing up here with a girl he loved whose mean grandfather wouldn't let them marry, and she'd have hidden them. You did, didn't you, Payson?"

Payson's face was brick-red but he answered firmly, "No, I never."

She sighed. "Well, I think you *will* admit because it will help about her murder. Mr. Vincentia, Viola was killed because she was going to be married and then Mrs. Vincentia wouldn't inherit your son's money. Mr. Aaronson told me if Viola died before she married, the money would all go to Mrs. Vincentia and I guess she thought that would be better than just counting on an allowance that maybe you could have stopped at any time. Buzzie says the police always wonder 'Who benefits?' when there's a murder. Well, everybody, in a way, benefited from Viola's death — well, I don't mean exactly that but the thing is that Mrs. Vincentia *really* benefited. I realized that after I'd thought everything over, before Antonio called me in here.

"See, Viola told Mrs. Vincentia 'everything.' She said that and you told me she called and wrote Mrs. Vincentia all the time. She'd asked Mrs. Vincentia to get her two rings, wedding rings, and Mrs. Vincentia knew she was in love. I learned that from, well, listening to them in the saloon that first night. But she didn't know who the boyfriend was; Viola hadn't told her *that*. I guess Viola thought she might tell you and you wouldn't let her marry a — well, a poor boy, not an Italian, either.

"So Mrs. Vincentia figured Viola would have to — to be killed pretty soon. The chance was good, last night, with Viola hurt and tied so she couldn't move and some of the people off the boat and the ones left worrying about those men on the island. And you were in bad shape, Mr. Vincentia, not able to watch over Viola. It was probably the best chance ever.

"So she and Mr. Cooper pulled that scene and he had her locked in her cabin so that the most likely person would be the one who couldn't possibly have done it." She became pensive. "He used me, you know, and I don't like that. And with Viola not able to talk,

270

they figured she couldn't deny their story. Oh, everything was going for them!"

"But," Vincentia put in, "Viola did write that she was going to be married and she drew that heart, with a *P* — oh, I see. Of course!"

"She *was* going to be married when she got off the boat — we asked her that, that way — and you just realized that *P* didn't stand for Paul. He must have been frightened, standing outside her cabin and listening to Mrs. Danniver and me talk to her. But it came out all right, for him, by bad luck again.

"Although," she added sadly, "Mrs. Danniver would say that you shouldn't have a similarity in initials, either, as well as names, but I can't help it. That's the way it happened. It's like when something strange happens to my cousin, who runs a movie theatre; he always says, 'Nobody would believe this script.'"

Vincentia was puzzled. She went on quickly, "And that scene they made in the saloon was certainly convincing. The way Mrs. Vincentia yelled, the way she rubbed her hands together — she should have been an actress."

"But she is," Vincentia said heavily. "She did Lady Macbeth with a heart-rending wringing and rubbing of hands. I saw it with Monica and she wept. And that animal was an actor; that's how she met him."

"I thought she was a singer! Viola said something about her singing on stage. If I'd realized she was a professional actress—!"

"She may have sung, in some light play. But why didn't Monica recognize the Macbeth touch? Oh, *yes;* she was with me when they did it. Enough of them and their pathetic performance! Payson, is what Elizabeth Lamb said about you and Viola true? You need not be afraid to answer. I have a high regard for you; the child might have been happy married to you, in a few years. Happy — and now she is dead!" His voice broke and he pressed his fist hard against his mouth.

"Tell me, boy," he said very softly, after a minute.

"It's so," Payson answered dully. "It's all like Elizabeth Lamb said. But" — fiercely — "I — I never interfered, like, with Pansy, sir! I was scared you'd think that. She could have been rightfully married in her white dress! I loved her lots and I would've been real good to her.

"She was so sweet, like a little kid. I knowed she wasn't real smart or she wouldn't've bin at Doc Oliver's school, but I ain't smart, neither. Mumma would've helped us; you're right, Elizabeth Lamb: her and Pa knew. I asked 'em to git things ready fer us, the J.P. 'n' all."

"But, son," Vincentia said gently, "Viola was too young to marry in this country without my permission."

"You kin git married at sixteen in Maine, sir. It's what they call 'the age of consent.' That's why she brung her birth paper, to prove it."

"No, Payson," Elizabeth Lamb said, "no, that isn't the same thing. You have to be eighteen to get married. I know, because Dora's niece had to wait till she was."

"Then it wouldn'ta worked. Oh, God, I wouldn't even care if I couldn't marry her if she was alive and laughin' again, the way she did." He looked at Vincentia. "And so how do we prove her stepmother did it? How did she do it? We'll hev to git her inter jail, because I couldn't kill a woman, even a bitch like her." He blushed. "I beg pardon, Elizabeth Lamb."

"She didn't do it, Payson. Mr. Cooper did. He brought orange juice down to Mr. Aaronson to get a look at the set-up and decide how to do it. He must have been up and down all night, listening and maybe peeking in to see if Mr. Aaronson might fall asleep or, even better, leave for a while. When Mr. Aaronson went in to shower, he took his chance. Mr. Aaronson had had me take Viola's pillows away, to Persis' room, so he couldn't do it that way. He wouldn't have wanted to leave marks on her throat, by strangling her, so he did a clever thing. A clever but terrible thing—"

"Fer God's sake, Elizabeth Lamb, what did he do?"

"I'm trying to tell you, Payson. It's hard for me, because don't you see Mr. Vincentia will picture it, over and over?" She drank from her cup of cold coffee. Vincentia smiled a little: "I will no longer picture it when the *villano* has paid. And he *will* pay, and pay in full, Payson. There will be judgment. He will pay."

Elizabeth Lamb had been resting her head on one hand while they spoke. "You know, I feel terrible. If I'd been smarter about what I've said I thought, how I was pretty sure that Viola was in

272

love with you, Payson, and I'd told Mr. Vincentia, this whole thing wouldn't have happened. I almost did, yesterday morning, but I thought I might be wrong and I'd just get you and Viola in trouble. I should have spoken out — but I thought I'd be — oh, I do blame myself." Tears ran down her cheeks.

"It ain't your fault, Elizabeth Lamb," Payson said. He got up and clumsily patted her shoulder. "You didn't know them devils was goin' to kill Pansy. It ain't your fault. Jest tell us how he done it."

She rubbed her hands across her face. "Well, I stood outside Viola's door a minute this morning, and later my feet were cold because they'd got wet. And Persis said she stood there and said a prayer and her feet were wet, her socks. And Monica was there in her bare feet and they were the same as mine. And Carlo yelled at me a while ago to leave the plants alone, when he was watering the ferns down there. He had watered them last night, too.

"What Mr. Cooper did was take the green plastic bag that all the plant baskets are lined with from the one by Viola's door and put it over her head and hold it till she stopped breathing. I guess it probably took at least five minutes, maybe more. Buzzie would know. Viola's forehead had a smudge of earth on it from the bag. I wiped it off; I didn't realize. If Buzzie'd seen it— And her hair was damp when I found her, from the moisture in the bag. And her face was flushed, too, but Buzzie only saw it later. He said it was pale. Maybe a flushed face is a sign of suffocation, too? We should ask him."

Mr. Vincentia made a strangled sound. She went rapidly on. "So the water from the fern pot had leaked out on the rug and that's why our feet were wet. He must have done it just before I went to Viola's cabin, while Mr. Aaronson was in the shower, because when I ran upstairs a minute or so later, he was standing up in the vestibule, by the galley. He was clutching his arms across his stomach. Then he went into the lavatory in the galley. I made him come out because I felt so sick I had to go in there, and when I cleaned it afterwards there was a green plastic bag behind the toilet. I put it and a dirty towel and apron in the laundry bag on the door so Pietro wouldn't be mad.

"He might have done it ten or even fifteen minutes before I saw him. I mean, it must shock even somebody like him, to kill. He might have gone into the saloon first to hide the bag, but Jim was waking up. He probably planned to throw it overboard, but the Coast Guard boat had come beside us by then and people were on deck. He didn't have a cabin of his own where he could hide it. I guess, when Jim ran by him, he figured the galley, right in front of him, might be a safe place.

"And he's been trying to get into the galley the whole day. He tried to go into the lavatory, saying Mrs. Vincentia needed aspirin, but Pietro wouldn't let him and finally Pietro locked the galley doors. And, you know, Mr. Cooper's allergic to cats. I'd bet anything on that, and we could prove it. He was sneezing and blowing his nose, just like Annie was in the car with Cioccolato, Mr. Vincentia, but he said he had a cold. Cioccolato was under Viola's bed, or somewhere in the cabin, the whole time, you see. Mr. Cooper—"

"Don't keep callin' him that, so polite!" Payson shouted. "Jest say 'that bastard'!"

"Well, the murderer, I'll say. He wouldn't touch Cioccolato the first day, when he wandered in, at tea; said cats hated him. He'll never admit to any physical weakness, I heard you say, Mr. Vincentia. Chris and Jim do have colds and have been sick all day and not able to eat, but Mr. — the murderer got better and ate a lot of lunch and tea. Mrs. Danniver told me the signs of an allergic attack go away quickly, if you take something or the thing that irritated you isn't around any more.

"When Monica stood in the dining room a little while ago and put a basket of hard-boiled eggs she was hiding from Annie under her shirt and put her arm across her stomach under the basket, I realized that the murderer had been standing just that way this morning when I came up, with the bag under his shirt. His shirt was all pulled out and hanging loose; he didn't wear it that way before. And then he left the bag in the lavatory. He had to just throw it down because I was yelling to get in. That's what I had Antonio ask Carlo: 'Was the lining from the fern outside Viola's door missing this morning?' And he said it was.

"I guess I would have realized all this before, or most of it, but the murderer was just so *convincing*. The way he cried, and all."

"*Lagrime di coccodrillo,*" Vincentia said. "Crocodile tears. *You* have convinced *me, caro.* Now I must think."

"I believe you, too. But you said we could prove it, Elizabeth Lamb. How?"

"The same way the murderer was afraid somebody might, and that's why he kept trying to get the bag back, probably to throw overboard. His prints have to be all over the bag and Buzzie took everybody's fingerprints. You didn't — you didn't put that laundry you got from the galley into the washing machine, did you, Payson? Pietro told you not to."

Payson was already out the door, brushing Antonio aside as he raced down the passage. Elizabeth Lamb, exhausted, lay down flat on the settee. "I want you to pack, nevertheless, Elizabeth Lamb," Vincentia told her. "Your grandmother would certainly agree that this is no place for you."

She sat bolt upright. "But why? He isn't going to kill *me.* There's no profit for him in that. Now we know and can watch out for him. Oh, can't I go to The Bungalow *tomorrow?* I'd so much like one more night on board and Pietro's making a special dinner! I can stay out of the way when Buzzie arrests Mr. Cooper. Oh, please, as a sort of reward for figuring it out?"

While he hesitated, she asked for information that had been bothering her: "What — what will happen to Viola? I mean—"

Very calmly he answered, "Viola is not the piece of clay in Bangor. My Viola is somewhere else. Her body is to be cremated and I will carry the ashes back to Boston for burial in consecrated ground."

"But will the Church let you?"

"It is permitted. But if it were not — *caro,* I would still do what I think best for Viola, for me, for everyone. I have," he ended grimly, "done things that the Church did not permit. This is not one of them."

Antonio's voice was raised in the passage. "No one enters; only the boy, Mr. Aaronson. I have orders."

Vincentia moved quickly to the door. Jake came in, followed by Payson with the bag of laundry from the galley. "He saw me comin' from the crew's place, sir, and asked if you was back," Payson explained nervously. "I didn't know if I should say but I did."

275

"It is all right, Payson," Vincentia answered. "Sit down, Jake, and I will tell you how Viola died. And you cannot blame yourself, my old friend. But first I must do something." He reached into the desk drawer and brought out a large Lucite box of loose stamps and from among them removed a long, narrow pair of tongs. "It is lucky I am a stamp collector; now, Payson, pull open that bag and carefully ease everything on to the floor. And then hand me one of those trouser hangers with clips you will find in the wardrobe."

Very carefully he applied the tongs to a lower corner of the plastic bag that was in the middle of the pile. He pulled the bag out, opened a clip on the hanger, and snapped it on to the corner he held with the tongs. Then he pushed aside the clothes in the wardrobe and hung the bag at its far end. He selected a key from his chain and turned the wardrobe lock.

"What in God's name are you up to, Vito, with those dirty towels and things?" Jake had been watching in astonishment. Payson put back the laundry and stood uncertainly, holding the bag. "What do I do now, sir?" he asked. "Have you called Buzzie Higgins?"

"The Lieutenant stayed in Bangor to get some more information on a case he thought he had closed. He is conscientious; even though he is on leave he wanted to tie up the loose ends. I do not know how to reach him but he will be here after dinner. Maybe sooner, but I doubt it. Now, you sit down, too, because we must plan."

"Plan what, Vito? What do you mean, you'll tell me how Viola died?" Jake demanded.

"Jake, I will make it short. Paul Cooper smothered Viola by putting her head in that bag while you were in the shower this morning. Elizabeth Lamb deduced what had been done and who did it. Now—"

Jake sprang up. "What are you saying? Are you sure? You believe this child? Where is Cooper? What are you going to do to him? My God, if I can get my hands—"

"Jake. Jake! Of course I will do nothing to him. He will be brought to trial. We must go by the law." He looked over at Elizabeth Lamb and smiled reassuringly. "I've never seen him smile like that before," she thought uneasily. "And he suddenly looks so much younger."

"And of course I believe her. The evidence is strong and the proof will be that, although Carlo's and Elizabeth Lamb's prints are on that bag, his will be where he held it around her neck—" He was unable to go on.

"Are you lakes, Vito? He killed your own flesh and blood and you're saying you'll take him to court? That's not like you, mate. What's that Sicilian thing you've quoted: 'An old wolf loses his fur but not his vices'? Come off it."

"Ah, but I am not the wolf I used to be. I am tamed. What I want to say to you all is this: we must be as good actors until Higgins gets here as Cooper and that despicable Julia were. We tell no one else except Antonio and Carlo, so they, too, can watch him. We act as if we know nothing. We have a pleasant dinner. If I say anything that seems strange, wrong, to you, go along with it, in silence. We have another saying in Sicily: 'Silence is a friend that will never desert you.'

"Actually, I will not tell Antonio and Carlo why they are to keep an eye on him, though they may guess."

"You said 'you all,' Mr. Vincentia!" Elizabeth Lamb cried. "May I act too? May I stay till Buzzie comes? Mr. Cooper *used* me, you know, and I'd like to be here. Don't you owe me that?" Her tone became persuasive. "And, you know, if you made me go ashore, he might suspect something."

"That is true," he said slowly. "And I know I can trust you to act as convincingly as the rest of us."

"Then I'd better leave my notebook here and you can lock it up. I was writing down clues and who could have done what—"

"Oh, my God!" Payson burst out. "Elizabeth Lamb, you don't hev good sense! Nearly drownded she was, sir, four years ago, right by that reef in the cove, because she had to go and figger out who killed the old lady what lived in one of them cottages here. And—"

"Payson," Vincentia interrupted firmly, "she is older now. And I trust you to watch over her very carefully, but not noticeably. He will not possibly suspect what she has told us, you know. Nor what you have.

"But, Elizabeth Lamb, I want you to go to your cabin and rest, read; whatever you like. Then dress nicely for dinner." He pulled out his watch. "That will be in less than two hours, and, as you said, Pietro is planning a very good one. We must eat it with appreciation. You, Payson, take that laundry back to where you got it and then help Pietro. But first I want a word with you."

She picked up her notebook from the floor under the desk where she had dropped it when she came in and tore out a few pages before she handed it to him. "I could just draw the plans of the *Chianti* decks, couldn't I? It would be sort of a souvenir, and maybe Buzzie could use them too."

He nodded and blew her a kiss. "And please tell Antonio to come in, as you go."

If she had known, as she went deliberately casually to her cabin, loudly humming a tune, what he was saying to the three men, she would have given a year's allowance to be back with them. "Now, listen carefully," he began, "for I will tell you how we will do this. You will all help and, Jake, I especially need you. I will call Higgins, who is not on a case but should be back at his home by now, and put him off till tomorrow morning, when he can bring the detective who will take over for him. Antonio, find Carlo and bring him here. But first I will tell you why—"

Mrs. Danniver was in the shower when Elizabeth Lamb entered their cabin, noticing when she went through the lobby outside that Carlo had put another liner in the fern basket by Viola's door. She sat at the desk and began to draw the *Chianti*. She drew slowly, her tongue between her teeth, still bothered a little by Mr. Vincentia's smile. Amy had donned the black dress she had worn at dinner the first night out before she looked over the artist's shoulder. "Giving up literature for art?" she asked.

"For a couple of days. I can't think any more and drawing's easier. I put my notebook in a safe place, so don't worry; probably nobody killed Viola, anyway.

"We're going to have a really special dinner tonight, Pietro said, so I guess I'd better change out of my jeans. You look awfully nice, Mrs. Danniver."

"'Seen bettah; seen wuss,' as my first husband used to remark when I got all gussied up. He was a charmer. Well, I feel guilty about not getting over to your cottage to see Persis, but tomorrow's another day and I guess I'd better work up an appetite for the funereal baked meats, or whatever.

"So I'm off to the bar for a cocktail or two. I hope our shipmates don't read in your eyes all our suspicions about them we've been harboring. Mum's the word, remember." She touched up her lipsticked mouth, took her evening bag and left, leaving behind a strong scent of jasmine.

"You bet it is," Elizabeth Lamb murmured aloud. And then, "I hope Mr. Aaronson isn't allergic to jasmine." She giggled a little at the thought. She dressed slowly, pausing to add to her drawings. When she reached the saloon, Payson, splendid in a stiffly white jacket, was passing a large silver tray of thin strips of toast spread with caviar. Bowls of minced hard-cooked egg yolks and whites and wedges of lemon adorned his offering. Pietro came in with a bowl of chopped onion to add to the tray.

Paul Cooper and Chris Grenville were standing together, drinking martinis. They shook their heads when Payson held his tray before them. "No, thanks," Chris said. "I c-c-couldn't taste it. Wasted on me." He took a swallow of his drink, coughing. "Oh, dear," Elizabeth Lamb thought. "His stutter's come back." She whispered to Monica, who was in her favorite stance behind the bar, that she would like a Kir, "if there's cassis?"

"Really, V.V.," Paul was protesting, "caviar seems unnaturally festive, considering the circumstances." His voice broke effectively. He was wearing a narrow black band pinned around the left sleeve of his blazer. "Wonder if he brought it along on purpose, in hope?" Elizabeth Lamb thought, and then determined to do no more speculating: "It might show in my face, if I do much thinking about him." She carried her drink over to Amy and Jake, who were engaged in a low, lively conversation.

Vincentia was accepting a martini from Monica. "Well, Paul," he answered sadly, "Viola is dead and there's nothing to be done about that. We all grieve, and I know how you, especially, must feel. But my friend Moselli, who flew Annie up, sent along a pound of fresh Beluga as well as the squabs we are having for dinner. I thought good food might cheer us, and the caviar will not keep."

He signalled to Monica to refill his glass. "The living must live,

279

hard as it is. We can do no more than mourn her in silence." He lifted the glass. "But let us drink once to her, dead too young but now at peace. To Viola!"

Everyone drank and then those who had been sitting sat uneasily down again. There was no conversation until Annie asked timidly the question on most of their minds: "Vito, have you — have you heard how Viola died?"

He sighed deeply. "Yes," he answered sombrely. "Higgins called me with the report: a simple case of heart failure evidently caused by the trauma from the fall. The carbon monoxide level in her blood was slightly raised but that could be explained by the fall. It quite literally knocked the breath out of her. Her heart was not strong; I knew that. As her father's was not, as mine is not. If those madmen had not shot and, probably, caused her accident, her heart might have failed under some future stress, young as she was."

"But, Vito, you should do something about them!" Jake spoke angrily. "Not let them get away with it!"

"Higgins will deal with them. I have no taste for revenge; at least, not while I still feel her death so deeply. As I learned as a child: 'Revenge is a dish best eaten cold.'" He again extended his glass to Monica.

Paul, brushing his hand across his eyes, went slowly out to the fantail, where Carlo was doing a number of things (probably unnecessary, Elizabeth Lamb thought) to the plants there. Julia joined Monica and Vincentia at the bar. "I haven't seen the Captain for hours, V.V.," she remarked. She, too, had a third martini. Her face was drawn and her makeup not in its usual state of perfection. She spilled some of her drink on the bodice of her dress as she picked up the glass with an unsteady hand.

"I had arranged for a car to be delivered to Elizabeth Lamb's cottage when I was ashore," Vincentia explained, "since Knudsen wished to go to Bar Harbor and see Paulo. He will spend the night there. A Swede who is as abstemious as he is when he is on board must shed his sea-legs now and then and visit a bar or two."

Payson was offering a replenished tray of caviar to Amy and Jake. Jake looked disappointed: "No onion?" Payson was apologetic in manner though his eyes glittered strangely in his impassive face.

"Run out we did, sir, but Pietro's choppin' more. I'll git it in a minute."

"He's probably been crying," Elizabeth Lamb thought. "He must feel awful." She put down her Kir. "I'll go for you, Payson," she offered kindly. The culinary action going on in the galley was both disciplined and turbulent and Pietro announced she was to wait outside. Idly scuffing her heels and humming, she thought she heard a splash of water from the deck and crossed the vestibule to look out a door.

Antonio, far forward, was just raising a bucket over the deck railing. He unhooked it from a rope and disappeared inside, through the door opposite Vincentia's stateroom door. He soon reappeared and lowered the bucket again. "What are you doing, Antonio?" she called. "Fishing?" He started, turned, shook his head emphatically at her, raising a finger to press it firmly three times against his lips and then pointing it to direct her to go inside. "And say nothing of this," he said softly. "The *padrone* said you promised."

Handing over the bowl of onion, Pietro instructed her to announce that dinner would be in no more than ten minutes. Mr. Vincentia, receiving the warning, left for the galley after informing his guests that they had time for only one more cocktail. Monica firmly refused to provide a second Kir, and so Elizabeth Lamb wandered about listening to the various conversations, all desultory and uninteresting. Paul returned and made for the bar. Julia promptly left it and went to talk to Jim Darrow, who had been sitting alone in a corner drinking whiskey and frequently blowing his nose.

The dining tables were gaily set with flowered china on yellow linen cloths. Vincentia placed Elizabeth Lamb, Amy, Jake and Paul at his. "We will leave a place empty for the Lieutenant, in case he arrives. I invited him, for his courtesy." Annie headed the other, Monica, Julia, Chris and Jim joining her. Payson served them with small plates of sausages surrounded by greens. "*Cavoliceddi,*" Vincentia informed the diners. "Sicilian sausage that is spiced with fennel seeds, with wild mustard boiled and tossed with oil. I am obligated to Moselli for the mustard, too."

He had risen to take an opened bottle of Annie's favorite chianti from the sideboard and pour it for her table. "Only enough for one more in this," he said regretfully as he emptied the last of it into Amy's glass. "And it is the last bottle, alas." Payson handed him a bottle he had been opening. "Jake," Vincentia told him, "you and Cooper and my young friend and I must make do with this. Ladies always have preference," he told Elizabeth Lamb with a smile, "but older ladies have first preference."

The *cavoliccedi* was enthusiastically eaten by all but Jim and Chris and Julia, who had been sipping the chianti with restraint and a shaking hand. "But you must finish every drop," Vincentia playfully admonished her, "or I will finish it for you! It is too precious to waste. We will have a good burgundy with the squab and there is enough for all, I promise."

Payson removed their empty glasses and poured burgundy into the larger ones on the tables. As he did, Pietro put a large platter of squabs surrounded by broiled tomato halves on each table, along with a stack of warmed plates. Annie and Vincentia served the squabs. "Oh, these are divine, V.V.!" Monica exclaimed after her first bite. "Almost as good as the eggs Pietro makes for tea! I know the secret of those; he pierces the shell and then boils them in white wine. But how were these ever done?"

"I split the *coussin* and brush him with melted butter, *mam'selle*," Pietro answered her. "And broil. Then I spread with *moutarde* and roll in bread crumbs, again brush with butter and finish the broiling. Then I cook down vinegar, chopped red peppers and peppercorns, add to it tomato paste, meat extract and hot water and boil again. Then I make a *roux,* add capers and more *moutarde,* mix it with the vinegar preparation and pour over him." He beamed proudly. "I will be pleased to write it down for you," he called over his shoulder as he left for the galley.

"You're certainly doing an expert job of demolishing that poor little bird," Paul observed pleasantly to Elizabeth Lamb, who was eating with appetite, as was he. "A lady four times your age couldn't do it as fast or as well."

"That one was born four times her age, I think," Monica commented; "if not forty. And she'll never get any older, just as she was never really young. Didn't Freud say we all substantially stay the same age? But I approve of her." She raised her glass to Elizabeth

Lamb, who smiled happily, still chewing. Chris began to dispute with Monica about Freud. The rest listened as they ate their food in silence.

"Well, it's maybe my last good dinner on the *Chianti,* Mr. Cooper." Elizabeth Lamb's mouth was finally empty. "I guess tomorrow I'd better move ashore to be with my cousin. She's probably better by now, and lonely, and had a lot of fights with Grandmother's housekeeper. They both have terrible tempers." She smiled prettily at him as she sipped her burgundy.

Mr. Vincentia nodded approvingly. "But you must both come aboard for dinner every night, while we are here," he said. "We will enjoy having you back and it will be several days before the new fuel injectors will be installed."

"What was the matter with the engines, Mr. Vincentia?" Jim asked. "Could they tell?"

"Some impurity in the fuel, I believe," he was answered smoothly. "We filled the tanks at a place in Quincy we do not ordinarily use. I will have something to say to them about it, I assure you. Now, Payson, you may clear and bring the salad."

Each plate of dressed Bibb and Boston lettuce held a baby Brie cheese, its center hollowed out and filled with a *pesto* of oil, garlic, herbs and anchovies. "Although we usually have water with the salad course, I think a white Zinfandel might go well with this," Vincentia decided, motioning to Payson.

"Really, V.V.," Amy protested, "you'll make us drunk! I already feel I might fall asleep before dessert, what with all this delicious food and wine." She took a healthy swallow from her glass as she spoke.

"I don't think wine with this salad is quite the article, Vito," Jake said, and to Payson: "Would you find some water for me, please, son?" Elizabeth Lamb agreed. "Me, too, please, Payson. Grandmother doesn't let me have more than one not-quite-full glass of wine, and I've already had two big ones."

The salad was succeeded by champagne glasses containing a creamy pinkish mixture. "Oh, *zabaoine biscuit!*" Annie exclaimed. She had said little during the meal. "Pietro hasn't made this for a year!"

"It's absolutely the best dessert I have ever tasted!" Paul was also happy. "And he hasn't spared the Marsala! I'll forgive him all his temper tantrums for this."

He put down his spoon for a second and looked at his host. "You're right, V.V.," he said soberly. "Food does make one forget one's miseries, if only for a time. You are a very wise man."

Vincentia nodded as soberly as Paul had spoken. "Pietro will be indeed r-relieved to hear that you forgive him, Cooper," Chris commented drily. "It's w-wonderful, but even the aroma is almost knocking me out." He smothered a yawn as he finished his *zabaoine*.

"Couldn't we have coffee here, V.V.?" Julia asked plaintively. "I'm feeling almost too weary to walk to the saloon. Coffee might buck me up a bit."

"I am sorry you are tired, my dear." Vincentia spoke solicitously. "It is the strain of — of our loss beginning to tell on you." He rose, nevertheless. "But I think we must let Payson clear the tables and get to bed. He had a more exhausting night than any of us. He will bring coffee to the fantail first."

"Not a more exhausting night than the murderer," Elizabeth Lamb thought, following her elders. They settled in chairs as she went up the spiral stairs to the upper deck. Antonio was there, walking around slowly. He solemnly winked at her. The *Chianti* had swung at anchor so that the lights of The Bungalow were directly in her view. The two in the living room went out even as she looked. "Dora must be making Persis go to bed early," she thought. "She *will* be in a temper! It's barely nine o'clock."

Her thought was being echoed by Jim as she went down to join the company. "It's barely nine o'clock but I can't keep my eyes open," he was saying. He put down his cup. "I'd better say goodnight. See you all in the morning."

"I'm going up on deck for some air before I go to bed." Monica also rose. "Good-night, everyone. Want to come along, Annie?"

Annie got up slowly. "No, I'm going straight to bed. I hardly got any sleep at all last night, even though I didn't have the exciting experiences you all did." She gasped and looked contritely at Vincentia. "I didn't mean to put it that way, Vito. I only meant — that island — the shooting— You know."

"You are exhausted, my dear. Come, I will walk you to your room.

I need some paper for notes I will make tonight for letters I wish you to write tomorrow."

Chris drank his coffee and also left for his cabin, saying if people were thinking of waking him for breakfast, they should at once put the idea out of their minds. Julia poured herself a second cup of coffee, drank it staring out at the darkness and then, ignoring Paul, told Amy and Jake and Elizabeth Lamb as she left that a good night's sleep was what they all needed.

Amy, too, got up. "Elizabeth Lamb, you'd better come down soon. I'll leave a light on for you. You have to pack tonight or tomorrow, you know. I'm so sleepy I hope I have the strength to take off my clothes."

"I'd be delighted to help, Amy," Jake told her with a grin. She blushed as she answered, "Another time, perhaps."

"That's the first time he's called her by her first name," Elizabeth Lamb thought. "Persis' 'gerry-antic' sex is going on in more places than Florida!"

"What about turning on the telly?" Jake asked. "Since everyone's deserted us, Cooper." Elizabeth Lamb followed them in. "I hope the cook's left the kitchen door unlocked," Paul said as she and Jake settled themselves on a sofa facing the set. "I've got a craving for more of that dessert, if there's any left. Think I'll give it a try."

Elizabeth Lamb smiled as she watched him go quickly out. She erased the smile as Jake raised his brows and indicated she was to watch the screen. Paul was soon back, frowning and empty-handed. Vincentia joined them and they viewed an epic in which the actresses, all with acres of thick blonde hair, and the actors, very toothy, with carefully styled hair only a little less luxuriant, seemed to do nothing but mix themselves drinks and breathe heavily upon each other, changing partners frequently. They would then declare that "we mustn't feel this way" and then everybody went shopping at Neiman-Marcus. She yawned widely in boredom. Vincentia caught her eye and told her she was tired and he wanted her in bed and asleep in five minutes. "Or I will never let you on the *Chianti* again!" he said, in mock threat. "Give me a hug before you go, *caro.*"

As she started down the stairs, she glanced back into the saloon and saw Antonio and Carlo coming in from the fantail. Mrs.

Danniver was heavily asleep, but Elizabeth Lamb felt no similar inclination. She put on the desk lamp, looking over warily to see if the sleeper woke, but there was not even a stir. "I'm not a bit tired," she said aloud. She decided to draw for a while and then steal up and put on one of the late-night talk shows she was never allowed to watch. "Maybe they'll all have gone to bed by then," she thought, "and everything will be all dark. Unless Mr. Vincentia is waiting for Buzzie. I wonder why he didn't get here?"

After a little, she put one of the small flashlights with which every cabin was supplied in the pocket of her printed lawn dress. The stair lights were still on, and one of the lamps in the saloon, but no one was there. It was not yet time, as her new Cartier watch told her, for a late-late show. "I wonder if Monica's still up on deck?" she said aloud.

She found that none of the upper deck lights were on. She played the flashlight around the deck chairs to see if Monica had fallen asleep in one. There was a rectangle of light far forward, flush with the deck, plainly visible in the darkness. "Of course; that's the skylight in Mr. Vincentia's cabin," she thought. She wondered if Buzzie was there, arresting Paul Cooper. She took off her patent-leather slippers and carried them as she lightly walked the length of the deck to kneel and peer down into the stateroom.

Paul Cooper was lounging on the settee facing Mr. Vincentia, his hands in his pockets and a superior smile on his face. He was flanked by Antonio and Carlo, standing behind and to either side of him. Vincentia leaned back, one hand near the pistol on the desk before him, and appeared to be speaking very slowly. Jake Aaronson sat in a chair pulled up to one side of the desk, his head resting on his hand as he watched Cooper. Payson stood beside Mr. Vincentia. She did not see Buzzie.

Nor could she hear one word Vincentia was saying. The brass cleat that held the skylight shut was on the side of the frame near her hand. "I hope it's not locked from inside, too," she thought. She unfastened the cleat and was able to urge the skylight open, just a crack. It was heavy; she reached for her shoes and, holding the frame open with one hand, gently inserted one shoe into the aperture and then slid the other on top of it. When she lowered the

286

frame, the shoes held it open about two inches on that side. She lay flat on her stomach and put one eye and one ear to the opening.

"It is useless to continue lying, Cooper," Vincentia was saying. "Here beside me is Viola's intended husband. You killed her because she was to be married and your lover Julia would lose her inheritance. You may as well admit it."

Cooper removed his hands from his pockets and folded them contemplatively under his chin. "And you believe this rustic," he said calmly. "V.V., I thought you were shrewder than that. And you have not yet told me how I killed my dear Viola, either. Has he revealed that to you, too?"

"Carlo saw you coming up the stairs from her cabin this morning. He will swear to it. You have told the detective you were not there after you took juice to Jake, much earlier. Carlo saw you go into the galley and he and Pietro later found the bag with which you smothered Viola. They gave it to me, very intelligently, since it was something out of place and an unnatural death had occurred. I have it secure, and your fingerprints will be on it, in the right places. Pietro was amused by your repeated efforts to get into the galley to retrieve it.

"And Payson has letters from Viola, speaking of their marriage. A court will believe him and will understand your motive for murder. And Higgins will have Julia tried as an accomplice. Not pleasant, for a woman of Julia's delicate upbringing, to spend perhaps twenty years in a woman's prison. Terrible things may well happen to her."

"I'd like a drink," Paul said abruptly. Elizabeth Lamb could see Vincentia pouring a glass of brandy, which Payson handed over. Paul drained the glass. "Well, and what if I admit it?" he asked sullenly.

"I have told you." Vincentia reached into the desk drawer and brought out a typewritten piece of paper, a plain one, and a pen. "You copy this in your own writing. It is short. It says you spoke to Viola during the night, when Jake was in the bathroom — as he was, of course, when you murdered her — and she told you she had changed her mind about marrying you. Enraged, out of your mind with jealousy, you smothered her. And that you deeply regret it.

"I have promised you that I will have my friend Moselli fly you to Canada. You have friends there, I know. You have my word that I will never produce this paper as long as you never again make contact with Julia. She was my son's wife; she bears my name; I wish to protect it — and her from such as you. The case will be unsolved.

"Unsolved, although Higgins has a strong suspicion Viola was smothered. I did not tell the exact truth about the autopsy report. But he can not prove it without evidence and he can put the blame on no one, even Julia. He will have no reason to extradite you from Canada, nor from England.

"What do you say?"

She could almost hear Paul thinking. "You lied about the autopsy," he said slowly. "How can I believe you when you say you'll do nothing with what I write? And that you'll get me to Canada?"

"I give you my word. You well know I have never dishonored it yet, nor will I now."

Paul sat very still for a long minute. Then, still sitting, he suddenly lurched forward. Antonio and Carlo sprang between him and Vincentia, their eyes fixed upon him. Paul laughed spitefully. "A fine pair of watchdogs you have, V.V. I was only reaching for the paper and the pen." He leaned on the desk and carefully and slowly copied the typewritten page on to the blank sheet.

Vincentia put it in the desk and nodded to Jake, who rose to stand before Paul. "Get up," he said coldly. "Get up, you dirty bugger." Paul's mouth twisted. "Going to beat me up, Jake?" he asked as he slowly complied. "Try it and see what happens."

In two lightning moves, Jake reached to touch a spot just above Paul's belt line and one by the middle of his collarbone. Paul stood swaying, unable to move. Elizabeth Lamb raised herself to look directly down into the stateroom. Antonio and Carlo moved to stand beside Paul and hold him upright, each lightly clasping one of his arms as they leaned against him. Vincentia took something white from Payson's hand and came from behind his desk. "Remove his jacket," he directed. "Gently; don't bruise him."

He reached to place in Paul's shirt pocket what Payson had handed him and then rapidly touched his lips to each of Paul's cheeks. He pulled a handkerchief from his own pocket, rubbed it hard across

288

his mouth and then threw it on the floor. "I'm afraid this will be the first time Vittorio Vincentia has broken his word," he said slowly. Then he smiled, a wide, strange, chilling smile. "Take the piece of filth away. Handle him carefully. I will be in to finish it."

Payson ran to open the little door to the bathroom. Antonio and Carlo seized Paul, one under the armpits and one under the knees. They carried him to the bathroom. Payson closed the door and, as he did, glanced up at the skylight. He gasped loudly and pointed upward: "Sir!"

As Vincentia looked at Payson and before his eyes were raised, Elizabeth Lamb ducked out of sight. She ran to the forward port ladder and aft along the main deck. As she did, she heard footsteps above her, running forward. Terrified, holding her breath, she went into the door to the dining room, raced across it and down the stairs.

She did not breathe freely until she was in her cabin, the door locked. She quickly got out of her clothes and ran to the bathroom. She stood under the shower, her heart still beating frantically, and wondered what it all meant. "Oh, I've got such a headache!" she said aloud. Even before she looked for her pajamas, she took Amy's toilet kit from the bathroom shelf, found her aspirin and swallowed four. "I'll probably sleep till noon," she thought, as she pulled the covers up over her head. "I hope I do. I'm so scared. He looked just like a wolf when he smiled."

She did sleep soundly, almost until noon. When she awoke, Amy was not there and bright, hot sunlight blazed through the portholes. She cursorily washed her face, smoothed her hair and put on shorts and a thin jersey.

Carlo was watering the ferns in the lobby. He greeted her gaily. "They drink so much," he said, indicating the plants. "Almost as much as the Lady Monica.

"Pietro has made you a good breakfast. He is keeping it warm. The *padrone* say I am to pack your things for you. He say after you eat, he would like to see you. He say he is glad you slept so well. What we found this morning was nothing for a young lady to see."

"What did you find?" she asked apprehensively. He shook his head. "They will tell you, the others."

Payson, looking refreshed but solemn, went into the galley as soon as he saw her at the top of the stairs. Amy sat in the saloon, busily writing. Jim stood behind her, looking over her shoulder and murmuring. Jake Aaronson was reading a newspaper near them.

"The way you carp, carp, carp!" Amy turned to Jim and spoke explosively. "The coat of arms for editors should have a carp rampant! *And* a bar sinister.

"Well, hello, Elizabeth Lamb. I thought you were going to sleep all day. You missed all the excitement. You missed your friend Lieutenant Higgins, too, though he said he'll be back. He's gone ashore about the body."

"*What* body? Do you mean Viola?"

"It seems that Cooper guy suffocated Viola," Jim answered for Amy. "He got remorseful, I guess. He left a note, admitting it, right on that table over there. Mr. Vincentia found it this morning. Then he jumped overboard, sometime last night. Higgins spotted his body caught on that reef out there when he and another detective were rowing out to us. Early it was, around seven."

"What!" She looked questioningly at Payson, who was putting down a large tray containing a number of silver-covered dishes, a glass of orange juice, a silver coffee pot and a vase with one pink rosebud. He ignored her look. "You eat that all up, Elizabeth Lamb. The boss said to. He says people feel better when their stummick's full."

It was not one of Pietro's customary morning efforts. The covered dishes held pieces of crisp bacon, a little cheese and mushroom omelet, muffins split and buttered, blackberry jam, green olives and slices of anise-flavored, thick toast. There was a jug of warm milk to mix with the coffee. Although she was still dazed and not a little frightened, she discovered that she was also very hungry.

While she ate, Amy continued to bicker with Jim, Jake urging her on. He looked over only once at Elizabeth Lamb, a considering look, although he smiled as he spoke. "Don't bring that rose anywhere near me, dear," he said. "Even one makes me sneeze. Found that out last—" He returned to his paper.

Payson retrieved the emptied tray. "The boss wants to see you now," he said. Feeling better because of the food, but still frightened, she went slowly to Vincentia's stateroom.

290

He was writing at his desk. In the exact middle of it, her patent-leather slippers were carefully placed. She sat down, staring first at the shoes and then at him. He smiled at her. "You look well, *caro*. Well-rested and well-fed. I hope your breakfast pleased you?" He leaned back, holding his pen in both hands, his elbows on the desk. He regarded her steadily. "So you know?" he asked.

She found she was no longer frightened. "All I know," she said evenly, "is that Mr. Cooper drowned himself because he was sorry he killed Viola. Jim says his note says he was sorry. What I don't know is — did Mrs. Vincentia kill herself, too?"

"Julia is on her way to England, courtesy of my friend Mr. Moselli. Chris is accompanying her. A great-aunt of his heads a convent, a cloistered one. Julia wishes to enter it."

"She wants to enter a *convent!* I can't believe it. She's the last person — are you making her do it?"

"Let us say only," he answered carefully, "that although Julia is aware I would have scruples against harming a woman, scruples long indoctrinated in me, even a woman who conspired to kill my granddaughter, she is also aware that there are younger — ah, younger friends of mine who might feel an obligation to defend the honor of my family. They might not observe the nicety of letting her live freely after what she has done.

"I have promised her that she may leave in twenty years. That can be arranged; Chris will see to it. I gave her a choice — go free and perhaps suffer some misfortune, or enter the convent. She chose the latter. Of her own free will, I assure you."

"But that's like twenty years in prison!"

He smiled. "For her, since she has no religious calling, it is indeed. But she is still young. She will not be so very old when she gets out. Now, *I* am old. Monica's father, when he was dying, quoted Cicero: 'Life,' he said, 'is a play with a badly-written last act.'

"I had hoped, when we embarked on this voyage of the *Chianti,* that my last act would not be too bad; I had hopes that I would not have to play it out alone." He looked keenly at her. "What do you say to that, *caro?*"

"Well, my father says you can be young at any age. I guess that's all I can say."

"Ah, but when that is said, the one saying it is still young. You can say nothing else?"

She drew in a deep, deep breath and let it out slowly. "No, I'll say something else; I'll say I'm not going to tell Grandmother, if that's what you mean. I like you, you know. Persis likes you. And maybe Mr. Cooper did jump off the boat, after he wrote his note. About that, I don't have anything to say."

He jumped up, moved quickly around the desk and kissed her, holding her close. His face was wet with tears. "You are as kind, as good, as you are beautiful and clever and brave. I swear to you, that if what I hope can come true, your grandmother will never be sorry. And I can say this now, only now, only after what you have willingly said: that you, and Persis, too, will one day be very, very rich. Richer than you can imagine."

"That's nice," she said politely. "Persis will like that, but I won't tell her now. And I hope it won't happen for fifty years or so."

He still held her with one arm while with the other hand he took out a handkerchief and wiped his eyes. "Did you burn the one last night?" she asked curiously. He smiled. "Of course. But we will never speak of last night again. Do you promise?"

She promised, and they walked hand-in-hand to the saloon. Buzzie had returned and was talking to Monica, who was dressed in casual shirt and jeans. Several suitcases were beside the chair in which she sat.

"Just in time to wish me Godspeed!" she told Elizabeth Lamb. "Lieutenant Higgins is going to drop me at the airport when he leaves. I'll have a day in Boston and then — imagine! — I find my booking to Paris is on the same plane he's taking tomorrow. What a coincidence!"

"Indeed it is," Jake commented drily, looking up from his paper. "I thought you wanted to go to England. Oh, Higgins, thanks for bringing the newspaper this morning. Never saw such a fascinating periodical. They even have a column on what the weather was *last* week!"

"I hear Julia and Chris have already left," Monica went on, ignoring Jake. "And what a tragedy about Paul! Although I always thought he wasn't 'quite the article,' as a maid of mine used to describe some of my escorts. I met up with him once in Majorca" — Amy nudged Jim triumphantly — "quite by chance, of course, and I wouldn't say his behavior was that of a proper gent. He let me pay the — oh, I almost forgot: has anyone borrowed my bottle of sleeping pills? I couldn't find it anywhere when I was packing."

"Perhaps you used them all last night, my dear." Vincentia spoke smoothly.

"No, I was so tired I fell into bed without taking any. Funny; I felt just the way I've felt when I take a couple along with a lot of liquor. No matter. I can find some more in Boston.

"Well, Lieutenant, I'll get some sun on deck while I wait for you. And, Elizabeth Lamb, if you're ever in London, look me up. I'm in the book and it's #7 Thornhill Square, in Islington. You're quite my cup of tea. But don't bring your Aunt Isabella!"

"I'll wait with you on deck, my dear," Vincentia offered. "The Lieutenant wants just a few words with Elizabeth Lamb. You can have privacy on the fantail, Higgins. I'll have Payson bring you coffee."

Buzzie sat across from her, his face stern. "Well, Elizabeth Lamb," he said, "there's been mighty strange goings-on here, all things considered, wouldn't you say?"

"I don't know, Buzzie. If a man kills someone and then is sorry and kills himself, I'd say that wasn't so strange. You must have heard of that happening before." She drank from the cup of coffee Payson handed her and smiled at both men.

"You stay here a minute, Payson," Buzzie ordered. "Sit down. Now, I want to ask you both: what do you think of this Vincentia? You first, Payson."

"Well, I like 'im, Buzzie. He's fair and he pays good. And you know what? I'm goin' back to Boston with him. He's goin' to send me to school; Boston Latin, I think it was he said. He's goin' to have me work for 'im after I finish school." He blushed. "He likes the way I kin take orders, he said; the way I operate, it was. He says I remind 'im of himself, when he was young."

"Do your mother and father know?" Elizabeth Lamb asked.

"I rowed ashore and walked down and told 'em, early this mornin', even 'fore Buzzie got here. He asked me last night. They're real

293

pleased. There ain't many chances to become anybody on this island, if you're poor like me an' don't know much. They're real pleased."

He got up. "Kin I go, Buzzie? There's nuthin' more I could rightly say about Mr. Vincentia. I don't know 'im well, only met 'im in Boston jest 'fore we come up to the island, but I think he's a real good man."

"Okay, you can go. When you get to be a rich businessman like him, with a yacht and all, be sure you remember me, Payson. Now you, Elizabeth Lamb."

"Now me what? I like Mr. Vincentia, too. And so does Persis, and Grandmother. And you know she's pretty sharp, Buzzie. What are you getting at?"

"Well, probably nothing. But what did he seem to be like; what did he say to you, and how? When you were alone with him, maybe. Were you ever with him when he was alone?"

She broke into nervous laughter. "Buzzie, how could I be with him when he was *alone?* Honestly! I still want to know what you're trying to get at."

"Well, he's got a reputation for having been a mite ruthless, at least when he was younger. And you've got a reputation, with me, anyway, for finding out things. Now, I ask you straight out: did you find that feller suffocated Vincentia's granddaughter, and tell him, and did he take matters into his own hands? I'll tell you right now we're comparing the water in Cooper's lungs with water I took from this cove this morning. Not everybody knows it, but you can tell if a person was drowned in the water he turned up dead in. There wasn't a mark on him; nobody beat him up or anything and there was no mark of ropes or other signs that he was forcibly drowned, but I just wondered."

She looked at him, both astounded and a little frightened. And then she remembered the buckets of cove water Antonio had been taking into Vincentia's cabin. "Of course, to fill that big bathtub," she thought.

Feeling cold all over, she nevertheless smiled at Buzzie. "Well, I'll answer straight out." She casually put her right hand into her jeans pocket and managed to cross her fingers. "I'm not detecting anything on the *Chianti.* I'm writing a book, for school, and just enjoying the boat. Honestly, Buzzie, it's so luxurious! Mr. Darrow told me that Mr. Cooper wrote a note and said he killed Viola and was sorry. And then he turned up dead. I'd suspect suicide, if I were you, and doing your job. And that's all I'd suspect.

"I can't see how you could think Mr. Vincentia would have figured out something I couldn't and then gone and pushed Mr. Cooper overboard. Mr. Vincentia had a bad attack, an angina attack, and he wasn't doing a lot of heavy thinking. And he wouldn't have been up to tangling with a strong younger man, either." She uncrossed her fingers. "Although everything I've said is true," she thought; "I could've saved my fingers the strain."

Buzzie eyed her. "You know, Elizabeth Lamb," he said casually, "the note said she'd told him she wasn't going to marry him. But I thought she couldn't talk? Mr. Aaronson had told me that when I first came aboard, when he was telling what a bad fall she'd had."

"Oh, my God!" thought Elizabeth Lamb, who, unlike Persis, never used her Maker's name in vain. She spoke as casually as he had. "What did the autopsy show about her throat? *Was* the larynx crushed, like Mr. Templeton thought when we found her?"

"No," Buzzie answered reluctantly, "it wasn't. I guess it must have been shock that made her unable to talk, at first."

"Well, then." She crossed her fingers again. "When Mrs. Danniver and I went down to see her, she sort of mumbled 'hello' at me, when I bent down over her. And that was only an hour or so after she fell. Mr. Cooper must have seen her much later. You could ask Mr. Aaronson *how* much later; when it was he went into the bathroom. But she certainly would have been able to talk a lot better then than even when she spoke to me, earlier. The shock would've worn off more."

She took her hand out of her pocket and picked up her cup of cold coffee. "And God help me if he asks Mrs. Danniver or Mr. Aaronson if they heard her speak to me," she thought.

"Yes, you've got to be right," Buzzie said. "I'll report it as a suicide. That talking thing just sort of bothered me, a little." He surveyed the plants around them. "No wild rose bushes here, are there?"

"Why should there be? Or shouldn't?"

295

"There was a white wild rose in Cooper's shirt pocket. Seems funny. I don't like things about a suicide that seem funny, although, as I said, suicide is undoubtedly what it is."

"Oh, Buzzie! There's wild rose bushes, all colors, in bloom around The Bungalow. And out on the reef, too, on that little place that always stays above water. Maybe he swam first to the shore, or out to the reef, sort of out of his mind, as he surely must have been. And just picked a rose, the way you do when you're not thinking what you're doing. Sort of absent-minded, — out of it, like. I don't know what goes on in the mind of a person who's going to drown himself, or even just thinking of it. And neither do you." She almost choked on the coffee she was sipping. "Oh, I hope he doesn't ask if Mr. Cooper could swim," she thought. "But who's left here who'd know, anyway? Or tell?"

Buzzie got up, smiling at her. "I like the way you can figure things out. Well, I'd say the case is closed. And sort of neatly, for everybody."

"Except for Viola," she reminded him. She almost added, "And Payson," but stopped herself. "People never think of dead people as having any rights," she said instead. "You can't even sue for them, Persis' father says, if somebody writes or says something about them that's not true.

"Buzzie, I'm *glad* Mr. Cooper's dead; I don't care what you think. I *am*. Nobody should kill a person and not have to pay for it by getting killed himself."

"I'd like to see you on the judge's bench," Buzzie said. "I guess most policemen would like to have judges who think like that. But maybe you're going to be a writer? Did you say you're writing a book? At your young age, Elizabeth Lamb?"

"Yes," she sighed. "A dumb book for that dumb school I go to. But this year'll be my last one there, thank goodness. Grandmother says she's going to see that I get sent away to a boarding school. That might be worse, but I doubt it."

"I hope," Buzzie observed, "nobody gets killed in your boarding school. You do sort of attract it, dear."

"Oh, Buzzie! Don't worry about that. What you'd better worry about is getting killed by some driver in Paris. Be very careful crossing the streets. I really mean it. You have no idea."

He laughed. "What's Paris like, Elizabeth Lamb? What should I be sure to do or to see?"

"Oh, Monica will show you all the sights, I'm sure. If you're not too tired, that is. I mean," she added hastily, "there's jet lag and all."

Jim and Amy were still wrangling. Jake had finished the *Bar Harbor Times* and was doing a crossword puzzle. They pleasantly answered Buzzie's farewell remarks and wished him a happy vacation. "You're going to enjoy Paris, I know," Jim told him. "It's very different from Maine. Fresh fields and pastures new and all that sort of thing."

"Oh, my God!" Amy exploded. "That's 'fresh woods,' you dolt! Why can't I have an editor who's literate?" She stalked to the bar. Jim followed, raising his eyes to Heaven and asking it why he couldn't have an author who was both polite and a teetotaler.

"Well, goodbye for a while, Mr. Aaronson," Elizabeth Lamb said. "I'm going to be rowed ashore soon. Persis and I'll be back for dinner, though. I guess she's sick of the housekeeper's cooking by now. Pietro doesn't burn things."

"I'd get up and bow and kiss your hand but, one, this isn't a final goodbye and, two, I'm too old and lazy. I'll just say one thing: you're even more of a *mensch* than I first thought you were. A super-*mensch*, you are."

She giggled. "You said Mrs. Danniver was a *mensch*, too. Is Mr. Vincentia one?"

"We-e-ll, I don't know. Not exactly. He's more of what in his lingo they call an *omi di panza*. A 'man with a belly.'"

"Mr. Vincentia's got a perfectly flat stomach, Mr. Aaronson!"

"No, no; that's only what it means literally. What it really means is a man who can hold his tongue and defend his honor. Sort of poetic.

"And that's what you and I must do, *caro*. The first part, especially."

"I know. Well, I'm off to get my notebook from Mr. Vincentia. I'm going to start on my book this afternoon." He raised his brows. "Don't worry," she said quickly. "It will all be changed, all different. Different people and different events; no murder. I'll make the

297

mystery about a theft of a big diamond, or something. I'll just keep one thing."

"What's that?"

"I'll keep the title I was planning to use. I'll still call it *The Voyage of the Chianti*."

• CHAPTER 13 •

Some Time After

THE AGENT operating the wiretap in the basement of an unoccupied house on Mount Vernon Street was both young and
the recent father of twin boys. They were babies possessed of strong
lungs as well as the tendency to exercise them at night. He was
yawning, both from fatigue and the uninteresting conversations he
had been recording.

"Not one damned thing in days except talk about wedding plans,
and a bunch of Wop recipes getting exchanged. And some dull stuff
about book publishing and the produce market," he was thinking.
"It's pretty clear Redford was wasting his time looking for smack
on that boat; the old guy's obviously dead-set against handling any
stuff and won't let his troops deal, either. We did turn that up.

"So why'm I here, anyway? We'll never pin a thing on him, no
matter what info Redford thinks he got from that stoolie. Guy's a
perfectly legit businessman. Nowadays, anyway."

He yawned again and leaned back in his chair. He had a limited
view, through a small window high on the wall, of the base of a
little tree in the courtyard of the house. Its yellow leaves were
dropping softly, propelled down by a cold autumn rain. They drifted

and swirled hypnotically, to settle gently on the brick paving. He stared at the leaves, his eyelids half-closed. "Might try five minutes of shut-eye," he said aloud, glancing at his tape apparatus. "They can't hang me for that, and there's about an hour of tape left." He settled back more comfortably, his headphones still in place.

Three hours later, he woke with a start. A laugh had sounded quite loudly in his ears. "No, my dear Angelo," a strong voice said, "you are too complimentary. If that is the word I should use concerning such a sad, sad occurrence." The voice the speaker was responding to was so faint as to be almost unintelligible.

The strong voice went on: "To say that it reminds you of that time on the East End docks — no, I assure you it was not at all like those days — well, of course I remembered your instructions that time to be certain the water in the lungs was the correct type — yes, it was Antonio and Carlo—"

"Wow!" the agent muttered. "This is more like it! Water in the lungs? What am I getting here?" He looked over at his tape. One end flapped uselessly as the reel revolved. He looked at his watch. He slowly removed the headphones and put them on the table. He as slowly got up and stretched.

"I'll get Redford to meet me at Nino's," he thought. "I'll stand him to two or three of Nino's specials and then maybe I won't get my ass kicked from here to some East End dock. Wherever that might be."